"Not even the h
able to resist th
special hero."—

Francesca was furious when Arden took her up
to her room from the raucous tap room.

"Roxanne can stay?" she questioned furiously,
hands on hips as she stood with him outside her
door.

"Roxanne is older, and wildly experienced,"
Arden said flatly.

"Then," she spat, "maybe I just had better go out
and find myself an obliging gentleman tonight, for I
think it's only my lack of bed knowledge that's
making all my problems and I . . ."

She never finished the sentence. The last words
died against his mouth as he pulled her to him.
There was nothing gentle in this embrace. He
held her close and opened his lips against hers
to swallow up all her protests . . . except that
Francesca was not protesting . . . quite the
contrary—she challenged him to finish what he
had so forcefully begun. . . .

THE GAME OF LOVE

Edith Layton

A SIGNET BOOK

NEW AMERICAN LIBRARY

PUBLISHER'S NOTE

This book is a work of fiction. Names, characters, places, and incidents either are the product of the author's imagination or are used fictitiously, and any resemblance to actual persons, living or dead, events, or locales is entirely coincidental.

Copyright © 1988 by Edith Felber

SIGNET TRADEMARK REG. U.S. PAT. OFF. AND FOREIGN COUNTRIES
REGISTERED TRADEMARK—MARCA REGISTRADA
HECHO EN CHICAGO, U.S.A.

SIGNET, SIGNET CLASSIC, MENTOR, ONYX, PLUME, MERIDIAN AND NAL BOOKS are published by NAL PENGUIN INC., 1633 Broadway, New York, New York, 10019

First Printing, July, 1988

1 2 3 4 5 6 7 8 9

PRINTED IN THE UNITED STATES OF AMERICA

"Masters, you ought to consider with yourselves: to bring in—God shield us!—a lion among ladies is a most dreadful thing . . ."

"Therefore another prologue must tell he is not a lion."

"Nay, you must name his name, and half his face must be seen through his lion's neck: and he himself must speak through, saying thus . . . 'Ladies,'—or 'Fair ladies—I would wish you,' or 'I would request you,'—or 'I would entreat you,—not to fear, not to tremble: my life for yours. If you think I come hither as a lion, it were pity of my life: no, I am no such thing: I am a man as other men are . . .' "

"This Lion is a very fox for his valor."

—WILLIAM SHAKESPEARE,
A Midsummer Night's Dream

1

THE DARK was not quite light enough; it was difficult to be sure of anything in the room except for one's hand in front of one's face. There may have been a thousand candles in the several chandeliers, but they cast their harsh and wavering brightness only on those persons clustered in small rings directly beneath their sharp circles of light. All the others in the room swam secret as sharks in a fathomless sea, becoming only passing shapes of shadows, outside those pools of light.

The gentlepersons gathered in the ornate room didn't complain; they may have been unhappy about a great many things, but the deceptive light wasn't a concern of theirs. They paid little attention to anything but their hands in front of their faces anyway, and if they could see them, or the dice or cards or piles of chips there, they were content. Or as content as gamblers could ever be, since from the look of the avid faces watching the fall of a card, the spin of the wheel, or the final resting place that an ivory die tumbled toward, it was clear that contentment was not an emotion any gamester in the room had ever aspired to.

So it was as well for the two gentlemen who slowly prowled the outer edges of the room that they couldn't be seen too well, for they were watching the other gamblers, searching for a particular face. And they particularly didn't wish to be seen doing so.

The larger of the two men was larger than most of the men in the room, even stooped and halt as he was with age as he made his laborious way about the room, bent over his heavily chased silver-headed cane. He was almost as broad in the shoulder as the width of one of the wide doors that had admitted him, and equally large in the chest and across his waistcoat too, as if many long years of luxurious living had padded him lavishly, besides having encumbered him with the gouty foot that necessitated his painful passage. And a lifetime of indulgence in wines as fine as the linen in his white cravat had doubtless colored his nose and his

7

cheeks so cherry red, or else his snowy white box wig, as
out of style and likely old as he was, only accentuated his
high color. A huge old gentleman, and from the tone of the
deep grumbling voice which sometimes could be heard, a
testy one too, and it was as well that his youthful companion
seemed as well-tempered as he was well-looking.

But that would scarcely have been possible, for had the
young gentleman that accompanied the cross old gent possessed a temperament to match his looks, he would have
worn a pair of wings and should have been able to find his
way about the room by the light he gave off from himself,
for only an angel could have looked so. Yet only a mortal
man could have made all the females in the room who were
not gambling look so when they noted him, which they did
immediately.

He was somewhat above average height, and his elegant
evening clothes—snugly tailored black velvet jacket and
skin-close breeches—showed an athletic, lithe, proportion-
ate form, just as the flat abdomen and long muscular legs
told of athletic pursuits more profound than following an
ancient, ill-tempered old gentleman around the circumfer-
ences of midnight gaming houses. As did his clear white
complexion, lightly gilded by the touch of sun and wind.
His forehead was high, the shapely nose and cheekbones
subtly sculptured over perfectly crafted lips; a firm chin with
a light cleft in it, to add charm to resolve, completed the
symmetry under that tender yet masculine mouth. In the
darkened room his long tilted eyes took on the gray of cat's
fur, yet when he passed gracefully beneath the candles now
and again, they grew light as the first rise of dawn. In sunlight they'd look so light as to be blind; in moonlight, they'd
be shadowed silver as the moon's path on water. The slightly
overlong gold hair was thick and straight, except where it
lay in tendrils about his strong young neck, like the curls
of a young vine, almost as if, high white cravat and fashionable get-up of an English gentleman or not, he were the
carved statue of some gloriously lusty young Greek god.
Certainly he resembled classic statuary far more than common flesh; mortals were seldom so perfect, modern gentlemen seldom so startlingly handsome. And that modern word
itself, "handsome," scarcely conveyed the full force of his
appearance. No, he was, in the fullest meaning of that an-
tique word, beautiful.

Now he scanned the room and then paused and inclined

his noble head and spoke to his aged companion quietly, in a dulcet tenor voice no less attractive than himself.

"Over there?" he asked softly. "The fellow in the blue with the lady all in golden gauze . . . or," he added with a hint of laughter, "rather, the lady not quite in all the golden gauze?"

The old gentleman looked up. There were dozens of well-dressed persons crowded into the large room, and yet despite the dim candlelight and the further impediment of blue cigarillo smoke eddying as it rose from several locations, his quick and sparkling hazel eyes followed the direction of his younger companion's gaze immediately. He saw the lady in her insufficient gold gauze gown instantly, sighed, and then replied in a low rumble, "No, no, my boy. Never. The gent has a diamond at his throat, and the lady several more at the breast she's about to drop on the table along with her wager. And real ones at that."

"Well, obviously," the young man said with a great deal of admiration, "I've seldom seen finer. I'd be pleased to take her bet myself."

"I meant the diamonds," the old man said with what might have been a chuckle that soon translated into a cough, "and I'll wager you this night's work her bets have already been covered, and often, by every gentleman in this room, save for us. No, no, my Apollo, our bird has nothing so fine at his fingertips, or about his lady's person. He's a confirmed gamester, and so any diamonds he holds, in cards or set in gold, are gone from his hands almost as soon as he's been dealt them."

"Are you sure they are real diamonds?" the young man asked plaintively. "I think we ought to go closer for a better look."

"And put you off your favorite game forever? No, lad, I can tell a true gem from thirty paces, and I assure you that the lady's jewelry is real as her complexion, hair, and figure are not. Bend but one of your dazzling smiles upon her, Julian, and you'll find that as soon as you've gotten her out of her gown, you'll have to free her from her stays, and that would be as much work as and even less pleasure than getting me out of mine. Ah yes," he said as he limped on and they passed the table the lady played at, "I see you've taken a closer look. Don't scowl so, it only makes you look in pain, and if you keep at it, we'll soon have all the females and not a few of the males in the room rushing over to solace you. It's being inconspicuous that we're after at the moment.''

''Damn your eyes,'' the young gentleman said pleasantly as they strolled past in the perimeters of light near the table in question, ''you're right again. She's old enough to be your grandmother, Grandfather, and you could cut glass with her smallest rings, dirty as they are. I still can't understand how it is that you can judge a jewel and a person from across a room, and a dungeon-dark one at that,'' he complained.

''My father, the Gypsy King, taught me,'' the old man commented absently as they walked   through a doorway to another of the salons in the noisy, thronged gaming house. ''And you know how dark those caravans can be. Ah,'' he said with some more interest, ''look there, in the corner, the fine-drawn old fellow in the biscuit coat, with the lively little blond party laughing over his shoulder. Our pigeons, or I'm really your grandfather. I'll lay a pony on it. And let's make that 'Uncle,' not 'Grandfather,' shall we? A wastrel uncle is very understandable, but corrupt grandfathers are not thick upon the ground even here in France, where almost everything else I can think of can be twisted interestingly. . . . Ah, piquet!'' he exclaimed suddenly in loudly audible tones as they walked toward the table he'd been gazing at. ''A good solid British game at last, Nevvy. Haven't had a hand at that in an age, b'God. I was used to be a dab hand at it in my salad days, or did I ever tell you?''

''I believe you did, Uncle,'' the young man replied with a patient sigh, smiling apologetically at the persons whose play their sudden appearance had interrupted.

Those persons—a small elderly, neatly gotten-up old gent with sparse light hair and pale eyes, the fashionably dressed fair-haired young woman in a deep crimson velvet gown who stood by his side, and the old fellow's opponent, another aged gentleman, this one with too many chins and not enough hair—all looked up at once, amazed, at the pair that had loomed up from the shadows to address them. For though it was a crowded gaming house, and though over half a hundred persons were in this small salon with them, few of the other gamesters had paid them any notice or could be expected to. This wasn't surprising; the salon was for the use of those interested in small personal wagers and games. And in a private *tripot* such as this one, a gaming house whose attractions included thrilling games of macao, baccarat, rouge et noir, faro, vingt et un, and the delicious, forbidden deep hazard, all games more treacherous and exciting than could usually be found at some of the most infamous clubs in London, not a great deal of interest could be expected to be taken in a private game of piquet between two elderly gentlemen.

Now that Napoleon had been bottled up again after his defeat at Waterloo, and this time on an island even more remote than the Elban kingdom he'd been able to slip away from last year, the world had come back to France to play again. Or at least it seemed that the English world had done so, and especially here, in this exclusive country hotel and gambling house. For though play was play, after all, wherever it took place, it seemed to have a more exotic flavor for the British here. As did all things French now, after having been in short supply for so long, from perfumes to cuisine, from fashions to the females who wore them. So although there were nationals from many lands come to lose their several monies here, the predominance of them spoke French with a Scottish burr, or a Welsh purr, or any of the several dialects of England.

Obviously, then, it couldn't have been the accents of the new arrivals that had startled the players. At any rate, the intrusion seemed to break the players from their concentration as well as their silence.

"Damme, sir," the fattish fellow grunted, looking up from his cards to his opponent in disgust, "mebbe I ought to throw in my hand and give this chap a turn, at that. My luck ain't in tonight, and if I'm to lose my sauce, I'd just as soon watch it disappear all in one stroke on the wheel instead of leaking it out drop by drop in this game with you."

"Why, I'd be pleased to raise the stakes if it would suit you, Henderson," the old gentleman said in a smooth voice, but then, being fixed by a long stare by the bright-faced young woman, he went on in more regretful, conciliatory tones, "but sure as the tides turn, your luck's due for a change, you know. Be pleased to have you sit in, friend," he added in an aside to the huge old fellow who stood staring down jealously at the table.

The young man solicitously fetched a chair for his gruff companion and brought it to the table with a particularly charming smile at the young woman as he did so. Then the old fellow he called "Uncle" sat, but with so many groans and grunts of effort and muttered curses of annoyance at his own bulk and his bandaged foot, and, it seemed, his life, as he did so, that he almost drowned out the declarations being made in the game he wanted to watch.

The stout gentleman playing cards groaned as well, if for a different reason.

"A point of four!" he said, scowling, and all the young woman's sympathetic smiles could not seem to raise his spirits as his opponent answered tonelessly, "Good."

"A point of five. I score five. A quart," he intoned, still frowning ferociously, as though none of the pretty young woman's warming smiles could be seen, as though it wasn't a triumph as well as a major modern miracle that she completely ignored the gloriously good-looking young blond man who had just joined them so that she could continue to smile down upon him from across the table instead, and he a stout, balding, five-jowled fellow with more decades to his name than he had jowls, and her own gentleman's opponent, at that.

For she was a pretty and lively-looking young creature, with a neat figure and a set of small even white teeth. If her nose was a shade overlong, her chin a trifle too decisive, and her frame more sturdy than sinuous, and overall, her looks as common as meadowsweet in the June fields of her homeland, still she was pretty enough, with eyes like bluebells and ringlets more blond than brown, and a dimple that was surprised from hiding in her fair cheek when she smiled. If she wasn't spectacularly beautiful, she was a true English rose, and so as exotic here in this gambling house outside of Paris among international lovelies as a dancing girl from Carthage might be in the heart of Sussex.

And not the least interesting thing about her, the old gentleman who watched the game go forth noted, was that though the fragile old gentleman whose side she hovered at was likely her relative or protector, she ignored him entirely and reserved all her winsome smiles and coy glances for the stout fellow who played against him, even though that fat fellow did nothing to encourage her, but only grumbled at his cards. And this, even though her party had just been joined by a young man whose looks made marble statues blink.

"How high?" the frail old gentleman asked evenly.

"Jack," the stout fellow replied nervously.

"Not good," his opponent said softly.

"A pair of queens," the other spoke up immediately.

"Not good," the older fellow said again.

"Damme, no point in going on, I concede it," the other declared, casting his cards down. "You've left me only the lint in m' pockets, Wyndham, I'm gone. Perhaps we'll meet again tomorrow. Change my coat, change my luck. Never know, what?" He dug a wallet from a tight inner jacket pocket, and after sorting through it, cast some notes down atop his discarded cards. "That should settle it," he grunted. "Till then," he said as he rose, and then, casting a full and meaningful look at the young woman at last, added, "Madam. You'll let me know if your friend changes his mind, eh? I'm still at the Deauville Hotel, near the Palais Royal . . . in my own set of apartments, too," he added pointedly, but then, recollecting that he'd an interested audience to his awkward attempt at setting up a meeting with the young woman, he bowed abruptly, and just as gracelessly left them.

"Well, then, sirs," the older gentleman said with a smile, deftly scooping up the cards in his long white fingers and rising to bow to the gentlemen that had joined him, "I'd be pleased to have a game with you. No, no, pray do not," he protested as the huge old man began to try to struggle up to return his bow. "Let's not be so formal as all that. I am Sir Geoffrey Carlisle, Baron Wyndham, from Norfolk, and I'm pleased to make you known to my good friend Mrs. Cobb, from the Isle of Wight. Her late husband," he said somewhat more gravely, "was a friend to our family for many years."

"Pleasure," the old man said in acknowledgment, nodding and setting back in his chair after his abortive attempt at rising. "I'm plain John Tryon, my lord, out of London this sennight, and here's my right-hand man, my nevvy, m'late sister's boy, George Tyler. Say hello, Georgie," he ordered, just as though the young man were three instead of the thirty he might soon be, but before the handsome young man could do so, he went on, "I'd be pleased to try a hand with you, Lord Wyndham, but I warn you, I'd be a flat if I didn't wager only for pins to begin, and I ain't known for a flat, I can tell you. Mind, neither am I a skinflint, but it's been a generation since I played this game, and seems to me you're a regular Trojan at it. Well, my only interest's been my farm and my prize bulls and getting them to market, do you see, and would still be if my blasted sawbones hadn't physicked me to death and ordered me on this repairing lease with young George here. So I'll say it

plain in case you want to take on someone more your
weight—though I don't lack blunt, no, for I'm warm enough
in the pocket and I haven't spent any in a generation neither,
living alone as I do, and secluded, except for Georgie here.
But I ain't in practice, my lord, not at cards, nor any sort
of play. Well, butchers can't be chosers, can they?'' he
asked, wheezing at his own wit even before Mrs. Cobb could
recognize it as such and join him with her own silvery
laughter.

"My dear Mr. Tryon," Lord Wyndham said amiably,
"never fear. I'm here for my health as well, unfortunately.
Heart," he explained solemnly, tapping his waistcoat with
one long white finger, and after the company had a second's
silence to acknowledge the diagnosis, he continued, "and
I'm not at all an adept at the game either, I only played to
oblige Mr. Henderson. And he, poor fellow, had himself
forgot half the rules, but he'd such a bad run of luck at the
wheel and with the dice that he wanted to try something
'tamer,' as he said. But, poor gentleman, his mind is so
taken up with his dear wife's recent demise, he couldn't
concentrate on anything. Lucky for him," Lord Wyndham
said wisely, "that I insisted we play only for pennies, for
the pure sport of it.''

If Mr. Tryon had noted that the banknotes, which had
disappeared as if by magic into Lord Wyndham's own pockets seconds after they had touched the table, had amounted
to a great many "pennies" indeed, or that Lord Wyndham's
state of health didn't seem to influence the steadiness of his
hands as he absently riffled the cards through them, or even
that Mr. Henderson's leers at Mrs. Cobb as he'd left her had
not looked anything like those of a man still grieving for
his departed spouse, he said nothing at all, but only grinned
widely, rubbed his huge hands together, and promptly settled himself, with a great deal of creaking from his suffering
chair as well as his stays, for a "good round game of piquet," as he put it.

They played for laughably small stakes at first, just as
Mr. Tryon had asked. And they played cautiously even after
they'd made sure they'd the rules right. For Lord Wyndham
had hesitantly explained the game as he knew it, and Mr.
Tryon had corrected him on only one or two points, frowning as he tried to remember them exactly.

They seemed evenly matched, at the start. They both
played fumblingly and so badly that at first it was a contest

merely to see which would lose to the other the fastest. It was so much good fun, and they were so equal in their skills, or lack of them, that soon they agreed to raise the stakes, since they had to add some interest to the game, and it was clear neither would beggar the other. And even then, as they upped the ante again, and yet again, and a treble time, until they were playing for quite respectable amounts of money, they seemed equal in skill and intent. Until, that is, they then looked up and about them, as though the silence there were loud enough to distract them, and saw that their spectators had begun to play as well.

For Mrs. Cobb, it appeared, fantastically enough, had suddenly been possessed by a singularly strong attraction to Mr. Tryon. Or his hands, he thought, or his cravat, he thought again as he noted the general direction of her unrelenting gaze, for his face, red and rounded and wrinkled as it was, could never have attracted the interest of anyone but a surgeon or an artist drawn to the naturalistic and grotesque. Yet when his unusually sharp and knowing hazel eyes beneath his bushy white brows met her wide and unabashedly direct blue stare, she smiled, and then dimpled and ducked her head, only to raise it to bat the lashes above that sky-blue gaze, but never so much so that she ever left off looking upon him with what seemed to be coy embarrassment and absolute invitation. And this, while all the while young George, who had himself, as ever, attracted interested stares from females clear across the room, both smiled and stared and gazed amazed, with something very like the look of a starveling puppy, or a gentleman who'd been instantly smitten, and very hard at that, at Mrs. Cobb. Who, in turn, noted this adoration, but then proceeded to completely ignore him as she continued to ogle his ancient uncle. While her gentleman friend, Lord Wyndham, looked up once, twice, and then again at the byplay of eyes above him, and so could not help but see young George's worship of his young companion, as clear as it was profound.

If Mr. Tryon could be expected to find it difficult to concentrate while being openly admired by such a charming young female, it would be only understandable that Lord Wyndham would discover it hard to assess his cards while his lovely ladyfriend was being so blatantly sighed over by such a manly young paragon. And so it was even harder to understand then why neither gentleman playing cards made so much as one miscall, or lost count of one card taken in, even as they each took in the situation, or forgot any other card his opponent dealt out, even as all this was going forth.

In fact, it was only after a particularly sharp play by Mr. Tryon that Lord Wyndham gazed at him narrowly, and then only when Lord Wyndham tried an extraordinarily observant ploy that Mr. Tryon laid down his cards and stared at him pointedly. And then the huge old fellow began to grin hugely, showing for the first time a set of strong, even, and dazzling white teeth. And then Lord Wyndham cocked his head to the side before he too laid down his cards and began chuckling. Young George left off languishing over Mrs. Cobb as he noted this, and after a quick look to Mr. Tryon answered his unspoken question, he threw back his golden head and began to laugh outright. At the last, when the other three were all so merry, Mrs. Cobb looked shocked, then annoyed, and then, relenting, gave way to an attack of giggles herself, and the sound was far more infectious than her usual practiced silvery ripples of laughter.

"When did you twig to it?" Mr. Tryon asked at last, wiping his eyes with the back of his hand.

"That last call," Lord Wyndham admitted a bit breathlessly, "and young George's soulful look. Good heavens, Roxie's a pretty enough chit, but why on earth an Apollo on earth would be consumed with passion for her so suddenly was more than I could discern."

"Ah," young George put in sweetly, seeing Mrs. Cobb's amusement dwindle at the comment, "but that admiration was entirely genuine."

He followed the compliment by immediately assuming a look of such outsize and pained devotion that Mrs. Cobb, who had begun to preen and look at Lord Wyndham with great affronted dignity, gave it up and began to giggle again.

"Well, as for that," Mr. Tryon said merrily, "her flaming passion for me was a bit much. There's only so much lust a pocketbook can generate."

After their laughter had been spent again, they settled to an awkward, edgy silence. Lord Wyndham, who had been absently shuffling the cards, straining them through his hands until they performed like acrobats there, assuming a dozen different formations, held them quiet at last, and broke the uneasy peace.

"We don't look either that affluent or that wet behind the ears, friends. What made you chance to try to pluck us?" he asked softly.

"We were looking for you," Mr. Tryon said quietly, as Lord Wyndham's shoulders gave an involuntary leap and Mrs. Cobb's merry face grew cold and wary.

"As a favor," Mr. Tryon explained seriously, and seeing their reaction, raised one enormous finger to silence them stiller than they already were. "But calm yourselves, we're no sort of law. It's only that my friend and I happened across a wretched young countryman of ours the other night in the gardens of a hell very like this one, near to Fontainebleau. He was, we thought, either attempting to discover how long his pistol's barrel was by measuring it with his tongue, or more seriously set on self-annihilation. Fortunately, he was too castaway to have remembered to loose the lock on it, or this weary world would have had one less young gentleman in it tonight. When we sobered him up enough to be coherent, he moaned that every last cent he owned was now in the keeping of a shrewd gamester who had plucked him bare. That wasn't our concern—the world is full of foolish boys with too much of Papa's money and too little sense to stay out of the hands of sharpers. But when young Lord Waite let fall that he'd also staked and lost the title to his ancestral home in Surrey, and he an orphan, and that the sum of his inheritance, we paid a bit more attention."

The quartet about the table grew grave.

"And," Mr. Tryon went on relentlessly, so far from a smile that it seemed his face had never framed one in the whole of its long life, "he described the dapper old gent with the charming young filly at his side. And she, he mentioned when pressed to think on, was not only so taken with him he could scarcely keep his mind on the cards he held, but she often strayed from the old fellow's side to drift close to him. Or else, he remembered, he wouldn't have noted that her perfume was lilies and roses intermingled, and that it made him drunker than the wine the lordly old fellow kept him so well supplied with. Now I," he added lightly, "am wounded. I didn't get a sniff of the posies or a sip of the wine. Did I look too old for the one and too hardheaded for the other?"

Mrs. Cobb opened her pale pink lips to speak, but Lord Wyndham silenced her with an upraised hand. His austere face was so still that it seemed he scarcely moved his lips when he spoke. But speak he did as he rose from his seat, quietly but firmly biting off each word as if he were slashing it out in bold black ink.

"I may," he said coldly, "use the lady's charms as a distraction for the opposition now and again, when needs must. But only that. And only for distraction. I do not scruple to win young men's fortunes from them if I can do it, nor old ones' neither, if it comes to that. But I do not bilk them. I am a gamester, sir, entirely, that is true. But never a thief. And certainly not a procurer."

He paused, and never taking his gaze from Mr. Tryon, took a swallow of wine to wet his lips before he went on. "I do remember the young fool. And I did take his purse, because he was as unlucky as he was impulsive, and played like an ass. And I took his bit of paper in settlement of the larger debt he still owed. Here it is," he said, reaching into an inner pocket and withdrawing a folded yellowed sheet of vellum before he flung it carelessly to the tabletop, "although I didn't believe it to be more than the paper it was printed on, and was in fact prepared to wager it off again if I could find someone foolish enough to want it. I can't return the money. Indeed," he said regretfully, "I lost it just last night to a better dicer than I've met in months. Hence Mrs. Cobb's cooperation tonight. I must make up the room rent, sirs," he said on his first half-smile, "but if the young idiot had told me the whole, he would've had the whole of it back. No," he corrected himself quickly, with a rueful grin, "not the whole, for we needed a good breakfast, but the most. For I'm not in the business of fleecing ewe-lambs. It was a very black sheep I thought I was clipping, my friend. And you?" he asked suddenly. "Is it Robin Hood and his merry man I address, then?"

"What, when the only deserving poor we concern ourselves with is ourselves?" Mr. Tryon laughed as he took the deed and tucked it away in his vast waistcoat. "No, not at all. Sit down, my lord, please. We, my cohort and I, are not in the habit of rescuing damsels or fighting dragons in the natural way of things. Say we are, rather, soldiers of fortune in the ongoing war against our own poverty. Only now and again we feel we must lend a hand when one is needed. Come," he said then, extending his own hand, "take mine, and let's cry truce. Mr. Arden Lyons at your service, my lord, and my good friend Julian Dylan, the Viscount Hazelton."

"And I," the old gentleman said, taking that large hand in a firm grip, "am actually Lord Wyndham, and the lovely lady is truly the widowed Mrs. Cobb, although," he said with a slightly wicked glance as the blond young man took her hand, "her husband never knew anyone in my family, or we wouldn't have let her marry away from us in the first place."

After they'd shaken hands all around, Mr. Lyons called a waiter and asked for some wine to accompany the light dinner he ordered for all, not as penance, he insisted, but because he was hungry too.

They chatted as they waited for their supper, and amused each other by comparing notes on a great many of the same people that they'd met in their travels across the Continent. And if Mr. Lyons and the Viscount Hazelton were not specific as to exactly where they'd passed all of the past year, Lord Wyndham and Mrs. Cobb were never precise when they documented what they did with those they'd met.

"No," Lord Wyndham said sadly at last, "I'm not very successful, I suppose, because I fancy myself a gamester, not a trickster. The truth is that the luck is seldom in the cards for me—for long. I've had more fortunes in my keeping than a shilling-a-sitting seer at a country fair, but I've lost more than I can remember having, too. I cannot," he sighed, "resist a good wager."

"And cannot," Mrs. Cobb put in with a little smile, "make one neither. Why, Geoff, you wouldn't know a good wager from a fool's errand, and you never wait to tell the difference."

"Roxie's not a gamester," Lord Wyndham explained, not in the least offended. "She likes the traveling and the excitement surrounding it, and doesn't understand the lure of it in the least. In fact, she'd not wager a pin to your gold watch that the sun will rise tomorrow. A good cautious lass. And yes," he said with not a little regret in his voice, "she's only window-dressing for me, Viscount, as much a daughter to me as my own, though if I were a decade or two younger . . ."

"And I the greatest fool in creation . . ." Roxanne Cobb laughed.

When the waiter arrived with their dinner, Mr. Lyons heaved himself up and begged their leave to freshen up before he dined with them. He left the remaining three at the table, waving away the baron's help, declining the viscount's company as well, and leaning heavily on his cane, sighed, and, uncomplaining, or at least, complaining mutedly, made his way out of the salon to his room abovestairs. His company made themselves so busy when he left, between the wine and their increasingly entertaining stories, that they didn't begin to miss him until the waiter appeared and began to fret over the chicken growing cold and the aspic growing warm. Then Lord Wyndham eyed a cutlet as wistfully as he'd ever studied an odds sheet at the races, and seeing the cover raised off a steaming stuffed goose, Roxanne Cobb swallowed hard and took an extra long swallow of her wine.

The viscount immediately began to serve out the food to the others, explaining, as he also heaped Mr. Lyons' plate high, that his friend was not such a gourmet that he'd mind a tepid dinner, which he deserved if he didn't shake a leg. It was while both Mrs. Cobb and Lord Wyndham paused, digesting this unusually callous remark about the lame old fellow along with the first bites of their dinner, that another, even more remarkable thing made them pause, forks falling unnoticed to their plates as they sat openmouthed.

For, quite suddenly, a complete stranger paused at their tableside. And then, without a word, had the audacity to pull out a chair, swing into it, and without so much as a "pardon me," picked up the cutlery and proceeded to dine on the absent Mr. Lyon's dinner.

Lord Wyndham, the first to collect himself, drew himself up and, swollen with outrage, exclaimed, "Excuse me!" in an awful voice.

"No need," the stranger said amiably, as best he could around a mouthful, "the capon is excellent, thank you."

It wasn't so much the viscount's smothered laugh as it was the stranger's familiar bright hazel eyes that made Lord Wyndham pause as he was about to call the waiters to eject the presumptuous young fellow. Then he sat back and stared, and slowly he too began to laugh. Roxanne Cobb didn't. She only sat, her napery to her lips, and finally gasped, shaking her head in astonishment, "Well, I never . . ."

"But he always does, you see," the viscount whispered in her ear, but she was still so astounded at what she saw that she scarcely noted he left his lips close for an extra second, he so liked the rose-and-lily scent he detected there.

The stranger grinned at them, seeming well-pleased at their reaction. He was a huge but trim and fit fellow, as tall as a young oak, and almost as wide at the shoulders as a tabletop made of one. Before he'd seated himself, Lord Wyndham had briefly noted that his figure tapered from a barrel of a chest to a trim waist, washboard-flat abdomen, neat hips, and then to broad, long muscular legs. A thick neck supported the well-shaped head, his hair was a thick and springy ginger crop, his face tanned, unlined, and smooth with craggy features that seemed hewn from stubborn rock, from wide brow to straight nose, from generous mouth to jut of chin.

He was a man of Promethean proportions, but although he was not in the least fat, there was nothing at all lean about him. Although an expert tailor had fashioned his correct evening wear, it would have taken a magician to make him resemble a gentleman of fashion. For even though he moved with a curiously easy grace for a man his size, he *was* his size, and so nothing in the style of the admired gentlemen of the day; nothing of a languid man of fashion, of a town, or, for that matter, country beau, either. There was simply too much of him, and every inch exhibited a vigorous and robust hardihood. Neither was his face anything in the acceptable style, but that wasn't to say it was unhandsome. Clearly, it could be jovial or threatening or even oddly attractive, and all at its owner's wish. He didn't remotely resemble the footsore old man that had grumbled his way from their table earlier, but it was the same wise and amused hazel eyes that gave the game away.

"I *am* impressed," Lord Wyndham said, when he could.

"And I am reeking of spirit gum. Julian, what did you do with the skin cream we bought in Paris? Fellow's vain as a peacock, hides away anything to beautify himself with, not that it will do him the least good when he's with me," Arden Lyons confided loudly to Roxanne Cobb, as she, finally accepting the inevitable truth of his identity, sat back to stare at him with shock and delight.

"A lot of padding . . . well"—he grinned as he explained to her—"perhaps not *such* a lot of padding, but a great deal of acting, and the will to appear to be different does the trick as well as the putty and paint, for it would never do for us to go about clandestine business in our usual fashion if we want to be discreet. We are, you may have noted, each singularly remarkable, although distinctly different in our manly beauty."

His guests stared and reflected on the truth even in the jest of that, for if the Viscount Hazelton resembled a young god, his companion was surely a Titan, or if described in mortal terms: one was a young Hercules to the other's Adonis, for there was certainly something mythic, even fantastical about the pair. Of course, they'd always be memorable. But the giant gentleman didn't give them time to reflect on it for long.

"And, yes," he said, leaning toward the blond young woman and gesturing with his fork toward the viscount, "you've guessed it, my dear. He's actually seventy-five if he's a day, bald as a day-old chick, and knock-kneed, to boot. Amazing what some spirit gum and padding will do, isn't it?"

Their meal was passed in joviality, all past accusations and suspicions laid to rest. The fair-haired young woman had two gallants to butter her up more than they did their bread, and the Baron Wyndham was receiving more information, he ruefully admitted, about men he'd mistaken for gentlemen before he'd lost several of his fortunes to them, than he'd ever imagined. They were all so in concert, so content with each other, that they were pleased to sit and chat long after they'd done with their meal.

It was surprising when the Baron Wyndham stopped speaking in the midst of a story about a certain mad duke with a fondness for wagering on any horse with three white socks, to look up with an arrested expression to the doorway he'd been idly watching since he'd demolished his dinner. He'd seen dozens of persons entering and leaving from it as the night had gone on, and yet now he paused and smiled. But so did many another gentleman in the salon.

A stout middle-aged couple, almost equal in height and girth, both overdressed in the latest fashions, as similar as any fraternal twins or long-married pair might be, stood there looking about eagerly. Between them, a vision that stopped most of the gentlemen who were not rabid gamesters in mid-wager stood shyly, protected on each side by the oddly matched couple. The young lady was all in white and her long golden hair lay neatly all in a coil on one of her white shoulders, reaching to just above the peek her demure but fashionable gown permitted at the rise of her shapely little uptilted breasts. Her long-lashed eyes were cast down past her divinely rounded form to her satin slippers, but not a few inveterate gamblers in the room wouldn't have hesitated to wager a week's wages on those lovely orbs being cornflower blue when they at last opened wide, for such a little beauty would have everything she ought. Behind her, a long Meg of a chaperone stood stiffly, white-faced and all in black, and glowering, it seemed, at every

man in the room, but especially, if one were of a mind to
tear one's eyes from the little enchantress newly arrived in
their midst to notice, at the Baron Wyndham.

But that gentleman only smiled widely, and rising, raised
his glass to the persons in the doorway.

They smiled back at him in turn, all save for the dour
chaperone, and began to approach his table.

"Ah, good, my daughter has arrived," Lord Wyndham
said comfortably, as proudly as any father in the land might
do.

"That little beauty?" the viscount asked softly and wonderingly of his friend Mr. Lyons, as they too rose to their
feet.

"No, no, he'd have lost her in a game of whist long since.
It's the duenna with eyes like thunder," his friend replied
absently.

"A baron's daughter a servant?" the blond young man
hooted softly.

"I've known viscounts' sons to be coachmen," Mr. Lyons
replied easily as his friend smothered a laugh, before he
added piously, "and my own papa, the sainted vicar,
would've been shattered had he been unlucky enough to live
to see his only begotten child a wicked gamester. No, she's
his chick, all right: they've both got clean, sharp lines,
they're fine etchings, the beauty's all pastels, a watercolor—
twelve to one on it, and a case of my favorite champagne
besides."

"Done!" the viscount said for his ear only. "And I'll
enjoy every drop I drink of it, Arden, for I've got you at
last, it's cheese to chalk, and they're nothing like."

The wager had been made impetuously, more in an attempt to confound his friend for once than out of absolute
conviction, and so the viscount eyed the chaperone more
carefully now after his sudden rash claim, for he wasn't in
the habit of noticing servants too closely, especially when
they had deliciously nubile young charges in tow. It was true
she was more youthful than she'd appeared at first stare; in
fact, on closer inspection it was clear that she, too, was
quite young. And her features, on second glance, could be
seen to be as finely drawn as a cameo's, although he'd seen
few cameos with such full and tempting lips. She was, in
fact, remarkable-looking, and could, he realized with growing interest the more he looked at her, be magnificent-look-
ing, but then he couldn't judge more, for she'd turned away.

Yet she'd looked nothing like the Baron Wyndham, for she was tall, with large speaking eyes as dark and secret as a quarter-past midnight, and her bound hair was black as the night shadows behind her. Lord Wyndham was a small man with pale eyes, and what little of his thin hair remained had the dusty look light brown takes on with age. Satisfied with his wager then, the viscount stood back respectfully, waiting for the introductions and his rare moment of triumph to come.

The middle-aged couple, soon discovered to be the "estimable Mr. and Mrs. Deems, from London," were just as respectful in turn, equally awed by Mr. Lyons' size and the viscount's comeliness, before they were thrilled and gratified to monosyllables by the viscount's title.

"And here is lovely little Miss Deems, gentlemen," the baron said teasingly as the tiny beauty in white dipped a curtsy to them. "If she were any more handsome, the Deemses would have to hire a dragon to guard her, and not just my own lovely daughter. And now, Viscount, Mr. Lyons, I'm pleased to make you known to this other beautiful lady, the Honorable . . . ah, I always will forget, won't I? It's still hard to admit to your growing up, I imagine. Forgive me, sweet . . . gentlemen—Mrs. Francesca Devlin, my daughter."

They made their bows to the golden-haired beauty, but when Francesca Devlin inclined her long black-draped body stiffly toward them, the viscount couldn't repress a sigh.

As soon as he was able, while the baron was smiling at Miss Deems and complimenting her parents on the child's great good looks this night, the viscount remarked resignedly to his friend, "Done and done in again, Arden. I doubt you still cast a shadow, because you have the devil's own way about you, but you'll have the champagne in the morning. You win."

But then he looked hard at Arden, because he didn't celebrate his victory. Instead, he stood unusually silent, gazing thoughtfully at the dark-haired, dark-eyed chaperone. For he too had seen the fury in her eyes as they'd been introduced. And then had felt the scorn in the cold and withering glance she'd given them before she'd concealed all, and let the emotion leach out of those great dark eyes, to leave them bleak as her pale face had been when she'd deliberately turned her back on them.

"Ah, no, Julian, my boy," Arden Lyons said slowly, still

bemused, watching her as she glanced back once over her shoulder toward them, only to fix him with a look of unmistakable loathing before she took her charge's arm to be sure she didn't also dare a glance back at the two remarkable gentlemen studying them.

"Wrong again," he went on, but on a sigh. "It's clear I've only just lost again."

The viscount looked at him quizzically.

"The Beauty or the Dragon?" he asked.

"Why, neither, I think now," the large gentleman replied on a half-smile, recovering his usual poise and bantering manner. "After all, you know my prodigious charm, and I've just decided I've been fairly and truly challenged," he explained unnecessarily, seeing he was already guiding his friend with him as he strolled past the glowering chaperone to the beautiful Miss Deems's side.

2

THE BEDCHAMBER was among the best that money could buy in France these days, because once it had been among the best that a gracious and noble host could have offered to his guests. A revolution had spared the great house and its contents only because a clever revolutionary had coveted and claimed it well before the mob had, and by the time they did, he'd already risen from their masses to become one of their leaders, and so as untouchable as its original lordly owner had once been. When his leader had fallen from his pedestal in turn, he'd at least been clever enough to retain his head in many ways. As a republican at heart, if not in practice, he wasn't averse to opening his home to the public, at ridiculously high fees, for the purposes of play, and so had held on to it as well as his own cool head.

It was a room redolent of roses. There were improbable blue and gold roses in the carpets, their buds everywhere upon the draperies; fanciful carved roses adorned the bedposts; tiny representations of them climbed up the walls on their stretched silk arbors, looped around the edges of the ceiling in intricate plasterwork, were strewn in the upholstery of all the fragile chairs, and echoes of them, outlined in gold embroidery thread, were embossed upon the white swags of the great bed's canopy. The young girl whose head was emerging from the white nightdress she was being helped into was no less of a lovely and blooming wonder of nature, and her mama nodded in satisfaction as that perfect cheek blushed a more tender pink at the words she'd just heard.

"Aye," the stout lady said as she perched upon an edge of the high bed and watched her daughter's maid brush out her golden hair, "depend on it, Cee-cee. Both of them were struck to the heart, but because they're gents to their fingertips, and men of the world with it, you'd never know. Never a stare or a pinch, nor a stammer or a foolish brag, nor will either of them pour the butter-boat over your head, but they never took their eyes off you for a moment, nor did they ever leave your side, neither. I thought that Mrs. Cobb would bust," she gloated, "when the viscount asked how long we were staying on, and then that lovely Mr. Lyons said 'how fortuitous!' since they was staying on for just that long too. As if they didn't decide on it the moment they got an eyeful of you, my dear," she chortled, swinging her short legs back and forth over the side of the bed as a girl might do at the thought.

"Which of them do you like better, Mama?" the lovely girl asked, watching her mama's reaction in the glass as her maid lovingly drew up her golden tresses and began to braid them for the night.

"Early days," her mother answered thoughtfully, "because the viscount's a treat to look at, without doubt—but a girl might be foolish to wed a gent that beautiful, since the gentlemen age better than the ladies, and that's a sad fact, and even get to be better-looking as they get older. Besides, who wants a husband who'll outshine you in looks if you don't take care even now? Still . . . he's a pleasure to rest your eyes on, and a viscount to boot. And the large gentleman, that lovely Mr. Lyons," she went on, ignoring a gasp emitted from the corner of the room, "a grand, big fellow, and, your father gave me to understand just before we left the gentlemen tonight, with a walloping big fortune to match. Well-connected as he is well-mannered, I'd wager. It's never necessary to hold a title to be high in society. Just look at Mr. Brummell himself, a valet's son, they say," she sighed happily, thinking with pleasure of how far impudence could rise in this modern day. "And with such a husband, you'd never have to worry about being outshone, would you?" she continued enthusiastically. "Those big chaps are so protective, I've always had a soft spot for them, still—a viscount, and with such looks combined with yours, my dear, imagine the children. . . ."

As Mrs. Deems grew silent, with a reflective smile at the happy choices she'd just described, her daughter grew pensive as well, and so both were a little startled by the vehemence in the voice which intruded on their reveries. Francesca Devlin leapt to her feet and gave a gasp that converted to a croak when she began to speak, and that in itself was odd, for Mrs. Devlin had the loveliest, most soothing deep and whispery voice in the usual way of things.

"Mrs. Deems!" the dark haired chaperone cried, "I beg of you, don't even think of it! . . . After all," she said, in as much of a quieter tone as she could manage despite her agitation, because she became aware of the sudden amazed quiet that had fallen over the room at her impulsive cry as mother and daughter Deems stared at her. Even the maid had left off her work, and stood, three hanks of Cecily's hair suspended in her hands, stopped in mid-braid by surprise.

"I mean," Francesca Devlin went on in her more normal husky tones, "you hardly know the gentlemen. Indeed, you scarcely know if they are true gentlemen at all. After all," she said in an appeal to Mrs. Deems's home wisdom, since that lady only looked at her oddly, "fine feathers do not make fine birds, and you've only just met them, and in a gaming house at that, and abroad as well. Pray don't consider either one as Cee-cee's future husband after only such a brief acquaintance," she begged, and then, realizing that she was being more than presumptuous by Mrs. Deems's growing truculent stare, she concluded more softly and a little desperately, "for Cee-cee can have her pick of the gentlemen, here and at home, you know."

"No, that she cannot, Mrs. Devlin," Mrs. Deems said indulgently, finally understanding and so relenting after being just a touch annoyed at the chaperone's interference, and after exchanging a knowing look with her daughter, she went on in kindly fashion, as though lecturing a child, "for we tried and we couldn't get a toe into anywhere fashionable

in London, you know, even with Cee-cee's looks and Mr.
Deems's money. We got invitations, but to trumpery masquerades and public entertainments; we met gentlemen, but
they were scramblers or old jades or younger sons with no
prospects or no sense, who'd do Cee-cee a favor by marrying so that she could settle their debts and feel honored
to do so again and again. No, no, my dear, we're here to
ensure Cee-cee's future, and we shall, my Sunday bonnet
to your shilling on it. The best of Britain is in France this
Season, and society here is freer. We'll catch us a worthy
gent, never fear, and one that will suit Cee-cee, Mr. Deems,
and myself, at that. Cecily Deems will wed into fashion,
and never doubt it. Mr. Deems is a canny gent, as clever
with reading people as he is with making money," she
chuckled. "And," she added comfortably before the chaperone could speak again, as she clearly wished to do, "remember, your own dear papa introduced us, didn't he?"

The dark-haired chaperone became very still. Nodding
triumphantly as she climbed down from the bed to kiss her
daughter good night, Mrs. Deems added, "Thanks for your
concern, Mrs. Devlin, but you were a young lady of fashion, and so you wouldn't know what it's like to be on the
outside looking in. But never fear, we'll get Cee-cee on the
inside, and sooner than you think."

And why not? she thought as she bade the governess good
night too and went off to her own rooms for the night with
everything in train to marry off her exquisite, well-dowered
little daughter as she deserved at last: Cee-cee rigged out
in the latest fashions and looking like an angel, reservations
at the best hotels, a baron's daughter for a chaperone, and
the baron himself to lend them countenance. He might be a
gamester, true, and down on his luck at the moment, so far
down that his widowed daughter had to work for her fare
back home. But the true gentry were sometimes wild, after
all. And they'd been lucky to find the baron and his daughter
when they had. For though the baron's fortunes rose and
fell, his title and his address remained of the finest. And his
daughter, poor thing, if she'd nothing else left, had her manners and breeding. And just look, after only one week of
employing Mrs. Devlin, it had already netted them an introduction to two fine eligible gentlemen from her father.

Clever Mr. Deems, his wife thought as she went to her
room to prepare to greet him as such a canny gent deserved,
to reason out that a gaming house was precisely where one

might meet the most eligible gentlemen. And there, free of society's strictures, he might become besotted, for constant company with Cee-cee would turn any gent's thought to dalliance, and, once he saw that wasn't possible, to matrimony. Then they could nab him before he remembered responsibilities to the name and the family and that sort of rot, for foreign travel altered one, just as Mr. Deems claimed, bless his heart, she thought, feeling strangely young and giddy herself because of tonight's events. Then, so content she began to cobble up an imaginary dress for the wedding for herself, she went to her room, her only present doubt being as to which of the two fine gents would make a better husband for her daughter: the charming, beautiful viscount or the wealthy, manly, jovial giant.

"I think the viscount is amazingly handsome, but do you think he would outshine me in time?" Cecily asked her chaperone as that lady made ready to bid her good night.

"I think," Francesca said determinedly, "that you do not know anything of him but his face, and so you should not even think of 'time' in regard to him . . ." And then, noting the maidservant's displeasure at her direct disobedience to Mrs. Deems's obvious wishes, she added weakly, despising herself but seeing the need, ". . . yet."

"But your papa introduced us," Cecily said smugly, as though reassuring herself so that she could go to bed allowed to dream of amazingly beautiful viscounts in peace and obedience.

"So he did," Francesca replied tersely, thinking that her papa would have introduced them to a man-eating lion if it served his purposes, and knowing that if she said that she could never go on in the Deemses' employ, and oh how she needed to. She sighed heavily.

"Oh, Mrs. Devlin," Cecily cried out in her little girl's voice, swinging round in her chair in front of her dressing table so quickly that her golden braid whipped out like a lash, "I'm so sorry. Has all this talk of weddings made you remember your own dear Harry?"

"No, no, I'm only weary," Francesca reassured her, feeling dreadful about her several deceptions, for with all her loveliness, Cecily had no more cruelty than the lovely flower she resembled; it was only unfortunate that she had little more wit than one. "Thoughts of Harry only bring me happiness," she lied, "and so it is—if you wed someone you have known well and for a long while."

She could do no more just now, Francesca thought angrily as she left Cecily's room, but, she resolved as she strode in a most unladylike fashion to her father's chambers, she was about to do a great deal more. She was so full of what she'd say and how she'd put it, so ready to rage and so justified in it too, that she didn't look where she was going and found, after she'd turned the corner of the corridor, that she'd walked straight into a wall.

And then the wall put out two strong arms to hold her upright and keep her from reeling, and leaning down, inquired in a smooth deep rumble of a voice, "Are you all right, Mrs. Devlin?"

She looked up, and then up further, and then up even above the white neckcloth so vast and so exquisitely fresh that it glowed like a beacon in the dim hallway, to see a concerned pair of eyes watching her carefully.

"You came around the corner so quickly . . . ." Mr. Lyons began, and then added ruefully, "and I tend to fill a corridor rather completely. There was, you understand," he explained further, when she didn't reply, "nowhere for me to go to avoid a collision. But don't concern yourself too much," he added in amused tones when he saw from the tightening set of her lips that she'd begun to recover enough to realize who he was at last, "I'm not too shaken, although I confess I'm a trifle concerned because I tend to bruise so easily. But no doubt after a nice little lie-down I'll be myself again, thank you."

He grinned at her and she gave herself a tiny shake, and then, when he still didn't move, she looked down at her arms rather pointedly. Only then did he release her, and she felt curiously light and insubstantial after he'd done so, for his hold on her, though light, had anchored her completely.

"I beg your pardon," she said properly, "it was entirely my fault." After a pause which he did not fill, and seeing that he still filled her path entirely and was making absolutely no effort to remove himself from it, she went on coolly, "I was on my way to see my father, who is just down the hallway, so if you wouldn't mind . . ."

"I wouldn't mind in the least," he said amiably, "but he isn't just down the hallway. He's downstairs with my friend Viscount Hazelton. I've only just left them together. Talking," he said at once, when he saw her sudden look of alarm. "We've done with wagering for the night. Only a fool plays past the midnight hour anyway, and whatever the time, we're far too awake to the time of day, my friend and I, to dare wager any longer with your papa.''

He said it easily enough, and the light was too dim to make out his precise expression, but she'd seen the white flash of his teeth after he'd said it, and believed she was being mocked. For who would not dare to wager with her unlucky papa? And who more so than this professional gamester? That he was a professional Captain Sharp was a thing she'd have staked her reputation on, and she, as the long-suffering daughter of a gambling man, had learned to bet on nothing but eventual disappointment. This gentleman and his elegant friend were too at ease in this house, too at ease with her papa, and too at ease in their world to be anything but what she'd imagined them to be when she'd first clapped eyes on them tonight. And that was: exactly like her papa. For if they were cronies of his, then they must be gamesters, or worse, fortune seekers of some sort, although, from the look of them, obviously more successful ones than poor papa. Although that, she knew, was not difficult.

"I see," she said coldly. Not only did she detest him for what he was, she remembered precisely what she was now, baron's daughter or not: a woman in service, a supposedly impoverished widow in need of a secure position. Just the sort of female, she'd always heard, who could be expected to find herself being compromised by men of his sort. And she was alone with him in a darkened hallway.

He stared down at her, registering every detail of her appearance, and then, because her eyes were becoming used to the half-light, she could clearly see the warm look of appreciation in his eyes as he studied her. Half-terrified, she then realized she was half-thrilled, and then she was immediately vexed with herself at the sudden admission that it had been so long since she'd been looked at as a woman, that admiration from a rogue even of his low caliber had pleased her. That it could, even for an unguarded moment, in any fashion, upset her considerably.

She eyed him as warily as he studied her intently in those seconds that he loomed over her. He completely blocked her path, but the slight scent of spice and leather that emanated from him reinforced the sense of masculinity that emanated from him as well, and pleasant as it was, it frightened her even more. She swallowed so hard she was sure he heard the crash and founder of her gulp, as she did in her ears. But she had dignity, she couldn't run. Besides, she thought, she'd only one direction to flee in. But she'd a sharp tongue and could summon a satisfactory shriek if she was prepared to. And, she'd fingernails. She braced herself.

He spoke.

"Good night, Mrs. Devlin," he said in an amused rumble that sounded almost like a purr.

And stepped aside, and flattened himself as best he was able against the wall to make room for her passage. She was so startled by his entirely proper act that she hesitated before she held her head high and marched past him. Then he spoke again.

"Oh," he said as her shoulders went up, "yes. Sleep well, and we'll see you in the morning."

She wheeled around, but before she could ask, he explained, "Your papa and Mr. Deems kindly accepted our offer to show you and Miss Deems some of the sights in the vicinity of Paris tomorrow. It bids to be a cold day, I see," he said merrily, "so do dress warmly. Till then," he added before he bowed and walked off down the hall.

Francesca was thoroughly furious by the time she reached her room. The more so because she'd had to wait until she was sure he'd gone before she'd doubled back again, remembering only after her encounter with the vile Mr. Lyons that there was no point in going to her papa's room, and that her own room was on the other side of the house, where she'd just come from, near to Cecily's, only one floor above hers, as befitted a servant.

She locked her door behind her, although she ruefully realized there was little need of it; no one had looked at her as a woman since she'd come to this hotel, since she'd agreed to work for the Deemses—no one, that was, except for the villainous Mr. Lyons. It seemed to her that since she'd willed that they would not, so they had not. She'd wished to be seen only as a good and decent, meek and proper woman, and had found that acting as one and thinking as one, keeping her head low and her eyes averted and wearing black and being deferential, had done the trick. But then, since before tonight she'd never lifted her fine eyes to the gentlemen to see their reaction to her presence, she could be forgiven for having thought that, especially since she'd wanted and needed so badly to believe it.

She'd quite forgotten, she sighed to herself, that once she'd been thought of, once upon a time but not so long ago, as a beautiful woman. No, that wasn't quite true, she corrected herself guiltily as she came into the room and walked the few steps to her window, for servants' rooms, even upper servants' rooms, are not, even, or especially, in noble houses, anything like those for honored guests. The only roses in her small spare chamber were those that arose in her cheeks at the thought of her self-deception. For no, she'd never really forgotten that once she'd been considered lovely, and that, damn her vanity, she thought miserably, had made her present servitude all the more wretched for her.

"My own dark lady," Harry had called her. "My own dark beauty."

And that too added to her guilt. But then, in those lost carefree days she'd not cloaked herself in widow's weeds and avoided men's eyes, frowning at the mere thought of dalliance, walking head down and hesitant like a proper grieving widow ought to do. Only she wasn't, she raged as she struggled to unbutton the detested shapeless black dress hastily so that she could fling it off the faster, for she, a servant herself, had no maid to assist her with the many tiny buttons. Not meek, she almost wept, sending a pearl button flying in her clumsiness, not widowed, she snarled to herself as she tugged her bodice down, not respectable, she thought, stepping out of the dress at last, and leaving it, like a deserted shell, almost all of a shape, behind her on the floor.

Now calm, and merely sorely troubled, she walked to her window and gazed through a shining sheaf of jet-black hair she'd just released from its bonds, to stare at the ghost of herself reflected in her night-silvered windowpane. And that ghost, she grieved again, was likely all she'd ever know of happiness, all she'd ever have of life, unless her fortunes turned. Unless, she thought, resting her aching head at last against the cool pane, her father's fortunes turned again, and though they might, for all things were possible, she supposed, there was nothing she could do but wait. Because she'd already done all she could for herself, and that had netted her nothing but these useless tears she dashed away with the back of her hand; weak, self-indulgent evidences of her shattered pride that they were, she detested them as much as she did her helplessness.

She'd done everything she could think of to extricate herself from the situation she'd found herself in since she'd joined her father, only a few weeks that felt more like a few centuries ago. And she'd tried everything Father could think of as well—at least, she amended, with a ghost of a smile, those things she was willing to do. For she wouldn't take over Roxanne Cobb's position for any reason—standing about as a distraction and a decoration for lackwit boys and drunken gentlemen in gaming hells not being an occupation she considered either her vocation or her destiny. Only what those were, she couldn't say, any more than she could say what final folly had brought her to her own special sort of degradation of the spirit. Because for all that she refused to play at Father and Roxanne's games, and for all that she worked at the virtuous task of companion, still she had to lie, deceive, and playact to do it—just like Roxie Cobb, just like any cheat and scoundrel belowstairs tonight in the gambling salons.

For she was not Francesca Devlin, aged five-and-twenty, relict of the brave Lt. Harry Devlin, honorably fallen at Waterloo these ten months past. She was the Honorable Francesca Carlisle, called "Fancy" by her friends, aged only just one-and-twenty, and yet a maid, and very much one, for she'd no more been a wife to poor Harry than she'd been the lover that she'd sometimes been tempted to be to him. And she wasn't meek or calm or disciplined enough to be a fit companion to poor foolish Cee-Cee Deems either, not when she couldn't even reconcile herself to her deception. She was only a confused and silly chit herself, she thought furiously, in need of respectable employment so that she could earn her way home. For she was terribly homesick, that much was undeniably true, even though, she admitted on a sigh, she'd no home to remember or return to, and scarcely knew what it was she missed so badly.

Father had owned a home once, a great stone manor house built at the time of Queen Elizabeth. She'd heard about it so often she fancied she could picture it, but she didn't remember it at all, since it had been sold out from under her when she was only an infant. Father had gamed it away, of course. Just as he'd gambled away his only son's respect—because a father was supposed to hold on to his heritage so that he could pass it on as it had been handed to him; and as he'd gamed away his family's friendship—because the head of the family was supposed to keep the clan together, not to lose everything and continually come to them for more to toss away; and just as he'd continued to play and lost his wife's love—because a husband was supposed to find more joy in his bed with a live love than by clutching pasteboard pictures of painted queens to his thrilled and wildly beating heart.

So by the time Francesca had learned to spell her long name right and write it out neatly, the disillusioned son had taken up the army to make his fortune, the rest of the family had turned their backs on its nominal head, and the slighted wife had found a decent man forced to an indecency by his love and fierce feelings of protectiveness. For he took the baroness with him one moonlit night, all the way to an isle off Scotland's coast, and thence to wive without benefit of clergy, so that thereafter only far-off Britain knew of her bigamy and his part in it.

The boy was older and had a legacy, and was left to it. The girl child too had been left behind. Perhaps her mother thought that she might lead a better life so, or so she ever after tried to believe, or else she'd been left so that there'd be nothing to remind the mother of her failure, and no trace of her marriage with the baron to shadow her new life. At any rate, she was gone to the kindliest world of all, Francesca learned, while giving her illegal husband their third child, about the time she herself was learning to cope with her new woman's body. And once Francesca had mastered the way of walking and talking in her new guise as a tall and elegant young lady, and not just a leggy, misplaced child, the only son had finally found, if not his fortune, then his sad destiny, and not in gold, but lead, in the form of a ball to his lung, on the bloody fields of Waterloo.

And so, just as it had always been only Francesca and her father—and not even that, for whenever he was in funds, she was in a good girls' school somewhere, and when he was out of funds, she was in a mediocre girls' school somewhere—it remained so. But when she was too old for schooling, and dared to write to tell him of it, she'd received his summons to come live with him on the Continent. Astonished and delighted at her turn of luck, she'd forgotten that he lived by his turns of luck. Scarcely daring to believe that she could finally live with her remote and adored father, she'd packed and left England at once. Only to discover him impoverished again by the time she'd arrived at his side, by two chance things—a horse that decided not to run hard one hard day, and cards that had turned up eights, when they ought, by all calculations, to have been aces.

For all she'd dreamed of seeing Paris and Venice and all the sights she'd read about, she couldn't go on with him, not if it meant going as a gamester, not when all she'd wanted to do was to see those things with him as a daughter. But she hadn't the funds to go back after she'd paid her hired traveling companion the last of the money she possessed, so that that indignant matron, lured out of England on a fool's errand, as she'd complained, could return. She simply couldn't afford to go back herself, even if she knew to where she could now go.

For there could be a delay in placing herself. There might be a teaching position at some girls' school. There might be some relative to take pity on her and find her some other position. But such "mights" could be expensive, since she didn't even have a home. She wouldn't call on her old school friends, believing that the firmest friendship couldn't support the twin burdens of sympathy and guilt their better stations would produce in them. She'd have to find employment of some sort, although there weren't many choices open to a young woman, even one with some education. And she was wise enough to know there were even fewer for a good-looking but respectable one. Still, drudgery itself, or worse, pity, would be preferable to living her father's sort of life. She, a gamester's daughter who'd never gamed, had quite enough of games. Just as she, who'd never taken a chance, and so had never known all of physical love, knew she'd not have much chance of discovering that honorably now either.

Oh, she was well-enough-looking. She wasn't so modest that she was blind. She knew that much, without excessive vanity, and without exaggeration. Her eyes were large and darkest brown beneath thin winged black brows, her mouth generous but shapely, her nose straight and small, her skin clear with a russet blush when she was flattered by being told of its beauty, for it was brushed with gold even when it wasn't exposed to sun, and her long thick hair was ink on a cloudless night and shone with silver or fire, depending on whether it was sun or moonlight that touched its shining silken surfaces.

And her form, she thought, eyeing her outline in the shadowed pane, was long-waisted and slender enough for current fashion, which dictated wearing next to nothing, and yet she had curves at waist and hip, and full, high, pointed breasts that both pleased and sometimes even excited her with the possibilities she saw in men's eyes when they gazed at them. When they had looked at them, she thought, so long ago, last winter, when she was allowed to be young. She'd been touched by a man only once, and then only for a brief moment—before she took fright and he took a deep breath and remembered he was her brother's best friend—by Harry, when she really was so very young.

That year, by some monstrous good stroke of luck, Father had been in funds. He'd rented a manor house grand enough to house Queen Elizabeth in, perhaps as a nod to what he'd lost, and he'd invited his son to it for his leave, perhaps as another. It was to be a summer of reparations. Francesca had come home from school for the vacation too, and although she was rising eighteen then, it was only the third time she'd ever done so, and never to so fine a home, or to find such wonderful company within it.

Lieutenant the Honorable Bramwell Carlisle was tall, but fair and pale-eyed as her father, and he constantly teased his young sister about the ancient bold Gypsy in the family closet that peeked out at him from her eyes. Father laughingly protested it was actually that mythical Welsh highwayman that had stolen beneath some ancestral sheets, but when they were alone, it was Harry, her brother's best friend, who had sighed at her and said it surely was a Spanish grandee or Italian prince that had lent his grace and charm to his dark and lovely love.

They played at love that summer, she and Lieutenant Harry Devlin. It was more play than love, she realized now, as he must have then, at eight years her senior and with the experience of foreign nations and their women to his benefit. Pehaps that was what gave him his patience, and the control to give her only his light kisses and gentle embraces and accept her hesitant compliance and close-lipped chaste kisses in return. For the one time he relaxed, that night toward the end of their summer idyll, he taught her to open her lips beneath his, and when she did and came closer into his arms, his hands stole up to hold her more intimately, and then she didn't know who took more alarm first—the shy but excited young girl, or her rueful suitor, who remembered his stronger bond to her brother even as he felt the strong pull of desire for her.

Slender, brown-haired, and brown-eyed, with ready laughter and enormous charm to more than make up for the great good looks he swore he lacked, he enchanted her and she had, in her innocence, loved him. Then, that winter, when she continued to write to him, his prose became more ardent. Her feelings for him grew, and she began to believe that she could love him beyond innocence, and regretted that interrupted embrace in the garden, planning how to give him more when next they met.

But that would have to be in the next world now, she thought, deflated from present anger to indulge in past sorrow, for he'd perished with Bram, brothers-in-death as they'd been brothers-in-arms, at their unit's glorious victory at Waterloo.

His monument was not only in her heart but also in her assumed name. She'd taken it when Father had said, and said rightly, she knew, that she'd never be hired on, not even by the social-climbing Deemses he'd met at the hotel where he'd awaited her, as a companion for their eighteen-year-old daughter if she were scarcely past twenty herself, and an unwed chit at that. So if it was a small lie to add a few years to her name, it was, she'd felt, a tribute to add his memory and become Harry's wife as well, at least in death. For if in life he couldn't offer her the protection of his name that he'd sworn he'd give her when his tour was over, she knew he'd never mind giving it to her now when she needed it so badly.

She might as well take on the guise of a married woman, she'd decided, for she doubted she'd ever become one now. Even if she were of a mind ever to love again, a dowerless daughter of a self-exiled gambler was not likely to be in great demand in any social set.

The false Mrs. Devlin suppressed her tears. She was very good at doing that. She'd never had her own room before, except for those few times when she'd visited her friends or Father in his several rented houses, and so had learned that sobbing is no balm for a sore heart when it disturbs a dormitory full of sleepy girls, since lack of sleep eventually hardens the most gentle hearts. Nor would it help her now, she decided. She sniveled instead, and blew her nose, and, defeated and subdued, not even bothering to put on a nightrail, climbed into bed and pulled the covers over her head.

But being alone and awake beneath the covers with a warm naked body, even if it was her own, didn't help either, since it brought up thoughts she'd been forbidden to deal with, so she soon poked her long legs out from the coverlets and scurried to her wardrobe to get a nice thick long flannel robe to cover both her cold from the chill room and her warmth from herself. Then, perhaps seeking a way to divert her wakeful mind from its problems, she rehearsed what she'd say to Father when she got him alone the next day. She had to chastise him, but she didn't want to alienate him forever, and so was glad in a way that he hadn't been in his rooms tonight, even if it meant she'd had to deal with that monster of a man instead.

Thinking of the enormous Mr. Lyons refueled her anger. How could her father have brought such a man to the Deemses' notice? Rich as he was, and clever as he doubtless was, the rotund Mr. Deems knew business and ironmongering, but nothing at all about the sort of creatures that inhabited gaming hells, the sort that had drained her father dry for years. It was not only the loss of her own position Francesca feared, for all that she wanted to earn the generous wages the Deemses had offered her so that she might find her way home to whatever home she could find. But she fretted for the Deemses and their plans for themselves as well.

They'd dragged Cecily clear from Manchester to London, and from thence to France, where they'd met up with Francesca and her father not a week before. And, they'd admitted, in straightforward Deems fashion, with never a blush or a stammer, it was all to seek out a husband to get their dear girl into society. There were three older sisters with more intelligence than comeliness who had already wed from home to local lights, and two brothers who helped with the business and had taken good practical wives from similar families.

But they all wanted far more for Cecily. Perhaps because she was beyond beautiful, and as canny business persons it seemed uneconomical not to make more of her. Perhaps because she was as obedient as she was dependent, and the notion was irresistible once it had occurred to them. Or perhaps only because the Deemses, who found themselves thriving in these incredible modern times of discovery and invention, when any common man with wit could make as much money as any nobleman might have inherited a generation before, wanted to establish their own little empire now, with Cecily as the dowager empress. It might be a vain and foolish dream, for although Cecily was good and kind and sweet, as well as lovely, graceful, and flower-faced, she was so empty-headed that Francesca often found herself wondering what gnomish ancestor in the shrewd but squat and homely Deems clan had once carried off a thoughtless fairy child and so was responsible for her appearance in this generation. But for all her intellectual lacks, she was a dear child, and so it was irresponsible to expose her to smooth and subtle fortune hunters such as the incredibly handsome viscount and his huge and evil companion.

Not only did Francesca instinctively distrust such a glowingly attractive male as the viscount, but especially one met in a gambling establishment, so she doubted the viscount had more than his handsome person and his title to his name. And for all his cleverness, his gigantic friend couldn't hide all the keen intelligence in his searching eyes, and so whatever he said, she didn't believe he'd fortune enough to feed himself for a week,

Moreover, and overriding all other doubts and instincts, she thought on a sigh as she embraced her pillow with both arms and buried her face in its depths, there was one certain irrefutable fact that damned them utterly. It was the certainty that any friend of her father's was not to be trusted, and likely had his own little game to be played. Thus it was her responsibility, morally, and also as someone who had lost so often, to see that this time he lost too. She was not in the least a gamester, but still she responded to a challenge. There might be nothing for herself in winning, but it would be, she thought drowsily as she willed herself to sleep so she could be alert for the contest sure to come in the morning, pleasant to win for a change. Or, if she didn't quite know what winning would feel like, then, at the least, it would be novel.

3

THE HOUR was advanced; all the houses in the French countryside surrounding the great house were shuttered and still. All save for the elegant manor house that dominated the landscape, of course, for now it was a hotel for gamesters, and true gamblers didn't note the passage of hours by clock or sunrise or moonset. They were far more mathematical. Just as they counted every number on every card and pair of dice and wheel they watched, they measured out their time carefully too, but only by the amount of money they'd left in their pockets to lose. Even then, they left the tables to sleep only if they could no longer keep accounts, either because they'd no more money—no one to beg it from, nothing to barter or sell to obtain more—or because their traitorous eyes refused to focus on their sport any longer.

As Arden Lyons came lightly down the stairs, he found the several salons on the main floor as busy now that the new day had begun as they'd been when he'd originally come to the hotel in the early evening of the previous day. He headed for the small salon where he'd lately left his companion and their newly met friends, the Baron Wyndham and his pretty friend, Roxanne Cobb. But then he checked, frowned, and, remembering, patted his waistcoat pocket absently and turned round to step quickly to the anteroom where the reception desk was and where the clerk had signed him into his room so many hours before.

That room was deserted now. There were no new guests expected at one hour into the new morning, and as there was also no gaming to be had there, the chairs and couches and tables were abandoned, all save one. As Arden entered the room, that one was suddenly left too, as the slender, nervous young gentleman leapt to his feet. He wore a look of plaintive desperation, and his thin-cheeked face with its finger-fretted pompadour all in disarray about his high forehead gave him the look of an inspired poet or a madman.

"Mr. Lyons," he said at once, all astammer, with a look of hope and despair all intermixed in his worried eyes, "dare I . . . dare I hope?"

"Don't bother," Arden Lyons said coolly, but before the young man could let the tears which came so easily to those large liquid eyes fall, the larger man hastily pulled the folded sheet of vellum from his pocket and thrust it at him.

"Here it is," he said. "You've not lost a tile from your home's roof, nor a holland cover from the drawing room while it's been out of your hands. But for God's sake, Waite, see it don't leave your hands again, will you? This time, the chap who won it from you was an honest man, within reasonable perimeters, of course," he added with a genuine smile, "but he's by no means typical of the breed."

"Oh, never again, never, I vow it, never shall I let it leave my keeping again. I don't know what came over me, it was like a fever, I could think of nothing but the cards, all else became less real to me . . ." the young man babbled, holding the deed to his ancestral home tightly in his trembling fingers.

"Fine, fine," Arden said brusquely. "Now, go home, my lord, and leave this sort of play to those who can afford it, or who've nothing left to lose, in property or honor. Home to England, if you can. But I forgot," he muttered in annoyance, as if to himself, "if you'd the money, you wouldn't have bet the farm, would you have done? Here, then," he said brusquely, and withdrawing his wallet, he counted out a sum and handed it to the young gentleman.

"Oh, take it, take it," he said impatiently as the young man hung back. "We all of us are entitled to be fools in our youth—that's the whole point of being young, I think. You can repay me someday when you've passed those treacherous shoals. Here, it's no king's ransom, but enough for the boat and a coach to Lancaster again after, and a few meals to keep you together till then."

"How can I thank you?" the young gentleman cried as he clutched the bills and the deed to his thin chest. "How can I ever repay you? To think . . . to wager and lose my home, and where would my young sister be then? And what of my name, and reputation? Mr. Lyons, how can I thank you?"

"By going home," his benefactor said abruptly. "Good night, my lord, and good-bye."

But the young man had transferred the deed and the money to his own pocket and now took his savior's hand in his own two and wrung it there and shook it repeatedly as he kept vowing his thanks and his future virtue.

Arden snapped, "Good night, my lord, and good luck to you," and then quite literally tore himself from that damp clasp. And in a far worse temper than he'd been when he'd stepped into the room, he stormed out of it.

He took a handkerchief to his hands after he left, but that didn't help; he felt as though he'd been dipped in a vat of some sort of sticky stuff after his encounter with the young man. And for all he'd done a good deed, there was something about the young fellow's abject attitude, though understandable and certainly laudable, that was also disturbing. So he was in a vile temper and stamping toward the main part of the hotel when he abruptly stopped to collect himself before going to find his friends.

They were alone in the salon now, since most of the other gamesters there had already gone to their beds. Arden found himself as grateful for the relative quiet as he was for the genuine smile of greeting he received from his friend Julian and his new acquaintances, who were still chatting with him.

"I only just ran into your daughter, my lord," he mentioned to the Baron Wyndham as he settled himself in a small chair, folding himself up neatly, automatically tucking his hands and feet close, as he'd had to learn to do. "Or rather, she ran into me," he mused, "but she was looking for you. I told her we'd already secured your company, and she decided to retire, so I imagine it was nothing urgent, but I'd look for her early in the morning, were I you. And, considering her loveliness, even if I weren't," he added with a grin.

"Lovely, ah, yes," the baron sighed, "but much good it will do her, with neither a decent father nor a dowry to advance her."

"Her late husband made no provision for her?" Arden asked curiously.

"Ah . . . no," the baron replied hesitantly, looking so self-conscious that his new friends realized at once it must have been an ill-advised love match or some other sort of ramshackle elopement that the daughter, likely as impetuous as her gamester father, had plunged into.

"Ah, but . . . in truth, he may have done—for he was a good sort of lad, and a conscientious one," he went on to assure them after noting their reaction. For Arden Lyons seemed pensive and somewhat saddened, and the viscount frowned, looking so troubled that Roxanne Cobb had to bite her lip to remember that she ought not to give in to temptation and put a hand out to smooth that furrowed brow as she wished to do.

"It was very unlike him to leave her penniless," the baron confided hastily, as though making up his mind to be entirely candid with them, "very unlike. So much so that I've a man-at-law looking into it, never doubt it. His family . . . has not been too forthcoming, not that I wish to say anything . . . but there are several younger portionless brothers, you see. Still, she's young yet," he said at once, noting the silence that had fallen over the others, "and she'll come round all right, for she's got a good head and a loving heart and a great deal of sense as well as education. But pray don't put that last bit about, gentlemen—it would be ruinous to her reputation, you know.''

They all laughed with him, before Arden asked lazily, so carelessly that his friend looked up at him curiously, "Surely not that young, if she's a companion to that charming ingenue? Not that I wish to be indiscreet, and a lady's age, we all know, is as secret as the amount of time she must spend in front of her glass each morning before she emerges from her room so that we can recognize her from the night before, but still, consider—we can't have one ewe-lamb leading another—just think of the danger of wolves!''

For once, the baron looked flustered, and Roxanne Cobb's trill of laughter was a key too high, before the old gentleman recovered and said with a wink, "Ah, but you've caught me out. But don't forget: a young daughter makes a gent younger too, sir, the ladies aren't the only ones to have looking glasses in their rooms, even if some of us only dare to look into them at night, and without a light.''

Then he added, under cover of the general merriment, "She's five-and-twenty, my friend, but then, I wed from the cradle, you know,'' before he adroitly changed the subject.

All the four discussed in the next half-hour was the state of France these days, the other gamesters in the city of Paris now, their known weaknesses and foibles, and the permutations and combinations needed to win at a new version of pharaoh the baron had been particularly unlucky at learning. When the mantel clock in the salon chimed a second time, the baron looked up, exclaimed his horror at the hour, and claiming his age and infirmity with a twinkling smile, took his leave of them all.

Roxanne Cobb, left alone with the two gentlemen, rallied with them for a few moments about her own advanced age and poor condition, accepted their gallant denials and compliments, and then, sighing because she'd rather have been left with the one gentleman, and knowing no way to dismiss the other, pretended to realize the impropriety of staying on alone belowstairs with both. Then she took herself off to bed with many a backward glance, both to let them know this, and, as she had made a great point of staying on after the baron had left, also to reassure them as to the fact that she was actually repairing to her bed, alone, and was sure to remain in that virtuous state all night—unless, her wistful smile clearly said as she departed, someone was willing to try to change her mind.

"Another conquest, Julian?" Arden asked after the door had closed on the hem of her skirt. "A lucky thing I wasn't keeping count. I doubt I could calculate that high."

"If females were money you could," his friend said, stretching luxuriously.

"If females were funds, my dear Julian," Arden corrected him, "you'd be a nabob."

"You wouldn't exactly be a pauper, my lion," the blond gentleman replied, rising and roaming the room, and, after finding the last of a bottle of wine and downing it thirstily, jesting, "and all those questions about the baron's black-browed scowling daughter. Can you have formed a *tendre* there, I wonder?"

"Have you?" Arden asked casually, looking down at the long legs he stretched out at last.

His friend paused. This was the way they generally proceeded before one began to stalk a female, to be sure the other wasn't vying for the same lady's favors, as had happened once before in Spain. Then they had, unbeknowst to each other, both succeeded with her, but after they'd discovered that, after the laughter and the jests, they'd always been sure to clear the way for each other. For though they were good friends, perhaps precisely because they were such good friends, the idea of such sharing or comparing, either on their part or the lady's, was distasteful to them both. As it was only a matter of the flesh, it couldn't be as important as their friendship, which was a much more complex matter of the mind, and though they neither of them were sentimentalists, of the heart.

They'd been traveling together for less than two years, and had met only a few months before that. But as different as they were from each other in appearance, temperament, and history, and as much as they'd never expected to remain together beyond their passage out of England, it was just as a perceptive friend to both had noted when he suggested they try to take on the world as a team: they suited each other very well.

The viscount had just done with his seven-and-twentieth birthday when they'd set out from home, and had just lost the girl he'd lately come to believe to be the love of his life, and that only days after he'd lost the lady he'd always believed to have been the dream of his life. In his shock, for

he'd never been refused by any female creature before, and
in his disillusion, for he'd begun to see that he'd never really
loved either of them, but only the illusion of them, and in
his exile, for he was a convivial creature, he was glad of
company, any company. Even that of an admitted criminal.

And Arden Lyons, having just observed what he'd said to
have been his thirty-first birthday—and there was little reason to doubt that, even though he could impersonate a man
of any age—and having to leave England because of Bow
Street's attention to his many illegal activities, had been
glad of company as well.

They'd understood each other very well from the start.
Neither had wanted to leave his homeland; both had to—
one for the sake of his soul, the other to save his skin.

Julian Dylan, fifth Viscount Hazelton, had been the
adored and cosseted son of a fond mama and papa, and the
world had continued to pet and praise him from the moment
he poked his perfect nose from out of the nursery. Although
his family fortunes had come to ruin, luck and the efforts
of a good friend had retrieved much of it for him. But none
of it would have been possible without his own hard work.
He'd labored long hours at menial tasks despite the scorn of
more fortunate fellows who'd once been his noble peers,
not even sticking at driving a public coach. Nor had he
hesitated to take on any sort of labor until he'd funds to
invest to turn his luck again. Because, as those few who'd
come to know him well knew and appreciated, the man was
as noble and attractive as his incredible face.

Arden Lyons had a hundred childhoods, and a thousand
sires to account for it, and never tired of fondly detailing
all of them whenever he was called upon to justify himself.
Even his friend Julian couldn't tell which was true, although
he privately believed all were false. But some of the most
fantastic things he claimed were undeniably true because
Julian had seen them with his own wondering eyes. That
Arden had once ruled a significant portion of the London
underworld was so; that he could read and ride like a gentleman, and brawl and brangle like a ruffian was, as well.
And that he'd received an education as comprehensive at the
world's hands as he had in some superior sort of school was
self-evident. But it was also true that the viscount had seldom met anyone as kind, loyal, and completely honest to
those few souls on earth he trusted enough to call "friend."

They made an oddly well-matched pair. If Julian Dylan

had undertaken his exile to complete the process of his growing up, and Arden Lyons had left in order to preserve his life and ensure his growing older, they'd each found an able helpmeet in the other. And more. Of course they joked at times, when on opposite sides of a gaming table, that they were David and Goliath. But in fact, as time had passed, they'd also become David and Jonathan.

And, in the process, wealthy almost to the length of their wildest dreams.

In their time abroad they'd done things that had earned them a great deal of money, as well as gratitude. For they undertook tasks others would not—whether through fear or lack of enterprise, or lack of knowledge or daring. And though they were determined to stay within legal limits, Mr. Lyons having given up his life of crime and the Viscount Hazelton unwilling to embark on one, these were often things they didn't care to mention. They were tasks performed just this side of the law, and that side of sanity.

If certain French jewels or papers or persons escaped from Russian hands one winter, and other Russian treasures, animate or inanimate, later somehow turned up in France the following spring, and emigrants animal, vegetable, or mineral somehow managed to cross borders that changed as rapidly as their prices did in the unstable world of international politics all through that year of Napoleon's escape from Elba, the odd duet might well have been behind it. Or so it was rumored.

No one could be sure. Sometimes it was a gigantic old man and a comely youth responsible for some bizarre and successful scheme. Sometimes it was later discovered to have been a strapping young peasant and his smaller father behind some profitable treason or madness, at times it was an elephantine dandy and his mincing friend that were spoken of. And once, a time that reduced the viscount and Mr. Lyons to laughter so long it almost turned to tears whenever they were asked about it, when there'd been a shipment of arms meant for Napoleon's army gone astray, it had afterward been hinted that those responsible might have been a great gawk of a German boy and his beautiful fair-haired blushing bride. Who had, on closer inspection, poor child, tended to develop whiskers, fine golden ones to be sure, but whiskers nonetheless, as evening fell, before darkness and a convenient carriage had hidden them from sight forever.

Mr. Lyons and the viscount always vigorously denied the

tales, whenever, that was, anyone dared to broach them to them. But they were nonetheless famous in certain quarters, and wealthy in all sectors, and never far from events both interesting and daring.

Now Arden looked down to his boots after his exaggeratedly innocent question, and his friend raised an eyebrow before he replied, just as innocently, "Me? And the Widow Devlin? Lud, Arden, did you see that look she shot us? I've eyed vermin in my bed with better grace. She'd eat me alive. You're the Shakespeare fancier; I'll leave the shrew to you. Are you so jaded that you've tired of willing wenches?"

"Oh," Arden said, grinning then, "there's many a slip twixt the yen and the sheets, laddie. Any thoughts about that little pretty she's guarding, Julian?"

The viscount paused in thought. It was a deep game the Colossus was playing this time, and it tickled him. He'd no thought of indulging in his favorite sport with either female. For they both were too well-guarded, one by her parents and propriety, the other by her attitude. No, at this time in his life, as unresolved as he was about so many things, he preferred easier courtships, and since he was usually the one being courted, he preferred saying yes and yielding, to trying to persuade someone else to his desire.

"No, no," he replied, acknowledging this. "Handsome as they are, they're not my usual style, since they're too much effort, both of them. I've given up the chase, for now. I'll leave the storming of citadels to you. My desire is usually for whoever has already said yes to me. But both? My friend Lion, I stand in awe of your appetite, to say nothing of your pride."

Arden winced at this familiar pun.

"Which goeth," he murmured softly, "before a fall, as I recollect."

"Oh, but before you tumble," the fair-haired young man said negligently, although his handsome face grew grave, "I'd remind you that the papa of one is an English nobleman, and the parents of the other, however lowly, are rich as they can stare, and both here as well—standing behind, beside, and in back of her."

"That would make three parents. She's a wonder of nature, but not that marvelous," his friend rumbled, "and the parents will endorse any suit brought by a gentleman and a Midas, which I shall be for them. As for the other omnipresent papa, it makes no matter we've broken bread together if we break open a pack of cards with him. The baron is an English nobleman, but an ardent gamester too, quite a different story. He's as sick with it as a man might be with galloping consumption; it consumes him entirely. Make him an enticing wager and he'll give up his daughter, his honor, and his life all together, and then propose dicing for his shroud. In fact, I believe he likes the losing as well as the winning. There's no problem that I can see in either case. Unless, that is," he asked softly, too softly, "you resent my thinking of attaching an English nobleman's daughter, my lord?"

"Thank you," Julian said too sweetly, "for your confidence in me. If I haven't minded your attaching a marquess's daughter, a duke's wife, and a countess *and* her daughter in the past," he went on with a trace of rising temper, "it makes perfect sense that I'd suddenly stick at your casting your eye on a mere baron's get, doesn't it?"

"Then," Arden exclaimed with a show of great gladness, "it's a moral point our lad's come up with it, isn't it? Thank the Lord," he sighed, "all those Sunday lessons didn't go in vain, Mother."

But his friend didn't smile.

"We've befriended the baron, gamester or no, and his dark-eyed widowed daughter is as impoverished as she is sour. And the pretty chit is an angel, but she's an infant, Lion, up for trade, not loan—a ring for a night in heaven or nothing. But you know this. This isn't like you."

"Nor you," Arden said quietly.

"It's only that it isn't in our usual style"—Julian spoke roughly, as though impelled—"seduction of the innocent or the oppressed."

His friend sat upright and stared at him. In the time since they'd met, in all the hours they'd passed together, the viscount had never seen him so genuinely amazed. Then the dumbfounded look passed and genuine amusement set in, as the gentleman again earned the nickname his familiars used for him. For he looked very like a lion indeed as his great tawny-maned head went back and his white teeth gleamed in his tan face and then he roared with full-bodied laughter.

"I'd forgot. I forgive you," he managed at last. "After all, you've only lately grown a conscience, and like all new things, I imagine it occasionally pinches."

"And you've none to trouble you? This isn't like you," Julian insisted.

"I feel like the ninety-year-old parson accused of fathering the milkmaid's brat: I don't know whether to be insulted or flattered," Arden said gently then, sobering at seeing the viscount's rigid back and unsmiling face. "But for the sake of our friendship, I think I'm flattered—at least that you think it possible I might succeed. For all my charms, Julian, I'm not precisely a young maiden's dream, or a young widow's neither."

"You have been in the past," Julian said calmly.

"No, never a proper young maiden's," Arden answered seriously at last, "nor a decent widow's, nor any decent female's, my friend. Just so." He nodded as he saw his friend's concentration give way to dawning understanding. "We don't meet up with many, do we? And the fact that you've forgotten that makes my point exactly, for it may be we've both been at our game too long. But I remember them from childhood fairy stories, at least, and do recognize the breed. So respect your elder's fancies and fantasies and don't jump to rash conclusions, my boy," he said as he rose and stretched until his hands grazed the high ceiling, "for amazing as it sounds, I'm barreling into mid-life, and it might be that respectability would be an amusing new game."

"But before you order up either a stack of fuzzed cards or a sack of rice for me," he warned, "recall that I'm not at all sure of what I want, at least not just yet, or what there is to want just now, for that matter, or even if this yearning for domesticity all isn't some distempered start brought about by boredom. Napoleon's snug on another island now. The world's settling down from his interesting deeds of great infamy to its usual petty squabbles. So it might just simply be time for us to sail southern seas and get a look at those little yellow birds you used to go on about," he added, clapping his friend on the shoulder.

"Lord," Arden said around a huge yawn, "I must be aging rapidly, at that. I find I quite welcome my bed tonight, even though it's to be as empty as poor Mrs. Cobb's, alas," he added, tilting a knowing smile to his friend.

"And her cot will stay as narrow and pure as a nun's if it really is so," Julian replied pointedly. "At least she stands, or lies, in no danger from me. She's a pretty, merry eyeful, and I wouldn't mind at all, if that's what's on your lecherous mind, Arden, but I don't know enough, that's the point. And I'd like to know just how fatherly the baron is toward her, you see. But I thought you'd be off to Paris yourself now, and not your own bed. It's only an hour's ride, and Madame Marie-Anne probably has kept a lamp in her window burning for you.''

''No, I don't think she's taken to hanging out a red lantern, not just yet,'' Arden mused, thinking of his sometime mistress, and remembering that practical but promiscuous lady, he added thoughtfully, ''She may well be one of the reasons for my turn of mind too, for she's very good at what she does, but yet I find that though she's mistress of a hundred ways to please a man, I have interest in only five or six of them anymore . . . well, perhaps nine or ten, actually . . . but none tonight.'' He sighed over his friend's laughter. ''I fear I grow old.''

''At any rate,'' he said in heartier accents, ''we've an early morning, I recall, playing tour guides for the baron and the fillies. Speaking of which, shouldn't you be off to your latest mademoiselle now—the curly-headed one in the Palais Royal, if you want to be back by dawn?''

''Oh,'' Julian said negligently, swallowing the last of some port he'd found and looking regretfully at the empty glass and bottle, ''she isn't mine any more than she's yours or anyone else's who is in funds. And she'll keep. I'm to bed, and alone too. The novelty might kill me, but the ride to Paris and back would do it faster tonight, I think. You're not the only one aging, you know.''

Arden stopped at the door to the salon and turned round to stare, ''Ah, yes,'' he agreed gravely, ''nine-and-twenty, best order up some milk and sops for breakfast, the teeth are the first to go. But do you know,'' he said, with his head to one side, studying his friend carefully, ''I believe you're going to be one of those disgusting creatures who take on more looks as they grow older. You'll pare down and look ethereal into your dotage, so that all your granddaughters' friends will fight to visit and write bad poetry to you. There's no justice in this life,'' he grumbled, ''and little hope of earthly pleasures in the next. Where is the fairness in it that you should resemble something that ought to be standing naked in a garden with a lute strung over one stone shoulder and a pigeon perched on the other, while I look like the uncut block of marble they carved you from?''

''Another soliloquy about your size,'' Julian sighed.

''Easy for you to say,'' Arden commented wisely as he

held the door open for his friend. "Only place yourself in my large boots for a moment," he lectured as they trudged up the stairs. "You, my exquisite friend, can go about unshaven and in tatters, and I'll lay odds that seeing you brought so low, females would sigh and cluck their tongues and offer you a bowlful of soup and a soft spot in their hearts, or a warmer one in their beds. But seeing me in like case, they'd shriek and call the watch. No," he said, pausing with uplifted finger in mid-step on the stair, before his friend could stop laughing to reply, "there's no justice. Clear your plate and you're admired for your hearty appetite. I'd be called a glutton. You may lose your temper with any man. I must be sure I control mine with every man or be named a bully, and heaven help me if I so much as raise my voice to a female. You dance, I caper . . . you wade, I wallow . . . you sing, I bellow—and in the unlikelihood that all goes wrong in your beautiful life," he added, growing oddly serious for a moment, "unable to bear it, you may manfully weep, or grieve. While if I should chance to drop a tear, I'd be said to blubber. No," he said as they reached their landing, and he recollected himself, and so added with a mocking grin again, "a large man has large problems, my friend."

"And he makes sure that his friend does too. What's brought this about?" Julian asked lightly, though he looked hard at the strong, grave face before him.

"The same thing that's made you drink everything that can be poured in a glass tonight, in case you thought I hadn't noticed," Arden said, as Julian started and then flushed like a boy at the truth and the perception of it. "Boredom and thoughts of the future. Go to bed, lad. If we're lucky, Boney will catch a boat from St. Helena by morning and we'll have some sport. If not, we might well yet have to sail south until our hats melt, or else wed some luckless ladies and make our own diversion."

This time Julian clapped Arden on the shoulder, but then paused and asked, "Ah, yes, speaking of luckless. Young Lord Waite, the boy that brought us here—you've returned his deed to him?"

"Aye, but there's something I couldn't like about the lad. He's too grateful. He'd have wagged his tail if he'd had one."

"Not all noblemen are monsters of conceit like me," the viscount answered, his unseen smile apparent in his voice.

"No indeed," Arden agreed without a pause, "but I'll

wager we'll see him begging again. He's got the look of a man used to being beaten.''

"I hadn't thought so," Julian answered thoughtfully, "but then, I wouldn't doubt it. You're seldom wrong."

"Such praise! You're after my new cravat, I suppose. But you shan't have it. Good night, Julian," Arden said, and on a laugh, they parted.

But Julian found his bed hard that night, and harder still the thought that he'd have been able to sleep if he'd drunk enough, and hardest yet the realization that there'd been a time when he'd blown out his lamp and it had been a race to see whether the light or he would go out first as he sank to his pillow, and so far as he knew, he'd always won. But that had been when he'd looked forward to his future as he had to each new morning. Now he'd won each of the goals he'd set then, from making a fortune, to making Arden his new fast friend. And yet still he hadn't discovered the most elusive one—his true desire, whatever it was. He'd only his usual and petty ones and, he thought in self-disgust, turning on a bed that wouldn't be a restful place tonight, no matter how he writhed to seek a comfortable spot, those easy desires were usually satisfied with ease.

It must be, he scowled to himself as he turned yet again, that the facile attraction of his face and form spoke truly of the inconsequential man he was beneath, because it was hard to complain when he knew how very much he enjoyed the sport they provided him, however inconsequential it was. Because whatever else his turns of luck, simple satisfactions, at least the warm and eager and perfumed kinds, had always fallen to him with ease.

He'd discovered he'd never really loved one female so much as he'd wanted to love any one of them, and sometimes beguiled himself into believing he did. But sport was never love, and so he grew discomforted now without his best diversion, with or without the illusion of love. But he knew he'd only to wait. Whenever there'd been a gap in his life, a woman had happened along to fill it in. Lazy, he chided himself. Lucky, he realized. But it was so, and so never vanity to know it, any more than it was pride to know that the sun would rise in the morning.

Those thoughts made his repose no easier, and he barely restrained himself from throwing aside his resolve and waking Roxanne Cobb. He quelled that foolhardiness only by reminding himself wearily that the morning, like the future he was too jaded and discouraged to seek, would, as all simple things did, eventually come to him again without any effort on his part. The thought brought no great joy, but it did eventually bring sleep.

Arden Lyons settled in his bed and locked his hands beneath his head and stared up at the ceiling. He regretted for a moment that he'd not sought out his mistress after all. But, being the sort of man he was, lately he'd got to wondering at all the wrong moments if he was bringing her anything in return, and that had begun to ruin the best of her efforts for him. It might be that her time was up. Which meant, he thought, on the humor that was never far from him, that there were even better reasons than boredom for his seeking a wife now.

He usually had a mistress in keeping; sensual pleasure was a requirement of his life. With all his jests, he accepted that he was a man of large appetites, and yet precisely because he liked women very well he'd never cared for the idea of using anonymous females each time he desired one. He accepted desire, and permitted himself to think of companionship, but was never such a fool as to seek love; he was a realist, after all.

To court sleep, he tried to force himself to give up thinking of that entire enchanting gender, from the mercenary mistress he'd forfeited this night to the ladies of the morning—the baron's dark and scornful daughter and the Deemses' little golden beauty.

Just before he fell asleep at last, he mused that once he'd forgotten that one need, it really wasn't so unpleasant to be alone and celibate after all. Because it had the virtue of being novel, and the advantage, unlike all the other uncomfortable conditions of his life—his size, his past, and his probable future—of being eminently correctable.

4

IT WASN'T so bad, after all. The carriage was crowded, of course. Cecily and her mama sat side by side, and though Cecily took up little room, her mama made up for the deficiency, so Francesca had to draw herself up into a knot and try to wedge herself into the seat beside them.

But at least that giant of a man, Mr. Lyons, sat safely away, although opposite her. The amused look in his knowing eyes showed that he was well aware, even sympathetic, to her discomfort. Well, he would be, she thought uncharitably, from having to do the same all his life, and she tried not to meet his eye. His sympathy meant nothing to her anyway, she decided as she sat stiffly across from him in what she believed was becoming a medical-textbook case of body-cramp. The additional irony of it was that he was used to folding himself up, and so there was a world of room for Roxanne Cobb on the seat beside him. She, because she was not only a widow but also a woman of dubious morality, could sit beside a single gentleman with not a hint of discomfort, mental or physical. It might well have been that she'd have preferred to be squashed in as well, if it were to be between Mr. Lyons and his constant companion. But the glorious-looking viscount was riding outside on the high bench with the driver. From the moment they'd driven away he'd said he preferred to ride thus—''for old times' sake,'' he'd added on a grin to Mr. Lyons—and though she'd pouted prettily, Roxanne couldn't object in any other way. For it was a clear day in early spring, and though chill, it wasn't inclement, certainly not anything that ought to discourage a hardy young man.

But it might have been worse, Francesca thought, and withal, it wasn't too bad. Because apart from the understanding glance she'd gotten from him, Mr. Lyons ignored her entirely, and set about entertaining Roxanne Cobb and Mrs. Deems, and therefore Cecily as well. For Cee-cee seldom ventured a word, and only hung on everyone else's conversation, coloring or giggling charmingly whenever ap-

55

propriate or whenever she saw that the others were responding so. It was clear that if a fellow wished to speak to her
he had to do so through her mama, and so it looked rather
strange, because for all the world it appeared that the suave
Mr. Lyons was courting Mrs. Deems. That, of course,
amused Francesca enormously, and quite took her mind off
her increasingly physical discomfort.

"And so naturally," Mr. Lyons was saying in his deep,
smooth voice, "hearing the rumors of angry citizens looking for him, Napoleon forced the unhappy young officer to
exchange clothes with him. But when they had to stop at the
village square, he heard the crowd chanting, 'Let us see the
emperor, let us see the great man.'

" 'See? What are you saying, foolish persons? They still
adore me,' he told his advisers angrily, and began to step
out of the coach, smiling and waving. They didn't recognize
him, of course, and continued to call, 'Let him out to show
his face,' Before he could protest that they, lucky people,
were indeed seeing their emperor himself, one shouted, 'and
here's rope to hang him high enough so that those in the
back can see him clearly too!' and they all cheered even
louder.

"Then, they say, he grew quite white and said in a squeak,
'But no, *l'empereur* got off at the last stop . . . ah . . . to
use the convenience. Good day.' "

Francesca had to suppress her smiles, for really, the rogue
told a tale very well, not only changing his voice for each
character but also giving Napoleon such a nasal, nasty, ac-
cented squeak that one could swear he became a small
frightened ex-emperor himself. Roxanne laughed outright,
Mrs. Deems chuckled richly, and seeing that, Cecily smiled
enchantingly.

"You're a complete hand, sir," Mrs. Deems congratulated him. "I never heard a better tale. One might almost
think one was there, I vow, don't you think, Cee-cee?"

"Oh, yes," Cecily said shyly, and Mr. Lyons smiled
down at her until she colored up like a little rose.

Francesca decided that if she actually became sick and
cast up her accounts she could always blame it on the motion of the coach, and not the motives and movements of
its occupants. A glance toward Roxanne showed her that the
pretty widow shared her sentiments exactly, but her next
action, which was to tip Francesca a long, slow, unsubtle,
and conspiratorial wink, frightened her into immobility. It

was all very well for Roxie to show her amusement, Francesca thought, looking away and taking a deep breath to regain her poise. She, after all, didn't have to earn her keep by remaining impassive in the face of idiocy. She only had to flirt and wink and display herself to strange gentlemen every night in order to distract them from a foolish old man's poor game of cards.

Oh, it was a bad old world, after all, Francesca thought bitterly, wishing she could ask the coachman to set her down so that she might walk off into the countryside and have done with the entire lot of them. But then fortunately they reached their destination, so she could rise and take the cramps from her limbs and her thoughts.

But they didn't get to stroll as she wanted to. They'd come to an interesting-looking small city on the outskirts of Paris that she'd have loved to explore, one with cobbled and narrow streets and a great gray, grim cathedral with gargoyles frowning down from every high and ornate crag of it, and on the whole, it looked cleaner than Paris itself. But Ceecee took cold easily, Mrs. Deems warned, and from the way Mr. Lyons took alarm and then immediately swept them all before him into the inn, one would have thought he would have picked Cecily up and carried her bodily into it, given the least encouragement. Actually, Francesca noted narrowly, he was being given the most encouragement even as things stood.

Mrs. Deems smiled and tittered and positively glowed at everything he said and at every admiring glance he cast toward her young daughter. It was true that Cecily looked uncommonly well; when her fox-trimmed pelisse was removed, it could be seen that she wore a warm wool gown of oyster white to complement her golden hair, and all her blushes added a counterpoint of color, as did her blue eyes—that is, when she looked up from where she seemed to be forever studying her small white slippers. She'd a neat figure for such a little girl, with sweet round breasts above a curving waist and hip, and, at that, Francesca realized, it was a wonder that Mr. Lyons never seemed to note those entrancing features, nor send one warm or lingering look toward them. Because if he did, she thought wryly, with the way Mrs. Deems was carrying on, it wouldn't be amusing in the least. The mere thought of it reminded her of a forbidden picture she'd once seen that had found its way into a schoolbook because it was done by some Dutch master, before the headmistress spied it and tore it out, for it had been an ugly but masterful representation of a procuress, a young girl, and a prospective client.

But Mr. Lyons did nothing that any gentleman would not have done for a matron and a pretty child, and he did that charmingly. This in itself struck Francesca as passing strange, for she'd have sworn he appreciated women for far more earthy reasons; the look in his eye when they'd been alone that once had assured her of that. Of course, he'd not even glance to her now, she decided with an odd twinge of sadness for an insult not received, since, as a widow, she was clad in black—shapeless black because she was a proper one, and rusty black because, whatever else she pretended to be, she was undeniably a poor one. When her father had decreed her instant wedding and even faster widowhood, she'd owned no black, because young girls didn't. And they neither of them could afford good black gowns, because they hadn't the funds between them for anything but secondhand goods, and badly fitting ones at that. Roxanne, of course, had protested she wasn't the same size, which was true enough, though Francesca suspected it was even truer that she wouldn't have given up a hard-earned handkerchief for nothing. But she seldom wore black anyhow, Francesca sighed, seeing the petite blond widow as pert as a robin in her fashionable red frock, gathering up her skirts to sit, and dimpling up her cheeks as the viscount held a chair for her as she did so.

"But come, Mrs. Devlin, have a seat," Mr. Lyons' deep voice said near her shoulder, causing her to jump, for the last time she'd looked, he'd been playing courtier with the Deemses. How a man that size could move so stealthily amazed her, as, shaken and silent, she sat in the chair he drew out for her.

"And don't sulk," he said unexpectedly on a breath in her ear as she did so, "because that deep blue mood you're in doesn't suit you, and don't covet thy neighbor's frock either, for neither does that envious pea-green. But pink, I should think, would, and your papa says you'll be out of your strict mourning within weeks. I can hardly wait to see the transformation," he added on a smile as innocent as if he'd only just mentioned some commonplace pleasantry before he returned to sit between the two Deems ladies for luncheon.

She could only hope red suited her, she decided, for that

was the color she was sure she turned in her rage at him.
She sat and fulminated all through the luncheon over those
things she could have said in reply—if she weren't an oppressed servant, if she were a lady, and if, she had to admit
eventually, she'd only thought of them in time. Consumed
as she was with frustrated bile, she could scarcely reply to
the viscount's pleasant commentaries, which pleased Roxanne as much as it must have puzzled that blond gentleman.
For he sat between herself and Roxanne, and his friend, just
across the table from him, was so occupied with addressing
conversation to Cecily on his right, only to hear the expected replies from her mama on his left, that the novelty
of it alone must have been what was engrossing him to the
point that he didn't speak to anyone else at the table. Or so
Francesca thought, as he glanced toward her again, as he
did every so often, as if to verify his own amusement at it,
before she quickly looked away, as she did each time.

But then she couldn't help looking back again, and so she
couldn't avoid seeing his every gesture. She focused so
completely on her host that she also didn't miss one word
of his charming and witty, thoroughly inconsequential conversation. She shamelessly eavesdropped, though in truth
she wondered if it really was eavesdropping when a chaperone listened closely to everything being said to her charge.
And acknowledged guiltily that it had nothing to do with
her charge, but only an aching desire to score something, if
only in her own spiteful interior commentary, over the presumptuous, duplicitous Mr. Lyons.

"Now, then," that gentleman said at last, looking up to
the rest of the table as he finished the last of his tart, "that
was a first-rate meal, perhaps too much of one. I believe
we ought to have some exercise now, or at least I ought, or
I'll have to hire on two extra horses for the coach in order
to get myself safely home."

Mrs. Deems immediately began to exclaim about how she
liked a man with a hearty appetite, as the viscount, with an
unholy look of vast amusement, said dryly, "See, my dear
Arden? The way to the lady's heart is through your stomach,
after all."

"Then I'm most fortunate," Mr. Lyons said contentedly,
looking to Cecily, "for I've a tremendous advantage over
other gentlemen in that respect, haven't I?"

Cecily looked up from her ices at that, and gave him a
shy, uncomprehending smile, as her mama cried at once,

"Oh, no, Mr. Lyons! Why, for all your jokes, you haven't an ounce of fat on you!"

This praise and Mrs. Deems's spirited defense were almost too much for Francesca, and she was glad of a napkin she could hide her smiles behind. It even seemed to be too much for Mr. Lyons, for it stopped him in his traces. He paused for a moment before he shot a bright look across the table at a startled Roxanne, and at both the viscount and Francesca as they struggled to stifle their laughter, before he said suddenly in a smug, high, prissy voice, "Oh, do you really think so? So kind of you to notice. For I've the teensiest waist, you know. I daresay a girl could encompass it in her two hands if she'd a mind to, don't you think?"

"Two arms, maybe," the viscount managed before it became too much for him and he dissolved into laughter.

It was difficult to dislike him as much as she wished to, Francesca thought later, while she walked behind Mr. Lyons as he escorted the Deemses toward the cathedral. The viscount and Roxanne were also ahead, deep in conversation.

Mr. Lyons had a Deems female on each arm, but it was his wide frame Francesca trudged behind when she discovered how effectively it blocked the cool wind from nipping at her. She saw the tilt of the broad shoulders that strained the good wool in his blue jacket as he listed to one side to address a remark to Cecily, and noted his well-shaped head, with its fashionably overlong mane that strayed over the back of his high white collar as he turned to hear the reply to his remark from Mrs. Deems. He curbed his long steps to match their little paces, but his strong long legs could clearly have eaten up miles in his steady stride.

Although he wasn't at all handsome in the style of his magnificent friend, Francesca realized that he loomed so large one even forgot the beautiful viscount in his presence. And he wasn't precisely unhandsome either, she thought, remembering his blunt, even features. His size caught the eye, but then he held it.

Francesca frowned more fiercely as it occurred to her that he had literally blotted out all other thoughts for her today, even as he obscured the sight of the street before her. But he troubled her. Observant, but unobserved, she saw a great deal more now. Clearly, with each passing hour, Mr. Lyons was making a dead-set at Cecily, which was not exceptional, since she was a lovely young girl. But Mr. Lyons was very clever, and so could be under no illusions at all about the lovely young girl's intelligence. He was more amused than enchanted, more interested in Mrs. Deems's approval than her daughter's charms. And so, given this—his manner, as well as the manner in which he had met them—there was but one inescapable conclusion:

Arden Lyons might well have been infatuated, and that could be why the courtship had commenced. But it was love of Miss Deems's fortune, not herself. A gamester's daughter who placed no wagers, still Francesca was willing to bet her soul that it was Cecily's money that thrilled him, not her face, and the delicious figure he lusted after the most was on her bank statement, not her person.

And, of course, there was nothing Francesca could do about it.

Within the cathedral it was chill and the high vaulted ceilings seemed to hold the weight of centuries over them. The ladies' footsteps were reduced to a dampened shuffle, but the gentlemen's bootsteps rang out and seemed to affront the brooding silence. Occasional torches didn't reduce the grim gray dimness, the highly placed and colored stained-glass windows twisted the light into subdued and chastened tints before it fell to the great gray stone slabs of the floor, and even the decorations on the enormous stone columns failed to lift the mood of solemnity, for they seemed to have been tortured rather than chiseled into their odd and fretful shapes.

Francesca paused to let the others go on ahead. She pretended fascination with a carving on a pillar, and from the side of her seemingly abstracted eyes watched them out of sight, down a long gray alley of wall vaults with stiff stone effigies of knights and saints. The last she heard was Mr. Lyons as he lectured the Deemses, mother and daughter, on the history of the place, using terms and speaking of times they likely didn't understand any better than she could now, as she heard only the low rumble of his speech drift back to her and could make out nothing of the sense of it. Then the vastness of the place swallowed up the rest of the sound. There were no other tourists she could see, no priests or parishioners present; she seemed to be alone in a citadel that only an egotist or a very brave believer would dare utter a mere personal prayer in. The atmosphere suited her mood exactly. She was lonely and disconsolate, so much so that she took gloomy pleasure in roaming the place alone.

But after a while even the soles of her slippers grew as

chilled as her body, and even more uncomfortable than her thoughts, and she drew her pelisse about her and breathed a sigh that became a cloud of white before her face. She stood staring down at a bronze marker on the floor, wondering what the long-dead gentleman she was evidently treading upon would have thought of this, his gloomy last cold place.

"Myself," the voice at her side said in a rumble that scarcely disturbed the dust, though it seemed to vibrate through the very bones of the old cathedral, "I'd have preferred the shade of an old apple tree. But then, I am not a knight. Poor fellow, after all his wanderings in the sun, to have to spend his eternity here."

"I'd hope not," she answered slowly, still wandering somewhere in the back of her mind, and so thinking of the words and not the person voicing them. "That would be a poor reward for a pious life."

"Precisely what Cecily said," Arden answered pleasantly, "in context, if not text. For she went on at some length about clouds and harps and the like."

Francesca looked up abruptly, and then around. "Where are they?" she demanded at once, seeing no one but Arden Lyons as he looked down at her with the same bemused, considering expression that she'd had, had she but known it, as she pondered the fate of the man under the stone beneath her feet.

"Gone," he said simply. "I got hungry again."

She stared at him.

"Well, you looked at me as though I was an ogre and you believed every one of those stories they told you to get you to eat your porridge," he explained. "You couldn't expect me to resist."

Seeing her steady stare, he relented. "They're all snug in the carriage, wondering whatever became of the truant Mrs. Devlin. Cee-cee thought you might be saying a prayer for your husband," he continued, watching her closely. "I'm not at all sure you weren't. Should you like me to leave you for a little longer?" he asked gently.

The sudden heat in her cheeks dispelled all the cold in her body. The strong face before her was softened by sympathy and she felt a complete cheat. She swallowed so loudly that this time she knew he could hear it before she blurted all at once, "Oh, no. Not at all. In fact," she went on hurriedly, trying to rid those knowing eyes of their sad understanding, "I wasn't thinking of Harry at all just now. He's not . . . he wasn't . . . we're not of this faith anyway. I was thinking of the man I was standing on. The dead one."

"Oh, that one," he answered, a quirked smile appearing. "I'd imagine he's pleased with his lot, even if we're not, knights being the sort who enjoy sacrifice, you know," he said pleasantly as he offered her his arm. She took it automatically as he strolled on with her. "No idle lolling about under some fruit tree like yours truly devoutly hopes to do until Judgment Day, for that fellow. No, he's made himself useful here, holding the floor together, becoming something not only to tread on, but interesting to point out and talk about by tourists tired of exclaiming on how many years it must have taken to build the place. Why is it, do you think, that everyone always asks that in a cathedral? Just once," he mused, before she could answer, "I'd like to be told: 'Two weeks, sir. We'd an incentive for the workers, don't you know—only four whiplashes instead of seventy a day for a good quick job of it.' "

Changing his voice from the cockney slang he'd affected for the proud imaginary tour guide, he went on thoughtfully, "Although I'd imagine I had more in common with that fellow you were walking all over than not. I'm more in his style, you see. Warrior, crusader, armor and warhorses, and lopping off heads and the like. Well, it would be most disappointing to discover the Crusaders had all been spindly little persons with squints and round shoulders, wouldn't it?" he argued, although she didn't say a word to this flight, but only stared at him wide-eyed.

"No, no, they must have all been whopping big fellows like me. How nice it must have been for them," he continued as they reached the door to the cathedral, "to have been in fashion. I'm quite out of style, you see, and have been all my life. But I ask you, pretty as they are, can you see Brummell or any of our town beaus, all those lean and languishing lads, pounding along on a charger's back wielding a sword and harvesting infidel heads? No, no, it was chaps like me . . . the ones who could give the chargers a ride when they got weary . . . ah, but I'm born too late," he said dreamily.

It was too much. She began to laugh, as he had intended. They'd stepped out into the sunlight and she laughed as she hadn't in days. And only stopped when she realized he was not, but rather was standing looking down intently at her.

"Brown!" he said with an air of great discovery. "In the daylight they're brown, not black to match that witches's hair, as I'd thought, and yet in the full sunlight there's gold in the depths of them too."

He stared down at her, and his hazel eyes never left off gazing at her eyes, until they traveled down to study all her face, and then seemed to focus with especial interest upon her lips. He looked at her assessingly, questioningly, his invitation clear. Then, as her own eyes widened, he reached out one great finger and brushed it against the top of her cheek, and as she drew back, alarmed, he held the finger up before her eyes. One lash clung to it, a tiny curved black line that looked like a miniature scimitar as it clung to that great expanse of flesh.

"Blow on it and make a wish," he said softly, looking back into the shocked eyes he'd just been describing.

She looked beyond him to see the carriage waiting in the street, but realized its occupants couldn't see them—the supposed gentleman and the impecunious supposed widow he was dallying with—since they stood behind the pillar where he'd stopped with her. And realized too that he'd known that very well when he paused there.

"I wish," she hissed angrily, "that you would leave me alone!"

The force of her breath sent the lash flying and he looked down at his empty fingertip before he smiled at her.

"Oh, too bad," he said softly, still holding her arm gently, but so securely that she couldn't flee him. "You wasted your breath. You must never tell your wish, you know," he added helpfully as he walked her to the carriage.

". . . and then," Mrs. Deems was saying eagerly to Mr. Deems, "there's the shipyard in Southampton, and the two merchant ships he's got half-interest in, the land in the Caribbean they've both invested in—"

"Aye," Mr. Deems interrupted, for he was a man of few words, but he spoke up when he had to, "I've been offered shares in a new island they've been buying up. Seems profitable."

There was a respectful silence for that word, before Mrs. Deems hurried on, "And the mine in Wales, mind, and don't forget the mills."

"Shan't," Mr. Deems said seriously, nodding.

Francesca felt as though she might faint. She'd never done so before, not when she'd not been burning with fever, and never just because of words. Not even when she'd gotten the letter telling her about her brother, nor even when they'd told her next about her Harry. Those had been events to make one ill enough, but they'd been done, and over, and nothing could be done about them but grieving, so mere seconds of unconsciousness wouldn't have helped. But now she would have welcomed swooning, if only to escape the situation for a few moments. Although, perversely, she knew she wouldn't have wanted to miss a thing that was going on beneath her nose.

And this dreadful conversation was going on, almost literally, beneath her very nose. For Mr. and Mrs. Deems sat in Cecily's room and plotted how to nab Mr. Lyons for her wedded husband even as Francesca stood above them watching the child herself as her golden hair was being brushed out, as innocent and unaware as a pretty little white mouse being chosen for a snake's supper.

The Deemses were content with their daughter's large suitor. He mightn't be a titled gentleman, but gentleman he surely was. Mr. Deems had made certain inquiries and it seemed the viscount was by no means the only noble friend Arden Lyons had. No, his connections were as fine as his fortune, and if some were not, why then that was only another mark of a true gent. For only they, Mr. Deems said sagely, could afford to sink into such low company as they occasionally did.

It was almost more than Francesca could bear. In fact, it was. So much so that when the Deemses had done with going over Mr. Lyons' supposed assets, and had got on to agreeing that they were willing, his suit was welcome, and that Cecily should be permitted his constant company, and then rose in accord to announce their approval before bidding their daughter good night, Francesca lingered on with her.

Ordinarily she'd have been glad to leave too. Not that her duties were onerous or that she'd anything to do when alone but read or write letters, but because she'd seldom much to say to Cecily, and what conversation they had was usually uphill work. She'd known her charge for only a week, and they were far closer in age than the other girl knew, with only three years between them, but it might as well have been thirty. For if Francesca had discovered that Cecily wasn't precisely stupid, and was a sweet girl and a kindly one, she'd also realized rather sadly that there was really little more to know of her than that.

"Cee-cee," she said now, after the girl's maid had left her for the night, "may I ask you something?"

Cecily saw her companion's face in the looking glass before her and it was clear that Mrs. Devlin was troubled. She spun round at once, looking just as troubled as she said immediately, "Certainly, Mrs. Devlin. But I doubt I know very much. I'll try, though," she added anxiously, for she liked Francesca very well. Her eyes might have told her over and again that Mrs. Devlin was not that much senior to herself, but she never relied on their reports. She was a good girl and always went by what she'd been told.

"How do you feel about Mr. Lyons?" Francesca asked bluntly, knowing no other way to put it, and not wanting to hint at the subject, knowing Cecily and knowing she'd be at it all night if she did.

"Oh," Cecily said, much relieved. For a horrible moment she'd thought the question might have to do with mathematics or history. "I like him very well. He's very amusing," she added when she saw that Mrs. Devlin expected more.

"I meant," Francesca said, becoming bolder because she thought she'd right on her side, proprieties be damned, "do you know that your parents are considering him as a suitor for your hand? As a prospective husband?"

"Oh, yes," Cecily said.

"And how do you feel about that?" Francesca persisted, reminded again of why it was she always left Cecily as soon as she was dismissed for the night.

Cecily frowned. Francesca immediately began to plan for midnight coaches and wild rides to the coast and thence to the sheltering arms of some elder, wiser relative of Cecily's. But before her active imagination could plot past Dieppe and the ferry there, Cecily smiled. She'd only been thinking hard.

"I like him very well," she repeated. "He'd be an amusing husband. He's very wealthy. And very kind."

"But he's so much older than you!" Francesca blurted.

"Husbands are," Cecily replied, puzzled.

"But don't you want someone handsomer . . . ?" Francesca asked, wondering if she should mention "love," curiously unwilling to.

"Oh, like the viscount?" Cecily asked, and when Mrs. Devlin nodded, she said, "That would be nice, but I think Mr. Lyons is well-looking too. And I will never have to worry about him outshining me," she said, remembering her mama's clever comments. "And he's large," she added when she saw Mrs. Devlin's defeated look, and trying to cheer her, added, "Big men are very protective, you know. Was Mr. Devlin large?" she asked softly. "Do you miss him awfully?"

"No," Francesca said, rising, weary and frustrated, wondering why she wasn't satisfied, obviously Cecily would have been happy marrying an elk if her mama thought it a good idea, "not large. And yes, awfully."

Francesca went directly from Cecily's room to her father's to have a word with him. She noted that he must have been successful in the past few nights at the tables, for he'd a valet again. Her father's valets were a clear indication of his fortunes; as soon as he'd more than the lining in his pockets, he'd hire one. He'd no need of most worldly pleasures, aside from his gaming, but having been raised a gentleman, there were some few things he regarded as necessities. A valet and a good horse were the two things he considered indispensable, or at least dispensable only if absolutely necessary, as when he'd two aces and was sure a third lurked in the hand that was surely going to be dealt to him next.

"Fancy, my love," he said with genuine gladness, coming to meet her and fold her in his embrace.

It was at these moments, when he held her close, and she laid her cheek against his freshly shaven one, and breathed in the scent of his Parisian lotion, that all the old longings and memories came back, and she felt at peace, at home and protected, against all her hard-won wisdom, against all her real expectations.

And of course, it never lasted long. For as soon as she stepped apart from him, she congratulated him on his evident turn of luck, and he answered confidently, "Of course, my love, I never stay down too long. And I've Arden and Julian on my side, I swear they quite changed my luck, and things will turn round with ease. Why, I believe in a matter of weeks I'll be hiring a companion for you. So prepare to kiss that pretty little cit good-bye, 'Mrs. Devlin,' for I think you're about to lose your husband again.''

''You won't widow me twice, Father,'' she said sourly, hardening her heart and growing discouraged with him all over again, ''not with the same man, it can't be done. And it's Mr. Lyons and the viscount I've come to talk to you about. For I think my pretty little cit will become Mr. Lyons' pretty little wife long before I can take my own name back again. And he'll have all her money from her too by then.''

''It never does to be jealous, Fancy,'' her father said teasingly, waggling his finger at her, never believing a word he said, for he never believed there was a more beautiful girl on earth than his Francesca, if she'd only learn to smile again, ''and it's nonsense anyway. He could buy Mr. Deems and sell him back in an hour, he's so well set-up, and it's never Miss Deems he's got on his mind—I vow, Fancy, if you'd a mind to, you could stand at my shoulder and we could take him for every last penny, for canny as he is at cards, he'd never see his hand if you were before his eyes.''

''He's got what's in his pockets as he stands before you, Father, and nothing else,'' she raged. ''I'd swear it. And he might have his mind on me, but I'm a servant now, so all he wants on me is his hands,'' she cried, her voice breaking in her vexation. She didn't dare to tell him of the insult she thought she'd received, for she believed Arden Lyons would literally never have laid a finger on a protected young female, or let his unspoken invitation be read so clearly by her either. But she remained silent about it, half-afraid that as a gentleman her father would seek satisfaction from him, and more than half-afraid that as a gamester and a self-deceiver, he would not.

''Oh, Fancy,'' her father said softly, reaching for her as she pulled away from him and stood stiffly, not wanting his consolation, because she wanted it so much.

''But you'll see,'' he said, accepting rejection as he'd always done, by discounting it as an aberration that would pass—as a true gambler knew all bad runs of luck eventually would—''he's got his eye on you, my sweet, although as I'm your papa, he's scarcely about to admit it to me yet. But when he knows you better, he will,'' he said knowingly, as confidently as he always did when he was guessing or hoping for better things.

''You'll not tell him the truth!'' she gasped, for she

THE GAME OF LOVE 69

needed her post for as long as it lasted, and knew that for his own purposes Mr. Lyons might well use the truth to upset the lie that was keeping her in a respectable position.

"No, no," he assured her with some embarrassment, for he could hardly tell Arden the truth until Francesca was out of the situation of paid companion. Afterward, when his fortunes had turned, it could be laughed off as a mad start— a frolic—a mere jest. Now, while he was still at low ebb, it was undeniably lowering.

Then it was time for him to dress and prepare for his night of gaming, and time for her to return to her room to undress and prepare for her night of sleep, if she was lucky. For, she decided as she made her way back to her room, it seemed that if she had an enemy, he was all the more formidable because she had no allies, and so if she wanted to preserve her honor, and protect the innocent, whether Cecily or herself, she must prepare to fight on alone. As ever.

As Cecily prepared to sleep and her companion to plot through the night, the Viscount Hazelton lounged in his friend Mr. Lyon's room, and they discussed both young women before they went belowstairs to watch the patrons of the gaming rooms try their luck with that even more unpredictable lady. Luck herself.

"So you want to stay on then?" Julian asked.

"I'd rather, unless you've other notions?" his friend asked in answer.

"No, no, nothing's afoot, except for your mad courtship of the two charmers in question. That's amusing enough. Planning to run footraces between their bedrooms?"

"Sack races." Arden smiled, inspecting his cravat in the glass. Neither of them had a valet at the moment, but as they'd learned to travel in danger and without trust for any but each other often enough in the past, they'd both learned to care for themselves as well as or better than any man's man could tend to them.

"And as to that," Arden said, "I noted you sitting quite content in your sandwich of widows this afternoon."

"You were so busily charming the Deemses to an inch, I had to do the pretty with them," Julian protested, "and so far as a sandwich goes, since we stay on, I might just find Mrs. Cobb to my taste. A few more questions to be sure I'm not stepping on the baron's toes there, and I just might," he said reflectively. "But as to Mrs. Devlin, she was too busy staring daggers at you to notice I breathed. Then after our educational tour of the cathedral, she looked at you as though you'd leapt out of a tomb. What did you do to her?''

"I looked at her," Arden said simply.

Julian laughed. Arden shrugged; there was, after all, nothing so stale as truth.

"Your work's cut out for you," Julian commented. "One's more a challenge, the other's a surer bet, but either way, you'll win through. I've absolute faith in you."

"I've absolute faith in my purse," Arden said on a half-laugh, "even with my rare beauty and charm. Neither lady is precisely for sale, of course, but as one's on the auction block, and the other would like to eat regularly, I believe I have a chance."

"You will never see what others see in you, will you?" Julian asked seriously, shaking his head in sad wonder.

"I see I'm not cut out to be a lover, my handsome friend, and as I don't wish to be seen as a fool neither, I'll remain practical, thank you. Remember Sir Toby?" he asked.

As his friend began laughing, Arden sighed. "Ah, yes, we made a few piles of ducats with that great fool, didn't we?" he went on reminiscently. "What a pigeon ripe to be plucked they all thought he was. And indeed, what a gigantic idiotic fop he was, a shambling bear in silks and satins, clumsy and affected and foolish to the point of absurdity with his mincing steps and nice manners. I did him to a tee, didn't I? But all the while, I confess, while I played him unerringly to both our profits, somewhere in the back of my brilliant mind I somehow believed I was only recreating that which I always feared I might be, or seem. A large man must take great pains not to be absurd. Laughter is wonderful if you want to generate it, but a killing thing if you don't.''

As Julian, sober and disturbed, searched for words to convince his friend that he'd never seriously seen him as the simpering would-be dandy he'd impersonated now and then, Arden went on lightly, "No, no, the bard's King Richard Crookback had the right of it, some of us weren't '. . . shaped for sportive tricks, nor made to court an amourous looking glass.' Certainly we're not made for love words and romantic passions either, we elephantine lads. But don't fret, Julian, I know both ladies have more than a price on their heads. And know what I have to recommend me, beyond beauty, and will enjoy the challenge."

"And you will play the villain too?" Julian asked softly.

When Arden looked at him quizzically, he said off-handedly, because as well as he knew Arden, his present honesty as well as his criminal history, there was a great deal about him even Julian did not know, for Arden cherished his secrets and there was often a dark strain under all his laughter. So much as he wanted to trust his friend completely, and had done and would do, sometimes, as now, he wondered. For as there was still some mystery as to what Arden had once been, there was still sometimes a question in his mind as to what Arden planned to be.

"Well," Julian said, trying to say a dark thing lightly, "seriously courting two ladies at once might create a problem if you're entirely successful, I should think."

"Really? In the country where I was raised, in the harem my father kept, that is, two were considered a bare minimum. Actually, as I remember, that's how Father always kept them," Arden mused, "bare, or in a minimum of clothing. Julian, my innocent, my discreet and friendly conscience," he relented, laughing as he reached out to rumple his companion's golden hair, "I know the rules."

And as his friend relaxed and grinned at him, he added sweetly, "Even if I don't always choose to play by them."

5

THE BLOND gentleman made too many of the gamesters uneasy. He distracted their ladies just by walking past them, devastated them if he as much as looked at them for a few moments, and a fellow couldn't keep his mind on his game if he noticed his female companion expiring from desire. And so, being a basically courteous man, as well as one with little real interest in gambling beyond that which his profession now and again called for, and as he wasn't working this evening, Julian Dylan planned to stay out of the gaming rooms entirely. Instead, he decided as he approached the anteroom and saw Arden sitting there lost in thought, he'd pass the time with his friend, who might or might not have been working, albeit on his own terms and for his own purposes.

"Done up like a dog's breakfast," Arden said pleasantly, eyeing Julian as he sat beside him. "What lark has our lad in mind for the night?"

"Not done up differently than most nights," Julian protested, looking down at himself. "I bathed before I came down, instead of after, but I'm not such a stranger to soap that it should make all that difference," he added, puzzled.

He wore his usual evening dress: black velvet jacket and black satin pantaloons, white shirt and high white neckcloth, his only touches of color the gold in his embroidered waist coat and his hair. But then, he'd only checked his glass for neatness and order and never gauged his luminosity as others did, noting how his hair dazzled, his clear fair skin glowed, and how his light gray eyes gleamed like the sun on cloudy ice.

Arden sighed.

"The boy looks as though he stepped from out of Greek myth tonight, not his bath, and he don't take note of it," he complained to an invisible listener at his side. "I suppose that's the only fairness in it, because if he knew and appreciated how he looked, there'd be no bearing it," he concluded, for all the world as though he expected his absent audience to put in a few words too.

"Oh?" Julian said. "Then I suppose it's a case of an ill wind blowing some good, for if I've gotten nothing else this last week, I've gotten beauty sleep. A great deal of it. Acres of it," he emphasized, "for I've taken Arden Lyons' famous rest cure, don't you know? Off to France to rusticate in a lovely country hotel, with nothing to do but indulge in nourishing foods and the light activity of touring and strolling and visiting by day, and then early to bed and early to rise to do more of the pretty with respectable ladies again the next day. No profit in it any more than there's fascination, you understand, but it's a sure cure for whatever ails you: Dr. Lyons' cure for excess."

"But as I recall, there were some early bedtimes involving less-respectable ladies in the night," Arden said thoughtfully. "At least I think that was you that rode into Paris with me a few times to visit with some lasses who were more interested in touring you than their city. He looked a great deal like you," he mused, "though it was

so dark, mind, I couldn't be sure. Charming fellow at any
rate, never a word of complaint about boredom out of him.''

"I'm not complaining so much as I'm wondering," Julian
answered in the light tone he used when he was being the
most serious. "All the world is here in France now. In *Paris,*
France, that is. And here we remain in this admittedly
pleasant but rural hotel, a week and a half has gone by, and
for all the world, I can't see what's going on. It must be a
very subtle game this time. You flatter and smile, exposing
your charm and your bank statement to the point that Mrs.
Deems is ready . . . no, anxious, to leave you alone with
her pretty little Cecily, even in her bedroom, and in the
dark, for the night, with three locks on the door and the key
under the pillow. But you don't declare yourself anything
but charmed. And you don't get to be alone with her neither, for every time you move heaven and earth to maneuver
it and Mrs. Deems obligingly goes temporarily blind, the
baron's daughter is there between you two like a thorny
hedgerow separating the straying lamb from the wayside.''

"The rest has done wonders for you," Arden commented
approvingly. "Not only do you look marvelous, but it's
brought out the latent poet in you."

"And yet you don't seem to mind," Julian went on. "In
fact—"

"Did you note that strategy yesterday?" Arden interrupted him to ask. "There I was, subtle as a buttertooth
draper trying to convince the duchess to buy my best silk,
and I'd gotten Cee-cee to come walking with me to see the
deserted summerhouse by the lake. And took her little hand
in mine, and strolled on like a vicar on Sunday parade, only
to discover Mrs. Devlin, sitting composed, but disheveled
and winded as though she'd run a footrace, already within,
waiting for us. Almost as impressive as the day before in
the museum, when she'd bearded us behind that statue of
David, with never a blush for the naked gent she was lurking
behind, as Cee-cee and I hove into sight from behind his
left buttock. Or Monday, when she materialized in the carriage . . . in the carriage! When last time I'd looked, she
was still with all of you at the castle. And yet there she was,
sitting panting, yet triumphant, as I handed my unsuspect-
ing prey up into it for the moments alone with her before
the rest of you descended to interrupt my planned and imminent half-hour of rapturous despoilment of the innocent.
Or so,'' he said with a reminiscent grin, "one would have

thought from the look of victory the widow shot at me. What an evil-minded, interfering, meddlesome witch it is,'' he said, still smiling.

"So that's it," Julian said, laughing. "I thought so. You relieve my mind and I compliment your taste, and in that case I don't mind the rustication at all.''

"Indeed?" Arden asked with a quirked smile.

"And since they're all coming down tonight, to show Cee-cee her first night of real gaming—although I suspect really so that you can be alone with her someplace dark, you'll have ample opportunity to do what you wish at last. For Roxanne says they've let Mrs. Devlin have the night off as well, obviously so she'll not intrude. But she'll be down too, since I think she's as deep in your game as you've planned. I wish you luck.''

"But I don't need it tonight. At least not here. I'm planning on disappointing both ladies tonight. I'm off to Paris. There's a female there, you see, who plays entirely different games, ones I'm more in the mood for just now. Care to come along?—only so far as the Palais Royal, that is. She's faithful in her fashion, my wench, but you're enough to try a nun's resolve tonight,'' he said, rising and looking at his friend carefully before he added ruefully, "no, an entire convent's, actually.''

"What?" Julian asked, disbelieving. "Leaving just before the final curtain?''

"Lesson number seven thousand and eight," Arden said patiently. "When a gentleman woos a gentlewoman, you young ignorant brute, even in the final throes, he must be a model of restraint. I'm off to buy myself some restraint," he explained, "in the confident hope that my absence builds up a little less restraint in the ladies at exactly the same time.''

"The *ladies?*" Julian asked whimsically. "Come, my friend, the game is up. I'll swear it's just one.''

"You've twigged to me entirely. It's that fascinating temptress Mrs. Deems. If I only could think of a clever way to dispose of that husband and clear my way . . . ah, well, desire's half the fun of love, though, isn't it? Coming?''

Julian paused before he shrugged and answered, "No, thank you. I've my own plans in the matter of desires. The baron, it seems, continues to swear Roxanne is like a daughter to him, and has been hinting broad as a barn that her lively eye is, for once, fixed, and on me. I think tonight I'll sit still long enough to see.''

''And feel, no doubt,'' Arden said. ''Well, be sure to give them all my love, for I'm off to try to do just that, or the nearest reasonable facsimile that I can muster, with another.''

He winked and strode out the door.

Julian was left to wonder why a man who obviously desired one woman so badly would seek to slake his desires with an inferior other one just before he won his heart's desire. He shrugged to himself again. Arden, after all, might not actually be going to his mistress, since he was a man who rarely told the exact truth if he didn't feel he strictly had to. And this game he was playing was a deep one, perhaps the deepest he could play, for whatever else he concealed, the largest part of him, his heart, was clearly involved in it.

And Arden Lyons, striding toward the stables to get his mount, could only think that for once he'd spoken his heart and his mind and so likely Julian hadn't believed him. But this time he wasn't so confident as he pretended to be, and was determined to take no chances with his luck. To see her each day, to watch her every moment, yet be allowed to touch no more than fingertips when he was able, was trying more than his patience. And so, he reasoned, the woman of his heart must not be allowed to concern his body, lest he frighten her away before he'd a chance at winning her. He needed time as well as surcease, he thought confusedly as he strode toward visiting a woman he didn't want in order to try for success with one he wanted above all else. But he was at a loss to know what else to do. Because he knew very well that he mustn't allow a breath of passion to blow down his carefully constructed house of cards.

As Julian mused over his friend's actions, and his friend went forward with them as full of doubt as he was of desire, Francesca, for once completely free to do as she wished, sat before her mirror and mused over whether she ought to crawl into bed with the covers over her head.

She had the evening off. It was a rare and bold gesture for the Deemses to make. A companion, after all, might be given blameless Sundays and rainy mornings off, but evenings, especially evenings in the presence of their charge's most ardent suitors, should be their true workplaces. It was as much their field of play as a pickpocket's at a carnival, as Francesca's father was fond of saying about anyone particularly in place for his best work. But then, she sighed, it was entirely possible her work was done, simply because she'd done it all too well.

At first she'd been thrilled at being actually able to perform her job at last, when Mrs. Deems had stopped accompanying her daughter and had left all guardianship to her chaperone. Then, of course, Francesca hadn't guessed it was all because of the astute Mr. Deems's proclamation. For, that clever gent had ruled, insisting on his wife's retiring from the lists: "No gent can be natural with a girl whose mother's sitting on her shoulder." And, the canny fellow had said, clinching the matter, "He ain't going to try to lay a finger on her with you there neither."

So in the past week, left to her own devices and noting Mr. Lyons', Francesca had become as alert as Argus, as watchful as a lidless eye. Although she knew that Arden's intentions, however mercenary and dishonest, were honorable, at least toward Cecily, she knew he'd compromise the girl toward a faster resolution to his game if he could. And so, of course, it was clear to her that her job was to be sure he couldn't.

She became the perfect chaperone. Always and ever in the middle: when Julian and Roxanne were there, a fifth wheel; when they were not, a third party. Welcome as a mother-in-law in a marriage bed, she persisted. There was only one advantage. She'd nothing to fear from Mr. Lyons herself now, except perhaps, she thought, for him slipping a sleeping draft into her tea, not so as to have his way with her so much as to have it without her. For she saw he'd not a thought or a look for her now, except for when he was plotting how to get around her. Which was always. And oddly, for a girl who'd forsworn every form of gambling, it had become an intricate and somewhat exciting game. Which, so far, she'd always won.

There was that time at the museum, and the one at the musicale, the triumphant moment in the carriage, and the frightening near miss, that time when Mr. Lyons had mutely beckoned with a tilt of his mighty head, and Cecily had risen like a sleepwalker to follow, only to find Mrs. Devlin behind her like the train of her skirt when she'd gotten out in the corridor to join him.

And if sometimes Mrs. Devlin, that ever-vigilant guardian of morality (herself not much more aware of what would have happened in that corridor or in that carriage than her charge was), sometimes wondered at her own wholehearted fervor on behalf of Cecily's continued ignorance, especially since the gentleman's aim, however self-serving, was, after all, holy wedlock, she solaced her doubts by reminding herself that the gentleman was supposed to ask for Cecily's hand from her father first before he took her lips to his own.

But being honest as well as alone a great deal, she sometimes allowed herself to marvel at how much she was enjoying herself these days. For she couldn't remember ever having laughed so much before. Certainly not in all her years away at school, not even with her closest friends in their silliest secret deep-night conferences. Never in those few visits to whatever home her father had, for she'd been too thrilled at being there and too fearful about leaving as soon as she'd arrived to laugh a great deal, and though she'd loved Harry and had loved to talk with him, she'd never laughed so much with him either.

Arden Lyons might be a rogue and all sorts of a low trickster, but Lord, she'd think when she was consumed with laughter, or trying not to be, he was amusing! He'd a way of joking, a way of saying the most absurd things straightly, a way of seeing things on a slight tilt, that never failed to divert her. It had become easier to laugh as time passed because he never looked at her with the slightest awareness of her femininity again, and she'd come to think it all had been a product of her overwrought imagination that day, since she really knew very little of the ways of gentlemen. If he looked at her at all these days, she assumed it was to see how carefully she was watching him, or whether she thought something he'd said was amusing. She usually did. He was so witty that there were even times that she discovered herself, contrary creature that she was, feeling sorry for him, and not Cecily! Because if he were successful and was eventually allowed to be alone with Cecily until death did them part, she wondered how Cecily would know when to laugh when there was no one to watch as a guide—when at their breakfast table, for example, or even when beneath his sheets in their marriage bed.

Thoughts of beds made Francesca cast a wistful glance to hers; she was very weary with her week's exertions. But then she looked back into her glass and was so enraptured at what she saw there that she forgot her exhaustion.

The Deemses had freed her tonight, obviously to secure

Mr. Lyon's proposal without her interference. But Father had invited her to his tables, both dinner and gaming. She could go to a well-deserved rest. Or she could dress up and go downstairs as though it mattered not at all to her, as though she was a lady who wasn't afraid to lose a lucrative position or anything else. So she'd dressed up for the first time since she'd taken on her position, just to see the result, she told herself, and now she was enchanted with her reflection, as Narcissus must have been. And, she cautioned herself, she might come to the same sad end if she persisted in gawking at herself.

But really, she thought, she looked very well. She'd gotten into one of her old dresses, a lavender concoction the shade of dusty violets, with a high waist banded in deep plum. Entirely respectable for a young schoolgirl or even a widow said to be in half-mourning now, but as she'd grown up since she'd bought the dress, what the soft folds of the gown did for her body wasn't remotely respectable. Its modest neckline became daring as the fabric was stretched more than it had been intended to, and the rest of the soft wool clung to every other thing that had not been fully there when the gown had originally been designed.

Francesca piled her heavy black hair up on top of her head and held it there in one hand while she threw back her head, gazing at herself with what she thought was a look of sophisticated seductiveness. She would, she decided, eyeing herself through half-shut eyes, go downstairs tonight and show them, everyone, what they'd been missing. And if for a moment she wondered why a companion who was about to lose her post in the most natural way, because she'd become unnecessary, thought it important to show her charge's affianced what he'd missed, she didn't let on, even to the sultry lady in the glass. She was usually more honest with herself, but in all fairness, she was really, after all, very tired.

"Ah, too bad. Got something in your eye?" Roxanne asked, appearing in the glass behind her. "Here, let me have a look."

"Lud! Don't trouble to scratch at my door," Francesca said, one hand to her rapidly beating heart. "Just march in," she went on irritably, getting over her fright and reacting very like the Honorable Miss Carlisle and not a humble companion, whether she realized it or not.

But Roxanne realized it, and appreciated it, for she knew

there was no harm in the girl and that it was only a well-bred young lady's way of dealing with surprise, and like all things that she thought might eventually do her some good, she hoarded up the movement and the words, should she find she ever needed to play at being a fine young lady on a very high horse.

"I did," she answered simply, "but there was no answer. Your father wants you, his dinner's waiting for you too. I didn't want to stand cooling my heels in the hallway all night, so I came in. You might have been lying in a pool of blood for all I knew," she added, grinning.

"Drowning in a pool of conceit, more like," Francesca admitted ruefully, for she never took offense at what Roxanne said. She knew the young Widow Cobb had a shadowy background, a less-than-spotless present way of life, and shady motives for her future, but there was no harm in the woman. There were only four years between them—Roxanne was truly five-and-twenty—but for all that, they could scarcely be friends. Francesca admitted that the gulf between them was as wide as the one between herself and Cecily, and in any event, Roxanne never had any female friends. Still, for all they didn't understand each other, they tolerated each other fairly well.

"What? Oh, aye," Roxanne said, laughing. "Conceit? Likely, poor girl, having to wear that old-fashioned rag. Why don't you have the baron buy you something decent? He's flush right now, and generous with it, as always. Ask him for the price of a real gown tonight, before he loses it all. In the meanwhile, here," she said generously, taking a beautifully patterned paisley shawl from off her own white shoulders. "It's got lots of purple in it, come to think, and suits you better than me, and will cover that shabby old thing you're wearing well enough."

Francesca looked at the fashionable new French poppy-colored silk frock that Roxanne was wearing, and realized how badly her own faded, outdated, undersize muslin gown really looked, and feeling foolish, like a little girl caught peacocking in cast-off finery in the attics, she bent her head and flushed.

"No, take it, take it, I've heaps of others," Roxanne insisted, misunderstanding her embarrassment. "Don't you want to cut a dash tonight? Don't you want to show the Deemses it don't matter that they're giving you the shove? Don't you," she added slyly, in what she thought were airy, unconcerned tones, although she'd paused long enough to alert the densest listener, "want to impress the viscount, at least?"

Francesca grinned at Roxanne's attempt at subtlety. But she didn't blame her for the blatant preference she'd been showing in the past weeks. The Viscount Hazelton was shockingly attractive, and having been as omnipresent in Cecily Deems's company as his friend Mr. Lyons had been, she herself had often found herself gazing at him for the sheer pleasure of it. Having him around, she reasoned, was very like having a masterpiece of art in one's own home; he was always good to look upon. She'd found nothing in his character to contradict that, for he always treated her kindly and with grace, although at odd times he'd looked at her with a great and secret amusement brimming in his light eyes.

But she never presumed to think of him in the way Roxanne increasingly and obviously did. He was simply too handsome ever to think of attaching. She believed he wasn't interested in any female for more than the moment either. It was as though despite their obvious differences—he a titled gentleman in the thick of his social life, and she, a titled but drab companion on the fringes of it—there was an obvious commonality between them, aside from their noble backgrounds. For she sensed he was merely walking through life now, amused and interested, but as detached from it emotionally as she was physically.

"Thank you," she said, taking the shawl and quickly wrapping it around her shoulders, "I'd like to look well but I promise you I haven't the slightest interest in fascinating the viscount. But take care," she warned, rising and looking down into Roxanne's satisfied smile, "because he's got no more than that charm and handsome face, Roxie, and I don't doubt he's a Captain Sharp like his friend Arden Lyons, into the bargain, and bad company leading him astray or not," she said, lecturing Roxanne like a schoolgirl before she could protest, "you don't need that sort of trouble."

"Fancy," Roxanne laughed, using the baron's pet name for the younger girl, "step back, do! You'll drip all over me new gown, love," she said merrily, "you're that wet behind the ears. Why, where are your senses, girl? However they've got it, and I don't doubt those rascals could tell a rare tale or two, they're rich as they can hold together, the pair of them! 'S truth," she said earnestly, crossing her heart. "Old man Deems is no flat—he had them checked out by his man of business straightaway, his wife told me. Why do you think he's letting Arden get so near his little beauty? Why," she said merrily, watching the other girl's astonishment, "Arden's a regular Midas too, famous for it, didn't you know?

"And I sometimes wonder," she said, seeing something subtle shift in Francesca's expression at hearing that name, and being far better at reading faces than she was at any sort of book, she continued, "what it is he sees in Cee-cee, and being a famously canny gent, I wonder if it ain't something he sees next to her, and not in her, after all. Now, don't blush, girl. Lord, what did they teach you at that school? I've got some home truths to tell you, and as I've got to get another wrap in my room before we go down, come with me and don't say a word till I'm done, hear?

"I've a bit of advice for you," she said sternly, taking Francesca's arm as they left the room, "for dealing with Arden, or any other gent. You've taken on the name of a widow, and the least you can do is to use it to your advantage."

Holding her arm tightly, she walked the younger girl toward her room, leaning toward her as she did so, speaking low and urgently. Francesca listened, appalled and fascinated.

"A widow's got it all over a young unmarried chit. Because a young chit isn't supposed to know nothing more but that men aren't women, and woe to them if they so much as cuddle a chap to try to find out more. They're supposed to be untouched and untutored and unwilling. But a widow is expected to know it all, and more important, *miss* it all as well, if you take my meaning."

Roxanne could feel Francesca start at that, and she nodded wisely and went on, "Even if she don't, and trust me, but don't quote me, sometimes she don't. But nevertheless, she can be bold as brass, and come to the wedding bed as eager as her gentleman, and before her wedding too, at that, and still never feel a moment's shame for it. Funny, how losing a husband gains you a world of freedom, but there it is. So use it, Fancy. All Cee-cee can do is blush and shuffle and make sheep's eyes. You can do anything, and I daresay you ought. Arden's a catch. A big one," she giggled as they reached her room.

"And I am not a widow, and even if I were, three times

over, I wouldn't want Arden Lyons for anything, except if he were my husband, to do me the honor of making me a widow again," Francesca cried out wildly and irrationally in her anger, when she could catch her breath.

"And I haven't got eyes, neither," Roxanne agreed smugly. "Have it your way. But remember," she said as she selected another shawl from a welter of them in her crowded wardrobe, "like your papa would say, when you've got an ace up your sleeve, it's a crime against nature not to use it."

And as though to illustrate her point, in illuminated script and gold leaf, as soon as they reached the dining salon Roxanne proceeded to show Francesca exactly how a widow should behave toward the gentleman of her choice.

The Deemses were dining in gloomy state in one corner of the hotel dining room, the absence of Cecily's huge suitor a palpable presence at their table. The Viscount Hazelton was taking his wine with the Baron Wyndham, and though the Deemses looked over enviously from time to time, they'd made a point of taking a separate table an hour ago, and couldn't change that now without offering insult where nothing but having the unexpectedly vanished Arden Lyons to themselves was originally intended.

Roxanne took a seat next to Julian, and when Francesca sat next to her father, it was as though they were suddenly alone at the table. For Roxanne gave the blond gentleman a glance so warm, so replete with promise that Francesca, only half-guessing at what that promise entailed, grew warm about the ears. Then, with no more artifice, Roxanne proceeded to completely monopolize the viscount's attention. The baron noted none of it, he was so excited about his own prospects. He occupied himself by entertaining his daughter with his plans for the night, which had to do with gaming with a certain gent he swore was so foolish he couldn't win a wager on a snowflake falling on him in a blizzard.

At that, Francesca forgot the murmurous conversation going forth between Roxanne and the viscount.

"Father," she asked slowly, helplessly, "don't you think you ought to invest in something more tangible? Roxie tells me you're on a winning streak. Shouldn't you at least put aside half and wager only the rest?"

"Such a puritan," the baron said, smiling at her fondly. "Child, how did you come to be a daughter of mine? How will you get on in the *ton* when we return to England, for that matter? Everybody gambles, Fancy. Everyone. From the Regent to his barber. Open your eyes. The country's mad for gaming. Why, I daresay your schoolmistresses placed wagers on your grades, and the vicar put his shillings down on how many of you would show up for Sunday lessons. Yes, I've come into enough to change our direction, but the only way to do so permanently is to increase that bit. If a chap is winning, he has to ride with his luck. You'll see,'' he promised, and then made fast work of his soup and fowl and fish and passed on the sweet, so he could get to a table even more to his taste and tempting to his appetites.

He invited his dinner companions to join him when he took his leave of the table. But Julian demurred graciously, and Roxanne, with mock anger, reminded him she'd been given the evening off, and Francesca, closer to tears than she'd been in a long while, begged off with a letter to write, something she had to tell Cee-cee, a trip to her room to change her slippers. When Julian, seeing some truth that her father had not, asked her to stay on with them, she smiled at his concern, and then more genuinely at Roxanne's relief as she refused.

She went to pace the corridors, in her agitation preferring to drift alone downstairs than to return to her room to weep in disappointment as she feared she would. For her father was going off to likely lose the money she'd just heard he'd gained, before she could even dream on how to use it to better herself. And her post was rapidly becoming obsolete, she was back where she'd been weeks before, only with a few lies to her credit, and no-one, she thought wretchedly, to speak with. And no one, she thought, nodding as she passed the disconsolate Deems family still sitting frustrated with the absent Mr. Lyons dominating their somber table, to even fight with.

"The baron's a fool," Julian sighed as he watched her leave. "A charming one, but a fool."

"So am I," Roxanne said quietly, leaving off all her banter and light chat. And when he looked at her curiously, she said, "I've done everything but say it straight out, haven't I? And there's no answer for me, is there? So I think I'll leave now, as well," she said, and began to rise.

"Wait," he said, putting one well-shaped hand over hers. That light touch caused her to sink back into her seat.

He looked at her, and his steady regard held her immobile. Ah, she thought, he was a handsome creature. He'd been unfailingly polite and eternally charming, and she'd all but thrown herself in his face these past weeks, and tonight had done just that, deliberately setting out to find out once and for all if he was interested in what she so plainly offered. If he wasn't, there were a great many others who were. She wasn't killingly beautiful as he was, but she'd do; from experience, she knew she'd do. She'd had five other men, and it was a mark of virtue with her that she could count them so easily. When she no longer could, she supposed, it would be a warning to her.

It would be a pity if he preferred other gents, or was pining for another lady, or couldn't accommodate her for some other reason. But, she thought, staring back at him with the impassive face of a practiced gamester, her cards finally out on the table for him to pick up or discard, in any case she'd survive. It would only be a great pity. She fancied him. She wanted to know what those sweetly shaped lips felt like on hers, what that amazingly beautiful body could do. She was not mad for the games that went forth between a man and a woman, but they amused her, and she lived for amusement. More, she knew how important they were to the gentleman, and knew how to play well enough to hold a man fast. And she'd have liked to hold this man. She waited for him to speak.

Pretty little creature, he thought, gazing at her. Pert and chipper and tough, and yet curiously tender, withal. He liked her white skin and her neat figure. He liked her honesty in this. It amused him. He could do no less than she'd done.

"I can't promise you anything more than tonight," he said softly, as gently as if he were saying love words.

"Neither can I." She shrugged.

"But I can promise you an interesting night," he said, smiling, and she noted that all of a sudden he seemed to have shaken off his negligent attitude and become more alert, more awake, and this sharpened interest he showed for the first time made it seem as if he'd been sleepwalking all these past weeks.

"So can I," she answered, grinning, for he'd come to life completely now and was even more exciting with that glow in his marvelous light eyes, that consuming interest radiating from him.

"Well, then," he said, taking her hand to his lips before he arose with her.

There was only a second's awkwardness between them when they were alone in her room. It was not when she uncovered herself to him, for he'd stood and watched her undress and she'd known she made a treat of it, and knew she'd a trim figure to show him. Nor was it when he discarded his clothes and came to her, for no sane person could doubt the impact the sight of that perfect, sculptural body would have on an experienced female. Nor was it when they came into each other's arms, or when he touched her where she'd dreamed he would, or even when she put her lips to him where it pleased him so. It wasn't even when they finally achieved that most complete embrace they were capable of. It was a moment later, when he kissed her for the first time. And thought as he so often did these days, before he felt too much to think, that it was a curiously intimate thing, this kissing a stranger as though he knew her, as though he loved her.

Francesca was still entirely alone when she could bear no more of it, when the hour had grown so late and her father had still not returned from the small salon. She arose from the table where she'd been sitting pretending to play at patience, although it had defeated her from the outset, as all card games did. When she'd gone to see how he was faring hours before, when impatience had won again, he'd been febrile in his excitement, and flushed, and his opponent, a thick-set gentleman, had scowled up at her when she'd looked to their game of vingt et un. She'd left hardly daring to hope, yet had passed the next hours dreaming on what might be if he'd been right about his luck running on and not out. But now it was past three hours into a new morning and he hadn't returned to gloat over his triumph with her, and she began to entertain more familiar fears.

She knew how he was faring from the moment she entered the almost deserted salon again. He was still excited, but now his forehead was pale and damp, his hands shook slightly when he picked up his cards, and she knew, without seeing his cards, that he'd lost nearly all she'd seen him win earlier.

So when Arden Lyons came into the room with a weary tread, only for a moment to see if his friend Julian might be there before he took himself off to his own hard-won bed, the first thing he saw was Francesca as she swung her head around and looked to him. And her look was as clear as a cry, and so he was caught in his tracks.

Nothing about him changed dramatically, except he no longer so much as glanced at her. He continued to shamble into the room, looking burnt to the socket and only mildly interested in the game going forth. But even though he said nothing, only watched with great interest from a vantage point near the thick-set gentleman's shoulder, it was impossible to ignore a man his size, and his silence was as enormous as he was. Eventually the heavyset fellow looked up. And seemed to pause for one startled second before he regained his composure and stared a pointed, annoyed question at the intruder casting a shadow over his game.

Arden wore a look of almost bovine innocence.

"Oh, excuse me," he said with great contrition, moving a step aside, amiable stupidity positively shining forth from him, "I couldn't help watching. And then I noticed . . . oh, am I interrupting the game? Anyway," he said, while both players paused and stared at him, so blockheaded as to rumble on while they clearly wanted only to get on with their game, "I couldn't help but notice your ring, sir. Very like the one the Earl of Darnley wears. Could you be any relation? South of Chichester, Darnley Hall. Went to school with my father," he added helpfully.

When he'd got no answer, he went on chattily, "I thought you'd rather speak with me about him than play now, anyway. The ring, you see, so distinctive, you do understand . . ." he concluded, letting his voice trail off.

The heavy gentleman grew red-faced and looked furtively at the few interested spectators still watching the game.

"Very well," he said, and to Francesca's amazement and her father's complete confusion, he laid down his cards and looked hard at Arden.

"Very wise," Arden said approvingly. "Let's have a little game ourselves, sir. But as the hour is late," he said thoughtfully, "let's make it a brief one. I tell you what . . . Have you a coin? I'll call it for the pot. For the entire pot," he said more briskly and a little impatiently, "that you've won from my friend Baron Wyndham this night. I'll not ask for a cent more, nor," he said with a hint of steel in his low voice, "a cent less."

To the absolute wonder of the spectators, the thick-set man, frowning fiercely all the while, fumbled a coin from out of a waistcoat pocket. And then, as the implacable Mr.

Lyons watched silently, he put it in his palm and thrust one thick thumb beneath it, sending it spinning into the air. It landed on the table. Before he could call the coin, before anyone could see which side it had landed on, Arden's hand shot out. He placed his large palm entirely over the coin. He smiled.

"Heads," he said.

The thick-set gentleman grew redder, and as he reached for the coin, Arden fingered it thoughtfully. Then he smiled again. "Neat work," he complimented the other. "Only a hairbreadth. But I've decided I lied. All the baron's coin . . . and this. As a memento. So I may remember you, should you be unlucky enough to encounter me in a gaming hell again. Anywhere upon this earth."

After the losing gamester had restored the baron's funds and stormed out of the salon, the baron and his daughter looked the same question to Arden Lyons.

"Simple stuff, really," he said with a shrug, "if one was watching, not playing," he added, for Francesca's benefit and the baron's pride. "The ring," he explained. "It was truly distinctive, only a disk with a faint coat of arms in gold, the rest polished, shining, bright and smooth as a looking glass. Ah, yes," he agreed with the baron's dawning comprehension, "and so loose it frequently slipped round on his finger. He knew every card he dealt, every card you held. He knew of the Earl of Darnley too—the fool was thrown out of every club in London as a Captain Sharp. A hundred years ago, it's true, but such legends are current as yesterday to those of the criminal fraternity."

"And the coin toss?" Francesca asked as fearfully as if she expected Arden to retreat into a bottle if she spoke too loudly.

"Shaved," the baron said confidently.

"Just so," Arden answered, examining it again. "The rim, so it would always land heads. Very nicely done, too."

The baron thanked him fulsomely, and only resisted offering him a share in the funds when a look in Arden's eyes warned him off.

"Shall I escort you to your room, my lord," Arden asked, "and help you protect your gold? Or may I escort your grander jewel to hers?"

The baron checked, and then remembering Francesca, he beamed. "If there's no one dicing on the stairway, I'll do

well enough," he said with something of apology. "Please
do watch over my greater treasure instead, sir."

There were a great many clever things Francesca wished
to say when her father left and Arden began walking her to
the staircase, but it was late, and her thoughts were disordered in any case. The only things she could think as they
mounted the stair and he gazed down at her quizzically had
to do with the miracle she'd just beheld, when her future
had been put back into her father's hands by this knowing
stranger.

"How could you tell it was heads-side-up?" she asked.

"Oh," he said, grinning at her wonderment, "smooth
hands. Not just dandies have sensitive fingers. I can read a
coin blindfolded. Yes," he went on conversationally as they
went up the stairs and he watched her raise her skirts a jot
too high from her slender ankles in carelessness brought on
by weariness, "it takes all the senses to game well. I don't
take snuff or a cigarillo into a gambling establishment, because then I couldn't scent the tallow used to wax the cards
so they can be dealt or sleeved more easily. I don't drink
more than a bottle or two neither, so that I can watch every
subtle movement. And so I can listen closely to hear how
the dice are weighted, how the cards are dealt, and how a
coin rings when it hits a tabletop. In short, I don't have
much fun in a gambling establishment."

"You only make a fortune," Francesca said, unthinking,
as she realized that despite his kindness tonight, this man
was a gambler, very like her father, only cleverer.

"At least, I don't lose one," he said. "Nor," he added
with a touch of temper when he saw her face as she stopped
at the top of the stairs to look at him, "do I let friends lose
theirs either."

They walked down the corridor to her room in silence.
When they reached her door, she bit her lip, turned around,
and looked up at him. "I'm sorry," she said simply, her
husky voice a shade lower. "That was badly done of me.
You deserve my thanks, not my disapproval. It's only that,
given my circumstances," she said, avoiding his eyes as she
spoke the essential truth she owed him, "you understand I
would find it difficult to approve of a gambler."

"But, my dear lady," he replied, looking down at her
fondly, for really, it was late and he was tired, and it took
more control than he knew he had to keep from reaching

out for more than the hand which he drew to his lips, "I am not a gambler."

And then, as she gazed at him, puzzled again, he regretfully relinquished the slender hand he'd swallowed up in his and added that old, familiar truism so that she might understand him, in this, at least. "Gamblers," he explained, "don't gamble, not ever, you see."

He went to sleep that night with the sound of her throaty laughter still ringing in his ears. He was delighted with the way an unsuccessful night had turned out so well. For he'd lied to Mrs. Devlin. He didn't take tobacco, but he'd still the smoky taste of it in his mouth. Marie-Anne had it on her tongue and he'd tasted it when he'd come into her flat and taken her in his arms and then possessed her mouth in a long, deep kiss. And then he'd put her aside ruefully, for her curved body had felt very good against his.

"I came too late," he'd said, touching her cheek gently, "and that I would have understood. For I never asked for fidelity any more than you have asked it of me. But please," he'd continued as he turned and picked up his hat and went to the door again, "let the poor fellow out of the wardrobe before he suffocates from his cigarillo, will you?"

But the loss of a wayward mistress was easily forgotten as he lay back and thought of what he might have gained tonight.

And Francesca, in her own bed, thanked several patron saints, but fell asleep thinking of a very wicked mortal, and smiled as she thought of him.

So for all Julian and Roxanne continued to wrap themselves into new and complex configurations in their search for gratification, it well might have been that Arden Lyons, alone in his bed, and Francesca, isolated in hers, were closer, even so, at heart, to each other tonight.

6

It wasn't at all a lovely day, Francesca thought when she arose early to look out on a spare, cool gray morning. Yet, whatever it looked like, it was a magnificent day for her. It was so early in the spring that the trees hadn't got word of it yet, and neither had the sun or wind. But even if the calendar hadn't insisted, she'd have known. She didn't need flowers or songbirds in order to celebrate the season; it was a time of rebirth for herself as well. Because suddenly, after a drear winter of hopelessness, it seemed there was enough sun in her own heart to light all of France.

For not only had her father gotten his ill-gotten gains back last night, but this morning he'd also sent her a note, with some more legal ones from France accompanying it, along with instructions to order up some new frocks for herself. It wasn't love of the latest fashions that then made her waltz barefoot and alone the length of her room and back again. It was the thought that her fortunes were changing again that caused the impromptu dance, and the sudden joy of it that also made her whirl to a halt and impulsively hug her dancing-partner pillow. But she didn't see its bland white featureless face as she gazed at it, and its blameless blank surface was never the reason she suddenly sobered and placed it on her bed again, pensive at last, wondering how an enemy so quickly could have become so important an ally, even an ideal, when nothing had changed but her fortunes because of him.

He certainly had not. Arden Lyons was still Cecily's suitor. Still a shadowy fellow with talents a genuine gentleman ought not to have. And the look he'd left her with last night was no less an admixture of sensual appraisal and approval than it had been when her father had not the penny to ask for her thoughts on fashion or any other matter. And yet, against all reason, when things had been at their lowest ebb and she'd seen him, she'd wanted to run into his arms for comfort. There'd been no logic to it, or help for it; there it was. Perhaps Mrs. Deems's odd theory of the protectiveness of large men had truth to it, for he had helped her. But, both wiser and having to be wiser than Mrs. Deems was, she knew that if she'd entered those arms later that night, as she'd been more than half-inclined to do, he wouldn't have helped her to anything but her own well-deserved disgrace. Oh, it was a good thing, she thought resolutely as she dressed, that with only a little more luck she'd soon have her own funds again to help her seek her own fortune again.

And of course, he was there, as constant as Cecily's smile, standing at Cecily's side, waiting for her when she reached the reception room of the hotel.

"We're going to Paris today," Cecily told her at once, with wonder, as though they hadn't visited there every third day, as though she'd never been there at all before. "I'm having some new gowns made," Cecily said again, as though she didn't have a new gown ordered up for every look Mr. Lyons bent upon her. "And a new bonnet too," she added in an unusual burst of loquaciousness, for purchasing clothes clearly spurred her to high flights.

The smile that Francesca was about to give to Arden, both in tolerance and amusement for Cecily's excitement and as a continuation of her own excitement and gratitude for his part in the evening just passed, faded entirely as she saw the smile he gave to Cecily as he took her hand and placed it on his arm.

"But where is Roxie? And the viscount?" Francesca asked abruptly as she straightened her bonnet and her proper, company face.

"Mrs. Cobb has decided to sleep in this morning, I understand," Arden said blandly, "and Julian is resting."

He decided it would be impolitic to mention what Julian was resting from, or upon, or even that it was unlikely he was resting at the moment. He doubted that Mrs. Cobb was getting much sleep either. Julian had, of late, the habit of plunging very directly into his new relationships, Arden thought wryly as he helped the two ladies to his carriage. It might be a few concentrated days before the blond gentleman emerged from his room again, after having literally exhausted all possible permutations and combinations of pleasure with his new interest, before, if he were running true to form, he'd discard her.

He hoped this time it wasn't true, if only for Julian's sake. There might not be much of love in such diversions, but

Julian was the sort of fellow, Arden thought, who needed
at least the illusion of it, and that he no longer sought so
much as that wasn't a good sign. When the viscount had
left England he'd been bruised by what he'd thought was
love. Though he'd not been hurt since, or at least in no large
way that his friend had seen, he'd evidently been wounded
often—in a thousand ways, in the sensibilities he swore he
didn't have—by the quick succession of the many brief and
careless lovers he'd taken without a semblance of love. He
would bleed to death from those thousand cuts, Arden
thought, unconsciously frowning enough to terrify Cecily,
if he didn't take care. Because it seemed to him that Julian
only came fully alive these days when he was in action of
some sort, whether it was facing danger or lovemaking. All
other times he seemed to be afflicted with an unnatural careless languor, which was never like him. It was far better to
have one's heart neatly pierced all at once and die complete
than have your soul leak away the slow way that Julian's
seemed to be doing.

No, Arden thought, it would be neck or nothing for himself, and literally so, for when he declared himself he would
leave no option and present his neck cleanly on the block
to the female of his choice. And too, he never expected to
find the grand passion and complete soulmate that Julian
obviously still sought or dreamed about, to his continual
disappointment. Far more realistic because he was older or
more worldy wise, and ready to retire from his roving, Arden had decided he'd be pleased to settle for an amusing
companion who'd either feel passion or care enough to simulate it, and whom he could please in turn by being himself.
Which was why, he thought, finally noting Cecily's frightened expression and her chaperone's puzzled frown, he was
going about things precisely the way he was now.

"We wait," he said in answer to Mrs. Devlin's unasked
question, "for Mrs. Deems to join us."

"I can't buy dresses without mama," Cecily explained.

"Oh, naturally," Francesca said, while she shocked herself with the sudden spite of her next mute sentence: or pick
a husband neither.

Mrs. Deems arrived at last, magnificent in purple, plump
as a grape, and scented liberally with heliotrope. She
crowded next to Francesca, suffusing her entirely in her
scent, stray gauze from her gown, and folds of her cape,
and taking up her attention completely with her conversa-

tion as well. She was suddenly friendlier to Francesca than she'd ever been, and surprised her considerably by beginning to chat at once about what sort of dress she thought might suit her Cecily, but so loudly and incessantly that had Mr. Lyons wished to entertain them, he could not be heard, and had he any interest in hearing Cecily's usual replies, via her mama, he'd miss them, since she ignored him and her daughter entirely. This was, Francesca finally perceived, after Mrs. Deems asked her third rhetorical question and burbled on without answer, evidently so that Cecily herself could bear the full force of Mr. Lyons' attentions.

"Don't look good to ditch the baron's daughter yet," Mr. Deems had ruled after much thought the night before, after reviewing all the possible reasons why Arden Lyons had not shown up at their table to take either their dinner or their daughter. "Too brash, and he's a gent likes the conventions, for all I doubt he's lived by 'em. Reformed rakes is the worst," he'd said wisely, but then warned, shaking a cautionary finger at his wife's nose, although she only lay on the next pillow absorbing every word of wisdom emerging from under his nightcap, "Keep the baron's daughter on, for the look of it, understand? But keep her close to you, away from Cee-cee till he pops the question. Far away. And keep yourself away too, my girl, or we'll share no wedding cake this summer."

But as they entered the city of Paris, a quick listen and glance showed Mr. Lyons wholly involved in recounting a tale about a horse to her enrapt daughter, and so because Mrs. Deems's idea of subtlety was not saying a thing more than three times, and mostly because she was on pins and needles lest her husband's excellent advice not be attended to, she suddenly leaned close to Francesca's ear and whispered, in a gust of candied violets, "Hist! Mrs. Devlin, don't be narked, love, but it would be best if you'd manage to let the two lovebirds be this afternoon. Let them alone, understand?"

Then she swayed right back upright, as though only a lurch of the carriage had brought her lips to Mrs. Devlin's ear, satisfied by the shock on the chaperone's face that her message had been heard clearly.

"Why . . . of course," Francesca managed, as horrified by the terminology, as she was staggered by the request, but as Mrs. Deems's eyes flashed a warning at her using a normal tone of voice to answer, she foundered only for a sec-

ond before she went on in lower accents, ". . . of course
. . . and so you may refuse, madam, as is your right, of
course, but I was wondering if I might have some time off,
for myself, in Paris today, as I'd like to order up some new
gowns for myself. I know it's a presumption," she went on,
warming to her theme and salvaging her pride by lifting her
chin proudly, "but I so seldom have the time to visit a dressmaker, they're all of them off to church on my half-day off,
you see, Sunday not being a day for trade."

"Why, what a treat for me," Arden said heartily, causing
everyone in the carriage to look at him. "Two lovely ladies
going for gowns today to offer my advice to. I'll be glad to
give my opinion," he said comfortably, as though he'd never
been deeply involved in a story about a horse, as if it had
been stony quiet in the jouncing coach so he'd been able to
hear Francesca's hoarse and broken whispers as well as a
shout.

"I'd think," he went on reflectively, "as I've already told
her, that Cee-cee would do best to have something done up
in white, for her golden hair, but as Mrs. Devlin's complexion is the creamy color of a camellia, white would be insipid
for her. Gold, I think, or green . . . yes, olives and sunlight,
something Italianate, or an Egyptian motif would suit. I've
been told I've an eye for color, though I can't paint a thing
except the side of a barn, and even there, I tend to go outside the lines." He grinned.

No one else did. Mrs. Deems stared, Cee-cee seemed
uncertain because her other guide, Francesca, was both annoyed that he'd heard and astonished that he'd been absolutely right. And absolutely wrong, she thought as she
recovered. Not for being *au courant* on female fashions.
Some gentlemen, she'd heard, enjoyed such diversions; in
fact it was exceedingly fashionable to be an expert on female fashions, and was quite the thing to do for a beau in
London. But those were gentlemen who lived for fashion,
decking themselves out in similar finery, making a life of
what was stylish, and occupying themselves with such delights as collecting fobs and snuffboxes and adorning boxes
at the opera.

Mr. Lyons, although always well-kempt and dressed, neat
and clean as an army officer, and obviously home to an inch
with gamesters and horses, did not remotely look like such
a gentleman. But even as Francesca's lip was curling over
her reply, he added softly, for all the world as though they

were alone in the coach, "The most romantic poet I know is the strongest swimmer I've ever seen, the best poet I've ever met resembles nothing more than a pugilist, Master Shakespeare himself, I understand, looked like a glove-maker. Take care, Mrs. Devlin, that you don't trip over a sharp preconception in your hurry to correct me."

She paused only a second before she said, as sweetly and innocently as Cecily might, but with a world more wickedness, if only because of her naturally husky, seductive accents, "I never doubted your talents, sir, but I fear you've overestimated my resources. I'm sorry to disappoint you, indeed," she said charmingly. "I shall be bereft without your kind counsel, but M. Louis Hippolyte Leroy's establishment is far above my touch. I'll seek a competent but far less extravagant seamstress for my wants. I'm not in society, sir, after all."

"She's in mourning too," Mrs. Deems shot back, visibly unhappy with the odd, half-understood conversation going forth. For the half she did catch sounded like something Mr. Deems would hate. "Don't matter who tailors a black gown, we'll be pleased to set you down anywhere, Mrs. Devlin, only shout it out as we pass," she added helpfully.

It was difficult to be angry when one was so hard pressed not to giggle and the only person who seemed in similar case was the gentleman one was angry at, Francesca thought, clearing her throat over rising laughter.

"My dear doting mother isn't the only one who wishes I'd been born twins now." Arden sighed. "How shall I resolve this problem? For I've offered myself and my advice to two charming ladies who are splitting to go in opposite directions, and though I'm a man of my word, I can't do the same without dangerous surgery. I have it," he said, brightening. "I'll accompany Mrs. Devlin on her mission, both to advise her and so she doesn't have to go unescorted in wicked Paris, and I won't have to worry about Cecily, for she's got the services of her mama and her coachman. And then, because I humbly believe no one sees dear Cecily as I wish to do, I'll be done in time to restore Mrs. Devlin safely to her, and offer up my advice before a bolt of cloth is cut, as well."

He sat back smiling, vastly contented and entirely pleased with himself. Everything he'd proposed was unexceptionable, inarguable, neatly arranged, extremely proper, and entirely unsuitable to everyone else's purposes but his own.

Exactly as he most liked things to be, Francesca thought in great annoyance, searching for a loophole in his reasonings and finding none.

A widow could go off with a gentleman alone, and aye, a proper widow ought to have an escort in a strange city, Mrs. Deems thought furiously. She ought to have thought of that.

And Mrs. Devlin should have some advice, since she looked a quiz half the time, poor lady, with clothes out of Noah's ark, Cecily thought, almost as pleased with the arrangement as Arden, if only because she never saw ulterior motives, singular motives being quite enough for her to comprehend.

"Ah," Arden said, peering out the window and slapping his hand on the roof to get the coachman to stop, "Madame Renaud's establishment, perfect. I'll wager that's precisely where you were bound, Mrs. Devlin," he said as he swung open the coach door. "Indeed, your papa mentioned the place to me, it having been recommended to him as a superior sort of establishment for ladies of taste, and so certainly suitable for one who's coming out of mourning," he added on a charming smile to Mrs. Deems.

"We'll meet again at M. Leroy's," he added as he took Cecily's little hand in farewell after he'd helped Francesca out of the carriage. For really, she thought as she stood on the sidewalk thinking rapidly as he made his arrangements to meet up with the Deemses later, it wouldn't have done to struggle, and would've looked ill-bred to argue, and moreover, and most annoying, she'd not the slightest idea of where to buy a gown in Paris.

She'd visited the city so many times in the past two weeks she ought to have noted where every interesting shop was. But she'd deliberately looked aside at first, for she'd had no money and hadn't wanted to tease herself, and then after Mr. Lyons had roared into their lives, she'd been so busily doing her job and being an expert watchwoman that she'd had eyes for nothing else but her charge and that gentleman. So for all her pains, she thought in disgust now, not only was she being eased out of her job, but also she knew Arden Lyons' profile better now than the shape of the Arc de Triomphe Napoleon had built.

Looking up at that human, but no less formidable profile after the Deemses' carriage rolled off with a merrily waving

Cee-cee and her stricken-looking mama, Francesca spoke coldly.

"My father," she said determinedly, "never mentioned any dressmaker."

"Care to wager on it?" he said with interest as he took her arm securely. "Now, come along, having your dowdiness removed shan't hurt a bit. And you can't hit me," he said pleasantly, "not only because we're in public and you are a lady, but because I'm bigger. Ah, here we are. Now, stop scowling or you'll frighten Madame—she finds the British terrifying anyhow. She came from a staunch republican family and doted on the little emperor and most patriotically wouldn't even smuggle her designs to us. That's why she's known only to the French, but as most of them still haven't even the little that you've got in your pocket right now, she'll be glad enough to design for you. The war's over, after all, and she is French, and so, above all, practical. And don't fret, she'll do a gown that would make Louis Leroy weep with envy, that is, before he buys it up and adds a bow or two to salve his conscience before he puts his name to it.

"Ah, madame, enchanté," he said as the proprietor of the shop hurried toward him. *"Permettez moi de vous presenter ma petite amie Madame Devlin. C'est important qu'elle ait une robe pour un ange, parce qu' elle est mon ange, comprenez-vous?"* he asked, sighing helplessly.

It was difficult to say whether Madame Renaud, who was carefully assessing Francesca's face and form, could have picked a proper color for a charming frock for a young woman who seemed to have a brick-red face, but then, since that face turned pure white with rage as Mr. Lyons finished with his speech, she might have guessed that the lady, so obviously English, had at least the civilization to match her beauty and so could speak French as perfectly as her escort did. And the lady, for some odd reason, disliked the gallant gentleman calling her his "angel" and announcing that she was his mistress. Ah, but she was certainly English, Madame thought, and therefore, of course, incomprehensible.

But, *"Mais certainement, M. Lyons,"* Madame said confidently, for whatever his jest, and the gentleman was known for his odd jests, he was warm in the pocket, and yes, she decided as she firmly towed a hesitant Francesca to her workrooms, still a connoisseur of females. Because for all the young woman was dressed as a frump she was, Madame saw, a diamond in the dustbin, trust the large gentleman to have an eye.

"And, oh," Arden called out, "no red. *Jamais rouge.*"

Francesca swung her head about to argue, for it had been red she'd been starved for after all these weeks of unrelenting black, and red she'd coveted as she'd gazed at Roxanne's dress.

"Too obvious, unless you want it to be obvious that you envied Roxanne to the point of madness, and have decided to take up her position when you lose your own, of course," he commented, stilling her protest at birth.

He ppr oved the yew green, and overwhelmingly approved the celestial blue, but just as she was about to protest that the cloth-of-gold gown was too clinging, as well as madly inappropriate for a chaperone, she saw his eyes widen and saw him at a loss for words for the first time since she'd met him, and so cried, "I'll take it," before he could recover himself. It might hang just as beautifully in her wardrobe as it did from her shoulders, and then cling to the contours of her valise as closely as it did to her own more sinuous curves, and do so until she grew too old and not just too timid to ever wear it again, but it was magnificent. And it was worth having if only for that dumbfounded expression he'd worn as she'd modeled it for him. But it was most important to have, because although she forgot it as often as she wanted everyone else not to know it, it was a beautiful, unnecessary frippery and she was only just one-and-twenty, after all.

She carefully counted out the sum into Madame's hand, and it was a generous one to be sure, but she'd enough, though it left her with very little.

"Don't vex yourself," he said kindly as they left the shop after she'd given Madame the direction for the gowns to be sent. "It was a great deal of blunt, but not wildly extravagant. One of Cee-cee's gowns would pay for the lot. And your papa really did suggest I guide you to a fashionable modiste, you know."

"Oh, doubtless," she sighed, "after it was pointed out to him that I looked frightful. I know," she went on quietly, "I really do, you know."

". . . that he loves you? Or that he does not?" Arden asked softly.

"Oh," she said, her odd husky voice breaking. "Both. All. He loves me in his fashion. I can't ask for more."

"Although you want more," he commented as they walked slowly down the avenue. "Did you find what you wanted with Devlin, then?"

She couldn't be angry at his presumption this time. It was too personal a question, to be sure, but it was too kindly put, too gently framed in that great, gentle voice, for her to take offense. Rather, she found she grew angry at herself for having to deceive him in her answer. So she kept her head down and answered him with as honest a lie as she was able.

"I lost what I wanted with Devlin, then," she said.

They walked the next streets in companionable, thoughtful silence. Until they reached M. Leroy's establishment and before the door was opened to them, she looked up and saw the sympathy in his eyes and the warmth of his smile, his look filled with fellow-feeling and not a trace of lechery. Then she was abashed and almost glad when Mrs. Deems rushed to greet them and carried him away.

They secured three new dresses for Cee-cee too, and then four dishes of ices at a café and it was not until they were on the way back to the hotel as she watched Cee-cee explaining to them all just why she liked her new frocks so very well, that Francesca realized she'd just passed yet another day in the fabled city of Paris, and still had not seen it.

Francesca had no new gown for that evening, but at least she'd still her post, and the Deemses had asked for her escort for Cecily at dinner. So she threw her old shawl about her shoulders, and seeing Roxie's paisley one folded on her chair, caught it up to return to her before she joined the Deemses downstairs. She hurried through the corridors, for once not looking forward to an evening in France just to see it through to its end. She hurried because she didn't want to stop and question herself, or her new excitement and hope, to find out why a mere day purchasing gowns, however lovely, should have set her to humming all the while she'd dressed, should have got her heart to beating so, should have made her so interested in living every moment before her again. A body in motion, she repeated to herself, as she'd been repeating all sorts of quotations and silly shreds of songs, as though words could block out the questioning words beginning to form in the back of her mind, tends to remain in motion. A body at rest, she went on, blithely missaying her lessons, tends to sulk. She was actually giggling to herself when she came to Roxanne's door.

And so she didn't notice how long it took Roxanne to answer her door. Nor did she note the interested looks she'd received from various gentlemen as she'd come down the hall to stand at the door. For her color was high, she held her head up, and her eyes sparkled, and, sad old dress or not, she was in as high good looks as she was in spirits. But Roxanne, she finally noted, when the door cracked open at last, did not look herself at all. She did not look badly, only entirely different.

Her blond hair was not carefully, artfully disarranged as it always was, rather it was prettier, although in true tousled disarray. She wore none of the subtle cosmetics she usually took trouble to apply, but her lips were swollen and blushed pink, as did her cheeks, and her blue eyes were dreamy as though she'd been interrupted from sleep, though they were more unfocused with some inner, dazed content than seeming to be confused at a sudden transition to wakefulness. She looked warm and pleased and secretive, and she clutched a wrapper closed at her neck and looked at Francesca with a smile.

"Your shawl. Thank you," Francesca said, suddenly afraid of something she knew but would not recognize, thrusting the shawl at the petite blond woman. "Are you coming down this evening?" she asked as Roxanne took the shawl but still said nothing in reply.

"I hope not." Roxanne laughed, her voice almost as low as Francesca's usually was.

"Are you all right?" Francesca asked nervously, anxious to be away from something unknown and personal that she thought she ought not to be seeing.

"Never better," Roxanne replied, and then when a voice behind asked a soft question, she spoke back to the room, "Only Mrs. Devlin. I'll give your love."

And then she looked at Francesca again, and unable to stop herself in her happiness, and perhaps because she wanted to boast, added, grinning, "And neither has he been, I'll reckon. So tell Arden and your papa that his lordship won't be down tonight either. If I can help it," she said on a wink, and closed the door on Francesca's wide-eyed dawning disbelief and comprehension.

"That was unnecessary," Julian said, annoyed, beginning to rise from her bed as she came back into the room.

Roxanne flung the shawl across the bed, taking care not to cover his nakedness. She did that in another, unexpected fashion.

"And is this unnecessary too?" she asked when she moved her mouth from him again.

"No, damn you," he said softly. And forgetting his annoyance, he remembered what he liked most these days—oblivion—and, relaxing, let her remind him again.

But Francesca couldn't forget. She'd seen nothing that was going on in the room, but could imagine it all. Or rather, she could not imagine it all, which made it even worse. Roxanne had taken a gentleman to her room, she'd always suspected she did such things, but knowing the gentleman and knowing Roxanne, she couldn't take it with the aplomb she wished she had. She felt betrayed, as though the grown-ups had done something she wasn't supposed to see. She felt complicitous for having seen it, and somehow less virtuous herself for knowing, however obliquely, just what it was. And she was frightened, for if Roxanne could so easily take the charming, civilized, amusing Viscount Hazelton and bring him to her bed, and reduce him to a sexual jest—as he would no doubt similarly estimate her—then she herself was vulnerable. If not more so, since she knew nothing of the matter as Roxanne so clearly did.

In order to rid herself of the distaste and fear and childish unease she felt, she focused instead on what she knew, and what she could judge. The viscount had taken Roxanne as a lover, and that was wrong. He, or any other gentleman, would not have dared take Cecily or any other protected female. He wouldn't have even walked her unescorted through the streets of Paris. It wasn't difficult to reach the next natural conclusion, so she hurried downstairs so that she might have enough time to roundly snub Arden Lyons before dinner.

She saw him at once; indeed, the only benefit she perceived in knowing him now was that he was always so easy to locate. He was deep in conversation with a tall, thin, distraught-looking young gentleman. She was so eager to engage him in dispute, or get his reaction in any way to the scandalous message she bore, all the while half-hoping he could somehow laugh it all away as she badly wished to do, as he was always so very good at doing, that she walked straight up to Arden's broad back as he stood listening to the young man.

But then she stopped abruptly as she listened too.

"Please," the young fellow was pleading in a quavering voice, his face white, his Adam's apple bobbing as he swallowed hard. "Please, Mr. Lyons, I must have that deed back. Indeed, I was badly foxed the other night, I ought never to have sat down at the table, I mislaid my reason with my coins. I'd foresworn gambling entirely, only the drink led me to it, that, and the ease of the game. And now . . . It's not the money I ask for, that was fairly won, and I'll not dispute it. But my home!" he cried in pain. "My legacy, my birthright! Gone. And what's my poor sister to do now? Sleep in the gutters that I have brought her down to? Oh, please, Mr. Lyons, I must have my home back again."

In his despair, he clutched at Arden's sleeve, his thin hands showing white knuckles, and tears starting in his wide, frantic brown eyes.

She couldn't see Arden's face, but she could hear the cold contempt in his deep voice, and she could all too clearly see the way that large tanned hand callously plucked the thin and shaking one from his sleeve and flung it away, and then brushed off his cuff as though it had been dirtied by the young man's desperate hold.

"It was not just your money you lost, I remind you," Arden said, "as it was not just your house, as you say. No, no more. Go home, Lord Waite, I'll have nothing to do with it, or you."

"What's the point in living, then?" the young man cried, fumbling in his jacket pocket.

"So you can lose again, I suppose," Arden said, shrugging, and lightly, as lightly as though he were taking a dance card from a lady, he plucked the chased-silver pistol from the young man's hand as it emerged from his jacket. He examined it, and then handed it back, laughing as if he'd been told some enormous joke instead of seeing a man half-crazed with despair. "And hope to earn enough to buy a better firearm. The only way you could destroy yourself with this, my lord, is if you beat yourself repeatedly on the head with it. It might do, if it knocks some sense in," he added as he turned to walk away.

And then saw Francesca standing staring at him as though he were rising from the young man's blood-spattered corpse, rather than simply cutting him dead in a hotel for gamesters.

Something flickered in his eyes as he took her arm and

led her away as well. But it was only concern and deep sincerity she saw as she gazed up at him.

"The boy's a gambler," he said as she looked back to see Lord Waite, white-faced still, and still as the grave, standing staring after them. "He'd gamble his homeless sister away as well, if he could, if she were here. I helped him once, and see the good it did. Good God, girl! The way you look at me! He applied to me because I won it back for him once before. Credit me with some sporting instinct, if not morals. I did not win it from him," he said urgently, shaking her arm slightly, to take her gaze from the boy.

"Everyone here gambles," she said, trying to understand, for when she was with him she badly wanted to.

"And everyone here drinks. And dances. But some can live without it," he said carefully, watching her closely.

She nodded, thinking about this, and let him lead her toward the dining salon.

"Oh," she said then, the confusion in her face causing that hard, impassive face that turned to her at her slight utterance to look down with a deep frown. "Yes. Roxanne told me to tell you that the Viscount Hazelton won't be down tonight. If she can help it," she added, turning her eyes away, sorry she'd mentioned it.

She missed his wince, but heard the anger as he said abruptly, "There are all sorts of addictions, aren't there?"

And then Mrs. Deems spied them, and took his arm and led him to Cecily, who stood, as shy and expectant as a bride, waiting for him, as he bowed down low over her hand.

All through dinner Francesca kept to her silence, but then, there was nothing remarkable about that; that was her place, after all. But she never so much as laughed politely as a spectator should, for she wasn't attending to the conversation despite the fact that Arden had the Deemses and her father aroar with his humor tonight, while all the while he watched to see if he could get her just to smile. But she was listening to her own inner counsel now, and it was a harsh and hurtful lecture she heard, and all to do with what one got for putting faith in gamblers, cheats, and easy gentlemen.

She stood at her father's side that night after Cecily had gone to bed ablush from Arden's gallantries. She stood where Roxanne usually stood, but didn't mind, because she didn't notice, she was so involved with her own thoughts.

So much so that her father realized the beautiful but silent woman in black at his side was not only distracting his opponents as much as he'd wish, but even more so, but deterring them from playing with him, since few men choose to game at a funeral. When he dismissed her, she wandered off, but before Arden, who'd been watching thoughtfully all that time, could reach her, she stopped and stared into the crowd like a woman who'd had an amazing revelation. And when he did reach her, she was trembling.

But she said nothing more than that she was tired, and she so clearly was that he was only too glad to escort her to her room. He was only sorry that she didn't seem to wish to listen to him tonight, for he tried to open the subjects of Lord Waite and Julian again, however explosive they were, just to clear the air. But though he broached both topics a dozen times, she wasn't attending to him.

He didn't take her hand to his lips at the doorway this night. Instead, he reached out and held one large cool hand against her forehead. When she looked up at him at last as though she finally saw him again, he sighed.

"There's no fever," he said gently. "Go to sleep. Other sorts of healing often come with sleep too, you know."

And then, as naturally as he would if she were a child, he bent and brushed a soft, cool kiss against her cheek before he left her.

But there certainly was something terribly wrong, she thought, closing the door behind her. She was too frightened to weep, or to tell anyone about it, for she'd heard all the tales about Bedlam. Because tonight, when she'd been so grieved with herself and the life she found herself in, she'd begun to remember, there in the noisy gambling room, what had been and what might have been. The click of the wheel had become as soothing as the trickling of the stream they'd stood by, the laughter of the excited gamesters very like the bickering birds that had been calling in the trees around them, and the warmth of the blatantly lit circle where she stood, in the midst of vast darkness, like and unlike the sunlit clearing they'd been within. But for all her fantasy, she couldn't forget that she was lost now in a strange land, surrounded by gamblers, seducers, liars, and cheats, so confused she'd begun to turn to the worst of them for comfort. She was homesick to the heart for the home she'd never known. And she thought so hard about Harry then that she almost wept aloud.

She'd turned her head to the door to leave, and through her drenched lashes had seen him. Seen him clear as day, clear as night, clear as any reality she'd ever known. Seen Harry himself, whole and live and as sick with longing as she was, standing there staring back at her. So she'd blinked and blinked, and then Arden had come, and Harry was gone.

She sank to sit on her bed, and wondered if madness began this way, from the need of it, to escape real sorrows by retreating into truer ones that the heart at least knew were past, and so could bear. And she looked up at last, though a misery now too fearful for tears, to see, at last, the slip of paper glowing white upon the floor.

She was afraid to read it, but when she'd done so several times, and felt the crispness of the paper beneath her fingers, and heard it rattle in her shaking hands, she knew that this, at least, was real. And so was joy.

"Francesca, my darling," it said, "I am here, I do live, I must see you. But I must not be seen by your father, nor anyone else, not just yet. All can be explained, all *will* be explained. I'll meet you tonight. Stay awake for me. There is a garden here, behind the kitchens. Come at first dawn. Trust me. For I have not forgotten, any more than you have, 'Mrs. Devlin,' my own, my darling."

And it was signed, unmistakably, for she'd saved and memorized each and all of his letters: "Your devoted Harry."

7

THE NIGHT was loath to leave, or so it seemed to Francesca as she hurried down the stairs in the odd quiet of the dark hotel. For though it was almost dawn, the darkness clung, as did an eerie silence. It was always noisy here; it had always been filled with people morning to night, and the bustle and voices and the several sounds of gaming, or gossip, or people entertaining themselves, had been as much a part of the furnishings of the hotel as any carpet or couch within it. Now it seemed oddly empty and echoing, for in this last hour of night, in this breath before dawn, all the guests and servants were equals: those who'd frolicked all night had gone off to bed, and those who'd soon arise to ready the place for tomorrow were deep in slumber, just as unaware of the approaching day.

Still, even if there'd been anyone awake, it was doubtful that the whisper of her slippers could have been heard as she raced through the main floor of the house to discover a back entrance, because she ran so quickly it was as though they touched ground only for an instant before they slid away again. She'd been pent up in mad imaginings all night, and so as soon as she'd seen the blackness of night begin to transmute to a blearier, unfocused sort of darkness, she'd leapt to her feet to keep her appointment with the dawn.

She'd sat up all through the long night, wondering at what cruel hoax, what odd jest, or what mad imagining had produced such a letter. Harry was dead. It was as much of a fact as the name of the king and the state of the nation. The government had declared it, his friends had mourned him, she'd written and gotten acknowledgment of her sympathies from his bereaved family. Though she'd never seen his grave, she knew it lay in Belgium. She knew of no firmer truth. Yet here was a note, in his hand, to hers, which said he was alive, and would be here with the coming of the new day.

She couldn't find an exit from any of the main rooms, and so she crept through the cavernous kitchens, glad of the increasingly milky darkness which gave a luminous glow to the room to help her find her way as she made for the back door to the garden the note had promised was there. The kitchen maid sleeping on her pallet near the stove only sighed as Francesca tiptoed past her, as though she really were in the dream she had begun to believe she was in, and the great door sighed open at her touch, as a door in a dream might, as she stepped out into the cool dying night.

She could see nothing but shapes at first as she pulled her shawl around her and looked out into the rising mists. Then she ventured to walk further from the door into the garden, but hesitantly, as if she were entering unknown waters that grew deeper with each step. There was no sound; even the birds had only just begun to sense the coming dawn, but the grass was cold and wet beneath her thin slippers, so she began to believe this was real.

Then she saw a different shape, a shape that might have

been another human, looming up from the gray mists. She stepped further forward and peered intently as first dawn came rising to release the birds from night's silence and a faint cool morning wind began to blow the mists away.

"Harry?" she whispered into the increasing light. If she were mad, she would be entirely so, she thought as she dared to whisper again, "Harry?"

"Fancy?" the apparition said. "My Fancy?"

And hearing that voice, muted as it was with wonder and secretiveness, she knew. She fled into his arms, and they came round her, real as anything in her life now was, and they held her close against living, breathing warmth. And if nothing else convinced her this was real here in the blank chill morning, the scent of the gaming house that still clung to him, of tobacco and tallow and lingering spirits she detected as he breathed her name into her ear with wonder, did, even before she raised her eyes to his face and cried, "Harry!" as though without being pinned to reality by his spoken name he'd disappear into the mists again.

"Hush!" he said, warning her to silence, and he held her wordlessly until she stopped shaking and could look at him and speak with reason again.

He was the same, she thought as she stared up at him and let her doubting fingers touch his cheek, the same, only different in this colorless bleak light, for there was no sunlight to enhance the straight light brown hair and lift it from the commonplace, and no brightness to light the subtle attraction of that lean sensitive face. There was nothing about him to distinguish him, he'd so often jested, from the common run of pleasant young men. He was slender and graceful and very ordinary, he'd insisted, but she'd always thought he'd been wrong, and knew it, and that was part of his charm. For there was enormous charm as well as self-mockery in the warm brown eyes, and the straight nose and smiling mouth were uniquely his, and no other gentleman she'd ever met had that ironic expression that lent such an elegant cast to his even features. No, it was Harry, unmistakably Harry, and if he were dead and risen, then death had not altered him, nor diminished him.

"Here," he said in a whisper as he wrapped his arm around her and walked her to a corner of the garden where there was a bench. "We've a little time to talk before the servants stir and I must go."

When he felt her start at that, he held her closer to him

so that she could hear his words exhaled on the slightest breath and began to speak at once.

"I won't go until I've explained," he said, and as she relaxed, he laughed lightly and added teasingly, " 'Mrs. Devlin.' "

She flushed, but before she could explain that she'd never thought she'd have to explain to a ghost, he went on, "Thank God you took my name, Fancy, or I'd have never found you. But Madame Renaud has a seamstress who . . . ah, knows me, and so she mentioned the irony of her having to sew up gowns for a lady with the same name. I was about to tell her that there are a thousand of us Devlins in the world, when she added 'Mrs. Francesca Devlin' and I knew in my heart that incredible as it was, it could be no other. I asked after you here at the hotel and found the truth in your lie. Then I saw you, then I found you. God," he whispered wonderingly, hugging her, "how lucky I was that one maudlin night I'd let fall my real name to the wench."

"Why?" Francesca said when she could. "Why, Harry?" she asked, pulling from his embrace at last, and facing him. "Why were you dead? Why do you hide now? Why are you here?"

"I'm here to see you and find out what's going on with you, my girl," he said sternly. " 'Mrs. Devlin' is flattering, I'll admit, but why in God's name are you all in black and with your hair like that, all in a dowager's knot?" he said scornfully, leaning back and scrutinizing her until she looked away. "And creeping about with that vulgar family of cits, in the company of a brute like that Arden Lyons, and a care-for-nothing like his hedonistic friend the viscount?"

"I had to work," she said desperately. "Father has no money left, and I didn't know, for I came here to be with him when school was done, and I couldn't stay on in Roxanne's post, as a gambler's assistant, and so I was glad to find respectable employment. But the Deemses wouldn't have hired me as I was, not at my age or in my single state, so I added some years, and your name. But I had to do what I could, for I'd nothing else, don't you see, Harry? Bram would've helped, but he died with you . . ." She stopped and stared at him then. "What happened, Harry?" she asked again, not defending herself to him any longer, as soon as she realized the absurdity of it, when she didn't even know why she was able to speak with him.

"I didn't die," he said. "I refused to die."

But he grew very distant and cold as he said that.

And though she began to suspect his escape had nothing to do with luck, she refused to think of it, and only asked, at once, "But, Harry, how wonderful! Then why didn't you tell us?"

"Because they wanted me dead," he said in a flat voice, before he mocked his own words. "Ah, no, they'd never say as much, but it's far better that they think I'm gone, for I'll swear, I never had a chance to live, and they won't thank me for saving myself. I saw Bram die," he said angrily, "saw him fall from his horse, by my side, and die. You've never seen a thing like war, Fancy, pray God you never do. War?" He laughed. "Not really, not like the illustrations we saw in books, not the glorious warfare we studied, no, for all the bombs and smoke, drums and uniforms and banners, it was more like a charnel house. No, a slaughterhouse. The ground was slippery with blood, men's or horses', they ran together, and both were without value or meaning. I left, Francesca, when I realized that. I left, and so I live."

"You ran away?" she asked, incredulous.

"I rode away," he corrected her sharply.

"You deserted?" she asked, shaking her head. "You deserted," she said at last, accepting that when he didn't contradict her again.

"Would it have been better if I'd died?" he asked with barely controlled rage. "I was not born to be fodder for the cannons. I rode away until I thought to stop and change clothes with an obliging Frenchman—a dead one—God knows there were enough of them. He rots in Belgium now under my name. I found my way to Paris, and I live. Can't you rejoice for that?" he asked, gently again, as she sat staring at him.

"Can't you go back and explain it all to them now?" she asked. "Surely they'll understand," she said, looking for a way out of this coil.

"Certainly," he agreed, "they'll understand as they put my back to a wall and put in the bullets I neglected to have added on the field of Waterloo. No, Fancy, I can't go back, not as Lieutenant Harry Devlin. That man is dead. Someday I may go back, someday I likely shall, with a new name and with the new face that age will give me. I knew what I gave up in order to live, and I regretted only you. Now, since fate has brought you to me, it must mean it was meant to be, even as I thought. So stay with me, Fancy,'' he said suddenly, taking her hand tightly, and smiling again, ''until I have that age, and then come home with me too. But as 'Mrs. Devlin' in truth this time.''

When she remained silent, only looking at him with those huge dark eyes that became soft brown as the night faded from around her, he added, less lightly than he wished, ''I've funds. Funds enough, since I got word to my family, and they continue to send them to me secretly. We can live very well, never doubt it, 'Mrs. Devlin,' '' he added on that warm and charming smile, as though it delighted him merely to speak the words.

''No,'' she said very slowly, wishing there was more time to think, more time to understand why she'd gone from utmost joy to grief again in moments, and hating to speak even as she reacted, ''never as 'Mrs. Devlin,' Harry,'' she said, ''for he's dead, you said so yourself.''

''Where is the honor?'' he demanded icily, all at once, ''in useless death?''

''Not honor,'' she said, tears coming to her eyes as she tried to find the words to explain, and spilling when she finally did, ''but there was a necessity. Napoleon would've won if it weren't for fodder for cannons . . . like Bram. He shouldn't have died, and maybe there wasn't a scrap of honor in it, but he did so that Napoleon could be set down once and for all.''

''And so the world goes on without him, and Napoleon still lives,'' Harry said, spitting the words out, ''and the victorious British rush to France and drink their wines and buy their clothes and women and make them fat and rich again. Is that why Bram died? Well, Harry Devlin died then too, but he's a wiser gent, for he rose to live again,'' he said, himself rising and looking down at her, and then away from her tears. ''And if you're wise, Francesca, you'll accept it and come with me. I offered for you once, but decided to wait because you were so young. You're not that young anymore,'' he said plainly, ''and now I offer again.''

''No, Harry,'' she said softly, ''because I knew that Harry Devlin, and I don't know whoever you are now.''

''Do you think to catch Arden Lyons? Oh, yes,'' he said wisely, ''I saw him escort you to your room last night. But he's a villain, worse than me. And he's after the pretty little rich cit, my girl, for all he'll stoop to dally with you. I offer wedlock, at least.''

"And I am sensible of the honor, but I decline," she said, not stopping now to think of her words, only knowing they were right as she spoke them, "for I'd never be able to forget, Harry, never.''

"I'd make you forget in time, I swear it," he said, pulling her close.

"You don't understand," she answered, turning her head from his lips. "It's Bram I'd never forget. And I don't believe you'd like me any more than I'd like myself if I did.''

"I'll make you forget everything but me," he vowed as though he swore at her, and brought his lips to hers.

But he stopped and drew back with a start as she said, just before he kissed her, "I hear someone coming, Harry.''

The cool, deadened tone of her voice should have warned him, but he heard only the words and so released her immediately and jumped away, looking about anxiously for the nonexistent intruder she'd warned him about. Then, when he looked to her, the sad, pitying knowledge in her eyes told him the truth.

"I've got to leave anyhow," he said coldly, straightening from the half-crouch he'd automatically, unknowingly assumed, "but I warn you, Fancy, I'm your last best hope. We loved once, we can again. You've no money and no prospects, and before long will have no reputation either. And soon you'll have no more time. I'll be back to ask once more. But only that. Good-bye. And, oh," he added, turning back after he'd turned to enter the remaining mists at the margins of the garden, "I ask you, out of charity, and for that honor you are pleased to insist upon, to tell no one of our meeting.''

But before she could promise him that, she heard a noise that could be another person coming, and by the time she turned back to warn him truly, he'd gone.

She stood alone, looking after him. He'd faded like a dream into the receding night. But he'd been real, it had been Harry, although she'd scarcely known him. And then she remembered, only the pain of it quelling her rising wild laughter, that as she'd forgotten to ask, she no longer even knew his name.

The kitchen wench was alarmed to find the lady wandering in the garden, for only the servants' privies were so far from the house, and the lady might be drunken or mad, or both, from the look on her face. But as the lady then smiled weakly and whispered something reassuring to do with such a fine morning, the little maid was only too glad to agree, and bob a curtsy, and forget her so soon as she'd gone back to the hotel again.

They became separated just after they'd rounded a corner and gone down the steps toward the embankment. Francesca didn't know how it happened, she'd not been paying attention, in truth it was her fault, she thought with rising panic, but suddenly Cee-cee and Mrs. Deems and the maid weren't there before her. There were dozens of Frenchmen and women, the crowds of them shopping and haggling at the many outdoor vendors' carts were thick, but they were all of them drably dressed poor Parisians, and the richly attired Deemses would have stood out among them—almost as distinctively as Arden did, she thought, as she looked about once more, to find him standing right beside her. But they ought never to have come here, she thought wildly as she realized she'd lost her employers, even though Arden had gone on about the charms of Paris' outdoor pet market until Cee-cee, usually so obedient in all things, was on fire to see the dear little caged birds and the wee kittens he'd waxed so lyrical about. For this wasn't a place for tourists, and the Deemses, she remembered, couldn't speak a word of French, except for ''How much?'' and ''Are you sure it can't be gotten more cheaply? . . . that's all I have with me just now, and I promise you you won't find a better offer, I wasn't born yesterday, you know.''

At least, that was what Arden claimed they could say when she told him her fears. And then he laughed at her expression before he assured her that Mrs. Deems, at least, could find her way to safety if she were stranded in the sea with nothing but a ravening horde of pirates and a shark about her.

''She was most likely attracted by a bargain on a cart,'' he said, ''and her hunting blood was up, so she stopped short to haggle whilst we strolled on ahead. But never fear, there isn't a less helpless female in Christendom than Mrs. Deems, she'll likely shout a 'halloo' at us any moment, so let's go on. Well, we can scarcely stand here until we become landmarks, can we? I hardly think you want to eventually overhear some ardent Frenchman saying to his m'amselle, 'Ah, but, my love, I shall meet you by moonlight tonight by the embankment, as usual, beneath the large Englishman and the beautiful lady in black,' or do you?'' he asked curiously.

She didn't laugh as long as he'd wished her to, and her haunted expression returned as soon as she was done. But then, he knew he'd never have been able to disengage her from the Deemses so easily if she'd been in her right mind in the first place. He'd actually planned on loudly whispering an invitation to a covert *tête-à-tête* to Cee-cee so that Francesca could overhear and try to spoil sport, and then be well-served by finding herself alone with him instead. But she clearly was falling down on her usual excellent job. One look at her distraction this afternoon had showed him that if he'd shouted his nefarious plans aloud, she'd still have missed them, and he'd have been well-served by being stranded with Cee-cee instead. And that would have ended the game immediately and would never have done, for it wasn't nearly time for that yet.

"It is possible, you know," he said, taking her arm as he strolled on, "to enjoy the sights of Paris without keeping one eye on me. No, I don't find it flattering in the least," he went on as she almost stumbled, "since I know it's all duty. I don't expect it, you see, since few females have found me so rivetingly interesting as you've done, you know," he explained. "Beguiling, yes," he said wistfully, "amusing, certainly, sensuous, brilliant, and handsome, of course, but never so endlessly fascinating."

"I share that same intense interest with Mrs. Deems," she retorted, without thinking, jolted from her inner conflicts by his presumption to become presumptuous herself.

He nodded approvingly; he'd brought her to life once more, and dragged her back from whatever dread things she'd been contemplating. With that father, and her duties, it was a wonder to him that she didn't fall into the sullens more often.

"Ah, but Mrs. Deems, bless her mercenary heart, would be entirely taken with my charming fortune, and would look sharp to see it don't slip away," he said, with a note, she noticed, of true admiration coloring his voice.

She, of course, couldn't dispute his assessment of himself without seeming to be as fascinated by him personally as he'd implied, and neither could she agree without being even more presumptuous. So, as usual, as she'd trained herself to do since she'd taken up her lowly position in life, as all servants must, she did nothing but pretend she hadn't heard or understood. She walked on silently with him. And he looked down upon that dutifully bent head with its primly drawn-up mass of shining ebony hair and he yearned to shake it free from its bonds even as he itched to shake her bodily from her reverie. And then, sighing, he diverted himself instead by acting as a tour guide, until she looked up and about herself with interest again.

It was a lively section of the city, and an interesting one. And one, as he'd said and she had to admit, that few fine lady tourists even knew existed. It wasn't a low slum; he knew precisely where that was and would never drive her in a coach within shouting distance of there. But it was a neighborhood for the common man and there'd been a war on. All manner of things were being raucously vended from the lines of carts by the left bank of the Seine, and that filth-choked section of the mighty river was no ranker-smelling that the refuse on the streets that hadn't been swept into it as yet, and the cast-off, foraged refuse passing as merchandise on so many of the carts.

But the section they strolled to was cheerier, if only because there were so many little wooden cages filled with small birds and animals ranged everywhere there. For, as Arden commented wisely, now that the citizens no longer had to keep from starving by using their little furred and feathered friends in the desperate way they'd had to do during the long wars, they were pleased to have them to dinner in the best meaning of the word again.

She'd stopped to poke one gloved finger through a cage for a tiny orange kitten to bat at, when she heard the sound of crying, so muted it sounded as though some little animal had begun to weep human tears at its homelessness. A very little girl stood near a double row of cages, crying helplessly, and worsening matters by rubbing at her eyes with a dirty fist to keep from weeping more, only to have the tears stream as much from the pain of this fresh irritation as they did from her original misery. Although her hands were filthy, she was plainly but neatly dressed in a faded blue smock, and though her shoes were mended, they were also clean, as was the dark curly hair that had been done up with a tiny bow. She was, even in her distress, far tidier than the hordes of ragged children Francesca had seen playing or scavenging by the riverside.

As she watched, a businesslike woman in black paused

by the child and demanded to know what the trouble was.
When the little creature only wept the harder, the woman
shrugged, and hefting her basket, went on. There were more
children than rats in the gutters of Paris, and if one were
foolish enough to decline help, she muttered aloud as she
indignantly walked away, then an honest woman hadn't the
time to bother with her.

Francesca forgot her own sorrows and was beside the
child in an instant.

"There, there, my dear, are you lost?" she asked as she
knelt by the child, only to cause the girl to go off in positive
transports of unhappiness, until Francesca remembered to
say it in French. But even then, despite her gentle voice and
manner, the child refused to answer. She had begun to think
the little thing was a mute, until she heard a sigh of great
annoyance, and found herself, although still kneeling, prac-
tically face-to-face with Arden as he too knelt on one knee
in front of the hysterical girl.

"Here," he demanded in excellent French, "has your
mother gone off and got herself lost again?"

The silence that greeted this was as great a relief to Francesca's ears as it was to her mind. The child grew very still
and wide-eyed, and nodded.

"Well, then," Arden said brusquely, "now I suppose it's
up to you to find her again, isn't it? Isn't that just like her,
though? Turn your back for a minute to look at a pretty
thing, and she's off and got herself lost," he sighed in exasperation.

Unmistakably, the child giggled.

"What shall we do, do you suppose?" he asked.

The girl looked as though she were about to speak, but
then grew very still and wide-eyed.

"I don't expect you to speak with me," he said impatiently, "I'm a strange man, of course. I'd be shocked if
you spoke to me. Tell the pretty lady here, instead."

After a moment's thought, the child spoke up.

"Find her," she said, between a sniffle and a hiccup.

"Oh, yes," Arden said in disgust, rising to a stand and
looking far down at the child as though he were vastly disappointed in her. "Can you imagine what will happen if we
shout. 'Maman!' here? Every second woman here will turn
around and say *'Oui?'* all at once, and we'll have our hands
full. To say nothing of the noise. What other name does she
have? And where did you last see her?"

"Madame LaSalle. And I'm Sophy. Sophy LaSalle," the child answered obediently, and pointing one grubby finger, added, "That way, monsieur. Ah, madame," she corrected herself, looking up to Francesca again.

"Aha. Well then, come along," he said in matter-of-fact fashion, and pointing one huge forefinger, held it out to the child. She clung on to it as naturally as though it were a lifeline, and the two began to walk down the crowded street together, Arden pausing only to inquire after a "Madame LaSalle" as he stopped at every cart.

It wasn't long before the frantic young woman pushed through the crowd and with a great cry of "Sophy!" fell upon the child.

"I heard a gentleman was asking for me. I cannot thank you enough, indeed, monsieur I turned my back for only a moment, and she was gone," she babbled, clutching the child, but not so hard that the little girl couldn't squirm, so as to give Arden a gaptoothed grin at that. "And the good Lord knows the dangers there are for children here, especially a pretty one like my Sophy, a thousand thanks, monsieur," she went on, and Arden stood patiently impatient until her praises wound down enough for him to acknowledge them and bid the pair a gruff good day.

"It's a matter of experience," he said before Francesca could speak, and he led her on down the street again. "I grew up in a huge family, you see, and my father ran the local orphanage, to boot. You have to understand children to help them. She was far too decently dressed to be on her own, like the other urchins, and though not so entrancing as her fond mama thought, still undoubtedly in danger, and so rightly sworn to silence should a stranger attempt to speak to her. Until her mother's foolishness was pointed out to her. Children are far too honest and logical to be trusted, you know. For example, she was told not to let a strange man take her hand, no doubt, but was never told not to take hold of a strange man's finger. And all the while, she felt secure enough to do so, since it was clear she could always let go if she wished. But she wouldn't have been able to if I were the sort to have beguiled her for nasty purposes."

Francesca remained silent, remembering how oddly and yet how nicely he and the child had looked together, even though Sophy had scarcely come up to one of his waistcoat pockets and it had taken her whole hand to wrap around his one finger. Francesca smiled at him at the thought, and seeing her expression, he said, just as sweetly, "There are loopholes in every security system, you see, and it's always been my job to find them. Be warned, Mrs. Devlin, for I'm very good at what I do."

"But I'm not a lost little girl," she said, annoyed at being caught in so sentimental a mood, annoyed that he'd caught her at it.

"Oh, but I believe you are," he said with sincerity.

She began to frame the rude reply she couldn't make to him at that, but then was caught by his gentle smile. He was such a big man that his broad shoulders cut off all the view behind him, and he stood before her like some benign Colossus, towering above the mere mortals scurrying about the busy streets around him. There was wry acceptance of her hesitation to be read in his rough-hewn face, and he waited as he watched her with the eternal resignation of a man who wouldn't be surprised at whatever his fellowman or woman did to him, and was prepared to bear all, whatever came. There was such a stillness at the bottom of his eyes, such a kind and questioning look on his face, along with the beginnings of something more, something both comforting and exciting to see, that she wanted against all reason to confide in him. And might well have done so, blurting out her troubles impulsively as they trembled on the tip of her tongue, if Mrs. Deems hadn't come panting up behind them at that moment and cried out in triumph at finding them at last.

All the way home in the coach, Francesca sat silent as Mrs. Deems marveled endlessly on how she'd no idea of why she'd lost them there in broad daylight, and Francesca silently thanked her for finding them in time. For she'd been about to extend not merely a hand in confident trust, just as the child had done, but more than that as well, and she might have followed Arden Lyons wherever he led then, even though he'd specifically warned her that it was unwise to trust so logically.

But now she didn't know what was logical or not.

Her world had been turned upside down in almost every way. Everything she knew about Arden Lyons still clearly told her to mistrust him. Yet, increasingly, everything she saw about him contradicted that.

8

"I'M SO GLAD you decided to rejoin the living," the gentleman sitting before the window commented, but he paid more attention to his steepled fingers than to the blond young man frowning at his cravat in the looking glass, as he continued, "And I don't wonder you've forgotten how to tie that thing. I doubt you've worn anything more than a Hottentot might in the last few days . . . no, I believe they, at least, affect some sort of grass skirts, don't they?"

"Loincloths," Julian said absently as he pushed a pleat into place in his high white neckcloth.

"Ah, well, I suppose you're right, you are the resident expert on loins, aren't you?" Arden grumbled.

"You *are* annoyed," Julian said in some wonder, turning from the glass to scrutinize his friend. "I wasn't imagining it. Why?"

"I've joined the League for Public Decency," Arden answered.

"And please don't make me pull it out of you inch by inch. Out with it, please. What have I done to offend you?" Julian said in some exasperation, running his hand through his fair hair to neaten it, and disarranging it unintentionally, but so fashionably that several gentlemen later that night, seeing it, would threaten their barbers with lawsuits if they couldn't emulate it.

"Your descent, or ascent, into the realms of pleasure for so long a time made it a bit more difficult for me, but I suppose you haven't offended anyone but yourself, actually. And Francesca Devlin, I'd think," Arden answered thoughtfully, but when he gazed up from his fingertips to see his friend's steady icy stare fixed upon him, he went on. "Well, it strains even my creative efforts to think up a new and nonsalacious reason for your absence from our congenial little group for three consecutive days and nights—whilst Mrs. Cobb, coincidentally, was similarly incapacitated. Good God, Julian," he said in more lively accents, "you acted like a devout honeymooner, you know. The Deemses were deliciously shocked, but they've given up on you, so they can afford to be. But Francesca was mortified, and has been watching me like a hawk to see if I show similar inclinations to snatch up a female of my choice and hide in my den with her until the food runs out. Why don't you take up racing, or horse breeding? I heard building model ships is quite relaxing.''

The fair young man looked abashed for one moment, before he spoke up angrily. ''I held no one against her will, you know. I . . . suppose you're right, Arden,'' he said, deflated, as he leaned back against the chair he stood beside. ''I found pleasure in it, true, but you're right, not so much as to warrant such total immersion. I was bored, I suppose. And at loose ends. And the lady was exceeding willing,'' he added on a shrug.

''And you're done with her now, I suppose?'' Arden asked quietly but with censure underlying his question.

''Actually, no,'' Julian said, cheering up, ''not at all. But don't beam like a maiden auntie, Arden, it's not love eternal, for neither of us. It's just that Roxie's very amusing, even when not . . . otherwise occupied''—he laughed at his friend's appreciative grin at his choice of words before he went on carelessly—''and I like her very well, and I amuse her too. That's enough, I should think, for any reasonable man, isn't it? I thank you for your concern,'' he said with real sincerity, ''and you'll be pleased to know that I think the present arrangement will suit me nicely—at least, I won't disappear like that again for a while. But I seem to have been gone long enough to have missed one important step, haven't I? *Francesca* now, is it?'' he laughed. ''Arden, whatever became of the travesty of your courtship of the little blond Venus?''

''It goes forth,'' Arden said on a yawn.

''But it's the smoldering widow you're after, after all. I can see you having the one without a fuss, but can't imagine why you continue to do the pretty with the other.''

''Wrong,'' Arden said sharply, not laughing now, giving his friend a warning look, which caused him to look back at him oddly. ''I wouldn't find it easy to 'have' the one. She may be a widow, but not a sportive one. She, you see, is a lady.''

''Good Lord, Lion!'' Julian shouted, in his merriment coming up with his friend's oldest nickname. ''You're caught! At last! That I have lived to see this day!'' he laughed, and the more because for the first time since he'd known him, his huge friend seemed decidedly uncomfortable, and his tanned face, although studiously impassive, was, in fact, amazingly enough, growing darker, but not with rage.

"Ah, well," Arden said, rising and going through a semblance of a lazy stretch as he collected himself, before, as a master of dissembling must, he diverted himself from his true emotions by assuming other ones. He laughed as well.

"You've found me out, lad. She's won me entirely. It seems I find the word 'no' stimulating, 'no, no' enchanting, and 'no, never' positively enthralling. I thrive on rejection, my lust grows with every snub. I'm so afire, in fact, that I believe I just may propose to her. Yes. Wedlock. You're not the only one at loose ends, my boy. I've made my fortune, after all," he said, looking away from the startled expression on his friend's face and walking to look out the window at the growing evening instead, "I'm grown no younger in the process, and with wars over, both international and private, I think at last it may well be time to go home and raise those evil children I've always threatened that I would."

"And it's to be Francesca Devlin?" Julian said wonderingly, thinking about what he knew of the widow. She was comely, or at least he thought she could be; perhaps she could even be beautiful if she could be anything but an impoverished chaperone. She'd been born a lady, and behaved as one, and seemed to hold herself in careful check because of her position, but he'd always thought she smoldered with unexpressed passions of every sort. Oh, yes, he thought, smiling to himself now, Arden was a knowing one who always saw beneath every surface. He'd be sorry to lose his friend's company, but yes, he acknowledged, this might well be just the lady for him. He only wondered how deeply involved Arden really was, and realized he'd likely never know, as Arden turned back from the window with an expression that was a great parody of an enraptured swain's.

"Francesca Devlin, it is," he said on a gusty sigh. "How can you have doubted it for a moment? She's tried to stymie my every evil intention, and has, without doubt, planned to thwart some even more wicked ones that I haven't yet dreamed upon. My friend, she's made for me. Hair like midnight on the high toby, the grace of a footpad—why, man, she moves with the stealth of a burglar, and thinks like one too. Yet when I catch her at one of her schemes to cross me, she speaks up her innocence like a magistrate, but all in the voice of a drowsy child . . ."

He paused then, and it might have been that there'd been some deep sincerity in his voice, before he caught himself and went on with is mock paean to love. "Yes, she's got the hauteur of a hangman. And the form of a courtesan with the stated morals of a nun, yet her eyes hint at more sins than even I have to my credit. Oh, yes," he said as he turned his eyes rapturously toward the ceiling, "a face like a saint's, with a mind as devious as a dog's hind leg behind it. She's more than I deserve, which is, of course, why I must have her. In holy, or in our case, surely, unholy wedlock."

"Bravo, Arden!" Julian applauded. "I can't wait to dance at your wedding."

"Put by your dancing slippers," his friend answered, suddenly serious. "It may never be. But I've at least a chance. She's in an unenviable position now."

"You've more to offer than escape from an unenviable position, Arden," Julian answered, equally seriously.

"Have I?" Arden said, looking hard at his friend, his face suddenly no longer amiable, suddenly again as it had been when they'd first met: hard, guarded, closed, and with more than a hint of menace in it. "I don't think so. I've lived an unadmirable life, Julian—trust me to have had enough decency to at least know what I did, if not to have stopped me from doing it. No, I deserve very little, but it's no insult to Francesca to hope I can win her, even so. Whatever I am, at least I'm better than servitude to her inferiors, or loss of honor with her reckless Papa. I may be her inferior, but I'll not ask servitude from her. And I plan to be less reckless, after, that is, my one last wild stab at fortune—when I offer for her."

"Arden," Julian said earnestly, angry at his friend's estimate of himself, for whatever his past, he'd been one of the most decent and honorable men he'd ever known, "you're no one's inferior, and whatever your background, I believe you could win your pick of wives, from the most dewy misses to the most upright matrons in England."

"Oh, good, I did hope you'd say that," Arden answered with great eagerness, "so I believe I'll toss Mrs. Devlin over and have a go at Princess Charlotte. She'll shed that Dutchman like a shot if I hint she can have me—is that what you're saying, I hope?

"No, no," he said, as Julian laughed again, "it's the Widow Devlin for me, for a mulitiplicity of reasons, not the least of which is that I believe I'm better suited for a widow—some experienced and clever lady who's done with 'true' love and is more than willing to settle for security and some mutually interesting passion. Despite your adoration, my friend, I'm not such a bargain for some virginal 'dewy' miss. At that, I can't for the life of me see that having such wetness in bed is any great treat. I scarcely want an infant just out of diapers in my sheets—how perverse, Julian," he said with admiration, glancing to his friend, "I *am* impressed. But aside from the obvious matters of expertise, I'm too jaded a hack for a novice driver, and too devious myself to tolerate an innocent for longer than an hour, even in verbal sorts of intercourse."

"And yet," Julian said, puzzled, "you'll still go downstairs tonight for all the world as if you're set on courting that pretty idiot Cee-cee Deems?"

"Certainly," Arden said in surprise. "Why, you don't think the crafty Deemses would stay on here at this rural hotel and gambling palace otherwise, do you? Or do you believe they're so charitable they'd remain all this time so that the wealthy gentleman they've their eye on can have a chance to court their daughter's companion? I'm amazingly lazy—like my soulmate Falstaff, 'I'd rather be eaten to death with rust than to be scoured to nothing with perpetual motion'—and I don't feel like chasing my lady the length and breadth of the Continent, you know."

Seeing Julian's raised eyebrow, he went on more thoughtfully, "And too, I do believe I get to see her more when she thinks she's spoiling my chances at despoiling her innocent than I would were I to come out and declare myself to her. That, I must take time and care to do. She's clever, Mrs. Devlin. She don't trust me as far as she can throw me. Although," he said, smiling with affectionate remembrance as he clapped his friend on the shoulder and they went to the door, "I don't doubt she'd be very surprised to know just how far she's already done that."

The Baron Wyndham scarcely had a word for his daughter, he was in such a state of high excitation that his normally pale face showed a ruddiness to suggest he'd been out-of-doors for all this cool spring day. But the rash, oddly distributed patches of color on his cheeks and on his neck gave the lie to that, and the rest of his countenance looked exactly as a devout gamester's should, pallid from the bleaching of a hundred nights beneath blazing chandeliers, rather than so much as a day's ride in the wan sunshine. His hands shook as he lifted his wineglass to his lips, but it was not that sort of spirits that made them tremble.

Arden narrowed his eyes as he noted all the signs of the man's excitement, and when he looked to Francesca, as she seemed to be earnestly attempting to convince her father of something in this hour before dinner as the guests stood and chatted in the main salon, he was suffused with a deep and sudden pity for her. For the baron was obviously not listening to her or even thinking of his coming dinner. He was, as he'd been the night before, and the night before that, on fire to go to the tables again—any table: for dicing, or a spin at the wheel of fortune, or the turn of the cards would do for him. He'd won at everything for a succession of days, and doubtless was telling his daughter how right he was in attempting to use that newly got money to get more money and increase their fortunes while his luck held, for she nodded at last, and seemed hesitantly acquiescent. But Arden grieved for her complaisance. As a man who knew the many ways in which men indulged their many weaknesses, he knew the baron was as eager to lose as he was to win now. It was the play itself that was the point of the game for such men, Arden thought as he watched Francesca, before he tried to decide when he could make his own next move tonight.

Tonight, he was all eyes for her every move, although anyone watching him as he sat at dinner with the Deemses, Francesca and her father, and Julian and Roxanne Cobb, would have thought he'd no care for anyone but the charming young fair-haired girl who'd been maneuvered to sit at his side. And tonight he made sure to be all ears, as well, though anyone observing him would scarcely have thought it as he told his droll stories and met the viscount's humorous observations with his own absurd commentary. And tonight, since all his thoughts were about love, or variant substitutes for it, he was remembering his own past one, although for all the world he seemed to be interested in nothing but the present. But he was an amazingly versatile gentleman, to his regret, for he could dwell on the past even as he prepared for the future. Indeed, he could scarcely help it, though he often wished he could.

For remembering Meggie still caused him grief, though the boy that had known her was as lost to him as she was now, and she, poor child, had been dust for a generation of men. And she *had* been a child. Meeting that lost infant today had brought that back to him clearly. She'd been a few years older than that waif, of course, but now, looking back, he was ashamed to think of what a babe she'd been, only fifteen when he'd met her, only sixteen when she'd died. But that, he reminded himself, was this ancient three-and thirty-year-old gentleman's conscience speaking, a conscience that would deservedly have been shamed for bedding such a girl. The boy who had loved her, the boy he'd been, had been sixteen when he'd met her, and a hundred when she died.

Although in some ways she'd always been older than he was, he remembered. She'd led him from the moment they'd met, leading him to a safe place to sleep out of the street after she'd come upon him hunched in a doorway, trying to make himself comfortable enough to doze off for a few moments. Leading him into the twisting alleyways of St. Giles, away from predators that would have twisted him or torn him and robbed him of more than his meager supply of money or his enormous innocence, despite his already impressive size, for he'd been innocent of her city then. And leading him to her own bed in time, to show him what physical love was, teaching him far too well, so that he'd never forget that the physical act was only half the pleasure, and love that made it beyond pleasure.

Not that she'd known very much more about it than he learned in their first hour. For all her experience, and it was considerable, since she'd been selling her spare body in the streets for six years before they'd met, the nature of that occupation, of course, had been such that she couldn't teach him very much about the ways of a man with a maid beyond the direct act. But in those months they'd been together, his own love and concern for her had taught him far more, for it showed them both the role that gentleness and consideration and desire for the other's pleasure could bring to that basic moment.

Meggie had introduced him to less gentle arts as well, for she'd shown him the skills he'd needed for survival. She showed him how a bitter runaway boy could stay alive in those lowest of London's gutters. And after he'd learned that honest labor paid little, he'd discovered the thousand other ways to earn money there at the bottom level of mankind. His strength and size helped him perform a dozen tasks where a broad back and a strong stomach could earn enough to fill their empty stomachs. But before long he'd seen that a clever mind could make more, and it took little more time to understand that nothing could earn a man as much as a clever mind and a strong back, and an acceptance that fine principles were a luxury he'd have to earn, and then, at last, he'd been able to keep them both in fine style.

They'd made quite a pair. Odd, mated and mismatched ginger twins. She as diminutive as he was large. Bone-thin but bonny, with a thatch of taffy hair and a raft of freckles he teased her about. And a smile that was so wide and infectious it redeemed that plain, tough little face that touched his heart so completely that with all the money he'd earned, and the opportunities it had bought him, he'd never bought one since he'd met her. For he'd never thought another female lovelier then. Or since.

It had all come too late for her, of course. She'd flowered quickly, growing up between the cracks in the grimy paving stones of London's worst stews. But it had been a forced, unhealthy growth, and all the warmth and comfort and good food he'd been able to provide her hadn't been able to compensate for those years of privation. She'd begun to cough one winter day, and like a wise woman with child in the earliest moments, had known from the first feeble stirrings within her what it was that she carried—not a life beneath her heart, but a death that shivered directly within her thin chest. Perhaps that was why she hadn't fought it, perhaps she couldn't have fought any harder, for all it had taken her so quickly. And the greatest gift he'd given her at the end, it seemed, had been the tears he'd fought so valiantly to hold back, for she'd touched them on his cheeks and sighed in wonder, and told him that no one had ever cried for her, never, and she was that sorry for him, but that proud.

He'd left then. Gone back to where he'd run from, having learned that there were far worse things to bear, and having borne them. Having learned mostly the value of all sorts of education. Now he was a fine gent, and here he sat in a luxury hotel in the heart of France, well-traveled, well-breeched, well-educated in a great many things, the sort of a toff whose purse she'd have been proud to have lifted. Much good it did him. For she'd left a void the years hadn't filled.

He wasn't a sentimental idiot. He knew very well that if
he could transcend time and death as the poets he loved to
read often did, and could return to her, he wouldn't have
had a thing to say to her, nor a thought in common any
longer. Indeed, though she'd been sharp and knowing, even
then their youth and their need were really all they'd had
together. And yet he couldn't stop thinking about her, even
as he planned how to offer another female his name for the
rest of his life. For she'd really loved him, and loved him
entirely, and he'd never doubted it.

But Francesca Devlin, he thought, wrenching his thoughts
entirely back to the present by main force, really needed
him. And that, he decided, was almost as good.

He didn't take his eyes from her all night, although he
never looked at her directly. He knew well enough he
couldn't stalk if his prey caught him at it. He stayed down-
wind from her at the dinner table, showing his white teeth
in laughter at everything his dinner companions said, and
listening to Cecily Deems's light prattle with the interest of
a grandfather with his first grandchild. Mrs. Deems swelled
with happiness, even Mr. Deems grew a slight ghost of a
grin, and yet Arden never missed a thing that Francesca did,
nor a word she said.

Not that she said much. She was unusually still tonight.
She was trying so valiantly to act normally with Roxanne,
seeing the blond widow for the first time since her disappearance with the viscount, or at least, she thought wretchedly, seeing her fully dressed for the first time, that she
failed utterly and chatted with her with all the ease she'd
have felt if it were the queen come to dinner. And when
Roxanne, amused and proud, but finally bored, turned to
join in with the gentlemen in their more lively conversation,
Francesca sank back into thoughts of Harry again, only
jumping up with a start when she thought in her distraction
that Julian was a mind-reader when he said "Devlin." She
relaxed when she discovered he was only asking her if she'd
like another slice of the excellent beef she'd evidently
cleared her plate of, without tasting a morsel of it.

So, of course, she'd no awareness of being so carefully
observed, just as she'd not the slightest idea of how she was
being studied later, as she sat and seemed to watch Cecily
trying to learn a simple version of euchre from Arden Lyons.
And after she'd endured an evening of that, and then seen
Cee-cee to bed, and had come down again to fidget and fret

for her father's gaming, and had seen the viscount and Roxanne think they were subtly stealing away together, she'd no
inkling of how she was being circled. And when her father
completely ignored her and she stepped out of the crowded
main salon to wait for him in a cool anteroom, she'd not
the smallest notion of how she'd been tracked, with padded
tread, to her corner.

Her thoughts were so bedeviled that when she heard a
slight cough and looked up to find Arden standing next to
her, she was genuinely glad to see a real and familiar face.
And for the first time, jolted from thinking of Harry and the
shock she'd had from him that morning, she looked up at
Arden with some real pleasure, although she was grateful
he didn't know it was only because she'd decided it was
better to pass time with the devil she knew than the one she
didn't. But he might have suspected it. For his tawny eyes
lit with amusement as well as interest as he took a seat
beside her.

"Gambling hells," he said ruminatively, without pref-
ace, "are much like wedding nights, are they not? In that,"
he continued, without waiting for an answer, "they aren't
much fun unless you're participating in what they are best
at providing. I could name some other, less tame analogies,
and will, you know," he threatened amiably, "if you don't
say something soon, or at least acknowledge my wickedness
by flying into a huff. I was trying to shock you out of the
sullens, you see," he said as she began to grow a little grin
despite herself. "Ah, yes. There's nothing like naughtiness
to get a proper female's mind off her own problems and onto
creating someone else's. Oh, better," he approved as she
laughed at last.

"I wasn't sulking," she said, and he amazed her by interrupting and nodding as he said, "I know, you were remembering.

"Come along," he said then, rising and offering his hand,
"you've a shawl, you'll need no more, it's a mild night,
let's perambulate. There's a poor kitchen garden at back,"
and when she started at the reference, he misunderstood,
smiled ruefully, and said, "But I won't entice you into the
back garden for my seduction, I'll ask you to walk out into
the front drive and down to the road for that. And," he
said, holding out his hand imperatively, "for the purposes
of blowing away the clouds of tobacco, candle smoke, and
blue dismals that have settled, wraithlike, about your head."

She took his hand, and rose, without another question.

It was cool, and quiet, and the further they walked down the gravel path that led from the circular gravel drive in front of the manor house, the dimmer both the torchlights in front of the house and the sounds from within it grew, as their footsteps crunching the gravel beneath them became louder and the stars waxed brighter above them. She walked at his side and drank in great gulps of the tart, sweet air, and then, feeling that she was coming alive again, if only because she was moving again, and in caring human company again, and out in the clean air again, she sighed deeply and said, "Thank you."

"I bottled it expressly for you," he answered, his voice a low rumble above her. "I'm pleased you like it. Two parts earth and a fraction of rain, a *soupçon* of brine, from the west, from the sea, and just a touch, no more or the effect would be ruined, mind, of early violets. Not so heady as mid-May, or near so intoxicating as June, but for our purposes, a presumptuous little brew and more than adequate, isn't it?"

She smiled a reply that she remembered he couldn't see, but before she could speak again, he did.

"One of the advantages," he said conversationally, "if not the only one, of being my size is that I can be of enormous help to ladies in distress. There used to be a great many more things a fellow like me could do on your behalf, of course, but even though they've decimated the supply of dragons, and ogres are not too active this time of year, I still have my uses. Is there anyone you'd like me to thrash for you?" he asked hopefully, peering down at her. "Any insult I can avenge? You'll note I do have more than an adequate shoulder to cry on—indeed, a legion of depressed ladies could gather there for a good lament. How may I help?" he asked in a less jocular manner.

"Thank you," she said again, sincerely again, "but there's no way, I'm afraid. There's nothing that you can do, but thank you."

Her husky voice always enchanted him, but when she spoke, there'd been an odd catch in it that caused him to stop in his paces. It was time.

"It's your Harry, isn't it?" he asked softly.

Afraid to answer, afraid to look up to him, she could only nod, for he'd no idea of exactly how right he was.

"It is," she managed finally, when he stopped and waited for her to speak.

They stood alone in a corner of the graveled drive, and though there was no other living being in sight or within call, she was not in the least afraid of him. In fact, she might well have been a bit fearful of the complete darkness of the profound night surrounding them, and of what real or imagined dangers might lurk in it—she'd always been foolishly afraid of the dark—but his large frame reassured her. It would indeed have taken a dragon to overwhelm him. No, now she was only terrified of herself, and how very much she wanted to confide in him.

"I can't wrestle a ghost," he said, and looking up, the starlight enabled her to see that he wore a rueful smile, "but I've learned that one oughtn't to try. Some ghosts should be made welcome, and asked in to tea, because only by entertaining them can we live with them. And some, we should definitely live with, if their presence is comforting. But we living have to go on living too, you know, and sometimes we linger too long with them when real life becomes too confusing. So," he said gently, looking down at her until she could swear she could see his light hazel eyes glow in the faint light, "the only cure I know for a surfeit of ghosts, is an abundance of life, don't you think?"

And he smiled so sadly at her that she nodded again, oddly comforted by that deep, soft voice and the concern it voiced. Then, very simply and entirely naturally, he bent his great tawny-maned head to kiss her. He hesitated only for a second to gauge her reaction, but she didn't move away or try to evade him, for she remembered thinking that it would be a kind, and brotherly, and entirely comfortable thing to have him do.

It was not.

His lips were cool and gentle on hers for only an instant, and in that instant it was as though something had sparked there between them, tingling like some sort of tactile starlight at the slight touch of his lips. And then he took her up in his arms and kissed her deeply, and she found herself yielding to far more than a desire for sanctuary as he held her closer than any comforter might, moved beyond mere sympathy to deeper needs. For all his strength, she was aware only of wanting to be held closer; for all his control, he was aware only of wanting to lose it entirely. At the same moment that she discovered herself shocked to be so lost to his embrace, he ended it. And stepped back to look down at her with an unreadable expression on his craggy face. But before she could begin to fear him, or herself, he spoke again.

"I didn't lie, you see, I did mean seduction, just as I promised," but there was no laughter in his husky whisper, and none at all in his eyes.

"But don't say a word just now, please," he said, putting up one huge hand. "Think on this tonight. And tomorrow. Until we meet again. And then you may slap me or challenge me to a duel or call me a beast, or even, if you like, kiss me again. But for now, please, just think on it, will you?"

Before she could reply, he took her hand, and in the most conventional way placed it on his arm and walked on with her as though for all the world they both weren't, each in his own way, completely and entirely staggered by what had happened.

After he'd left her at her door, she went within and prepared for bed, still dazed by the encounter. For he'd made her forget Harry entirely. It had been as if Harry hadn't existed at all, but had only been some pale daydream of her youth. She went to her bed for once exorcised of his demanding ghost, only to be visited again and again in the night by her thoughts of the substantial and vigorous reality of Arden Lyons, whom she might not trust, but now believed she would never forget.

Arden lay awake for a long while as well, considering how to proceed. She was far more than he'd thought, and just as he'd told Julian, far more than he deserved. He'd meant to court her more subtly, he'd even meant to quote poetry, but she'd overset his plans long before she'd overset him so completely. The sight of her uplifted face had robbed him of speech and he'd had to use his lips to better purpose. He was grateful that she wasn't some dewy miss who'd have taken alarm at his ardor, and glad he'd enough experience himself to have ended it before she'd time to question her response or fear it, or him. There were many things he was grateful for tonight.

He blessed her foolish father for casting her in his way, as he lay and rested his head on his arms on his pillow and stared at the night, seeing only the way her great-eyed face had tilted to his and still feeling the warm sweetness of her generous mouth, the way her body had shaped to his, and the way her hair had blended with the night to sift like night mists through his fingers. He had a silent thanks for Harry Devlin too, for he well knew that without that poor devil's death, he'd never have had a chance at Francesca. She might never love him as she'd loved Harry, but she'd need him now. He'd told Julian no less than the truth of that. Because if she weren't world-weary, and lost, and in need of a man to shield her again, he'd never have begun his campaign for her. He'd not have asked for anything from her. He'd not have dared.

Deep in Julian's arms, pleasantly weary and quite content, Roxanne nestled her chin on his chest and sighed. "The baron's on a winning streak," she said, "ever since I left his side. Do you think that means he'll decide to be shut of me? And then what shall I do?" she hinted, as she traced a teasing question mark in the golden down beneath her cheek with the tip of her finger.

"Not to fret. He'll be on a losing streak soon." Julian yawned.

"Poor Fancy, then," she said, seeing it was too late and too soon to pursue the question of the duration of their affair. He'd only promised her a night, she'd gotten near a week; she aimed at longer, but knew how to bide her time.

"Fancy?" He frowned in incomprehension.

"Francesca," she explained, "that's what the baron calls her. What shall she do if he goes to pieces again? And the way your friend Arden's after that mooncalf Cee-Cee, it looks like poor Fancy'll have to find herself a new post soon enough. Speaking of that . . ." She raised her head, and seeing the slight smile he wore, poked him with her finger. "Here," she complained, "I've got me ogles, laddie. One minute the giant gent's sighing over the sapskull blond, and the next he's staring at Fancy as though she was the dog's dinner. Which of them is he after, eh?"

She didn't really care. She liked Francesca well enough, but while not precisely selfish, she never bothered herself over the fate of another female for long. She'd herself to lookout for, hadn't she? And who'd ever helped her? But Julian never spoke about himself or his friend, and not only would a bit of gossip bind them closer, for nothing ties a fellow to his wench like confidences, she knew, but also an interesting tidbit would please the baron, and perhaps she might find out something for his daughter too. Fancy had an eye on the big gent, whatever she pretended. Roxanne was selfish, but tonight, in this golden gentleman's arms, she could afford to be generous.

"Arden's a man of his own mind," Julian said obliquely.

"Ah, poor Fancy," Roxanne sighed, fishing. "With funds, she might dress up a treat; without, the big man mightn't even consider her for a fancy piece. Not that she'd consent, mind," she said primly, "since he won't get her as easy as you got me, m'lord. She's a good, decent, pure girl," she added mockingly, so he could congratulate her for not being one.

"I sincerely hope not," he laughed, "for her sake, since it's her experience that interests him. There's quite a market for widows these days, you know," he said, wrapping one long hand lightly about her neck and giving her a playful shake, which pleased her enormously to turn into an excuse to bite his shoulder in reply.

"Oh, yes, widows are what every gent wants to wive," she said, daring an outrageous, and likely just as outrageously ineffective, hint under the cover of her laughter.

"In my friend's case, yes," he answered thoughtfully, stroking the neck he'd just mock-throttled as he pondered what he'd said, "although, whatever his intentions, I doubt he'd have the time of day for her if she weren't. Widows seem to thrill him. At least, despite her other obvious charms, and she has not a few, that seems to be one of her largest attractions for him, if not her chiefest one," he said in some wonder, before he recalled whom he was speaking to, and never wanting to betray any confidence of Arden's, he veered from the subject, and leered on a whisper, "and I can see why."

"Oh, Lor'!" Roxanne breathed, dismayed, suddenly realizing the coil the baron had got Fancy into, and, "Oh, Lord, love me!" she groaned, realizing, too, that the baron knew far too much about herself for her to betray the charade to her own benefit, before, "Oh, Lord, yes, love me that way, do," she sighed again, when, much to her pleasure, she found he'd misunderstood her, delightfully.

"And then?" the gentleman urged tensely.

"And then, monsieur, he kissed her," the busboy reported, scratching his head and yawning, for really it was very late, and if it weren't for the extra coins he needed, he'd be asleep and not here in the kitchens talking to the English gentleman.

"Kissed her?" the young gentleman asked, his face growing gray.

"Perhaps 'devoured' is a better word. What an embrace! Right there, in front of the hotel, before my eyes."

"And she struggled?" the young gentleman prompted, his white hands turning to fists.

"All my women should struggle so, please God." The busboy winked.

"And then . . . ?" came the terse question.

"Then?" The busboy shrugged. "What else can I say? The big man and the Widow Devlin walked off arm in arm, back to the hotel. I can watch the hotel and the grounds, monsieur, but I cannot peek through their keyholes. Please understand, the manager is always after me!" he protested, seeing the look on the gentleman's face. "To say nothing of the large gentleman, should he catch me! I am afraid. You should understand," he said slyly, or matter-of-factly, the gentleman could no longer tell.

The busboy caught the thrown coin in one hand and smiled, although to the gentleman it looked more like he sneered, just as it seemed to him that all men who looked at him directly did, these days.

9

IT WAS PRECISELY the sort of gala, lavish, festive ball that had started a revolution. Now, of course, some of those who'd been servants a generation before were dancing in silks and satins, while some of those lucky few who hadn't been forcibly separated from their titled heads were covetously watching from the shadows or the servants' quarters, so all was well and egalitarian and *comme il faut* again.

"Democracy in France does not seem so dissimilar to democracy under the old regime," Arden Lyons commented to the Viscount Hazelton. ". . . except for the powdered wigs," he corrected himself thoughtfully, "which are vanished, because I suppose they were a mark of decadence. But the servants look as underfed as they might have before the glorious revolution for all that they've earned the right to call their employers 'brothers,' though not aloud in company, I suspect."

"Cynicism becomes you," Julian answered idly. "That must be why you never leave it off—actually, now that I think on it, I've never seen you wholly enthusiastic about anything. Except that"—he looked a pointed glance across the room before he smiled into his glass of champagne as he drained it—"and I can scarcely blame you."

Arden frowned, but didn't look to the lady Julian indicated as he stared through his glass.

"So apparent as that?" he asked, troubled.

"Only to me, my dear mountain. To anyone else I imagine it seemed as though you merely noted her. But I saw your lids open that extra fraction when you greeted her, and saw the ferocious glint in your eyes revealed. Such passion, my friend—I'm amazed at you. But why don't you want her to see even that paltry salute? She's magnificent tonight and deserves much more. That new gown has created a new woman, or is that all there is to it? She's looked to you often tonight. I wonder where she looked last night." He grinned at his friend's impassivity before he went on. "Whatever. She glows, Arden. You were right. But then, I believe you could find a diamond in a coal heap."

"I wish she'd remained in one, or at least in the nearest representation of one—one of those sad black old rags she was used to favor. You forget, my rash youth, that the Deemses wouldn't be best pleased to see Your Devoted slavering over dear Cee-cee's companion. So the lady will just have to appear to be wearing sackcloth and ashes as far as I'm concerned tonight. My eyes will not widen enough to let in a slit of light again until darling Cecily dances into my line of sight. Ah, there she is. Behold me enraptured," Arden said as he put down his own glass and greeted Cecily as she emerged from a dancing square.

He had to pass right by Mrs. Devlin, where she stood by the wall, to reach the little blond girl, and he did so without so much as a glance to the widow, though it was like trying to drag his eyes away from the sunrise in order to look at his shoes. She was everything he had dreamed she could be when he'd first seen her. And she was not even gotten up in highest style or her best new frock.

She wore the yew-green one, for a chaperone couldn't appear to be trying to outshine her charge. It was a dense color, the green of mosses and certain deep-woods ferns. It wasn't half so low in front as most of the other gowns to be seen at the ball, even though, since it was stylish and French, it exposed the top of each high, pointed breast so that an observant gentleman could see how they rose from her slight rib cage to tempt the fabric of her gown to an indiscretion and the observant gentleman to far more. The green gown clung to her waist, though it had none, being belted below those impudent breasts, just as it then flowed down her rounded hips and outlined her long legs. But it was a discreet hue and exceedingly ladylike, unlike those more fanciful gowns worn by luckier females who didn't have to work for their livings, or if they did, then worked (even though their protectors wouldn't have cared for the word) at exactly what their gowns implied, with their bright colors and scant necklines.

Even Cecily Deems, who was always done up as a positive paragon of virginity, wore her white gown with iridescent sequins upon it so low at her bosom that her thoughtful maid had brushed some spangles across the expanse of bare skin she displayed, so as to give the lie, or tease at the truth of all the available flesh a gentleman saw. But the white flesh of the little breasts bobbing above the sequined gown only made Arden think a great many basically decent iridescent fish had died in vain as he bowed over the little white hand. But then, his eye had been ravished by subtly golden skin that glowed—Julian had the right of it—glowed like a flush of sunset over a yew-green gown.

Cecily's hair was a wild French fantasy, all bows and curls and random spangles and ribbon-wrapped flowers amidst the flax, so that the gentlemen might know it was a very young girl who'd put on a giddy show. But even as he complimented the display again, as he'd done when he'd first shown her into her carriage to come here, Arden remembered the more sober style her companion had worn, only enlivened this night, as he'd noted immediately, by allowing the mass of it to depend in inky curls from high on the back of her proud head, above the swept-up, brushed-smooth nape that he'd longed to brush with his lips. He yearned to look back at Mrs. Devlin in her new green gown and golden-skinned splendor tonight, even as he took the pastel Cecily into his clasp for the waltz she'd promised him, but brave as he was, he dared not. He'd too much to lose, and being a cannier man than the ill-fated Orpheus, he thought, he dared not glance back to the lady he wanted so intensely lest he lose her forever. He would wait. He could endure. He was, after all, very good at that. But he'd not forget.

He'd walked right past her. She didn't expect that he'd have stopped to chat, not really, Francesca thought as she turned away as though she'd seen something immensely interesting on the hem of her gown. He'd greeted her at the hotel, and shown her into his coach with Cee-Cee and the others, and then not directed another word to her as they'd ridden to Paris. And now that they'd arrived, when the music was struck up he'd walked right past her to select his partner, with not a word of notice or remembrance of the night before.

But she was, after all, a servant, she remembered. He might have grappled with her in the pantry as soon as embraced her in the cool darkness. With all his gentle kindness, there was really, after all, she thought, staring ahead and trying to pretend she'd smiled at someone who'd been standing behind him, little difference between what had happened between them last night, however profound it had been for her, and a pinch and a tickle or whatever a gent could get from the downstairs maid. Servants were fair game to the gentlemen, and the pleasure they managed to take from them in passing was as soon forgotten as the ease of the getting of it. And it had been easy for him, she thought in disgust, for no scullery wench could have yielded more easily. Or, she thought in shame at herself, could have wanted to yield more.

He'd comforted her and then disturbed her, but both things had given her pleasure. She'd found that his soft words had eased her mind even as his embrace had not. For she'd become aware that the strong mouth could be as gentle as the words that had issued from it, and far more than a shoulder to lean on, the long body had communicated a world of sensation as its taut, tightly muscled length was pressed to her. But there'd been no force used save for desire, because he'd held her close with great care and no hint of his complete capture of her, and the second she'd thought to hesitate, she'd found herself free.

Still, she'd gone to sleep last night entirely captivated by him. Everything about him enchanted her—his strength, his control of it, his eyes, now intent, now full of understanding, even his scent had intoxicated her, she'd begun to imagine that perhaps some great good turn of luck of the sort her father had always believed in, which she'd always dismissed as foolishness, had finally found her. Perhaps, she'd thought, she'd found herself a mate—for her soul and her body and her life. Because she'd never doubted his intelligence and had come slowly to learn of his compassion, and had begun to dare to believe in his honor, against all rational evidence, against all her doubts. But now she knew that whatever else he had, he'd no honor at all, at least, none in his dealings with females. There were, she understood, a great many gentlemen who didn't consider females as quite human, and servants, of course, as not even precisely animate beings.

Now, as she watched him stride past her so as to take Cecily Deems into his arms, she realized he had been toying with her, of course, amusing himself cruelly, like the great cat he resembled might when bored, never thinking of her as an equal in anywise, but only as his rightful prey. Perhaps the most bitter realization she came to as she watched him waltz with his chosen lady, the one that finally made her turn her head away, was that however angry she might be at him, she had to admit it had been her own need that had sent her into his arms, her own loneliness and fear that had seduced her as effectively as his talents had almost done.

Still, "almost" was the word to fasten on, she remembered, lifting her chin, since "almost" never hanged a man, or compromised a woman, however foolishly she'd behaved. And she almost succeeded in believing this as she stood and continued to watch the gala ball swirl on around her.

Arden waltzed with Cecily, Julian danced by with Roxanne, the Deemses stood at the sidelines and congratulated themselves with identical knowing smiles. Only her own father was absent. He, of course, was still in the gaming rooms somewhere in Paris tonight, even as they were, but as he'd gleefully whispered to her before he'd left the coach they'd all come in, he was going to dance only after he'd built their fortunes higher, as he was sure to do this night.

They'd all been asked to this ball, finding the cards of invitation on their breakfast trays, not because, as the Deemses assumed, they were friends of a baron and a viscount and a man-about-the-*ton,* but, as Francesca suspected, because they could afford the rates at their hotel. So far as she could discern, for all its splendor, the only entrée necessary for this ball aside from a title was a full purse. Because although the ball was held in a grand ballroom in the heart of Paris, in a home that had belong to a *duc,* then a citizen, now a descendant of a *duc* again, it was as widely attended and as various a company as any she'd ever heard of at one of London's scandalous public subscription masquerades. Those well-advertised, well-attended occasions were where she'd heard that the nobility, disguised in every meaning of the word, consorted with the common herd, and masked commoners also became elevated in many several ways. Although drunkenness was not so obvious tonight, the costumes she saw before her were almost as fanciful as at any masquerade, for all that they'd been meant to be fashionable. Since persons of all ages, ranks, and financial circumstances were crowded into the room together, the effect was more motley than *à la mode,* and there was just as strange a mixture of classes as costumes.

A varied lot had been invited, from the ranks of the new regime, the old regime, and any regime that looked possible in future, including any wealthy visitors to France. These turbulent days, no one was sure who ought to be invited, only that it was prudent to exclude no one who might be, or become, important. Napoleon was gone, the king had returned, but nothing was certain except for money and power, and to judge from the past, even those two constants were remarkably inconstant. Here, Francesca thought as a merry young gentleman took his polite refusal from her with good grace, even a chaperone might be invited to dance, and invited to more, of course, she thought wretchedly, by a gentleman in the dark and in secret.

That was why she indignantly turned her back upon the waiter who seemed to be trying to signal to her from across the room. Because, she thought, it might be that her situation was clear to persons of the male gender from any rank, and she might as well be being enticed by a waiter as by a gambler or a gentleman. But when she saw Arden Lyons chatting comfortably with the Deemses as Cecily stood by, blushing and radiant, for all the world as though her papa were a minister, her mama a maid of honor and she were being wed to the large gentleman as she stood at his side,

Francesca spun round once again, and so almost collided with the waiter, now bearing a tray of napery.

"Madame," he whispered as he appeared to be adjusting the tray on his shoulder, "please, there is a gentleman who wishes to see you. Now and at once. In the garden. If you please, madame, he says it is of utmost urgency. *Vite! C'est important!*" he whispered harshly, abandoning his labored English before he bowed and made off into the crowd again.

She thought of her father. He was the only man left who might have something important to impart to her, for he was the only one she trusted now. He held her future in his two hands, along with his new fortune and whatever cards he was dealt, she thought in fearful acknowledgment of the tenuousness of that future. If he were physically hurt or in danger, there'd be no need for secrecy; that he summoned her alone into the dark terrified her. She raised the hem of her skirt and rushed from the room, ignoring a footman who pointed out the ladies' withdrawing room to her. She asked instead for the location of the garden. He grew a shadow of a smile at that. Ladies, after all, did not seek out the gardens at balls except for purposes most unladylike, but reluctantly remembering his place as he ogled her, he bowed and pointed out the long door at the end of the hall, and the torch-lit gardens beyond.

There was a small flight of steps leading from the terrace, and then narrow paths circling a few trees in tentative bud, several shrubs and benches, and a great many white marble statues. In the leaping torchlight she could see there were also several shapes that could only be couples perambulating and whispering together in the darkness, and other shapes that could only be couples, interlocked, saying nothing but sighs.

Her slippers made little sound as she stepped out on the flags, and it was so secretive there in the cool, murmurous night that she gasped when she felt a light touch on her arm.

"Please," Harry said softly, "say nothing," and led her by that one touch down the path and to one side, and through a gate, until they stood outside the garden in a darkness lit only by the moon, as were her eyes with tears. But these were tears of indignation.

At first she'd been frightened, and then her instant reaction had been one of joy at seeing him again. He stood before her in his neat evening clothes, his familiar, long-remembered, and loved face so full of concern that she longed to forget the present as well as the future. But then she grew uneasy with all the things she hadn't come to terms with, and frightened of everything she denied. And so, trying to deny all, she grew angry at last.

"What is this?" she whispered furiously. "I have a position I must fulfill. Do you mean to have me lose it?"

"I've come to tell you it appears that you have already lost it, if not more. If you can't open your eyes to the truth, Fancy, I must do it for you. I was going to leave you time to think, but then I discovered you've been doing far more active things than that," he said coldly, and when she fell completely silent, guilty and amazed that he could have known of her one transgression, he nodded, and went on with bitter satisfaction, "The nights have as many eyes as stars. Think of that next time you steal out for a secret embrace, my dear."

But now her anger overcame her shame. Her meeting with Arden might not have been correct behavior, but neither was his spying upon her. She'd not let herself think too much about Harry since yesterday; there were too many dreadful, profound things to take in all at once in what he'd said. And Arden had chased all those thoughts away; in fact, she wondered if she'd not welcomed him as much for doing just that as for himself. That thought alone made her feel stronger now.

But there was still, at the surface, her new anger toward Harry, for he'd betrayed her as well as his country. She'd grieved for a man not dead, and rejoiced at his living, only to realize, at once, before all else, before any thoughts of his cowardice or lack of honor came to bedevil her, that however he'd survived, he had, and yet hadn't sought her in the year since his supposed death. Not yet daring to contemplate the fact of his desertion entirely, she seized upon the simplest hurt: he'd only found her out by accident, the accident of her weak and sentimental gesture in taking on his name, the name of the man she'd mourned in all innocence, and in all innocence, loved. And that man, surely, *was* dead.

"You've no right to lecture me!" she hissed at him.

And he, who hadn't sought her in that year because he'd been thinking only and ever of what he'd done that June day, as he'd done and tried not to do since that day until he'd heard her name again, looked at her again and saw a new reason to live, a new cause to continue outside of himself, and so contained his temper.

"No," he said calmly, "I have not. Except that I can't help it, Fancy. Someone must care for you. Your father won't, you know, and Arden Lyons certainly will not."

"I know that," she said furiously, knowing more than that, "he's a beast. Perhaps the greatest beast in nature. I'm well aware of that. Have you come to tell me that? Then you're far too late."

When he only stared at her steadily in the darkness, her face grew red as she heard her own words echo in her ears and she added haughtily, "Not *that* late, of course. Unless you call a stolen kiss a lady's virtue."

"No," he said, enormously relieved at her denial of the other man, as well as of any further intimacies with him. "No," he said, "I know you better, my love," he lied, for he did not. "But what shall you do when you lose your position when he weds the rich little cit you're employed to protect?" he asked. "And what shall you do when you lose your position as well as your good name when he lures you to an indiscretion again? What shall you do alone, Fancy? For I swear you haven't anyone but me."

She shook her head, but before she could deny him as well, he spoke again.

"I may not be what you'd dreamed when we were young, but you didn't know reality any more than I did then. We're neither of us that young anymore, my love, though I'll swear I love you just as much, if not more now. I'd give you the time to grow up, years of it, and gladly, but you haven't that much time, Fancy, not anymore. Events move too fast for us, for that luxury. I'll come to see you again—when you most need me, I'll be there for you. And I'll be the only one that is, my poor dear. Then I'll ask again, but then I think I'll know your answer too. God keep you, love," he said fervently as he took her hand before she could withhold it, and kissed it before she could pull away, and bowed and backed into the shadows and was down into the dark at the end of the street before she could tell him: No, never. Before she could even say: Don't bother. Before she could say: Good-bye.

She didn't return to the ball immediately, though she knew she ought. The town house held laughter and light and as much betrayal as the darkness had, but at least she was alone with her sorrow here. So she trailed back to the garden, and moving stealthily as a shadow, made her way to the terrace to stand near the windows so that if she were discovered she could claim a sudden light-headedness, and seem to have been seeking nothing but the cool night air. Not that the Deemses would likely do anything but rejoice at her disappearance tonight, or call it anything but tactful and inspired. She was as invisible and useless here with the clandestine lovers of the night as she was within the bright and noisy house, but at least here, she thought wretchedly, there was no need of artifice.

" 'She walks in beauty, like the night of cloudless climes and starry skies; and all that's best of dark and bright meet in her aspect and her eyes' . . . so why then, I wonder," the deep voice asked, "is she weeping?"

"Am not," she muttered rebelliously, feeling very foolish as she rummaged through her reticule to find a handkerchief, and having to resort to snatching the huge white one proffered her, like a white flag waving in the blackness, before she could say something really cutting. Because it seemed he was right and her face was streaming with tears so that she could scarcely speak, much less clearly see the man looming over her there on the terrace, although he stood not inches away.

"I was going to quote that last night, though it's lamentably modern," Arden went on thoughtfully. "George Byron recently penned it, you know, and so, lovely and popular as it is, it's not tried-and-true. So I'd decided on using that line about the Ethiopian's ear instead, you know, that bit from Romeo and Juliet . . . 'she hangs upon the cheek of night like a rich jewel in an Ethop's ear . . .'—because it was a beautiful night and the context of the play would have been most apt, but your face as it looked then took the words from me entirely. A singular achievement," he said admiringly when she only stared at him, her eyes dark and damp and wide above the handkerchief he'd handed her.

"Very nice," he said, when she remained silent. "You look very like an Arabian dancer just now. Are we doing charades, then?"

"That you dare . . ." She struggled with the words, and then hearing them muted as well as glutted with tears, she lowered the handkerchief from her mouth and blazed up at him in a strident whisper, "that you dare mention that night now!"

He gazed down at her and his smiled slipped slowly. She was in pain, just as he'd thought. And for all she looked adorable and he wished to go on teasing her, she grieved, as much as he'd suspected she had when she'd stared after him and Cecily, and then when she'd flown out of the room like that . . . And so while all the while not attending to the Deemses' light babble, he'd decided.

He'd had a careful plan and a beautiful scheme concocted. But a crafty general, a clever gambler, and a considerate lover all had to know that the best of finely wrought, practiced schemes must be put aside when events turned quickly. He'd seen the hurt, and had known at once that he must act quickly to prevent the hate that would surely follow. Even if it didn't, he admitted he could not bear to see the hurt. He would do as he'd done since she'd come into his ken: he'd act on his desires.

The game was ending now, and he was glad of it, for he was as weary of the banality of his courtship of Cecily Deems as he was of the banality of his life, it seemed. And too, although he doubted the blond infant had more than her mother's desire for him, and was sure she'd no more sensibilities than that would-be lady, he wanted to spare her embarrassment at least, and discomfort as well. She was, after all, as harmless as she was witless. Very unlike Mrs. Devlin, who could wound him as well as be wounded. For it hadn't only been her intelligence and her beauty that had attracted him; he knew he'd also been drawn to her sorrow. That had always been a lure. He bowed to the inevitable.

"Francesca, listen," he said with such urgency and seriousness in his deep voice that she stopped struggling as he gripped her elbows and held her fast.

"I've had to court Cecily, or seem to be doing so, so that I might continue to see you, foolish girl. Did you think me in need of money, wit, or a doctor? I'm a villain, admittedly, but not a fool, an idiot, or a pauper. Did you really think I'd want such an angelic little fribble for a wife? Lovely opinion you have of me. But, consider, my dear, would they have stayed on even so long as they've done if I hadn't shown some interest in her? I'd have asked Julian to do the pretty to divert them and buy me time with you, but he'd already noted Roxanne, and even if he hadn't, he's not the man, for a great many reasons I'm not at liberty to divulge, to ask to pretend to love."

When she continued to stare at him, uncomprehending, he allowed himself a little smile before he said, gently and clearly, "Mrs. Devlin, my dear, you've enticed me entirely, and although I know it's early days, I can't go on with this charade of mine. I won't hurt you any longer, nor tease myself, neither. In the best of worlds, you'd have the leisure to get to know me, and trust me. This is, as I know you've also found, not that world. So I must act now, but better too soon than not at all,'' he added, half to himself.

He looked at her steadily. ''Both of us have been around long enough to dispense with the veils around our emotions, or our motives. You need a protector, and it seems I need someone to protect.

''Francesca,'' he said softly, still holding her, though she'd ceased to wriggle and stood looking at him with her head to one side, ''there's only one hope for it. If you're going to be anyone's widow, I'd like you to be mine.

''Ah . . . that's a proposal of marriage,'' he added when she only gaped at him.

10

THE WALTZ MUSIC ended and the musicians began to play the undanceable strains of one of Mr. Haydn's more complex compositions to signal that a light dinner was to be served. It became evident that in France there were certain priorities that transcended love, for as Francesca stood on the terrace and continued to stare wide-eyed at Arden Lyons, a slow procession of couples cleared the garden and filed past them to reenter the house. Although they stood in a shadow, still Arden took her hand and walked her, unprotesting, to a more deeply shadowed alcove, away from the steady file of lovers hungry for more than each other's lips could provide.

''My timing is dreadful. Should you rather have a plate of lobster?'' Arden asked, motioning to the couples entering the house as Francesca continued to stare at him, amazed.

''Well, if you were French, you obviously would,'' he went on, ''because for all they go on about *l'amour*, it appears they're more interested in *la carte*. Just look at that thundering herd rounding on the canapés. Ah, well, I imagine once one appetite is sated, there's always another to consider—they're a practical people, after all. Perhaps you'd like me to come back next week?'' he asked pleasantly, after a pause, ''so you can have a bit more time to think it over?''

''You asked me to marry you?'' she asked, her voice husky and strained.

''Why, yes, I believe I did,'' he answered, smiling. ''It seemed the sensible thing to do, since I'd like very much to marry you, you see.''

''You don't know me!'' she cried.

''Oh, but I do,'' he said, suddenly more serious. ''I know you're beautiful. And brave. And clever. And longing for a place in life again, one that you can fill with honor and pride. And before you go on to say you don't know me, I'll immediately grant it may be so, and though I'm tempted to jest it's far better that way, I do want you to say yes. So I'll repeat that I doubt that we've time at this time in our lives to remedy that without legal recourse. I doubt you'll come to me without a clergyman's blessings, nor do I ask it of you.

''But I'll supply some details on pertinent matters to speed things along. I'll tell you straightaway that I'm exceedingly wealthy, I've a manor home in England that wouldn't shame you. I'm neither cruel nor in the habit of beating anything but the odds, so you'll never fear violence from me, and as to odds and evens, I've no more interest in gaming than in flinging my money off high bridges for amusement. I'll promise to be generous and I'll try to be understanding, and I'm seeking a mate who will share my advantages and be clever enough to ignore the disadvantages. To wit, since I'm determined to be honest: I'm not beautiful, nor am I in the first flush of youth, nor have I an admirable background. Very much the reverse, in fact.'' He frowned, before he remembered this was a proposal, not a confession, and continued, ''But my past is passed, along with that tender youth, and I don't claim to be the answer to a maiden's prayer. Which, I might add, is why I never sought a maiden, however my friendship with Cecily appeared to you.

''And,'' he said softly, looking at her with great tenderness, ''I'm not French, after all, so there are some appetites I find canapés will not fill. But I believe you share them, and indeed, may miss that dish in life's menu, and so we'll suit there too. I'll never be unfaithful, Francesca, because I'm basically a simple man, and,'' he added more lightly, ''an exquisitely lazy one, and you know the time and trouble slipping about on a clever wife takes.

''So then?'' he asked, standing back and watching her closely.

It was, she discovered to her amazement, precisely what she wanted. It was too precipitate, true. But he was quite right, there was no time for the trimmings she'd have wanted, although, she thought, if she gave the answer he wanted, there well might yet be a way to delay the vows until she was absolutely sure. If, she amended, she wasn't already absolutely sure. There hadn't been a word of love, but he wasn't a sentimental man, and if she refused him, that would be embarrassment enough; she could scarcely blame him for not wanting to put his heart as well as his life under her foot for her to trample. It was enough that he'd asked; he was still unwed and it wasn't likely he'd been turned down often, so it wasn't likely he'd often asked. She never doubted other women reacted to him as she had, and so was as flattered as she was amazed. It was true he wasn't a youth, nor was he a beautiful man, nor, from his many and varied odd talents, did she doubt that he hadn't a checkered past.

But he'd not been deceiving her, all his interest had been real, he'd never played her false, and that made her joyous. And when she thought of the reasons for that sudden joy, she began to understand that he was, and had been, precisely what she wanted. And would be even if she were not in distressed circumstances. She gazed at him and found that strong, hard face one she'd seek in any crowd, that huge frame one she'd shelter beneath in any storm, that shrewd eye one she'd trust to see truth, and that humorous mouth one that would always speak words she'd want to hear. He was, she dimly began to perceive, the home she'd always longed for. She was one-and-twenty, and understood all at once that she wanted to pass the rest of her years with this man for all the reasons he'd not stated: for his honesty, for his kindness, for his wit, and for the passion she knew he controlled so well. But as she thought of what he'd said on that score, her slight, growing smile froze fast.

His smile had begun to grow with hers, and then, seeing her sudden discomfort, he grew grave as well.

"Is there another man," he asked softly, "aside from Harry?"

She startled, and then wanted to laugh wildly. "Oh, no," she managed, "I promise you there's no one aside from Harry."

He relaxed. The gentleman she'd met tonight in the garden and then angrily dismissed had no claim on her then, just as he'd thought when he'd observed them from the shadows.

"Mr. Marvell had the right of it, you know," he said, reaching out a hand and brushing back a bit of her hair that had come free to coil beside her cheek, " 'the grave's a fine and private place, but none, I think, do there embrace.' I don't mean to be callous, for I've left a love beneath the earth myself, but I'd thought we'd both agreed, admittedly in unspoken fashion, that life must go forth."

"It's never that!" she said at once, upset that she couldn't tell him everything, but still so confused about Harry that she couldn't admit a truth to him that she'd not yet accepted herself. "It's one or two other things," she said hesitantly, guiltily remembering her chiefest lies, not so much that they were dreadful truths she had to tell, but only wondering how he'd feel about any lies she'd told.

He repressed his smiles. He'd wondered about that. And wasn't at all unhappy. One or two was what he'd expected. She'd been married during productive years, after all. Her papa had said she was almost six-and-twenty; one or two children at the very least was what he'd imagined. As an impecunious widow with a careless father, she'd likely had to leave them in England under some relative's care while she tried to earn her keep. That wasn't unusual or unexpected and it was fine with him; the more he could aid her, the more he could shelter her and her children, the more he would deserve her, and win her gratitude. And he liked children very well. He only wondered what they were—a boy and girl, he guessed; trust her to do things symmetrically.

"I haven't told the strictest truth," she began slowly, before she went on rapidly, her great dark eyes searching his face as she spoke, "but indeed, it was Father's idea and I don't blame him, for he was entirely right, I needed a position and was ill-prepared the way things were . . . no, not ill-prepared, but considered so in the eyes of society, you see, so I had to lie about some things, and you must know of them if we are to marry, of course . . . I was never really married,'' she blurted.

It had been many years since he'd been shocked. He'd seen things in his time that had made strong men faint and gentle women curse, but he'd not been shocked since he'd been a boy. So he didn't know how to react to the new emotion her words brought to him. He simply grew very still and stared at her just as she'd gaped at him moments before. But he was never without speech for very long, even though he realized he was speaking from the shallows of his mind since the rest of it was numbed with disbelief. Not so much, perhaps, at her state of moral grace, as at his own uncharacteristic misreading of her character, of any other being's character, for that matter.

''I understand,'' he said, desperately trying to, and as the reasons flitted through his mind, he uttered them: ''Some family disagreement? He was already wed? He had to leave to join his company before the words could be said?''

''We didn't want to, because I was too young,'' she said, not very sadly—not sorrowfully at all, for the first time—as she realized now that it had been absolutely the right decision.

''But surely,'' he said, wondering about the children with some growing alarm, ''as the years passed . . .''

''Only a year passed,'' she replied, and then, seeing his face, she bit her lip and said in her foggiest broken voice, admitting to her other lie, ''I'm no more five-and-twenty than I'm a widow, you see. That's the other thing. I've only just had my twenty-first birthday, which is why I came to see Father, because I'd finished with school and there was nothing else for me to do . . . Arden?'' she asked, for he stood and looked at her, and as she watched, his gaze became a glare.

''One-and-twenty?'' he asked stiffly, one sandy eyebrow rising. ''And never wed? I suppose next you'll tell me you were never lovers either, and that you're as pure as a snowdrop . . . or Cecily.''

''Twenty-one, yes,'' she said, wondering why he was glowering down at her, his face as immobile as if just carved from ice, although his words dripped sarcasm and his tawny eyes blazed, ''and never wed, and no, never lovers. What sort of a female do you think I am? But no, not pure as a snowdrop, for I did kiss Harry, and often, and perhaps a jot more . . .'' she quavered, lowering her eyes, thinking of embraces that had gone beyond kissing until Harry had groaned and stopped, "but, no, never lovers, you needn't worry about that," she said staunchly, although she was as uncomfortable now as she'd been then at Harry's touch on her breast, remembering how she'd been shocked both at him and at the thrill of it.

It was the way she lowered her eyes that convinced him. He didn't even take the time to frame a careful reply. "Are you mad, girl?" he thundered at her. "To even think of marrying *me?*" he boomed in his fury, so that several persons near the windows looked out to see what sudden storm had broken out-of-doors.

The faces at the windows made him recall himself, and he took her by the arm again, less gently, and dragged her to the deepest shadows on the terrace, too angry to stroll with her politely. One deep breath contained his rage again, another controlled his voice, and the third brought his wits back, along with his customary eloquence.

"I don't understand," she was saying. "I told you Harry and I were not . . ."

"Child," he said softly, calmly, yet from such a distance she could scarcely believe he was the same gentleman that had just made such a warm and witty proposal to her, "I know you 'were not . . .' as you so delicately put it. Now that I know all, of course, I see all too, clever fellow that I am." He spoke in scorn to himself, but when he spoke to her again, it was with the sad, patronizing patience of an elder gentleman lecturing an infant.

"I didn't mean to shout, Francesca," he explained, "but you did take me by surprise. I apologize then, and beg your pardon, and hope you'll forget everything that went forth tonight, and last night too, of course, please. I would not have spoken or acted so, had I known."

It was so astonishing a turnaround that Francesca could only stammer, "But . . . then . . . you don't want to marry me after all, is that it?" And when he didn't answer straightaway, she said, with more heat, "You were only jesting, only having a bit of fun with me, is that it?"

"No, no, child," he replied at once, holding up one huge hand. "That proposal was sincere, and I meant it entirely. But the lady I proposed to was not . . . real, you see. Francesca," he said rapidly, for he'd looked to the windows again, and one of the faces peering out into the darkness could unmistakably be recognized, even through the old distorted glass, as belonging to a suspicious Deems, and so he knew he must have his say quickly. "You can't pretend that you love me madly. And yet I believe you were about to accept me. No, no," he said as she lowered her eyes, "there's no shame in that. I understand completely. It's because I understand now that I withdraw my offer.

"If I were as beautiful as my friend Julian, I'd not question your acceptance. The boy," he said with rueful amusement, "catches hearts through the eyes. But I do not. Neither do I believe it was my wit that snared you, because, child, fair ladies seldom elope with the jester, for all that they may laugh at him. Neither do I believe it to be because of my affluence—you work for the Deemses, you're not one of them. No, Francesca, in me I believe you behold a safe harbor, a snug resting place—an understanding friend and a kind protector—and don't turn up your nose, these are all good things, indeed fine things to find in a mate . . . if you were what you purported to be.

"But precisely because you're not, you can have far more. You can find a husband you can take with love and passion and all the foolish, delightful things the young are supposed to have. And that you ought to have. Do you see?"

He spoke so gently she wanted to weep at the tone of his voice as well as the words. But she drew herself up and determined to be as cold, calm, and sensible as he was being now. Though events were moving swiftly, she perceived that she'd a great deal to lose if she didn't speak up quickly. She hadn't the time to wonder if it was his low valuation of himself or his high estimate of her that was about to ruin her chances at happiness.

"Arden," she said with as much steadiness as she could muster, lifting her head and looking him in the eye, "do you think I'm so young and foolish that I don't know what will bring my own happiness? After all, you're speaking of only a few years between what I am and what you thought I was."

"A few years, my dear?" he said quizzically. "Say, rather, a few lifetimes. I thought you were seven or eight years younger than myself, not a dozen. I thought you were once wed, and had known sublime happiness, and had lived more than a dozen, dozen months with a man, and so were now ready to settle for comfort and compassion, having once known complete love and passion."

"Do you think I couldn't feel that for you?" she asked
in wonder.

"Passion? Oh, aye," he said with a sad smile, reaching
out to run the back of his fingers against her flushed cheek,
"I might be able to give you that, teach you that, but complete love? Francesca," he said in a hard voice, the sudden
voice of a stranger, "I'm no man for a young girl to take to
her heart. I've led a bad and a wicked life, my dear, and
have forfeited the right to a great many things in so doing.
And one very beautiful thing," he whispered, as if to himself again.

"And so, after all this, it's only that? Beauty? Is that all
you ever saw in me?" she asked in hurt amazement.

"Oh, no," he answered low. "In you I saw everything
that is there, and it's everything I could want. But I also
saw what was not there, which was, even then, almost more
than I deserved."

She reached up and captured that large hand, and was
about to try to dare to answer him with her lips, without
words, for even in her confusion she could sense his great
hurt and disappointment. But he stepped back as though
he'd read her mind in her eyes, even in the darkness, and
then she noticed that the darkness had been suddenly sliced
by a wedge of light from the opened terrace door.

"Mrs. Devlin," Mrs. Deems said in an awful voice,
"might I have a word with you? That is to say, if you're not
too terribly busy, of course?"

"You look as though you've gotten your tail caught in the
door, or is it a thorn in your paw that's troubling you, Arden?" Julian asked as he came into his friend's room without bothering to ask, and settled himself into a chair near
to the desk where Arden was working, scowling as he wrote.
He studied Arden at his task and noted how the big man's
tanned face was yellowed with fatigue, a faint rusty stubble
dusted his clenched jaw, and there was a distracted look in
his shadowed eyes.

"You didn't get in until dawn, I know, for that was when
I made my weary way to my own little bed," Julian said on
a yawn, though he continued watching his friend carefully,
"and though your apparent exhaustion was a comforting
thing to see, since it usually speaks of hard and interesting
play, as you passed me by on the stair, without a word, I
could tell . . . no . . . say more honestly, my nose could

sense, immediately, that it had been from exerting yourself with a far more literal sort of filly than I thought you'd been out riding all night. Ah. Now I see that the speechlessness last night wasn't just because you didn't see me. Is that an invitation to a duel you're laboring over? Don't bother, then, my eyes are too bloodshot to make it out, pick up a glove, here's my left cheek—you'll have to make do with it, my right one's on the other side and I'm not moving—and then tell me straight out how I earned your royal displeasure. And make it pistols, please, or better still, cannons, because I'm too tired this morning to direct my sword to a target even as large as you.''

"Conceited pup," Arden muttered, blotting the note he'd just done with writing and liberally sanding it before he reached for another sheet of paper. "I'm writing to my sister."

Julian's light eyes widened at that; he'd never known Arden had a sister, or rather, he'd heard that Arden had a dozen of them, ranging from the first one he'd been told about, the Spanish dancer, to the most recent, the nun in her cloister in Rome.

"Ah, might that be the mother superior or the cossack's fifth wife?" Julian asked curiously.

"It might be either, but it isn't, it's the one in Scotland," Arden answered as his pen waved furiously. He wrote a tight, neat hand, and he covered the sheet with speed.

"Ah, one letter for each eye, very thoughtful," Julian commented, craning his neck and trying to read over his friend's shoulder, but finding the pen racing too quickly in the huge hand it was in to make out the words clearly.

"And one," Arden said patiently, "to our old friend the Duke of Peterstow in Gloucestershire—yes, I'm sending off a line to Warwick too, and as soon as I've done, I'm off to Paris—on your horse, I think, since mine, who'd have your head off your shoulders if he knew you'd referred to him as a 'filly,' is likely too tired from last night's wild ride. We covered many acres," Arden murmured as he sanded his second note, "as I composed these letters in my head."

"On a hired hack, I think," Julian corrected him, "because I'm going with you on my horse. I need the ride," he said negligently as Arden turned his wide neck to stare at him.

"Yes, likely. You're so jaded I wonder you can sit a chair, much less a horse today, and what man wouldn't want to haul himself out of a merry bed after an arduous night to go cantering off to Paris?'' Arden sighed. "No, don't worry, lad, I'm not up to bad business again, for either of our profit, or to any danger to myself. It's actually good business I'm after this time, and not in the least to my own benefit, believe it or don't. And,'' he added in a muted voice, "the only danger to myself is past.''

Julian sat quietly as the second letter was prepared, and when Arden looked up again, he found himself staring into a pair of icy gray eyes as unblinking as if it were a pistol, and not just that affronted, intimidating stare that was being leveled upon him. Although Arden remained still and his eyes didn't so much as flicker, he finally sighed.

"All right,'' he said quietly, "it seems that last night I offered for the baron's beautiful daughter. Offered marriage, Father, don't fret yourself.''

"And from your lack of laughter,'' Julian said lightly, yet he was surprised to find how badly he ached for his friend's sake at the news, although he'd never pitied him before, "I take it she turned you down. Well, small loss, she likely has her eye on some other swindle, a gamester's daughter, after all—''

"Julian,'' Arden said softly, "leave off ripping up the lass, eh? She said 'yes,' or was about to, anyway. I was the one who respectfully declined the honor paid me, et cetera, I was the one who said 'no.' ''

He rose from his seat and paced the room before he turned to his friend and shrugged.

"She had, after all, led me on. Shamefully. Actually,'' he said on a chuckle, "I'm proud of her—she deceived me so well . . . not many have, you know. Maybe I am growing old. Maybe she is my match, for all that she'll never be. She purported to be my ideal, you see: a worldly-wise widow of some five- or six-and-twenty summers. But it appears she's only one of your famous dewy misses, who not only has never been wed, but never even shared her bed with so much as the kitchen cat, and has only just twenty-and-one springs to her credit. It was all done, the hasty imaginary wedding and bedding and widowing, along with the extra years thrown in for balance, in order to ensure her getting that wonderful post of chaperone from the Deemses. And all because Papa can't support her, and I suppose she can't support acting in the capacity of his lure as your enchanting Roxie does so well. So, of course, why wouldn't she leap at marrying me? I spoke nicely to her, and, I suppose, am the perfect papa she never had.''

''You're far more than that to her,'' Julian protested. ''You yourself said she was wise.''

''Almost supernaturally so, now that I know her true age,'' Arden agreed on a smile.

''Why, then, I should think you'd be delighted to find her so young and so untouched. She's an even primer article than you thought,'' Julian exclaimed in wonder at his friend's bitterness.

''Precisely. And I'm delighted to say that so far as I'm concerned, she'll remain in that pristine condition,'' Arden said forcefully enough to quiet Julian, ''because she deserves better. I won't take advantage of her any more than life already has done. She's not had the chance she deserves to find the man she deserves. Don't goggle like that, Julian. Think of your reputation—Greek statues do not sit about, however gracefully, with their mouths hanging open,'' he warned on a little grin.

''And I'm not the noble self-sacrificing saint you appear to be about to weep over,'' he continued with a sad shake of his head. ''I'm practical, as ever. Lovely for both of us, wouldn't it be, if I rescued her and carried her off on my Clydesdale—for if I'm in shining armor with her on my lap, we'd need one, a palfrey would never bear up under that weight—and after I've got her installed in my castle, she finds the parfait young knight of her dreams? What then? No, I know I'm too old, too steeped in sin, and although I've a plentitude of them, I haven't even got one real name to offer her. Julian, I'm never the man for her, she's far too good for me. She needs to be among her equals.

''So,'' he said more briskly, taking up the letters, ''since I've reason to suspect my declaration in the moonlight may well have lost her a position by this morning's light—the Deemses having noted our absence together from the ball— I'm doing what I can to find a better life for her. These letters are to assure it. I've not seen her since last night or yet today, and before I do I'd like to have a remedy under way. I've written to ask for one from my sister and Warwick, the only two decent, wealthy, worldly, and thoroughly crafty people I know in Britain.''

''Another position as chaperone is your idea of a better life than one with you?'' Julian scoffed.

''It's possible,'' Arden answered quietly, ''although that's

not what I'm asking them for. I'd more the idea of an introduction of some sort for her, a sponsorship and a little push
in the right direction. But I'm not at all sure a decent job
of work mightn't be better, at that."

He stopped in the middle of the room, his booted legs
apart, his hands at his sides, head high, as though facing a
challenge fully.

"What was I when you met me, Julian, however cleverly
I was it?" he asked suddenly.

As Julian sought the right terminology, the correct words
to soften the fact, Arden answered himself harshly.

"I was a thief. No, better. I was a procurer—no, more
than that. I was a burglar, a footpad, a resurrection man, a
cutpurse, a highwayman, a bully-boy, a fencing cully, a
cracksman, a dipping cove, a counterfeit, an out-and-out
Captain Sharp. Oh, I was a knowing 'un, laddie, living high
on the corners of Queer Street and Easy Street, and all for
them piles of yellow boys, and all for the gelt," he said in
self-mocking slum accents.

"But so I was," he said seriously, "all of those things,
because I employed all of those persons. I was a veritable
king of the underworld, Julian. You could buy a body or a
soul from me, cut-rate, I'd sell you anything you could afford to buy, and some things no man can. I know what I
was, Julian. So trust me to know what I deserve now."

"But that was what you were," the blond man protested.
"I was a callow fool and a dreamer when we met, but that
doesn't mean I can't and don't want to grow into being a
fuller, worthier man someday."

"A dreamer isn't a killer, lad," Arden said, his face a
mask, his loud deep voice dropping like lead to end the
conversation.

"Ah, well," Arden said after a moment, his voice again
his own, his expression again wry and tilted with a half-
smile, "it's only just as my father, the prince, so often said,
'When you make your bed, son, make sure you also know
who you want to lie in it with you.' A wise man, but given
to tedious maxims, perhaps that's why I never listened to
him. Come along then, Julian, perhaps a ride will do you
good, if it's a wiser, worthier gent you're after being. Because I don't think," he said as he picked up his letters and
folded them in his waistcoat pocket, "that the road to wisdom can be found beneath the sheets. Although," he added

thoughtfully, ''I've come across some interesting paths to exotic places there myself.''

They rode side by side to Paris, but they seldom spoke. Julian was too busily thinking up cogent arguments to broach to his friend after his initial reaction to Francesca's deception had softened. He knew it would be difficult to get Arden to change his mind, but knew that for all its usual steadfastness once it had been made up, it was a fine mind, withal, and so always one amenable to reason. He didn't know Francesca very well, but believed her to definitely be the right woman for his friend, if only because Arden had been so impressed with her, even more, because he could see how the big man suffered, feeling he ought not to have her.

Once, on that long ride, he felt a twinge of annoyance when he remembered that Roxie hadn't told him the truth he was sure she'd known, but then he shrugged it off. Roxie, after all, owed him no more than he owed her, and what they provided each other, although delightful, was never faithfulness or honesty.

Arden rode as swiftly as his thoughts did, and both his direction and his thoughts turned to the future. His past, after all, did not bear reexamining. Or, at least, knowing nothing could come of regret save more regret, he refused to look back again. But mainly, he admitted, it was because for all his courage, he disliked pain.

The inn was in the heart of Paris and was a gaudy one, furnished in determinedly charming provincial style. No French persons were in it except for the staff; it was thronged with wealthy tourists of the sort that saw the city with one eye on the town and the other on a guidebook, and Arden and Julian exchanged knowing amused glances as they strode to the front desk. A game of chance with any one of the fine gentlemen adorning the front parlor would have netted either of them enough for a month in style in the finest hotel in Paris. But they were done with that, their rueful smiles admitted, and were only here because the inn boasted the most coaches to and from its expensive precincts than any other lodgings in the city. This was the place many English persons on the move often requested their mail be directed, whether or not they were guests. For this inn was such a famous little outpost of their countrymen that a letter sent from here would go to England almost as fast as a man on a fine horse could travel.

It was after Arden had paid for such swift transport of his letters, and after he'd asked after any that might have been left for himself or his friend, that Julian noted the clerk nodding to a tall small-eyed man lounging against the window in the parlor. From the slight, almost imperceptible shift of his wide shoulders and the subtle rebalancing of his feet, Julian knew there was no need to warn Arden, for he was aware of the man from the moment he peeled himself from the wall by the window until seconds later as he came up beside him.

"Excuse me, sir," he said in a thick London accent, "but do I address Mr. Arden Lyons?"

"Aye," Arden said pleasantly, turning around, leaning on the desk with all the languor of a coiled snake, for all his assumed unconcern.

"Also known as Mr. Sean Ryan, and Mr. John Tryon, and Mr. Thomas Jameson and—"

"Aye, and five times over, my boyo, and what of it?" Arden asked with unrelenting pleasantness, so sweetly that Julian tensed as well.

"Well then, sir, I'm that glad I found you so easy, for I've been asking after you since I come here yesterday. I bear a message for you, sir," he said, reaching into his pocket and then dropping his hand from his coat, empty, as he jumped back, terrified when he saw the pocket pistol gleaming in Arden's grip, the other sprung into Julian's hand.

"No, truly, sir," he protested, both pale thin hands twitching and waving in the air like an upended beetle's legs, "I do. I bear a message from your sister, sir," he said faintly, "I do."

"Which one?" Arden asked softly, the pistol steady, but apparent to no one but Julian and the tall, perspiring stranger.

"Why, the Lady Millicent, sir," the man said as Julian's pistol dropped to his side at the words and he looked at Arden with shock clear in his light eyes.

"Oh, aye," Arden sighed, his weapon disappearing as quickly as it had been brought forth.

"She didn't want it going astray, it's that important, she tole me to get it to you soon as may be, sir," the tall man babbled, retrieving the note he carried and offering it to Arden with trembling fingers. "It's urgent, Mr. Lyons. She told me to tell you plain—no time's to be wasted. Please hurry. It's your father, he's taken to his bed and wants you at his side. I'm sorry, sir, but it looks like your father is dying.''

"Oh, my father,''Arden said, nodding, his face still. "Which one?"

11

IT WOULD BE difficult to be a chaperone if one were never allowed to be within ten feet of one's charge, uncomfortable staying on as a companion if one's every polite nod and smile to company was looked upon as an invitation to debauchery, and impossible to get a decent reference if one left a situation without being dismissed simply because one found it difficult and uncomfortable. But at least, as her papa had always said when he'd gamed away his night's lodgings but had a penny left in his pocket to try to win it back, there was a bright side. The anxiety over what she should do about remaining in her post diverted Francesca's mind from the bizarre proposal and rejection to her acceptance of it she'd received the night before. For there were periods of all of five minutes together today when she didn't think about it.

She could stay on, of course. The Deemses, finding her holding their daughter's best beau's hand in the dark, might think her a conniving back-stabbing seductress, but being endlessly practical, there was a sneaking admiration for her efforts in their attitude. And, for all their chagrin, it was clear they felt they could still use her. They, after all, monied or not, had only recently become so, and were trying to obtain a toehold in the upper reaches of society. And she, impoverished or not, had been born there. If she felt no advantage and had never known any in her father's title, she did now. Her employers mightn't trust her, but they respected her enough to keep her on, she realized, even if she should take to holding more than just a gentleman's hand in the dark. So long as it wasn't any part of that particular gentleman again; they'd made that clear.

Mrs. Deems had put it plain, and in so doing had set Francesca's cheeks aflame.

"Mr. Lyons," she'd said without preamble when she'd summoned Francesca to her room as soon as they'd gotten back to the hotel, "is a gent whose company we encourage, if you get my drift, Mrs. Devlin. No doubt it ain't a piece of cake being a widow, and I can't say as I blame you, he's a fine figure of a man and rich as he can stare. But hands off, my dear. Anyway," she said slyly, at the last, "it's clear it isn't a marriage bed he's thinking of taking you to, slipping around as he is in the dark with you. I can't blame him neither, he's got no ties, and a man will take what's offered for free, depend on it. So, if you want some advice, my dear, find a gent who'll stand with you in the sunlight. But on your own time, my dear, in future, understand?"

She did. Which was why she was packing. She was only going to move into another room in the hotel, though. And there she'd stay until her father moved on or could get her another post. He'd gotten her this one without references, he'd get her another, she'd no doubt, she hoped as she threw the last of her belongings together. He hadn't been in his rooms last night, and wasn't yet back this morning, but then, he often stayed out all night at the gaming tables, taking breakfast as well as his winnings at them until his eyes began to close of their own volition. Gamesters lived in a world where the sun and the moon became myth, and weather and seasons belonged to another world. But he was her father, and they were both all each other really had, even though he'd the cards, which had become his family and his life.

After she'd gotten all her things together, she nodded, looked about the room, cast a glance in her glass, and then went downstairs to wait for her father to arrive so she could tell him of her decision, the Deemses to awaken so she could renounce her position, or Mr. Lyons to pass by so she could ignore him entirely, or say something cutting, or pretend she hadn't seen him, she was so deep in conversation with some other dashing gentleman who might happen by. Such things, she knew, might happen in a busy hotel. Even if they didn't, something else could come up so that she could make him feel small and hurt as she did now. Because the more she thought of it, the more she realized it was patently ridiculous that he would refuse to marry her because she was young, a virgin, and had never loved another. Mrs. Deems had been entirely right. She would write him off entirely. He wasn't worth thinking about. She was very proud of the way she wasn't thinking about him as she went down the stairs.

But she saw no one she knew as she waited in the front room, and although a great many gentlemen tried to strike up conversations that would be enormously satisfactory to have Arden Lyons see her engaged in, they were of the sort that made Arden Lyons himself look like a recently beatified saint by contrast. For, as a gesture of her new freedom, and in a fantasy of making Mr. Lyons keel over from the force of his thwarted desire, she'd put on her new fashionable celestial-blue gown. Its cut made her figure look elegant, its flattering hue caused her hair to appear to shine like polished jet, her complexion to glow, and brought almost as much color to her cheeks as the glances and comments of the strange gentlemen who saw her did.

A chaperone who now saw she was in need of a chaperone, she finally arose and drifted to the back of the room, and positioned herself by a window. By gazing out of it as though mesmerized by the back of the bland drive, except when she glanced at the mantel clock every sixty seconds, she was so well-occupied that she was let alone and left to watch for the arrival of what she was so obviously awaiting. It was only too bad, then, that no one came.

The shadows in the weak spring sunshine moved from right to left and then disappeared entirely, only to begin to fall to the other side when they reappeared, as the sun rose to its zenith and moved on to the west. The Deemses must have taken their lunch in their rooms, Arden and Julian might have dropped off the face of the earth, Roxanne likely had decided to pass her day as she best liked, in her bed, alone or not, and not even her father's valet came belowstairs to enliven Francesca's day. She felt so alone that there were times when she wondered about her own reality.

That might have been why, despite all her plans and best intentions, when she finally turned to see Arden's huge frame filling the doorway, her first expression was one of enormous relief and spontaneous gladness. Then, of course, all her subsequent frowns and hauteur and the fact that she'd swung her head back to the window so quickly as to make her grimace as her neck pinched, did no good. He came to her side at once.

At least she spoke before he did.

"I don't want to hear it," she said immediately, addressing his cravat as he took the seat opposite her, his back to the windows. "I imagine, from your expression, there are a great many cunning things you've got to say. But please believe me, I don't want to hear them. It doesn't matter anyway. You don't have to worry about meeting me or seeing me everywhere, sir, for I've left the Deemses employ, or will," she said, correcting herself, "as soon as they wake up so I can inform them that I have. I'll be traveling on with my father, and it is a wide world, sir. And one in which I devoutly hope we shall not meet again. So good day."

And so, enormously relieved and pleased with herself that she could cry, she stared resolutely out the window again. Discovering that his wide shoulders now blocked that riveting view, she swung round to stare with great interest at the front parlor, in particular at the mantel clock.

"Francesca," he said in a deep soft voice, all velvet at its heart and reverberating so that she looked at him despite herself. She saw the sadness in his face and the eloquent futility he expressed wordlessly as his hands lifted and then fell to his lap again, for all that he, as she immediately reminded herself, trying to look away again, was as helpless as a thunderstorm, and about as predictable. Untrustworthy, she told herself sharply, and pursed her lips over the word so that it was there, at the ready, should she begin to waver.

"I never meant to make an enemy of you," he said soberly, more somberly than was his habit of speech. "Indeed," he went on in his usual lighter accents, "I don't need any more, thank you, my plate's already full. But aside from that, I consider myself your friend. That's why I can't be your husband, in all conscience, however much I might wish it. But I'd very much like you to consider me your friend instead. In time you'll see you've the better bargain, believe me. Ah, I see you don't. Believe me in anything, that is, or, at least"—he chuckled—"your profile tells me so. Nevertheless, I've been busy in your behalf today. I'd like to be that friend in truth, and do what I can to lighten your load and relieve your situation before I go. May I?"

"Go?" she asked all at once, forgetting everything she'd heard but that, finding a queer panic at the pit of her stomach at that one word.

"Yes, back to England, though it's the last thing I'd like to do. But my father's ill, and is having the relatives stage a classical deathbed scene, complete with willow branches and black-edged handkerchiefs handed out at the bedroom door, no doubt, and obviously has ordered up a fatted calf as well, for my delectation. I don't care to go, for more reasons than that, but I must. Needs must when the devil drives, and the old chap's driving me hard. I've a conscience these days, it seems, or perhaps it's just that I want to make sure he's mortal, after all," he added in an undervoice, scowling.

For all she'd planned a hundred ways to rankle and belittle him in the hours that she'd waited for him, she had to hold her hands tightly together to keep herself from saying what she impulsively wished to do—which was to ask him to take her with him. Not only did she want to go home again, to whatever home she could find in England, but she realized, amazingly enough, that she was afraid of being left here without him.

He may have seen all that in her suddenly white face and wide, frightened eyes.

"I've written to my sister and another good friend of mine. If I know them, they'll soon send a reply. I'd like to find you a position in one of their households. And not just as a jumped-up servant, but as a friend. With your charm and grace, education and birth, I know you can find an eligible match before the year is out. I'll dance at your wedding, Francesca, and you'll thank me for this day yet," he said with a smile crossing his weary face.

He *was* weary, she noticed; he looked tired unto death, and maybe because of that, or perhaps because she forgot everything but the fear of his leaving her here among strangers, she didn't flare up.

"Thank you. But I'll stay with my father," she said quietly.

When he looked hard at her, she said quickly, again, before he could interrupt with some excellent reasoning to make her change her mind, "I do thank you, Arden. But I think I'd be no better at taking charity than you would, sir."

Even he found that unanswerable. But after a pause, as he tried to think of a way to refute it anyhow, as she knew he would, she nodded sadly, and to regain composure looked back across the room again.

He hadn't thought she could get much paler, or tremble

more. But her face grew ashen and her hands clenched hard in her lap as she looked at the young man across the room who was looking at her. His gaze was not flirtatious or lecherous, rather he stood still and simply raised an eyebrow and wore a small wry half-smile before he turned away and went out the door. He'd been an unremarkable young man, neatly dressed, and with a thin, neat, ordinary face that Arden remembered immediately because it was his business to remember such things, and more, because once, in the dark, he'd seen Francesca angry with the young man, and so had memorized that face and filed it in his mind, never to be forgotten.

"A friend?" he asked her casually now as she stared after the young fellow.

The face she turned to him struck him to the heart. Her eyes were as terrified at his question as the eyes of one who'd just looked on death, but her face was composed as she answered, after a moment, in her huskiest tones, "Oh. No. Just someone I thought I knew. When . . . when do you leave, Arden?"

"Within two days. But not before I clear up some business matters. I'll ask you again, Francesca. I'm persistent," he said, rising.

"Godspeed then, sir," she said, arising as well and giving him her hand and a weak smile. "I thank you, and I do understand. But for all your persistence, I'm afraid I am resolved."

As she watched him stride away, she realized that she was just that—afraid. Yet she was no worse off, she told herself as she sank back into the chair and deep thought again, than she was before she met Arden. Except for the fact that in a few weeks she'd discovered how it felt to be a servant, as well as a rejected lover.

Now it was just herself and her father again. And Harry. And she didn't know how to go on and find another position, or handle the resurrected love of her life, and the one man she might have liked to ask for help, offered friendship . . . which she didn't trust him enough to give. All she had for him was love, which he decidedly didn't want from her.

As the time passed, Francesca realized that Roxanne wouldn't be seen until dark, and the Deemses were likely showing their displeasure with both Arden and herself by remaining in their rooms until evening as well. Then, knowing how the Deemses thought by now, she reasoned they'd likely issue forth with a flourish and Cecily in all her glory and be monumentally forgiving of Arden, so that, they'd hope, he'd be overwhelmed at their graciousness as well as at their daughter's loveliness. She could, of course, Francesca knew, seek them out in their rooms and give in her notice to them there. But there she would be alone, entirely at their mercy, and suddenly she was weary with being alone. She'd wait until she'd seen her father, she decided, and so might as well go to her room to rest until night, when it was inevitable that he would have returned.

But as she rose to take the stairs, a last glance to the window showed her what was unmistakably her father's valet walking at the edge of the drive, carrying his portmanteau by his side. She hurried out into the late afternoon to intercept him before he disappeared down the long drive.

"Madame," he said, bowing, perfectly correct, except for the excessive coldness in his face and tone when she'd stopped him by crying out only "Monsieur," because he hadn't been with her father long enough for her to have remembered his proper name.

"You are leaving?" she asked breathlessly.

"So it would appear, madame," he said icily.

"My father dismissed you?" she asked, hoping he'd say "yes" and stride away, and yet knowing with a horrible sinking feeling that he would not.

"He did not," he said, with the first suggestion of a human expression that he'd worn, but as it was a nasty smirk that played about his thin lips, she looked away as he continued, "I gave in my notice, madame, for I am accustomed to being paid for my services, not being," he said with vengeful spite, "accustomed to being a charitable institution. Good day, madame," he said, and bowed and left her standing in the drive, her eyes closed in pain.

And then she took to her heels. She only slowed when she reached the hotel, so as not to call attention to herself, but once there, she took the stairs with uncommon speed to make her way to her father's door. There was no answer to her scratching, or knocking, or shaking at the door, and so finally, looking up and down the deserted hallway to be sure no one else was there, she knelt and whispered at the keyhole, frantically, "Father, Father, it's Francesca . . . Father, it's me, please."

The door swung open. There was no one to be seen in

the room. But she stepped in anyway, and when the door closed again, her father was there, where he'd been standing behind it all along. She went into his arms in a rush, not weeping—she was beyond that now. Because she knew. Before he spoke, she knew.

"It was a great deal of money," he said wonderingly as he held her and felt her trembling. "I haven't had so much in years. I kept telling myself I would make it more, but all along I think I knew what would become of it. When I was young," he said wistfully, petting her hair absently, as he would any smooth and gracious texture beneath his fingers, "I would have held on to it for long enough to live in style for a while. But now, I imagine, my control is relaxing, even as my judgment is. I lost every penny. Every franc. And more. I'm sorry, Fancy, but I'm afraid I must be going now, while I still may. Debtors' prison is never a lovely place, but worse in France than at home, I've heard. In any case, I shan't remain long enough to find out for a certainty."

She disengaged from him and stood back, taking in a deep breath.

"Then I'll come with you," she said. "I was going to tell you I'm leaving the Deemses anyway. Arden Lyons, you see, offered for me . . . yes, he actually did, but then he changed his mind . . . it's a mix-up and a pother," she went on quickly, in what she hoped were dismissive accents, "but the result is that the Deemses have made their displeasure known, and though I can be a servant, Father, I truly can, I can't under such conditions. So I'll come with you tonight. What luck! I've already packed," she jested on a weak smile.

"No," he said, shaking his head, and smiling just as wanly, "I'm afraid you can't. Not only because I don't plan to skip out in the dark of night—what do you take me for?" he said gently, and as she flushed, he went on, still smiling, "Every innkeeper expects gamblers to sneak off in the night. Doubtless our host will have word of my dramatic fall by then and will be lurking, waiting for me to decamp all through the night tonight. No, I'll walk out in broad and blameless daylight, this very afternoon, sans baggage, and wave him a cheery greeting as I do, as if I were only going for a stroll. And then I'll never return, of course. A clever fellow can wear several changes of clothes at once—you didn't note I look a wee bit plumper today? All to the better, luggage is never so important as freedom. I've done it before," he said with a shrug, "a great many times before," he murmured as he turned away from her.

"And you can't come," he said more harshly, not looking back at her. "It wouldn't be safe. I know all about the Deemses, my dear, Arden spoke to me this afternoon, he only just left, in fact. He offered me financial help," he mused, and as Francesca's spirits began to lift, he continued, "I refused. I've some notion of being a father, Fancy, not much, but some. I won't have you in his debt through me. Not that I believe he'd take advantage of it, and not that I don't think he wouldn't be the perfect chap for you in any event," he said at once, wheeling around and looking at her keenly, "for he would be. Perhaps not if I'd been a proper father, true, for then you'd have had a come-out and a place in society and your choice of titled gents. There's no way to know now, of course, yet I believe even if that were so, he'd still suit you admirably. But never if you were in his financial debt. You may do anything for a friend or lover, but money changing hands changes everything," he sighed sadly. "No, he may well be wrong in thinking you're so far above him, but I won't have him ever thinking you're beneath him. It may all work out. In any case, I think you ought go with him to his friends in England, that's a favor that may be taken. Or stay on with the Deemses, if you prefer—they're crude, but not dangerous. Both are safer courses than remaining with me."

"Oh, Father," Francesca cried, catching her lower lip in her teeth to keep her startled laughter from becoming sobs, "how can you imagine that? You're my father. I'm not such a puritan that gaming distresses me to the extent that I'd leave you."

"But I am so much of a gamester that I insist," he said sharply. "Listen well, Fancy, my dear, you don't know what you're saying. When I'm at the tables I know nothing but the game. Honor, respectability, duty, and love are all one, and all mean nothing then. I'd knock down a man who dared to insult you with so much as a word in my presence. But when at the gaming table, with the fever on me, I'd put you up as a wager against a penny-piece to any man who had it in his pocket. Do you understand?" he asked, his eyes hard, his voice rising. "I'd never sell your honor, your name, or your body, when in my right mind. But I'm not in my right mind when I game. That's why I do. As I love you, I'll leave you now, Fancy, believe that.''

He turned once about the room as she stared at him, shocked.

''When I was young,'' he said, his usual gentle smile in place again, ''we all wagered, every man jack of us. At school, at university, and after. All the bucks of the *ton* would bet on anything. Lud,'' he said, grinning like a boy himself, ''and what mad wagers they were. I lost a packet on a race once, I recall—everyone was in on it, from Prinny to the Beau. I chose the geese to win over the turkeys,'' he laughed, ''and would've won too, but I'll swear someone lured them off the course. We played at everything, all of us, faro, whist, rouge et noir, hazard, deep basset, why, even patience, noughts and crosses, and jackstraws. Name the game, it didn't matter then, we'd bet on a card or a race or a number or even on who would marry first among us, and die last.'' He smiled reminiscently. ''All of us. Only some of us did it only as an amusement—and some of us couldn't leave off once we started.''

His smile slipped, his face changed, and he looked hard at his daughter. ''I don't blame your mama,'' he said, and she took in her breath, for he seldom mentioned her, ''for all she left me. For I lost everything we had, and then made one last wild wager and lost her. She had, you see, more honor than I, for all she left me to wed another while yet married to me. She was only a bigamist, you see. I was far worse. Don't ask more, Francesca, only believe me. And now,'' he said, clearing his throat, picking up his greatcoat and his walking stick, ''I shall hop it neatly, so that I can leave without too much further shame to you, and not so incidentally, also without incarceration for me. I gambled more than I had, and there are several debts outstanding. But the wheel turns, and when it does, I can pay my creditors back. Gamesters have convenient memories, and a full pocket always buys forgiveness. And I know from experience that one country doesn't cooperate with another in these matters, and that free, my luck may change . . . well,'' he sighed, ''it can't get much worse.

''I've something for you, my dear,'' he said, putting his hand in his greatcoat pocket, and withdrawing a small paper-wrapped parcel, he gave it to her. But she could only hold it and didn't try to untie the string until he urged her,

"Go on, go on." When she opened the parcel, she laughed, although she wanted to weep.

"Oh, Father," she said, holding out the pack of ornate and decorated cards to him. "No, these . . . these are your talismans, your favorite—"

"The luck's out of them for me," he said. "I never used them anyhow. I kept them close because you were too young before. Remember how I chased you away when you and Bram found them that time? And then how angry I was when I found you'd hidden behind a chair to hear me tell him how they were used?" He smiled at the memory, before he went on, "But now they're for you, it's time, you are one-and-twenty after all. And it's only fitting, for I had them from a lady to begin with. She was a great lady, very imperious, very imposing . . . except in private," he said with a smile that took the years from his thin face, "and one of the best dealers at the game. At any rate, it's a grande dame's, a lofty dowager's deck. That's how to use them, as she did, with absolute and perfect assurance and complete haughtiness, that's the key. They're not so bent as to land you in a Newgate parlor, but winners nonetheless, if you play them right. Even if you don't, keep them to remember me by. Not a very great legacy, perhaps," he said, his smile fading, "but an apt one from a gamester to his daughter."

He left her holding the packet in her hand, but paused at the door to look back at her.

"But I haven't a penny to give you, my dear," he said, "or one to bless myself with. Roxie's on her own now too, but she's got young Hazelton and she's experienced enough to find someone else by nightfall if he falls by the wayside. And never fear for me, neither. I'll find a mark before sunset, and who knows, I may be rich by next week. Come give me a kiss of peace and farewell. I'll write to you in care of your school, they'll forward my word, no doubt, wherever you are."

She walked to him hesitantly, and he kissed her cheek and hugged her once before he let her go. There may have been anguish in his eyes before he smiled again and tapped her cheek with one finger.

"Take heart," he said, "there's always a chance I'll be fortunate enough to keel over dead at the tables one day when I'm winning, and then I'll make it all up to you. I trust in chance, you know . . . ah, but you do know, all too well, don't you, my dear? I'm sorry," he said once, briefly, before he shook his head, and smiling sadly, left, leaving her alone.

He was gone for several moments before she accepted it. And then she walked raggedly into the hall, trying to contain her weeping until she reached her own room. All those who loved her were leaving her for her own good. How lucky she was to be so loved, she thought. And so when she discovered herself running blindly toward her door, only to run up against a warm, hard chest with a pair of strong arms wrapping about her tightly, she looked up into that craggy stern face and tried, through her tears, to tell him of all her good fortune before she laid her head down against Arden's chest and wept. It seemed there was nothing else she could think to do.

"Blast," he said, holding her close and trying to hush her broken sobs, "and damn propriety. I can't take you to your room, nor mine, and we must speak alone. Come, come along, Francesca—I have it—we'll go to your papa's room. He's likely gone by now, but I won't take advantage, I'll swear it . . . hush, do, your name will be safe, as you will be there, no one else will know he's gone if he is . . . ah, so he is? I know, I see, hush, please, Francesca, it will be all right, I promise," he kept saying in a murmurous undervoice as he walked her to the room she'd so lately left.

Once there, he closed the door and simply held her close for a long while, and told her to weep all she liked, and she did until it seemed she could cry no more. Then she continued to lean against him until she recalled herself, and then, suddenly, all in a flurry, she lifted her head, looked at him, and grew red with embarrassment.

"Here," he said, "another handkerchief . . . Lord, but you're an expensive chit. You baron's daughters think linen grows on trees—but it does, doesn't it?"

She gurgled something from beneath the large square of linen he'd handed her, and emerged at last, muttering something of an apology for weeping on him and something about how ghastly she must look, all red-faced and swollen-eyed and blotchy, as she protested, as though she couldn't make up her mind whether she was more embarrassed at having broken down in front of him or at having him see her looking so broken-down. But he remembered the warmth of her in his arms and the shape that he'd held so close and wanted to do nothing more than take those swollen lips beneath his, and take that long ripe form similarly, so he coughed, and

looked away and saw a pitcher and basin on a table and told
her there was no harm done to her pride, for hadn't he once
offered her his broad shoulder to cry on? And then told her
she could repair any damage to her face as he spoke to her.

She'd just immersed her heated face into two handfuls of
cool water when she heard him say it bluntly.

"You're coming with me to England," he declared, and
she looked up with sudden hope and then was glad her face
was blurred with streams of water when he added, "You'll
be safe from me, as well as from gossip. I'll hire on someone to act as companion, or, since I'm in such a hurry, we
might get Julian to ask Roxanne along, for the look of it.
We'll take on a maid for the form of it too. Actually, your
coming like this saves me time when I most need it, it re-
solves matters more than I could have hoped to do in the
next few days. I wouldn't have left things hanging, of course.

"You can't remain here," he said gruffly, "not alone,
and certainly not with the Deemses. Not any longer. Once
I've gone they'll be off about the Continent again, and with
your papa gone as well, you'd have no security from their
displeasure. I'll find a safe harbor for you, Francesca. I told
your papa that, and I promise you that too. Can you leave
day after tomorrow?" he asked abruptly, finding the im-
pulse to reassure her in more concrete fashion almost over-
whelming, aware of the door closed on their privacy more
than he wished to be as she finished drying her face on a
towel and looked to him with indecision.

"Arden," she said, her normally husky voice so low from
her weeping that it almost overset his resolve. It seemed,
he thought with grim humor, that this woman could reach
his body with her voice as well as her own sweetly curved
body. "Arden . . ." she said, paused, thinking rapidly, and
then, confused, beset, and weary with carrying her burdens
alone, she decided to trust him entirely. "There's something
else. I'd no time to tell my father—no, I didn't dare, I think.
I didn't know what use he'd make of the information. But I
do trust you," she said, but then hesitated, wondering if it
were fair to trust Harry's secret to anyone else, even this
admittedly wicked, strangely noble man.

So she decided to trust him only a little, only as much as
she dared, and went on, prevaricating, "I'd like to go with
you, if only because you're right and I fear being alone. But
I can't leave just yet. There's something I must do first. I
don't know how long it will take to find . . . I have to speak

with a certain gentleman before I go. I owe it to him," she said firmly, explaining it to herself as well as to him, as she thought aloud.

"The young gentleman you were staring at in the parlor this afternoon? The one you goggled at as though he'd just risen from the dead? Henry Durham?" he asked. And as she looked at him with incomprehension, he added, "A few coins to a few low-paid persons, and anyone's secrets are divulged. He's known as Henry Durham, and he's been uncommonly interested, it seems, in me, as well as in you. I'd planned to take certain steps, but from your expression, I wonder, ought I to be as alarmed as you, and go prepared for danger?" he asked curiously, as the color left her face.

"No," she blurted. "No, he means you no harm, Arden, please, don't hurt him—it was Harry . . . Lieutenant Harry Devlin. Ah," she breathed in dismay, closing her eyes, now that it was out so easily, wondering if she'd wanted to be tricked into revealing all, after all. "I think I wanted to tell you all along. It's my Harry," she said miserably, not noting how his jaw tightened at her possessive word more than any other. "He was never dead, it seems. Well, obviously," she added bitterly, "I only just found out myself, the other night. He . . . he left the battlefield at Waterloo, alive, because he wanted to remain so, he said. He wants me to stay on here with him. But I can't. Still, I owe it to him to tell him. I can't just leave without telling him."

"And do you love him still?" he asked quietly.

"I don't know if I loved him ever," she said wearily, "since I don't know if I ever knew him."

"Then would it be all right if I spoke with him? I promise to be good," he said. "I only want to let him know you're not alone and that my intentions are not dishonorable, or honorable," he added lightly, "but that I'll see to it that you're taken care of honorably. I can find him soon enough," he promised, "and I give you my word that's all I'll do."

"Yes, then, and thank you," Francesca said, looking to him with such gratitude in her great dark eyes that he immediately swung open the door, and after looking about to see if anyone was in the hallway, took her arm and led her toward her room again.

"Be ready to leave day after next," he said when they'd reached her door. "I'll have your dinner sent up tonight. Then get to sleep. Don't worry about the Deemses, you can see them tomorrow or pen them a note if you wish. I'm the one who'll have to duck flying crockery,'' he sighed, making her laugh, before he added, ''and I'll see your Harry before you leave. And, oh, Francesca,'' he said as she began to close her door, ''be easy. His secret's safe with me. I've neither the time nor the inclination to play informer just now. But more important, please believe all your secrets are safe with me.''

''There aren't any more,'' she said on a shaken sigh.

''Oh, no?'' he asked with great disappointment. ''And here I'd great hopes for you never boring me.''

''Oh, I'll try not to,'' she laughed.

''Don't try too hard,'' he warned, and left her then, and taking a last look at her weary, grateful face, was extremely glad he had, and enormously glad she'd shut the door just then, as well.

He found Julian at once. The fair-haired gentleman was in his room, grimacing over his neckcloth as he prepared to go downstairs for dinner, as he called for his friend to enter. It took only a few words to apprise him of the situation. Julian said nothing as Arden spoke, but his handsome face was eloquent. Lieutenant Harry Devlin wasn't the only one to be making a return to the living these days, Arden noted, for Julian seemed to be slowly coming back to life; the more they planned and plotted, the more lively and interested he became. When he heard of the baron's decamping, he chuckled and then grew thoughtful before he lifted one dark gold eyebrow at hearing of Francesca's accompanying Arden back to England, and then, at the last, when he heard of the fate of Lieutenant Harry Devlin, his gray eyes grew wintry and he became cold and still.

''I'll handle it,'' Arden said flatly. ''I promised to do it gently and in secret, for all that I understand, from the baron, that his son and our Harry were in the twenty-ninth Light Dragoons together. Yes, we do have some friends there, don't we? Or did,'' he corrected himself more soberly. ''Nonetheless, whatever we may feel, I'm a man of my word, so it's forgotten, eh, Julian?''

''What is forgotten?'' the viscount asked, returning his interest to his neckcloth.

''Thank you,'' Arden laughed. ''And are you coming to England, as well? You needn't, you know, if you don't choose to.''

''And here I thought it was till death did us part,'' Julian said in some annoyance. "Don't be a flat, Arden, I'm coming—as if I would not."

"And the fair Widow Dobbs?"

"As you say, you need a chaperone . . . Lud! You needing a chaperone!" Julian gave a shout of laughter. "This grows more entertaining by the day. I'd not have missed it even if you weren't my friend. And I do believe I will ask Roxie along, as well. Now that the baron's loped off, I think she'll be only too glad to seek new employment. But Roxie as a chaperone! That's almost as wonderful as you needing one."

"Be careful, my pretty fellow," Arden said seriously, "that she knows as well as you that it's only new employment. Because I think she'd go with you even if the baron won his fortune and asked her to stay on to help him win another."

"I am in many ways a fool," Julian said softly, "but I believe I can explain the difference between love and lust, employment and matrimony, to any female, Arden."

"Oh, indeed," his friend agreed, "forgive me . . . acting as a papa has quite ruined my judgment, I found myself carried away, that's all," he said humbly, before he added, ". . . son."

They parted laughing. Arden to go about his several self-appointed tasks to make ready for their journey, Julian to seek out Roxanne.

He might have wished his friend had been more forthcoming, Julian thought as he took the stairs to Roxanne's room to see her down to dinner. He would have liked to know what the big man meant by asking which father of his it was that was failing, he'd have preferred to know how it was that Arden had a sister who was a lady, he might even have wanted to know precisely where it was that they were going. But all directions were the same to him now, he reflected on an interior shrug, and he knew the past was the only thing his great-hearted friend had never offered to share with him. He respected him enough not to press the matter. In any event, he told himself, he'd soon know all. Curiosity was never why he was going with Arden. He was accompanying him because he had to; Arden was his friend and he'd never let him face that daunting past, or any present pain, alone.

Yet now, although he'd not thought to go home for all the two years that he'd been gone, he found himself growing

excited at the thought. He was as a boy in his sudden anticipation, filled with unexpected homesick yearning. He
wanted to go home again. It was time, he realized, and past
it. And so he was in high spirits when he tapped on Roxanne's door. He'd broach the matter to her at dinner, along
with a fresh bottle of her favorite wine. She was, he recalled
on a grin, always exceedingly compliant after her second
bottle was decanted.

She called for him to enter when he announced himself,
and when he did and closed the door behind himself as
directed, he found her room darkened, the curtains drawn,
and only a few candles burning. She had the headache, he
thought, sobered and disappointed as he drew near the bed
where she lay. But when he'd got halfway across the room,
he saw that she lay there entirely naked, except for a single
red rose, in a remarkable place.

"Good God!" he said, pausing and looking down at the
bed, caught between laughter and lust. "What if there'd
been a thorn?"

But he didn't wait for her answer before he plucked the
flower exactly as she'd intended him to, and so made her
forget the clever answer she'd prepared for his question.

It was more than an hour later, as he lay on his stomach
and looked ruefully to the ruins of his discarded neckcloth
on the floor, that he finally remembered to mention the matter to her.

"I didn't know the baron flitted," she sighed when he'd
done, pursing her lips in a whistle so that her breath made
his clean bright hair rise and fall even as his head did upon
her breast with every breath she drew. "I suppose it's in the
note he sent that I haven't read yet. Poor fellow, his luck's
run out entirely. But mine hasn't," she said gleefully, craning her neck so that she could plant a loud and merry kiss
upon his brow. "I'll come with you, Julian, of course I
will."

He stirred, and raised himself up on his elbows and
looked down into her face. When she wriggled suggestively
with his change of position he held her fast and frowned
down at her.

"No, listen, love," he said seriously, "and understand,
please. I intend to pay your way, food, clothing, entertainment, and anything else you choose, you understand? I enjoy your company and so I offer you a paying position now,
as my . . . ah, companion, as well as Francesca's supposed

chaperone. At that,'' he said, touching the tip of her nose, and grinning as she wrinkled it at him, ''it's an honor. Do you know?'' he asked, his handsome face grown grave with discovery, ''I've never had a . . . paid companion before. It's always been briefer or less formal arrangements that have suited me. So I'm impressed even if you aren't, wretch,'' he said as she stuck out her tongue. ''But listen,'' he added, serious again, hovering over her, straight-armed, looking down into her face with serious clear eyes, ''I won't lie to you. It's a paid position, and I think a good one, and I hope it lasts a good while. But I don't guarantee it. And I do not offer any advancement.''

''Oh, yes, yes, I know,'' she complained, ''talk, talk, talk,'' she murmured in a line down his collarbone and beyond, until he quieted her as he knew best how to do. And all the while, she grinned. And while he may have thought it pleasure, which it partly was, for she enjoyed this sort of thing more with Julian than she had with any man, it being less obligation and insurance than surprisingly pleasant in his arms, she smiled because she was remembering that once he'd promised her only a night, and now look what he offered. And now, she thought as she made him lie back, stunned with pleasure, she'd only have to be clever enough to ensure what he'd think to offer next.

12

IT WAS a narrow street crowded with tall old houses that tipped toward each other over the cobbled road as though they yearned to lean on each other for support as they staggered under the weight of the years. Arden had been directed toward the top floor of a gray and peeling house, and as he went up the curving flights of stairs as quickly and as lightly as a lass might skim down them, he kept his hand over his waistcoat pocket. This was not so as to feel his heart, which wasn't laboring in the least with the exertion, but to ensure that heart's continued beating by the expedient of keeping his hand near to his pocket pistol. He didn't know the man he had to face at the top of the stairs, but he knew enough about him to know that such a fellow would be most dangerous, if not *only* dangerous, if he felt he was trapped.

High up under the roof, where an artist or a stargazer would have celebrated the light or the freedom of the open sky, a deserter hid from view. Arden knew this, and yet he paused only to take in a breath before he knocked at the door. He tensed as the hesitant voice within called out a query in French, because he knew it didn't take a brave man to protect his own life, nor did only valiant men kill those that threatened them. So he spoke his answer plain and in a calm flat voice, in English, and at once, before Lieutenant Devlin could get anxious about a second's unexplained silence. This was no place for deception.

"It is Arden Lyons," he said coolly. "I've come to talk, only to talk, with you. About Francesca Carlisle. . . . We must speak, she wishes it," he added when there'd been no answer for long seconds.

The door eased open. Of course the slender gentleman with the white and strained face who stood there held a pistol, and of course it was leveled at his heart. Arden relaxed. It was all going as he'd thought it would.

"May I come in?" he asked, not so much as blinking or raising his hands a fraction from where he'd dropped them to rest at his sides.

A terse nod and a gesture with his head were the only answer he got. He strode into the room, and looked about impatiently, remembering that his security lay in his absolute confidence; unease or stealth would set this man off.

"Lieutenant Devlin?" he asked.

"Henry Durham," the gentleman answered quickly.

"Also Lieutenant Harry Devlin," Arden stated in flat, bored tones.

The young man hesitated. Then he asked despairingly, "She told you?"

"Scarcely needed to, I would have found out. But, yes, she did. I was sworn to secrecy, never doubt it. And," he said loudly and immediately, seeing how the young man began to grow white about the mouth and his upper lip grew damp, "once I swear to a thing, it is unalterable. I've no interest in you, Devlin, beyond Francesca's peace of mind."

"Francesca's peace of mind?" Harry said incredulously. "You care about that?"

"I'm scarcely after her money, all five pence of it, and her body, though entrancing, comes with too high a price on it for me to pay. No, she's a lady, and will remain one, and I, believe it or don't, am only after her happiness, whether I share it or not. Her father's cut the stick, he'd gambled away everything but his teeth, and I believe he's got a line of credit on them too. The cits who employ her won't be happy now he's gone, and as they'd their other eye on me and I have to return to England, her lot won't be comfortable with them neither. So I'm taking her with me . . . chaperoned," he added when he saw the look in Harry Devlin's eyes, "though she don't need protection from me. I know enough to keep my hands off m' betters, mannie," he said, touching his forehead and flashing his white teeth in a second's perfect mockery of a groveling serf.

"I offered her marriage," Harry said, sitting down at last, but still holding the pistol, laying it across his lap as he ran one hand through his smooth light brown hair.

Arden said nothing, but deliberately turned his back on the other man and gazed up out the skylight at the morning sky and the thin clouds scudding over it.

"I've funds," Harry said. "These are only temporary lodgings. I can get better anywhere in France, here in Paris or anywhere in Europe. I offer her marriage, a home, children. Once, she loved me. I wish to speak with her," he said with sudden resolution, rising to his feet, "now."

"She's an Englishwoman," Arden said softly, "who wants to live at home."

"A woman's home is wherever her husband is," Harry said defiantly as he struggled into his jacket.

"She doesn't want to marry you," Arden said very quietly.

"I suppose she told you so," Harry retorted with anger.

"She allowed me to come here today to speak with you. I doubt she'd have done so if she intended marriage with you. I think," he said reflectively, turning to face Harry, "that she's afraid for you. Not of you. She doesn't want to hurt you, but she don't want to marry you, that's certain. She wants to say good-bye. I've come to ask that you make it easier for her. She deserves that, at least."

Harry Devlin stood still, head high, and stared at Arden. He was not nearly so tall as the other man, but he was

slender, lithe, and attractive, the very sort of gentleman
Arden had pictured Francesca marrying someday. In his red
and epauletted uniform he would have been dazzling to a
young girl, an agreeable sight to any man. If he'd stood half
so tall on that terrible day last June, Arden thought, he
might have lived to carry the day, and then the world before
him. And even if not, still he'd never have had to hide his
face or conceal his name. He felt pity and anger, scorn and
sorrow for Devlin. All that Arden thought might have been
in his face as he looked at Harry. Or perhaps it was only
that Harry saw all that now in all men's faces. For he
winced, and then spoke out angrily in too shrill a voice for
the distance between them,

"How easy it is for you to disdain me! How pleasant for
you! But I tell you that it's easy to be brave when you only
have to think about what you might do in war. Any man can
be a hero in his dreams, every man is. But sometimes," he
said, pacing, and throwing Arden a bright look as he did,
"it's braver to walk away from madness than to join in it.
Sometimes, for all it looks like cowardice, sanity is the
braver course. I became sane at a bad moment, when everyone around me went mad. I don't think there's shame in
that. War is insanity. I learned that."

"Only a madman loves war. Or a conqueror," Arden said
unemotionally, "because it is, as you say, insanity. And
useless and cruel and stupid. But so is tyranny."

"Oh, bravo!" Harry called out, slapping his hands together. "Hear, hear! Well-said! And easily said," he added,
on a sneer, "when far from the cannon's mouth and the
blood and the screams of the dying. Are you going to lecture on honor now too? That generally comes next, I believe. The generals always went on about it. Honor," he
said as though he spat the word from his mouth. "Is it an
honor to be blown to bits, mutilated and left for dead? Thank
you, you can have it, I am on the side of life. There's a
word with a better ring to it than 'honor'—'life.' "

Arden nodded, and then quoted, " '. . . Can honor set
to a leg? No. Or an arm? No. Or take away the grief of a
wound? No. Honor hath no skill in surgery, then? No. What
is honor? A word . . .' "

Harry Devlin's eyes lit and he began to smile encourag-
ingly as Arden went on in his deep slow voice, " '. . . What
is that word, honor? . . . Everything,' " he misquoted, as
Harry's smile froze in place.

"They were true words, but you twisted them," Harry said, his face twisting as well.

"They were written as irony, I twisted them to truth," Arden said. "I've earned the right. I know them."

"As well as you know battle, as well as you know war?" Harry challenged him.

Arden merely shrugged. This wasn't the time to compare experiences; they were not two old veterans survived to settle into their chairs in front of the fire and relive the way they'd returned alive from the battlefield. Arden's face remained impassive as he stared through the dirty glass skylight at an oddly stained sky in order to avoid Harry's eyes, for it seemed to make him more nervous if he was looked at directly.

"Only a madman doesn't know what fear is," Arden said evenly, "but you have to know it entirely and then embrace it and swallow it down whole in order to live with it. And sometimes you must. Still, you've the right of it in that the dying doesn't take much thought, but it's a frightening business, this living. I only think we should make it a bit easier for Francesca. Let her go, Devlin. And let her go with an easy mind. It will take bravery, a different sort of courage, but I think if you give her that, you'll never regret it."

"Nor will you!" Harry shouted. "Oh, I see why you're so eager to speak to me about bravery and courage and honor, all so that you can get your great filthy hands on her. She said she disliked you. Why is she so suddenly agreeable to accompanying you? What hold have you over her?"

"It's not necessary to love a man in order to take his advice and offer of safe conduct," Arden said, and though the words stung, he wasn't surprised by them. She had disliked him enormously when they'd met, after all, and even if she hadn't, rejection never surprised him. "I've no hold but the sway of reason," he added.

"Oh, likely," Harry scoffed. "Sweet reason, is it? I can think of words far less sweet. Oh, I know about you, sir! You've a reputation. A dangerous man, they say, with a thousand secrets. She'll not become one of them, not while I live!" he cried out.

"I gave you my word—" Arden began to say, but Harry was furious now and cut him off abruptly.

"Your word?" He laughed bitterly. "The word of a common sharper, a trickster, a spy, and perhaps worse? An ox with the mind of a weasel, anything for profit is your way.

For all I did, I was only an Englishman who left the field. I never aided the enemy more than that!''

Arden's face set still and cold, and it took more control than he believed he had for him to clench his teeth hard and stop after taking only one step toward Harry Devlin where he stood before him, shaking with rage as he ranted. But that step caused Harry's eyes to widen and he took three paces back and flinched and snapped up the pistol and held it before him in trembling hands and cried out, "No further. No further or I'll shoot you dead.''

"Devlin!" Arden said in a great and angry voice, the tone so cold that Harry shuddered back another step. "Enough! I tell you I only seek the girl's future happiness. And I tell you I'm done with parley. Say good-bye to her decently, man, and give her a chance to build her life again. Give her a future, let the past go. We leave tomorrow and then we're for England on the first fair tide. You know her direction. You may seek her out tonight or in the morning. But I tell you this, unlike her papa, I cover all my bets. You may not see her alone again. Good day.''

And scarcely glancing at the man, or the pistol that wavered but followed him as he strode to the door, Arden left the room and went down the stairs, never looking back. But for all his calm and seeming unconcern, his broad back tingled all the way down the long flight of stairs.

There were worse things for a young woman of quality than being penniless, losing her post, being abandoned by her rakeshame father, and then having to travel alone with two gentlemen of dubious repute and a lady of admittedly light virtue. There was, for example, Arden thought as he swung up onto his horse again, Harry Devlin.

And so he told Julian that evening as he dressed for dinner, as the light-haired viscount frowned at the telling of it.

"A dangerous man?" Julian asked when he'd done.

"The Deems clan I'll be facing tonight frightens me more, my friend. Don't fret, the lieutenant don't worry me. I once lived in one of London's finer quarters, where a room with a bottle of blue ruin, a meal, and a female to share it and your floor with you all cost a ha'penny at high tide. I saw a great many creatures like Harry Devlin there. No, he's only dangerous to the helpless, or to any man if his exit's blocked and he thinks you're coming down into his burrow after him. Which I'm not about to do. Even if I strongly suspect there's more to his story than any living being knows. It wouldn't have been that easy leaving—you remember that night, Julian," he said softly, as his friend did, and wished he did not.

The viscount scowled at the memory of how he and Arden had heard of the great battle and ridden all that day to arrive in the night, only just in time to aid the wounded by killing off all the scavengers, human and otherwise, and trying to cheat death by getting as many of the crippled to the surgeons in time for them to use all their insufficient arts, as well. No, he'd not likely ever forget that smoking, malodorous night of pain.

"Yet, even then," Arden said thoughtfully, "if I did know of something more, and if I hated him for it, I can't think of a worse fate for him than being himself. He's bright enough to know what he's done. His only hope lies in being a little less honest and convincing himself that he's done right. And he's halfway there now. Forget Lieutenant Harry Devlin—I doubt he'll do more than say good-bye, and that, unfortunately, if he summons up enough courage or self-pity to do it, with the plea for her not to forget him that I specifically asked him not to make. Ah, but the Deemses now," he said, shaking his head. "I missed them last night, and I must face them at dinner—now, there I tremble."

But for once, Arden Lyons was wrong, a circumstance that his friend Julian was only too pleased to note and mention interminably afterward. For the Deemses took the word of his leaving with admirable calm, having already got wind of it from Francesca's carefully phrased notice the night before. Although the baron's daughter had not gone with them to dinner, her conscience had pricked her. She'd gone around to their rooms when they'd returned to them, and given in her softly phrased resignation, and the Deemses had listened closely and inferred even more from it than they had from the coincidence that both she and Arden Lyons hadn't come to dine with them.

They'd been too busy thinking up contingency plans to upbraid her or cite her ingratitude or treachery properly. Francesca had discovered why when she'd gone to Cecily's room next to bid her farewell.

"I'm sorry to leave you," she'd said.

"Oh, yes, I'm sorry to see you go," Cecily had replied, her delicate face a mirror of Francesca's assumed distress.

"But I think I'll fare better at home now," Francesca assured her with a confidence she didn't feel.

"Oh, of course, yes," Cecily answered, much relieved, taking her cue as ever from clever Mrs. Devlin's face and tone of voice.

"And I wish you everything that is as good and sweet as you are," Francesca said finally, exhausted, as ever, after only a few words with Cecily, but realizing even as she touched her lips to the girl's proffered scented cheek that there was no more harm than intelligence in the child.

"I shall have all that," Cecily said then, shocking her onetime chaperone by saying something unsolicited, and by sounding so gay and so smug about it, "for I've a beau."

Francesca's tender heart had frozen at that, and while she thought of how she might break the news that Arden Lyons was leaving as well, Cecily, once having broken one barrier, had spoken yet again.

"I hope Mr. Lyons will not be very unhappy. He's the kindest, most amusing gentleman, Mama says. But I like Jonathan better, even though we've just met, and Mama does too, for he's a lord. I think a baron, like your papa . . ." She frowned, thinking, but then brightened as she added, 'Papa says that taken in hand, he'll do. Mr. Lyons, he says, could never be taken in hand. Or be a lord, actually." She giggled. "Jonathan is splendid," she said softly. "He's very young. He says he adores me. He wrote me poetry."

She slid a page of carefully written lines to Francesca, and blushed, as though the words were naughty, instead of lovely words of love.

" 'There is a garden in her face, where roses and white lilies grow, a heavenly paradise is that place, wherein all pleasant fruits do flow . . .' " Francesca read. "Why, how charming. It's Thomas Campion," she said, breaking off and smiling at Cecily.

"No," Cecily said with a hint of truculence, "it's Jonathan, Lord Waite, my young gentleman."

"Cecily," Francesca said softly, "it's by Thomas Campion, a well-known Elizabethan poet," but then, seeing the girl's lower lip beginning to jut out and her lashes lowering over blue eyes now drenched with unshed tears of confusion and defiance, she went on bright, "but it's written out beautifully. My, but he has a lovely hand, why, just see how well his letters are formed, and how . . . neat it all is," she added desperately.

"So it is," Cecily noted, relieved. "He's remarkably educated. I noticed that at once. He had dinner with us," she said happily, the incipient stormclouds gone from her white brow, "and Papa was quite impressed. He's a lovely home, a mansion, near to Banbury, but some dreadful Captain Sharp cheated and won it from him in an unfair game of cards. But Papa will get it back for him," she added, "never fear."

Francesca assured her that she wouldn't, and listened to several more moments of praise of young Lord Waite, wondering all the while if the young man was the same crazed gamester Arden had dealt with. Even if he were, she knew better than to broach the matter to Cecily. If the question of the authorship of her love note had almost precipitated a crisis, she dreaded thinking about what such a claim would do. She'd ask Arden's opinion, she'd decided, and forgot the matter, for she was growing very tired. After listening to some more glowing praise of Lord Waite, she bid Cecily good night and good-bye again before she left for her own bed, relieved beyond words that the Deemses had forgiven her, if not already forgotten her.

She might even get a blameless letter of reference from them, she'd thought as she sighed and laid her head upon her pillow. Then she almost sat bolt upright again at the wondering thought of what she was actually going to do once Arden got her back to England, but she was very weary and confused, and for once, remembering his assurances, she was willing to leave her fate in his large hands—at least, she remembered thinking on an enormous yawn, for this one night.

But now the night had passed, and as she'd passed her day preparing to leave, she was edgy and anxious and unsure again. Roxanne had stopped by for only a moment at midday to assure her laughingly that nothing would keep her from coming along to England with her. "I hired on with your papa," Roxie had said with a grin, "and I'm staying on with his daughter, so it's all in the family, after all. Oh, never fear, duckie, I'll be a splendid chaperone"— she'd winked—" 'with me one eye on me own gent and t'other on me toes,' as the saying goes."

Before Francesca could assure her that there was no need, her intentions toward Arden or at least his toward her being quite otherwise, Roxie mentioned a dozen things she had to get together before she moved on, and laughing merrily, had left. But Francesca had everything in order, and so then had time and to spare to think and wonder and worry, and finally, in an effort to stop tormenting herself, an abundance of time to groom herself and dress for her last night at the hotel. So when Arden came around to her room at last to collect her for dinner, she was keyed-up and wary, uncomfortable and uneasy, suspicious and frightened, and absolutely lovely.

' She'd put on and taken off the same gown three times. As she'd only the three new ones she deemed handsome enough to wear, and a great deal of time, that had made a total of nine trips to her glass to judge what she'd looked best in tonight. Arden's arrival had interrupted her indecision, and it was the luck of the draw, a thing, she thought as she went to the door, that he surely would have appreciated had he known it, that she would go down to dinner in the gown she was wearing at that moment. Even if she'd had fourth thoughts on the matter of this particular one, it was too late to change again, and it was as well, for the look she surprised on his face when he saw her made it the right choice.

She wore the cloth-of-gold gown. It needed little other ornament because of it's exuberant color and daring cut, which was as well, since she'd no ornament to match it, her cameo and her strand of amethyst being insignificant against its glowing golden sheen. She didn't realize that her form itself was all the ornament it needed, for it clung to her every curve, and showed exactly how many there were, from the high tilt of her breasts to the softer subtle lines beneath them that dipped, like sighs, into the inverted stem of her waist, before flowing gently out to her rounded hips and then away in long supple folds, to the floor. She'd dressed her black hair high and smooth to lend the elegance that the gown demanded, and the only other thing she wore besides her slippers and undergarments was a wide tortoiseshell comb that held her heavy hair to its sleek obedience. That, and an air of uncertainty, for while she'd been flattered at Arden's eyes widening, he said nothing for a moment more as he looked down at her.

But she was all golden, he thought, using every device for control that he knew to take his eyes from her, so that he could take the avidity from them before he looked at her again. Her skin wasn't chastened by the high color of her gown, but rather blushed gold at how well it complimented her, and the color surprised echoes of golden sparks in her deep brown eyes. Even her scent tonight was cinnamon-tempered, the flowers in it spiced with Oriental attars and musks. For once, he regretted all his keen senses, for if he were to be this lady's benign protector until he could deliver her to safety, he ought not to be able to sort her scent note by note, or see every nuance in her eyes and lips, or feel, he thought as he took her hand, exactly how smooth its skin was, as he wondered all the while what the texture and taste of the skin he saw at her neck were like.

So, wishing he were blind and without senses, he almost flinched when her husky voice reached his ears and he remembered its power over him. He wondered, standing mute and wretched in that moment, if he would have to bind his ears as well, like one of Ulysses' sailors, so as not to hear her siren call. But he answered her as soon as he realized she was becoming as devastated by his unnatural silence as he was by her mere presence.

"I'm sorry, but you look so beautiful, you overset me, you know," he said, too astounded to attempt to dredge up a lie when he realized that he could not immediately. "I didn't," she said at once. "Know, that is. But I'm glad." She smiled because she was, and took the arm he offered her.

"I don't look anything like a companion or a chaperone now, do I?" she asked on a whisper as they went down the hallway.

"Not in the least," he assured her, "nothing like," and as she gave him a smug smile and then held her head higher and marched down the stairs like a grand duchess, he felt a little relief. This gloating over her transformation was very human and a bit conceited, and as he'd been looking desperately for any small flaw in her, he seized on it. But as he found even that endearing, it wouldn't do. Nothing would, he understood as he took her in to dinner, and as he knew he couldn't have her, and should not, at least not if he'd any of that debatable quality—honor—left in him, for the first time in his difficult life he found himself truly frightened, and not at all sure of how to cope with it.

Julian rose when he saw them coming to the table, and for a moment wasn't sure who the beauty Arden bore in was. So his smile widened, as did his eyes, and his face grew intent and he seemed somehow to flow into himself until he, all in his proper black-and-white evening clothes, appeared to glow as golden in his masculine beauty as she did in her loveliness, at least enough so as to make Roxanne hold her breath. It pleased Francesca enormously that he didn't seem to know her, and she smiled so widely that even before she neared him he realized his error, and left off his hunter's poise and gave her a grin of friendship with no trace of seduction in it as he bowed over her hand.

But as he did, Julian thought again how unfair it was that Arden had the knack not only of seeing under the surface of the human mind but also of judging physical beauty even if it were layered in ugliness. The man, Julian sighed to himself, had the soul of an artist as well as the luck of the devil. What was it Arden had joked to him once? "If I'd your face, my lordly friend, I could be king . . . of the world." And so he could, Julian thought as he sat again and felt Roxie's hand on his thigh.

She had worn a gown crimson as a pirate's sash, wearing so many trinkets with it that she might have carried a green parrot on her shoulder as well and completed the effect. But although she'd imagined it daring and delightful when she'd dressed, she felt tricked out like a show pony when she saw Francesca, but was honest enough and clever enough to say that straight out. So they all of them had great fun helping her to divest herself of various bits of her finery as dinner was served. She found herself the center of attraction, for all of Francesca's beauty, by helping Julian to her earrings during soup, handing Arden a bracelet with the butter, and slowly stripping off the rest of her jewelry as the night wore on, making them all laugh and conjecture about what she'd do once the jewels were gone, laughing even more at that thought, all the while she was the centerpiece of the meal, all exactly as she'd planned.

Arden, for all he laughed, wasn't having a delightful time. For all his wit tonight, in that central core of himself he was deeply troubled. Francesca Devlin . . . Francesca Carlisle, he corrected himself, was everything he wanted and nothing he could or should have. And while he was never so foolish as to torment himself by serving her up on a dish to another man, he was very shortly going to set her on the road to that end. And all for that word the love of her youth had scoffed at, that word that his favorite, Master Shakespeare, had mocking Falstaff call "air" for all he'd named it "everything" for Harry Devlin—honor. But it was, he decided on a sigh, forgetting his jovial pose for a second, very like he'd said, after all. If it were not for that word, he doubted any man would remain in any battle. And he, after all, had only to battle his oldest opponent—himself, this time.

Francesca, too, sometimes found herself laughing, just as Cecily had so often done, solely as reaction to everyone else's jollity. For now and again amidst all the raillery she realized how enormously her life had changed and was changing. Because, she thought with panic at those moments: to be abandoned by your father and declared for by a gentleman you would gladly have, only to have him deny you because you'd lied about your virtue and had been more virtuous than he'd believed, and then offer you only his help—and that by taking you away with him and his friend and his friend's lover—was not the most entirely comfortable thing in the world. She dimly understood that things had happened too quickly for her to be as frightened as perhaps she ought to be. Then too, she thought, breathing easier, Arden would be with her. But, she realized with distress, she'd no cause to trust Arden so implicitly, except that she couldn't help doing so. And that was no comfort either.

Roxanne laughed and teased and jested continuously, keeping the table in an uproar, and all so that Julian wouldn't take his eyes from her again. He was so handsome tonight, she knew every other female in the hotel envied her. So her every effort was for him, and the only pleasure she found in it was in success, and although the strain of it made her amazingly merry, it couldn't be said to be amusing, it was such hard work.

Julian had nothing to keep him from good humor. He'd a considerable fortune well in hand, a pretty little ladybird to ease his idle hours, a good friend at his side, and a damsel in distress for them to aid and comfort. He really hadn't looked for more in all these past two years. But now he was going home again, and perhaps that was why it all suddenly wasn't enough. When he wasn't laughing, he was wondering why this should be so, and why he found himself as restless and unsatisfied now again as he'd been when he'd left to seek his fortune originally. And increasingly he wondered this even as he was laughing.

The table with the four handsome, well-dressed persons, all enjoying themselves so much, was the envy of every other patron in the hotel, of course.

The Deemses saw them immediately upon entering the room, which saved them the trouble of looking for them. For then they acted in concert. The Deemses, Mr. and Mrs, who could be judged as one in all things except for his problems with costiveness and hers with bunions, took great pains to let Arden Lyons know how unaffected they were at his departure. They wished him well so often, and with so many secretive smiles, Mr. Deems going so far as to actually show his teeth in one of his smiles, that they were entirely sure he knew how well shut they were of him. For then they pushed young Lord Waite forward and he did the pretty with Cecily better than they could have coached him to do. He watched Cee-cee's every utterance leave her lips as though she could lisp his death sentence there, and sighed over her grace as she curtsied to them in farewell, and held her little white hand as tenderly as if it were a separate wounded thing he carried back to their table. And all, he thought triumphantly as he did so, to show Arden Lyons he'd landed on his feet after all, and didn't need his help now that he'd a rich cit in tow.

And Cecily, of all of them, was entirely happy.

"I wonder," Francesca said as Arden walked her to her room at last, after she'd made her good nights to Julian and Roxanne before they'd left the salon, so that she'd not have to pretend she didn't know they weren't going to separate bedrooms, "if it was right not to tell the Deemses about Lord Waite."

"Oh, old Deems knows," Arden said as he paused with her at her door. "There's no shrewder gent in France today now that they chased Boney away. He knows the boy's debts to the last shilling, he even asked me if young Waite 'was into me for summat' when we met up in the gentlemen's convenience tonight. Yes," he said, smiling down at her, "you ladies aren't the only ones to settle the state of the world and find out all the gossip under the guise of going to refresh yourselves, you know. And he don't care, because he thinks he can 'straighten the lad out.' Doubtless"—Arden smiled widely now, his teeth white in the dim light— "he will. Poor boy. Although Deems will get a run for his money, for a gamester's like a drinking man, and there's always a neat wager to be found, or a lottery ticket to be bought, just as there's always a chance for a drop of the grape, except in heaven . . . where I understand it's not neccesary . . . though I'll likely never know. So all's well that ends well, just as the master said."

"Is it?" Francesca asked softly, her head to one side in thought, looking so pensive he almost turned away from her to keep from turning to her. "I don't know. What of Cecily?"

"Ah, well, Cee-cee," he said with great heartiness to distract himself from her nearness and the spiced floral scent of her. "She's least to be pitied, for she thinks she's in love."

"Is she not to be pitied then?" Francesca said. "I wonder." Then, sad for a number of inchoate reasons, she shook her head and took his hand, and sighing, went into the room to prepare for bed.

Arden stood at her door and used all his self-control to keep from following her.

It was as well that he did, for in a second her door opened again. She stood there flushed and trembling. He took a step to her without thinking, and was glad that he'd been so many steps away when he noticed the note she thrust out to him between them.

"It's from Harry," she said on a long, shaking sigh, and then he knew why she'd looked up so often at dinner, and had gone so reluctantly to bed, even though he'd told her of their early start in the morning. She'd known of his visit with Harry, if not precisely all of it, and though worry for Harry was gone, she'd obviously been waiting for the end to the matter, a finalization as sure as the closing of the grave she'd been denied seeing, by Devlin's living, last year.

He scanned the note rapidly. It said all the conventional things, with nothing out of place, except for a renewed wish that she try to understand, and an address, from which, he vowed, word would always be able to reach him should she need him, should she want him. He looked up from the note to find her reading it again at his side, her dark head just beneath his shoulder. He pretended he'd not done with it then, and would have remained so, reading and rereading the note and not even caring if she'd wonder if his lips were tiring with the effort, whatever she'd think of his intellect, just so he could stand so, close to her, if she hadn't turned to him and asked softly, in her broken little voice, if she might have the letter back, to keep, please, her breath warm, her scent against his lips.

"It's done," she said wonderingly then as he stepped back so that she might have her letter and her safety.

"Over and done, don't worry any longer," he agreed, and gave her good night again.

Once left alone, he shook his head in wonder at himself.

For it wasn't desire or temptation to pleasure he fought, nor was it any physical need. It was, rather, an old enemy and ally: fear. And, he thought, backing from her door, just as he'd told that poor devil Devlin, the only way to deal with it was to swallow it whole, and live with it.

Because he, who'd faced every danger in his life with as much stoicism as he'd faced every moment of it, was amazed to discover himself living in fear now. He knew full well what the right thing, the best thing, and the damned honorable thing to do was, and feared not being able to do it. But, he told himself bracingly, if that craven Devlin had summoned enough courage to deal with her, then so could he. He would see her settled, he would let her be. And it wouldn't be for much longer, after all.

There'd be, he reckoned as he went downstairs again, only tomorrow and tomorrow and tomorrow, after all. One more night at another inn in France, and then a day for the cruise to England and a little sleep, and then a day for the coach ride to his friend Warwick's home. Failing to find her a refuge there, it was only a day or two more to his sister's. Only three to five more interminable days and dangerous nights and then he'd be free of her. Although, he understood as he went in search of something to drink that would speed the morning to him faster, of course, he'd never really be free of her, not really, ever again.

13

"YOU WERE made for the sea," Francesca laughed, holding the rail tightly and trying to steady herself and to repair the damage the whipping wind was doing to her hair all at the same time. "Look at you," she cried, "walking the deck as if it were a meadow, as though you were born to the sea."

"But I was," he said imperturbably, "on my mother's side. Owlers and smugglers of brandy, tea, and whatever paid best, sturdy, sneaky lads, the nemesis of the king's cutter fleet, all on my mother's side. My father's kin were the land pirates—they were the bad fellows who lit beacons for safe harbors that weren't there, wreckers and scavengers, the lot of them, with a few of them taking to the water only to sail sloops as revenue men, to have their wicked fun that way.''

''I thought your father was a duke,'' she giggled, ''yesterday.''

''So he was''—Arden nodded approvingly—''yesterday.''

She laughed again, and leaned into the wind, finding the mild spring air bracing and the entire trip home far more entrancing than her voyage out had been. It was more than the fact that the season had turned from that icy passage; it was the warmth of the man who accompanied her now most of all, she thought. To keep from thinking that, she glanced away from his stalwart figure, as he stood at case, his feet braced apart, rising and sinking with the motion of the ship as though he were part of it, and she looked out to the far-off outline of the shore they were rapidly approaching.

''Do you think,'' she asked, turning her head and trying to shout her question against the freshening wind, ''that Roxie will be able to leave the ship?''

But her voice wasn't made for volume and he had to move closer, against his will, in order to hear her.

''Oh, aye,'' he said, coming to the rail to stand beside her, ''for all she looks as though she's dying now. Once the motion stops, she will. And will rise and walk off this vessel under her own power, and consume half a cow and a few tankards with her dinner, as well, if I know my girl. There's some that can't take the sea, for all they have to take it, and they learn to live with it by enduring until they reach land again. Why, there was a first mate on our whaling vessel that weighed little more than a mackerel when we finally rounded the Cape of Good Hope. But after we'd anchored and taken on provisions, he came back on the ship so stout we had to roll him up the gangplank with the kegs of beer.''

''*Ar*-den,'' she said, turning to him, making his name distinctly two rueful syllables, a world of mock censure in her voice, a world of laughter in her eyes.

''Don't!'' he said so suddenly she paused, startled. ''I only meant . . . don't fidget with your hair anymore, let it be, the wind will always win, let it have its way now and enjoy the romp, there's a lifetime on land to straighten it after,'' he said, looking out to the horizon again, annoyed with himself for alarming her, even more uncomfortable with the way he'd loved seeing that black witch's mane of hers streaming across her sun-flushed face in the wind, as riotously tangled as he thought it might look in the throes of lovemaking.

"Yes," she said, and looked out to land as well, but then, discovering she could use her flowing banner of hair now as disguise, she looked her fill at him through the blowing strands of it as he stood by her side as they stood in companionable silence.

He was really huge, she thought again with surprise, as she often did when she realized the power of the man that custom sometimes made her forget, and he was burly and every bit as formidable-looking as he'd been when first they'd met. But now she knew the swiftness and grace with which he moved, and had seen how he was able to carry himself with all the economy and precision of a man half his size. And now she knew how that rugged impassive face could be shocked or startled into betraying some of the thoughts in that labyrinthian mind, and then only by watching those tawny eyes carefully, for they alone could betray some of his many secrets. Not many people knew that, she thought, but then, not many dared to look so close, lest those knowing eyes catch and consider and sum them up first. But when she looked at him, sometimes he looked away. And when she moved too close, he stepped back. And for all that she came only to his shoulder and his thigh was almost the size of her waist, she knew in some way he feared her almost as much as she, in some ways, feared him.

But gazing at that blunted profile, his ginger hair blowing back from his wide tanned forehead as he studied the shoreline, she knew that what she feared in him was not likely what any other being did. Because she was beginning to understand that she wanted what she feared, even as much as she was wary of it. She could no more forget his kiss than she could his kindness or his gentleness with her. And so what she feared most now was his leaving her. The more she knew him, she thought, or rather, she corrected herself, the more he let her know him, meaning to or not, the more she refused to think of parting from him.

So she would do with him, she decided, as she studied him through her cascade of hair, what he advised her doing with another elemental force, the wind. She'd enjoy it while she could, whatever happened, for she'd the rest of her life to mend matters. She really didn't know what else to do. Although perhaps, she thought on a grin, if it all became too difficult for her, she could do what she did with all her other problems these days: ask Arden.

It might have been that he felt her eyes upon his face as much as he felt the warmth of the sun on it, it might only have been that he couldn't look away from her for too long in any case, but as she stared at him he turned his head and looked back at her. For one moment, one quiet moment, neither spoke. And then he stirred and sighed, and looked over her shoulder.

"Poor Julian's a gentleman," he said, "and so is needlessly spending his trip below decks holding his lady's hand, or basin," he said on a smile, "for all the good that will do her, or him. She'd rather he was away so she could be ill in peace, that's why she chased you off as well—it's not pretty, being seasick, you know, or do you? You ride the waves like a stormy petrel yourself."

"I didn't know I could," she confessed. "This is only my second time under sail. But I quite like it. It's exciting. Roxie was raised near the water, on a little island, you'd think she'd be used to it."

"Exposure don't ensure comfort," he said, and paused, for he'd almost gone on to say that he'd seen her every day and yet couldn't get used to the pleasure of looking at her, could he? And so instead he said, lightly, after a moment, when she looked up at his silence questioningly, "Ah, excuse me, but I'd only naughty analogies spring to my mind just then. But trust me, if being used to something made it easier to bear, there'd be no point to prison, or torture, or even wedlock"—he grinned at how nicely he'd turned that, and added innocently, "now, would there be?"

But she didn't laugh. Her face grew still and she looked up at him, her brown eyes in the sunlight grown gold, her gaze softened as it roved over his face as she said very softly, "But once, I remember, you didn't object to wedlock, however it was like prison or not."

"And once, I remember, I thought your name was Francesca Devlin," he said harshly. "Listen, my girl," he went on tightly, taking her by the arms and glowering down at her, "constant exposure to something might not make it more comfortable, but it can make it seem more reasonable when it oughtn't to be. You're alone now, and you're very young. You seem to trust my judgment. Then trust me that you're better off knowing me in passing. You've not met my like before—pray God, you never shall again. You're very beautiful, and clever, and sweet, and a thousand gentlemen will want you as I do. And any one of them will deserve you more.''

He released her and put his hands on the railing and lowered his head.

''Francesca, or Fancy, or whatever name you choose to call yourself,'' he said softly, not looking at her, ''let me do one noble thing, please. Let me be your friend. And only that.''

She didn't know where she got the courage from, for she'd have sworn it was a thing she could never say. But one moment she thought it and the next it was on her lips.

''Be my friend, Arden. Indeed, I've never had a better one. But for all I'd like to make you happy, I can't promise to change how I feel.''

''Time,'' he said wisely, nodding at the sea, ''time will change that, my dear. Time will show you the difference between gratitude and love, or at least love of the sort you deserve.''

Time, he thought as she fell still and they looked at their homeland coming closer, time and the only other thing he could control in all of this: distance.

Roxanne seemed entirely recovered; in fact, she bloomed from the moment she stepped off the packet and onto dry land, and simpered becomingly as a sailor paused to admire her neat ankle when she did so. Julian, Francesca noted with a mixture of amusement and pity, looked dreadful—or at least as dreadful as he ever could. He was pale and haunted-looking, and had a slightly hunted expression in his pale gray eyes. He was still enough of a picture to make the barmaid at the waterside inn they stopped at stop in her tracks and gape, but he would be that, she thought, if he were dying, rather than only weary and still slightly queasy from his self-imposed ordeal of nursing Roxanne.

He was much recovered when she came down to join the gentlemen and Roxanne for an early dinner, and, now washed, shaven, and elegantly dressed, he was enough to make every barmaid in Britain goggle. It was odd, she thought as she smiled and took the seat he offered her, that for all his radiant beauty, she'd never thought of him as anything but a friend, and not at all in the way she had begun to think of Arden as one. Perhaps it was because he'd never acted as anything else, perhaps because she'd not for a moment considered that a man that looked like him would so much as notice her, or even perhaps because he was Arden's best friend, and so always in her mind an adjunct of him—first as an enemy, and then later as an ally, but never as a seductive male. And then, she thought, drawing herself up in her seat with the sudden aquisition of self-knowledge and self-praise, it might have been because she'd known intuitively, from his odd detachment and almost dreamy disinterest, that he was not the sort of man for her.

And then, slumping a little, she looked at Arden and thought: Of course not. After all, Julian wasn't a self-professed rogue, with a past he claimed to be every bit as wicked as it was mysterious. It was most likely, she thought then, looking so dismal that the company looked to each other at seeing her face, because there wasn't a reasonable reason on earth why one person was drawn to another, with or against his better or worst judgment.

Her wistful expression spurred Arden and Julian to new heights of creativeness that night. They saw to it that she and Roxanne became breathless with laughter. Arden had a whimsical and outrageous wit, but tonight Julian displayed his own dry and understated humor. Arden, she found, could mimic a hundred accents, English and foreign, and Julian could change his voice to a man or woman's of any age or condition, soaring up to a falsetto or dropping down to a dying frog's. Arden, she learned when the two gentlemen discovered a pianoforte in the common room, had a wonderful rich baritone and Julian a sweet tenor that could fly over it. And they both, she realized to her entire embarrassment and delight, knew not only ballads but also music-hall catches, and, as the evening went on, every verse to each of the increasingly salty tunes the local patrons began to harmonize with. And likely knew more too, she complained to Arden as he marched her up to her room when the company began to warm up to "The Mermaid's Complaint" and she was firmly banished by his edict.

"Roxanne can stay," she protested, hands on hips as she stood outside her room, arguing with him, she realized in frustration, as if she were a child sent to bed before the dancing began.

"Roxanne is older, widowed, and wildly experienced," Arden said flatly, though a smile played on his lips.

"Then," she spat, now roundly vexed with herself and her subservience, as well as with the world and especially with this implacable male, "maybe I just had better go out and find myself an obliging gentleman tonight so that I can live happily ever after, for I think it's only my lack of bed knowledge that's making all my problems, and I—"

She never finished the sentence. The last words of it died against his mouth as he reached down and dragged her to himself. There was nothing gentle in this embrace. He held her close and opened his lips against hers to swallow up all her protests, as well as her lips, and only drew back when he realized she was not protesting at all any longer, although she trembled, although she shook, despite how closely and firmly she was held in the vise of his arms.

"Damn you . . . no, damn me," he breathed, his hand coming up to his hair and dragging through it as he stepped back. "I'm sorry . . . ah, don't look at me like that, I ought to know better, I take you up here to keep you innocent and damn near . . . Go to bed, Francesca!" he boomed at her.

"Arden," she said as he opened her door and pointed like a very large, very irate archangel gesturing with a sword, "Arden," she said as she backed into the room, greatly daring after their evening, and because of the hour and because he'd almost closed the door between them, "Arden . . ." she said before she did close it, smiling tremulously, "I'm sorry. I liked it. Awfully much," she added, giggling at his expression as she closed the door, as amazed at herself as he was.

"No poplars . . . look, Arden!" Julian called to his friend as they rode ahead of the coach down the long shaded road into the heart of Gloucestershire, "and no cypresses. Oaks, my friend, good, decent English oaks, and look"—he slewed in his saddle and pointed to the forest as they passed—"beech and larch, and oaks again!"

"I didn't know you were a horticulturist," Arden commented, watching his friend's growing elation.

"England!" Julian shouted, standing in his stirrups as though he were greeting the nation, instead of only alarming the coachman and some birds at the roadside. "Dear England! Remember breakfast? No skimpy dry little loaves and a pat of butter with a cup of bitter coffee for us this morning, but porridge and kippers and eggs and rashers of bacon. Real breakfast," Julian laughed, "and real forests, and look there—a magpie! Real birds as well. Travel's enchanting, but maybe mostly because of the way it makes the familiar exotic and so treasured once again. How I've missed all this!''

''And real women?'' Arden asked, bringing his horse up closer.

''Well, you will note,'' Julian said on a grin, ''that I've an Englishwoman with me, as well.''

''A certain dreadful consistency, yes,'' Arden agreed, but more quietly, signaling Julian to hold back his horse so they might speak softly. For here in the early morning the quiet of the country road was complete except for the breeze and birdsong, and the passage of the two riders' mounts on the hard-packed road, and the steady clatter of the four horses pulling the creaking, rattling coach that followed after them.

''I'd not forgot,'' Arden said. ''That's why I wonder if you mightn't think it wiser to take Mrs. Cobb and Francesca to an inn while we visit with Warwick and his good lady,'' and when Julian frowned in incomprehension, he added negligently, ''seeing that your relationship with Mrs. Cobb, though intimate, is an unsanctioned one.''

''Good God, Arden,'' Julian laughed, ''he may be a duke now, but I've known Warwick forever, he isn't the sort to cut up over that, why, he's had far more obvious ladybirds in his keeping before he wed . . .'' His voice trailed off as he fell silent, thinking.

''Precisely,'' Arden said comfortably. ''Wedlock changes everything, and though Susannah is the kindest child in nature, Warwick might not be so forgiving . . .''

''No, you're right,'' Julian answered soberly, ''foreign travel's turned more than my perceptions, it seems to have addled my wits. Continental manners won't do here. One doesn't bring one's mistress to a respectable friend's home, and actually, oughtn't even to mention her in front of his wife. Thank you, Arden, for reminding me. We'll leave them at an inn. Francesca may be blameless, but Roxie . . . I'd not like to see Warwick's face when I introduced her to Susannah . . .'' He grew thoughtful again then.

Arden let the silence ride with them for a few more feet and then asked gently, ''Should you like to stay at the inn with them as well? I've a favor to ask of Warwick, after all. I'd like him to have Francesca stay on with them. It may be they can help her find her proper place in life, preferably a safe and married one.'' He frowned as though he'd found a flaw in this pleasant program, before he recalled himself and went on smoothly, "I know it's been two years since Susannah and Warwick wed, but I needn't mention you're in the vicinity at all, if you'd prefer."

Julian turned a face filled with surprise to his friend. He'd known Warwick Jones, Duke of Peterstow, since his school-days, and had indirectly been the reason Arden had met his best friend two years before. And it was entirely and too embarrassingly true that the only uncomfortable moments he'd had in all his years of friendship with Warwick Jones had been when Susannah Logan had chosen him for her husband, instead of himself. Indeed, the hurt of it was why he'd left England.

But he'd come to see, long after the painful necessity of watching their wedding, that it was his pride that had been hurt the most—and that it had been two friends he'd seen wed to each other, not a lost lover and a friend. For he hadn't really known her. It was true he'd thought he'd loved her once, but then, he'd thought he loved another lady the week before that. Now he saw that he'd loved being in love more, and the thought of seeing Susannah again, happy in her marriage with Warwick, filled him only with purest pleasure. And so he told Arden, seriously. But then he threw back his fair head and roared with laughter, explaining, be-tween chortles, that since Warwick had written that she was increasing now, the picture he suddenly had of himself, lovelorn and sighing, following an extremely pregnant Su-sannah about the house on his knees, amused him enor-mously. That was when Arden relaxed, and, two years after the fact, seeing his friend's genuine hilarity, believed him entirely over whatever had tried him so sorely at last.

They chose a neat inn, the Rampant Rose, and settled the ladies and their maid in it. And as soon as the two gentle-men cleared the dirt of travel from their clothes and faces so they could see their friends with only a single coating of road dust upon them, they rode to the Duke of Peterstow's ancestral home.

Arden whistled as they came up the long drive to the estate. "He inherited more than a title," he said after they'd announced themselves to the gatekeeper.

"But see how he remembers all his old and indigent friends," Julian jested after the gatekeeper got word of their welcome and permitted them entry to the road up to the great house.

"Well," Arden said thoughtfully as they rode alongside green and freshly scythed lawns to the sprawling gray castle, "if he changes his mind, he can always pour boiling oil on us from one of his parapets."

When they arrived at the front door to the great house, they saw a tall, lean figure running lightly down the steps. And so soon as he could, Julian leapt from his horse, and flinging its reins to a stableboy, walked to the gentleman and found himself clasped by the hand, and then by the arm, and then, with a shout of joy, the two men embraced each other and hugged each other hard.

"By all that's holy, it's grand to see you, Warwick," Julian said at last, when he could.

But he spoke to air, for a second later his friend grasped Arden by both shoulders and then those two grinned hard at each other, as well.

The duke was a tall, slender, high-nosed young gentleman with olive skin and nut-brown hair and an arresting face remarkable for its leanness and high cheekbones, and a grandly imposing nose. But withal, it was his heavily lidded knowing sapphire eyes which overrode all else in that elegant countenance, and they were wide and lit with real warmth and delight as he looked upon both of his friends again.

And then he drawled, with all the insouciance and boredom of a man speaking from the depths of his favorite chair at his club, rather than one who'd just danced wildly about his castle courtyard with a friend, "Just in time for dinner. How fine your timing still is, Julian. Come, Arden, we'll slay a fatted calf or two dozen for you."

"Ah, well," Julian said hesitantly, dusting off his knee with his riding gloves so that he could avoid Warwick's eyes, "it's early yet, we're used to Continental hours, can't possibly have dinner until ten. At any rate," he said in heartier accents, "we've only just come to talk, you see."

The duke nodded, and then looked his question to Arden.

" 'Ere, yer grace," Arden explained in the most bucolic of his accents as he shuffled his booted feet and turned his fashionable hat in huge hands, becoming an oafish yokel to the limit, " 'e's left 'is fancy-piece at t'inn, y'see, and she'll 'ave 'is pretty ears on a plate if 'e don't set down to 'is mutton wiv 'er tunnight. So, if it's all the same to you, yer grace, we'll 'ave a bit of a chat-up and we're off, and no one's sensitivities will be knackered, do y'see?"

"Unless he plans to have her for dinner, and on my tabletop at that, I do not see. Go fetch her, idiot," Warwick ordered imperiously.

"But Susannah . . ." Julian protested, and at that Warwick's midnight-blue eyes grew a softened expression, and for a scant second that Arden alone didn't miss, there was a flash of dismay and deep pity to be seen for his blond friend there.

"Never blame the lad," Arden spoke up in his rumbling voice, to dispel that look and that impression, "it was my idea. I thought now you're wed, it wouldn't be at all the thing for us to bring the . . . ah, lady, here."

"Unless she refuses to wear clothes, I don't see why not," Warwick said testily, "and even then, it might be enlivening. My lady's bored to pieces sitting here waiting to hatch out a new duke or duke's daughter, and if she discovered you'd refused dinner with us due to her supposed sensibilities, she'd slay me. Come, come . . . go, go. Turn round and don't dare return until you've got 'the . . . ah, lady' in tow."

"Two ladies: one 'ah' and one a baron's daughter," Arden corrected him.

"Two? In such charity with one another that they'll dine together? Lord, Julian," Warwick said with great admiration, "you *have* acquired Continental manners."

Roxanne trailed into Francesca's room without so much as knocking, but then, Francesca thought, watching the maid they'd acquired in Paris shaking out her gowns, the door *had* been left ajar. And Roxanne was the most casual female she'd ever met. But she'd actually never met a woman who was carrying on an illicit relationship with a gentleman, she realized, and was so enormously proud of her own exquisitely casual handling of it that she often bent over backward to excuse all of Roxie's other *faux pas* and nonsexual misdeeds so the sportive widow wouldn't think her snobbish or prudish or not liberal. She was, of course, deeply shocked by everything she imagined Roxie doing with Julian, but it made her feel extremely worldly not to show it, even to herself.

"If you've time on your hands, Marie," Roxanne said to the maid, "you can give my gowns a good shake-out too. Oh, and an iron run over the red one wouldn't go amiss either. Servants," she sighed, shaking her curly blond head as the maid hastened to her room to do her bidding. "If you don't tell them what they already know, they'd sleep all day and blame you for it, don't you know?"

But Francesca didn't, so she flushed and bit her lip and bent her head over the sundries bag she was unpacking. The girls didn't have personal maids at school, and her father, being a bachelor gentleman, had never had her home long enough to think to hire a lady's maid for her. And by the time he'd realized she was old enough for one, she was either gone back to school or his money had run out.

"I'm not accustomed to servants," she said honestly, when she saw Roxie watching her unpack her toilet items. "Father . . . you know. But did you have many when you were young?" she asked, and then was very sorry she had, for it wasn't likely, she thought, that a woman who'd do what Roxie did would have come from comfortable beginnings.

"Lud, yes," Roxanne laughed. "Ooo, just look at your face! You'd be as bad a gamester as your father! Did you think I was brought up by savages? No, Fancy, I had a grand house and a staff of servants, and that's no rumgudgeon I'm pitching you, it's plain truth. My paw had money, he was no less than a squire, we'd a snug house and a good many acres with it, on the Isle of Wight, as I said. Pretty place, and I lived high. But Gawd, after I was fourteen it was a dead bore. Not too much liveliness there, I can tell you. Teas and tame socials and a church dinner and dance every fortnight, need it or not. My father wouldn't let me go to the dances they had up-island for the naval staff based there, he thought them a ramshackle crew who'd not have much respect for an island girl, however well-off she was. He was a regular old tartar. I had to sneak out many's the night." She laughed. "Lucky thing I had friends whose folks were free traders. We could drift down the road like wraiths and they knew every back track so I could be home without being missed, by dawn . . . *if* I wanted to be," she said with a wink.

"But the old man was right in that, at least," she sighed. "It wasn't marriage they were interested in, no matter how interesting they found me. My father wanted me to marry a neighbor's boy, all teeth and red hair and talk about cows and barley, with turnips thrown in if he felt lively. I don't know what would have happened to me if we'd had to wed. He expected a good, calm, cow of a wife, and I'd already got a taste of the high life. Our wedding night would've been a shock to him right off, if you take my meaning.''

Francesca thought she did, and tried to look as amused as she was supposed to be, while all along she was staggered by Roxie's calm admission. The result, which she caught a glance of in the mirror, made her look as though she'd swallowed something nasty she was trying to proclaim delicious, and she was glad Roxie had a far-off look in her eye, so that she could compose herself again.

''Lucky for me I met Jamie, my dashing Captain Cobb, when he visited with a cousin who was my neighbor. We hit it off like that''—she snapped her fingers. ''What a lark! He was as ripe for mischief as I was. A dark little chap, never such a beauty as our Julian, but well enough in his way, and he understood me down to the ground. I married him to get off-island and he wed me to keep his family quiet about his wild ways and to have a wife who wouldn't hang on his sleeve or cut up his peace. We'd a modern marriage: I had my fun, and he his, and we never let it interfere with our fun together, neither,'' she vowed, as Francesca's eyes widened to huge dark windows of amazed titillation. ''Lud! What times! An officer's wife don't see the fighting, unless it's to keep some gent she don't fancy away from her dance card, and at that, Jamie saw more gaming rooms and assembly halls and bedrooms than he did battlefields, I'll wager. He was a real parlor general.'' She chuckled reminiscently.

''And so we would've gone on,'' she sighed, ''if he hadn't caught a bit of shrapnel fire one day. At least, it was over fast, they said.'' Roxanne went on after what might have been a second's pause for regret, ''And I was just about fed to the teeth with a double-dealing friend of his in Belgium I'd hooked up with when I ran into your papa and his offer of a job of work. Luck's always been with me,'' she said happily, looking to Francesca again.

Francesca waited. For all she'd known Roxie these past weeks, they'd never spoken so long about personal matters until now, and liberal as she wished to be, still she wondered if this sudden chattiness was brought on by the other woman's loneliness or the fact that she wanted something from her. She might not have been out in the world very long, but the girls from school came from that outer world, and so for all her past cloistered life, she knew females very well. It was plain Roxie didn't care for women too much— it was not so much dislike as disinterest—and so, Francesca reasoned, this sudden interest must have a purpose. She waited.

"Has Arden ever talked about me?" Roxanne asked, seizing up a nail file from Francesca's bag and attending to one perfect oval of nail with great concentration.

"Actually, no," Francesca answered, realizing this was so; the only mention Arden had ever made of Roxie was about her experience and situation, but as neither was done in a spirit of censure or praise, it was hard to remember any precise words he'd spoken about her.

"I mean . . . you don't think he don't like me, do you?" Roxanne asked, frowning at the supposedly offending fingernail as she sawed at the side of it. "That is to say . . . ah, might as well come clean," she said, putting down the file before she'd done a damage to her manicure. "I fancy our viscount, you know. And I've certain plans. But the gentlemen place great stock in what their friends say, even the best of them do. So I'd like to know what Arden thinks of me."

"I don't know, really, Roxie," Francesca admitted. "Do you want me to ask him for you?"

"Gawd, no." The blond woman shivered. "He'd know in a second if you did. He's up to all the rigs. If you want to know the truth, that's why I never looked at him twice, not that I'd the heart to after I clapped eyes on Julian. But Arden always makes me feel naked, and not in the nicest way," she added on an uncomfortable laugh. "Not that he isn't an attractive gent in his own way, and I can see what you see in him, but better you than me, Fancy. Don't worry, I'll never try to catch his eye—I don't like having a man know what I'm up to every minute."

Roxanne cut off Francesca's stammered denials of her interest with an amused, "Oh, yes, and the cat's not a bit interested in the cream neither—have it your way. It's no skin off my nose, just let me know if you ever hear something interesting, will you?"

As Roxie prepared to leave, Francesca couldn't help staying her for a moment. She'd not had a close girlfriend to talk with in months, and this rare moment of honesty with Roxie had showed her how much she missed such companionship. She felt bound to try to save the other woman distress. The petite widow's aim might be good, but her target, Francesca thought worriedly, was surely too high. Julian Dylan, Viscount Hazelton, was not a madcap army officer.

He was a nobleman, obviously adrift at the moment, but just as obviously used to a far better life.

"Roxie," she said hesitantly, trying to think of a neat way to put it, "I . . . I don't think Julian's very serious. Indeed, I think the reason they left us here now is so they wouldn't have to introduce either of us to their friends. After all, a duke and a duchess! I'm sure Arden wants to spare my feelings if they refuse me the house room he says he's after for me, and Julian, I expect, wants to prevent you from being similarly snubbed," she concluded, pleased with the clever way she'd hidden the fact that no gentleman she'd ever heard of would dream of taking his mistress into respectable society.

"Of course he's not serious," Roxanne laughed, "and of course, no real well-bred English gent would take his bit o' muslin to meet his decent friends in the *ton*. But I wasn't always his mistress, and I come from a good background too. And he's at a turning point now, and well I know it. Stranger things have happened. Dukes as near to the king as his elbow have wed actresses, taking them right from the stage to the altar at St. George's in London, and earls have brought their housekeepers from their beds to the church. It's not too much to hope a viscount will do as much, believe me. It's their sense of honor, you see," she mused, as though to herself, "that's the key."

She'd thought of it early, and she'd thought on it often. She'd wanted Julian Dylan from the moment she'd seen him, even when she'd thought him only a poor dupe for the old villain of an uncle Arden portrayed. She liked his style, his manner, his easy grace, and his ways in and out of bed. And his looks, of course. Gawd, she thought, those looks of his! It was as well he was used to being watched, for he didn't seem to notice how she feasted her eyes upon him, but then, she was careful about it. She didn't have to gape at him in public; then she could see him by reflection, in the eyes of all the other woman looking at her with envy. And in private she looked her fill when he least expected her to be watching him.

Even at his supreme moments during their bedwork, even then, when most men didn't, he pleased her eye. For he didn't frown or knot up his face, or grow a tight grin, or look angry or in pain as other men did when they struggled to achieve their final interior glory. No, even then, he managed to look even handsomer, for he'd throw back his head and, dazed, look glorified and ennobled, becoming something like pictures she'd seen of saints undergoing religious experiences, dazzling in his pleasure, never looking foolish or ugly. Those were her best moments as well, even when they weren't, and all for the look of him.

She wanted him badly. He mightn't want her now, indeed, she might tire of him in time too—constancy was something she expected of no one, least of all herself. But there was a world of amusement waiting for her off-island, just as she'd always imagined, and Julian Dylan, Viscount Hazelton, would be the perfect companion as she went through it. She didn't know him entirely, she accepted that she might never, for there was, for all his courtliness and charm, a certain coldness at his core, a barrier she always found at the center of his soul. But that was no problem, she didn't ask for his soul; his corporal person, and his name, would be enough for her.

There were more beautiful women, she knew it, but didn't think it vanity to appreciate that few attracted and then pleased men as she did; she considered it her talent. Many other men wanted her, and titled ones too. Even in the hotel they'd just left, there'd been an impressionable young Bavarian *Graf* who'd followed her from Brussels and vowed to follow her to the ends of the earth, and had actually gone so far as the dock at Dieppe to see her off, sullen and cheated by her refusal.

But a Germanic lordlet was never her goal. She'd set her sights high. Julian mightn't want her now, but she'd a plan and a purpose, and so far in her life she'd come far, and would, she vowed, go further. As far as she dreamed. For she believed she sailed through life beneath a lucky star. She'd have Julian as her constant companion and ensure it by becoming his wife. And as to being a viscountess? She grinned at the thought. She'd always liked an extra sprinkle of sugar on her dessert plate.

"Don't worry for me," she told Francesca brightly now. Poor Fancy, she thought, who had so much and didn't have a clue how to use it. "If you care, let me know what you hear. I can fight any enemy I know," she said. "And here," she added generously, "want to borrow that red thing I wear? Marie can let the hem down in a trice."

Francesca searched for words of polite denial, not for the gown, but for Roxie's own sake. She doubted anything but sorrow would come of her obvious plans for Julian. But even as she tried to frame the correct way of putting it so as to spare Roxanne present annoyance with her as well as future heartbreak from Julian, she heard familiar voices calling her and Roxanne. And then a thunder on the stair in the quiet inn translated to the vibrant figures of Arden and Julian, coming to a halt, both winded and both grinning, at her door.

''My ladies,'' Julian said with a deep courtly bow, ''the pleasure of your company is requested at the Duke and Duchess of Peterstow's gracious home.''

''And at once, and with your baggage, and so if you two prime baggages will bestir yourselves,'' Arden added as the two women stood gaping at him, expecting some joke to follow the pronouncement, ''we'll arrive in time for dinner tonight.''

Roxanne recovered quickly. She preened and shot Francesca a triumphant look. Because from the way her luck was running lately, she'd never doubted this moment, or at least never doubted she'd have been asked along, eventually.

But Francesca never noticed it, for in that moment she saw only Arden, as he gave her a slow, strangely sad smile which never reached the resigned expression in his grave eyes. For he'd a favor to ask his old friend Warwick tonight, and the way his luck always ran out, he never doubted it would be granted, not for a moment.

14

ROXANNE WORE a wine-dark gown, and did her hair with garnet ribands, and brushed on only subtle touches of rouge on her cheeks and lips, for she was going to meet the Quality and she knew how she ought to behave. But when a look into her glass showed her a petite and dignified lady who might very well earn the admiration of the gentlemen, but not so much as an urge on their part to tweak any part of her behind the backstairs or give her a second glance in a gaming hell, she perked up her ears with a pair of diamond

earbobs, and set her eyes to sparkling by applying a generous sweep of kohl to her lids and lashes at the last.

Francesca wore her dark-green gown and a faint appre-
hensive smile. She very much wanted the duke and duchess
to like her, but not so much as to offer her a temporary
home. For then she'd only enrage Arden by not accepting
it. She'd known that all along, but all the long ride from the
inn to the duke's home had made it a clear and immutable
fact. She'd decline respectfully but firmly. Not only did she
not want to be anyone's favorite charity, but she'd no wish
to be rescued from what she now found to be her chiefest
joy—Arden's constant company. While the others chatted in
the carriage, she was mute, going over a beautifully phrased
and well-thought-out disclaimer as carefully as any polite
lady might rehearse the way she'd turn down a respected but
unwanted suitor's proposal.

"He *is* a duke now, but though they dine on superior
stuff, I doubt any of them have taken to chewing up young
ladies," Arden said in her ear as they neared the torch-lit
castle. "Even if they did, this one wouldn't, for he has a
very toothsome duchess, you know, and since they've wed,
I hear he's become about as interested in other females as
he might be in lepers. No, I'm out there," he went on when
she didn't answer, "because being a charitable fellow, for
all his sharp tongue, I think he's far more interested in lepers now, actually. You haven't died from the excitement of
it all, have you?" he asked sweetly. "Now, that would flus-
ter even Warwick, if we came pounding up his drive with a
dead lady in tow."

"I don't wish to be an object of his charity," she said
softly and in terse accents, and then wished she hadn't, for
it was but a fragment of her really excellent speech, and it
was far too soon to give it anyway.

But hearing her hoarse, panicked, whispery little denial
quite took his breath away, so Arden merely nodded and
said casually, "Oh, good, alive-alive, oh," and let her alone
until he could recover himself as well.

There ought to have been trumpets, Francesca thought as
the great door swung open and they stepped in to the high-
ceilinged vaulted reception room, and then, divested of their
coats and wraps, were shown the way into the drawing room.
Roxie was breathless with excitement when they were announced, but Francesca only felt a dreary sort of expectant
panic as they stepped in to meet their host and hostess.

But their host was as unexpected a sight to the two women as the bright, warm room they were ushered into. There were highly patterned Turkish carpets and brightly painted yellow and rose-colored walls and ceilings, and the fires and lamps dispelled all shades of gloom in the huge octagonal room. And the Duke of Peterstow was every bit as elegant and suave as Roxie could have wished, but he was young and lean and well-dressed as well, and as he came forward to meet them it could be seen that his heavy-lidded eyes opened upon them to show sympathy and humor and a world of fellow-feeling in his clear dark blue gaze.

"The first time I was shown in here as a youth," he confided to Francesca as he bowed over her hand, "I fully expected to be knighted. Instead I was told to take a seat and a cigar, and was offered a glass of port. I was seven at the time," he mused. "My uncle, the late duke, was a determinedly eccentric fellow. I loved the port, but the cigar . . ." He shook his head and went on to be introduced to Roxanne.

She took the introduction in silence and gave him a dimple for his compliment on her looks, but she broke her silence against her will and better judgment in her surprise when she saw the duchess rise from her chair and come to take Julian's bow and then his hand.

"But . . ." Roxanne blurted as she saw the exquisite white-skinned, flaxen-haired young woman standing next to Julian, the two of them, light and fair and glowing like twin spirits together. "Are you two related then?"

"Ah," Julian said on a deep, exaggerated sigh, "no. But we might have been. Susannah, ah . . . beg pardon, my lady, the duchess broke my heart once upon a time, and look—she does it again now."

He held his hand to his heart and looked so stricken with mock regret that Arden and the duke laughed. Arden laughed with genuine humor. And the duke, with relief and pleasure at his friend's evident recovery, now saw what Arden had seen earlier. For no man who was genuinely heartsick with unrequited love could act it out so well.

"Oh, fie, you're only trying to make me feel better, Julian," the duchess refuted him, "because no doubt you've heard Warwick teasing me. He's constantly going on about me being in danger of being mistaken for one of those new hot-air balloons these days," she complained, raising her chin and trying to look vexed, and failing, for her piquant face was not made for sullen expressions. But there was some truth to what she complained of, for when she crossed her slender arms over her obviously burgeoning midriff, she looked as comfortable as a woman with her arms up on a shelf. She was exceedingly pregnant, Francesca thought nervously, wondering as she always did when she saw such women, what she would do if the lady suddenly decided to deliver herself of a child as well as a laugh.

"But see how you rise to the occasion," her husband commented as Julian immediately began to mutter loudly about challenging him to a duel.

"Never mind those oafs, you look beautiful, my lady," Arden said honestly, taking her hand and smiling down at her as she tilted her chin and looked a bright grin of vindication to her husband before she pointedly turned all her attention to Arden. "Yes . . ." he said consideringly, "even more so now that you've taken lodgers, I think."

"Oh, wretch!" the duchess cried, stamping her foot as her husband drawled, "Careful, my love, don't overdo. Arden's been many things, but never a midwife, I think."

"Now, there you're out," Arden replied, "for my grandmother was one, you know, and I often helped her at her chores. There was once a case of triplets, now—"

"Oh, never say, or it may be," the duchess yelped, and they all laughed together, even Francesca and Roxanne at the last, as they saw that these four people knew each other well, and well beyond the constraints of any formality they'd feared or hoped to find here.

In fact, dinner that night was nothing of the embarrassment Francesca had envisioned, or the ordeal Roxanne had feared it might be. There were laughter and wine and good food and fondness, all the luxury a duke of the realm could offer, and all the warmth of old friends met in peace again. Francesca forgot her personal problems enough to parry with Arden when he joked with her, and as the great table seemed to grow smaller as the night went on and the company drew together, she discovered that the duke and his lady had the same sort of absurd humor she appreciated so much in Arden and Julian. It wasn't long until she was joking with the duke and naming him "Warwick" without a stammer, and siding with Susannah in their teasing, without remembering to call her "my lady" as she did so.

Nor was it long before Roxanne gave up her staid and stiff ways and began to twinkle her saucy replies for Warwick's pleasure, and toss her head when she rolled her eyes in Julian's direction, the company so jovial and down-to-earth that she wasn't afraid to let anyone know just how well they went together and why they did. She was not so at ease with Susannah, never feeling entirely comfortable with any female so beautiful. Even as *enciente* as the lady was, she was surely the feminine equal to Julian's rare and startling beauty. Then too, it was clear from what lay beneath the conversation, and from bits and pieces that she'd gleaned before, that for all his jests, Julian had once thought he loved Susannah. That was enough to make her wary of the exquisite duchess for all time, however kindly a hostess she was. However blatantly expectant a mother the lovely lady was, Roxanne still considered her a potent potential rival. For Roxanne didn't believe in pure friendship between a male and a female, and doubted its very existence, never having known such, and never having wanted it.

So when the ladies rose and left the gentlemen to their port, as was the custom, Roxanne was glad enough to see to her toilette and let Francesca do the pretty with their hostess. Fancy knew where her bread was buttered after all, slyboots, Roxanne thought with admiration as she left for the withdrawing room; just see how the girl was chatting up the duchess, as if she'd borne a dozen brats herself and was eager to talk about it.

But as neither the duchess nor Francesca had yet birthed any babies, they were actually chattering on about something Francesca knew and the duchess didn't. They were speaking of France, which the baron's daughter had seen, and the duchess, as yet, had not. They found themselves amazingly compatible, but then, they were close in age and interest, education, and tastes, for both, it transpired, to Francesca's delight, liked Arden Lyons exceedingly well and appreciated all his many finer qualities.

But for all they gossiped, Francesca became aware that her lovely hostess never spoke about Arden in any detail. The duchess claimed this was because she'd known him for only a matter of weeks before he'd left England. Even if that were true, knowing that he claimed a mysterious and ugly past, Francesca knew she could hardly press the matter, so soon that topic of conversation dried up.

And as Francesca had actually seen very little of France, except in passing, unless the interior of a hotel for gamesters could be called a scenic and cultural topic, that too

soon became an extinct subject. When the duchess asked
Francesca how long she was staying on, and where she
planned to go from Gloucestershire, the dark girl became
so flustered and wretched, and unwilling to commit herself,
that that subject was also swiftly abandoned.

Without barriers, Francesca thought sorrowfully, the
duchess might be a lovely person to speak with. Without so
much that she didn't know if she ought to say, the duchess
thought unhappily, the Honorable Miss Carlisle might be a
charming companion to entertain.

So when the gentlemen joined them, the duke comment-
ing that he cut their time short for fear his wife's time might
be on her by the time Arden and Julian finished telling him
their exploits, the two ladies were sitting, looking rather
sad, and speaking in tentative fashion about baby clothing,
which neither was wildly interested in.

Things enlivened considerably when Roxanne returned to
find the gentlemen returned. As the duchess and Francesca
seemed to have fallen mute, Roxanne had the felicity of
setting the tone of their entertainment. And so instead of
talking, they sang, and instead of recalling the past, they
invented the present and told stories and entertained themselves merrily, but like strangers met to while away the
night, never recapturing the camaraderie of their dinner.
Francesca felt like a reluctant bride on her wedding night
when the duchess pleaded her condition as an excuse for
early bedtime. For the duchess, on a soft word from her
duke as he led her to the stairs, turned and offered to show
her lady guests to their rooms for the night before she retired. Although the gentlemen tried to hide it, they were
obviously vastly relieved. The ladies' absence would give
them the chance to confer long and quietly, as they might
have done after dinner had the duke not been unwilling to
leave his wife alone so long. Even Roxanne, who clearly
would have wished to laugh away the night with them, gave
in gracefully, and rose to be taken to her room.

Francesca left with many a rueful backward glance, if for
different reasons. She didn't wish to entertain the gentlemen, she only didn't want them attempting to settle her
future for her.

"My study, I think," the duke said briskly, when he'd
done bidding his wife good night, promising to come to bed
at a decent hour. "For all my domesticity, that's the one
place that's entirely mine. Mind," he said as he led the

gentlemen to the huge book-lined study made intimate by the staggering number of books that brought the walls inward upon them, and by the two fires burning brightly in the twin fireplaces on either end of the circular room, "it's a bit difficult to stage my orgies properly in here, and the light's more for reading than for a proper nude revel, but I make do. Here, have a seat," he said, dragging another leather chair up to the two arranged near a nicely mumbling fire. "No one will disturb us here unless Susannah decides to add to the company tonight. All my wild stories about the wild revels in here seem to discourage the servants. Or at least," he admitted, smiling gently as he sat in the middle chair, "I like to believe they do."

"You've taken to domesticity beautifully, Warwick," Julian said on a grin. "It's almost as amusing as it is incredible."

"I've taken to Susannah, lad," Warwick sighed, "and I find, like any wolf become a fireside dog, that being tamed is a small price to pay for my content. But one of the drawbacks of that blissful state is that now I have to live my daring adventures through these books, or through more venturesome friends. So not another word from me, gentlemen, until you tell me some of your wilder wanderings. Begin!" he commanded imperiously as his two guests laughed.

But it wasn't long until they did, Julian telling one tale, Arden another. Their adventures, Arden and Julian soon realized, became more amusing with the telling now that they'd lived through them, far better if only because they were more coherent than they had been in the living, and fueled by good port and a receptive listener, the night went by with laughter and thoughtful pauses and storytelling.

When the fire had burned low, they sat in companionable silence until Warwick said softly, "Admirable work. Within, yet without the law. Patriotic yet lucrative. Charitable and clever. Well done, my children. . . . And now? Come, every good saga has an ending sometime. But are your travels ended? I'm more delighted at your return than you can believe, for I've not so many friends that I can afford to have two of the best sort decamping for the Continent and leaving me here to wallow in domesticity alone forever. The best of treats are better shared. As are the most thorny problems."

He grew still, and then fixed his stern blue stare on Arden.

"For example," he said softly, "I understood from your letter that you've a gentlewoman to unload, Arden, but from the looks she bends upon you when she thinks no one watches, she no more wishes to be gone from you than . . . you wish to discomfort her," he finished politicly.

"Do you want me to leave?" Julian asked Arden, half-rising from his chair. "I could go through a charade of yawning, but I'm too tired to act that well, and, well . . . dammit all Arden, but I'd think hard of it if you banished me now. But I'd go," he admitted.

"And listen at the wall with a wineglass at your ear, just as I taught you," Arden sighed. "No, lad, stay. There's little I can say that you don't know, or won't know soon enough, and you've earned the right to my secrets."

"Thank you," Warwick said before Julian could speak. "I'm flattered to know you think I have as well, Arden."

"Ah well, Duke, you're a canny fellow, and I've always admired you. Had I your education, no doubt I could have risen high enough to become a duke myself, sir, but aside from the Bible, they only used books for pressing flowers at the orphanage, you know," Arden said wistfully.

"Arden," Warwick said simply, and only that, and after a moment Arden shrugged.

"My father is dying," he said at length, "the one that conceived me, that is. And I must to Cornwall to add to the lamentations. His, I expect, for I can't for the life of me think of anyone else that will regret his passing."

"And the lady . . ." Warwick prodded, and then paused before he complained, "You know, my friend, unlike you, I've had only one occupation—that of wastrel and gent-about-town. I've never been a tooth drawer. So please, spare me the effort, will you? You told your tales of derring-do in a way to make Mr. Keane weep with justifiable envy, and now, here, I can't get a few decent sentences out of you without cajolery. Coyness does not suit you," he snapped.

"I'd hope not!" Arden said, sitting up straight. "There are few odder sights, I'd imagine, than that of a coy elephant. All right, I'll be brief. I need to find a safe harbor for the Honorable Miss Francesca Carlisle. Her papa's sick unto death with the gambling fever and she's no other family, and thanks to him, no dowry or funds at all, of course. And yes," he said gruffly, staring into the fire, "she thinks she fancies me, but that, of course, only shows how abject and hopeless her position is.''

''Of course,'' Warwick said smoothly, even as Julian did, and though they looked to each other and smiled then, Arden only nodded and went on:

''But she's got good breeding and manners and education and staggeringly good looks, as you can see, even if she's momentarily deprived of good sense. So I'd be grateful if you'd think of some way, somehow she can find her proper place in life and make a good marriage. That's why I've landed on you so precipitately, for all that I love you, and that's why our lovely Julian's returned to England now as well. The boy's a bur,'' Arden said on a sudden thought, frowning. ''You never mentioned that when you suggested I travel with him, did you?''

''Why do you think I offered him to you?'' Warwick asked with even greater pleasure as he saw Julian's mock-affront. ''It was either that or try to pass him off as my shadow, and no one would ever believe I had such a paltry shadow. After all, one's shadow should have even a longer nose than oneself.''

''Quite impossible,'' Arden agreed. ''The poor lad is bereft in that department, obviously.''

Julian ran his finger down his classically perfect nose, and sighing, whimpered something about handicaps. They were all still laughing when Warwick said pleasantly, so unexpectedly that it even took Arden by surprise, so that he almost answered without thinking, ''And so, since it would be far simpler, why won't you take her to wive, Arden? She is, as you say, wholly admirable. Even at such short acquaintance, one can see her quality. She's very beautiful, bright, charming, and most old-fashioned and admirable of all, I'd venture she's a good person, too. So wouldn't that be the simplest solution, especially considering her one aberration—her obviously discernible and wholly unaccountable (to me, at least) prejudice for you? Or do you dislike her?''

''I expect you know better than that,'' Arden said after a pause to get his bearings, hunching his shoulders and sitting forward and shooting a knowing look to Warwick. ''You've a way of seeing around corners. But you're absolutely right and exactly wrong. In either case, it's impossible. Because I know very well that I do not deserve her, it was madness to try to attach her in the first place, and that was before I really knew her or her real place, which would never be with me. And before you hasten with a dozen arguments about my better noble nature et cetera to the point of nausea, as our Julian has been fond of doing, I'll say right off that it's my past—and it's more than you know and more than I think she could bear."

"However much more, I cannot say," Warwick said thoughtfully, "but she'd be marrying what you are now."

"No one weds the present without taking the past to the marriage bed as well," Arden said softly, becoming fascinated by his fingertips, "and, too, I fear the enemies of that past might someday reach out to harm her, the blameless, in order to harm me: the most blameworthy gent you know. For certainly," he said, so low both gentlemen in the room had to listen close to catch the low thrum of his words, "that would be the surest way to destroy me. So it would be a lie to say I don't know fear for myself, because for all I've never minded risking my own thick skin, I'm terrified at the thought of having harm come to her, through me most of all, but in any fashion at all.

"At any rate," he said more briskly, looking up at the duke, "I'm not willing to make that likely. Will you take her to stay with you, Warwick?"

"No," Warwick said calmly, and as Arden looked up in surprise, as did Julian, he added, "not yet. I don't ask to know all of your history, my Lion, but if you grant that I am, as you say, a canny gent, I'd be willing to wager—as willing as the Honorable Miss Francesca's father, and I'm not a gambling man—that the past is not quite what you think . . . if only," he said, forestalling Arden's objections, "because no man's past is just as he remembers it to have been. I won't go on to add that I believe it to be in your case the fault of your greatest handicap of all—that distressing rudimentary conscience of yours. Yes, I've noted it, despite all your best efforts to conceal it from me and yourself. It is that, I think, that makes you see the past differently from what it actually was. Take her with you to Cornwall, Arden. If I'm mistaken, there'll always be a welcome for her here with us. But first, let her see for herself."

"And London as well?" Arden asked with a mocking smile.

"And London," Warwick agreed.

"My London or yours?" Arden asked with a hint of quiet menace that made both his listeners remember how he could inspire fear in men with a single syllable. "Park Lane, Rotten Row, Hatchards, Almack's, and the opera dancers cavorting at the new Drury Lane Theater? Or Spitalfields, Shoreditch, Newgate, and the spectacle of men swinging by the neck at the new Tyburn Hill there?"

"Both," Warwick answered calmly. "You can protect her from everything, I think. Snobbery and thievery both. But with all your bravery, Arden, I wonder if it's fear of facing her judgment that makes you hesitate even as you claim to know what it would be. Could it be fear of her disliking you that you fear most of all, I wonder? Ah, yes," he went on as Arden stared at him, sitting still and alert as he did, "far easier, I'd think, to be noble and leave her all for her sake, although it might wound you and her. But I'd venture it would be even more painful for you to finally have her actually look at you with all the disgust you believe you so richly deserve."

Arden remained silent for a long moment as the last of the wood in the fireplace sighed warning of its imminent death.

"A very canny gent," he breathed at last, and then, fixing Warwick with an amused look, he shrugged.

"So be it," he said. "She's had enough of cowards, I think. Her first love ran off at Waterloo and left her brother to die alone, you see. Perhaps it *would* be better if she could forget me as a bad misstep she almost took than to grieve for the fantasy that might have been." He looked at his host quizzically. "You knew all the while that the certain way to make me do anything would be to call me coward, didn't you?" he asked wryly.

"Say rather," Warwick answered on a little smile, "that I assumed that if you let me live, you'd listen."

And as Arden chuckled, Warwick turned to Julian and smiled at him, but knowing the quality of that smile, Julian braced himself.

"And you, dear Julian," Warwick said sweetly. "Do you wish to leave your guest, Mrs. Cobb, here with me too?"

"Scarcely," Julian said, glancing away to his boots as Arden chortled low. "The entire purpose of our, ah . . . friendship is that she keep me company, you know."

"Oh, really?" Warwick asked with lively interest. "Is that why her title is always prefaced with an 'ah'?"

"You don't approve," Julian said flatly, looking beleaguered, "Why is it that I seem to have suddenly acquired more fathers than even Arden claims?"

"On the contrary," Warwick said, "I approve entirely. A sportive widow is just what you need right now. In fact, she's a perfect 'here-and-now' sort of companion."

"Just so," Julian said, relieved. "She's pretty, and gay as a linnet, and she amuses me. I really don't yearn for impending fatherhood or any sort of permanent arrangement right now."

"The thing that worries me is that she might not realize how fleeting a moment 'right now' with you is," Warwick said thoughtfully.

"I spelled the thing out chapter and verse, so plain that it even embarrassed me," Julian said doggedly. "It's completely a matter of gainful employment. Why, you didn't think I'd be a cad about it?" Julian asked in amazement.

"Lad," Arden said as Warwick poured himself another glass of port to drown his rising laughter in, "it's never your taking advantage of the lady we'd fret about."

"I am nine-and-twenty," Julian said haughtily, and with some real annoyance, "just as old as you are, Warwick, I remind you. And only a few years junior to you Arden. I don't know why you both worry over me as though I were an infant or a mindless clot."

His two friends looked at him as he rested his chin on his hand and looked sullenly into the dying fire. The glow of it fell on the planes of his face and form, causing his slightly overlong golden hair to seem to frame that beautiful but masculine countenance like a nimbus, and outlining his muscular form so as to set it off like a freshly cut marble representation of a sulking young athlete beloved of some god, or goddess, posed on his pedestal.

"It's because you're so damnably . . . collectible, Julian," Arden finally said on a sudden inspiration.

"Just so!" Warwick exclaimed. "That's it exactly. You are, you know, eminently so, Julian. And we'd rather, when the inevitable time comes and you decide to deprive the females of the world of your random attentions in order to concentrate on just one supremely lucky lady, that it be your choice, and not your trap, do you see?"

But then the duke could not see very much himself, as his golden friend lofted a chair pillow at him. Warwick roared with laughter as he dodged it, as Arden joined in, until the viscount grew a shamefaced, understanding smile as well.

"And now," Warwick said, stretching and yawning, "to bed, I think. If you'd rather, I'll look the other way and you can nip into your 'ah, lady's' room tonight, Julian. You can take advantage of my kindly offer only for a few more weeks, mind, because when I have a child about the place, no doubt I'll not let you so much as kiss her hand, in the garden, in the dead of winter, and in the dark of night," he said, his head to one side as he thought on it, "and at the eclipse. For I intend to be an uncommonly moral papa, the irony of it is too delicious to pass up. But you may visit her tonight, if you tiptoe," he offered as they all rose and went to the door of the study.

"No, thank you," Julian said loftily. "A duke's house is no place for fun, and well I know it."

"Indeed not," Warwick replied, nodding vigorously.

They parted at the top of the stairs, on a handshake all around, but Warwick walked Arden to his door, as Julian went off to his room alone.

"Arden," the slender nobleman said seriously, and in a whisper, as they paused in the variable light of a wall lamp, "Arden, my wise friend," he said gently, "only remember, if a man cannot come to terms with his past, he can't enjoy the present or hope to find peace in the future. And you deserve all that, whatever you insist on believing."

"But, Warwick, my clever lordship," Arden said in his rich and velvet undervoice, "I have come to terms with it— that's precisely the problem."

"Is it? Have you? I wonder," the duke mused, "if only because I wonder if you've ever seen it clear. A man may get so far from a thing that he needs help in seeing it. There are spectacles to use for the printed word, but only fresh eyes will do for the past. Take her with you, Arden. Even if you're right, it will do no wrong just to look."

"Isn't that what Pandora said?" his friend asked with a smile so filled with bitterness that it could even be seen in the diminished light. He sighed before he said, "Yes. All right. Let be. Have done. I shall. Damn you . . . your grace."

"Do you know," Warwick said, enchanted, "all the rigmarole and pomp and nonsense involved with acquiring the title is well worth it when I hear you speak like that."

It was as well that no defenders of rank were present in

the hall to see the huge man give the duke a single buffet on the shoulder, but it was a measure of his control and aim that the duke only laughed, and gave back as good as he'd gotten before the two parted for the night, in charity and in complete understanding.

"Warwick?" the duchess murmured sleepily when she felt the light weight settle beside her in bed.

"I should hope so. Whom were you expecting?" he chided softly, gathering her in his arms as much as her bulk would allow, stroking her hair, and giving her a light kiss on the brow before he admonished her. "You ought to be asleep," he whispered, "and for all I've never held with the nonsense of separate bedrooms for fashion's sake, perhaps you'd be better off if I made my bed in the old duke's room until you've done with all this breeding nonsense."

"Oh!" she cried, struggling up from a comfortable sleepiness to alarm, as she sat up. "Do I . . . does the sight of me distress you? For if it does, then I understand, and by all means—"

"By all means you are an idiot," he said on a smile, holding her and calming her. "It was for you, my dear fool. I'd prefer to stay here with you if you grew to Arden's size and I had to sleep on the floor. Rest easy, Sukey, and hush now, go to sleep if you want to produce a nice plump new Jones for me."

"Warwick," she asked drowsily against his chest, "Julian is over me now, isn't he?"

"I'm sorry, my love, but he seems to be, although I can't understand it."

"Good," she breathed. "And I'm glad you don't understand it too." Then she asked softly, "He's not interested in that . . . ah, Mrs. Cobb, is he?"

"No," he replied, grinning at the widow's commonly used impromptu title, "except, ah, for obvious temporary reasons."

"Good again," she sighed. "He deserves far better. And Arden," she asked with interest, growing more wakeful as she gossiped, finding tattle more diverting than sleep, "what seems to be the problem there? Francesca is the dearest girl, she's a delight and just right for him."

"And so she may be, yet," he said.

"Such good news tonight then," she said on a wide yawn, "because for all he's always gone on about his wickedness, he's never shown anything but a kind face to us."

"But he has many faces, love, and he does not always lie, in jest, or not. Still, any man may walk a higher path; there'd be no point to redemption, else. Why, look how I've reformed. I scarcely recognize myself—doting husband, preparing to be an absurdly proud father. If I weren't enjoying myself so much, I'd quite disgust myself. And now," he said firmly as she tried to conceal another yawn with her giggle, "not another word. Sleep now . . . time for chatter in the morning."

But for all she smiled, nodded, and laid her head down and began to drift off again, it was her husband who spoke again, fretfully, as he lay on his back and held her close with one arm around her, his hand resting on the immense satiny bulge that separated them as he stared at the ceiling of the moonlit room.

"The best things are worth waiting for," he sighed, as though to himself, as the expanse beneath his hand surged to one side at his touch.

"The babe is coming soon," she murmured, feeling his large hand rise to trail up over her swollen breast, hesitate, and then leave it to circle a caress upon her smooth shoulder instead.

"I wasn't talking about the baby," he said with enormous sorrow.

Understanding, she gurgled with delighted laughter, and circling her arms about his neck, breathed "Thank you" and a light kiss into his ear before, smiling, she finally went to sleep.

15

THE MORNING came too soon for Francesca. She dressed before her maid had rubbed the sleep from her own eyes, and then saw those eyes widen when the girl tiptoed into her new mistress's room to waken her, only to find her already washed and gowned. Even though Francesca knew she'd never win a servant's respect that way, she'd little concern for it; she was far too anxious to know what had happened in the night she'd just tossed and turned her way through. And so when her maid answered the door and took the message, and told her that her presence was requested in the morning room, Francesca leapt up and came down the stairs so quickly she almost collided with the large gentleman standing there waiting for her.

"We keep running into each other." Arden smiled. "Fortunately for me. But I thought you mightn't know where the morning room was after I'd found it myself—this house is handsome, but it's a regular warren. Warwick's children will be able to play champion games of hide and seek, and woe betide their nurse when it's time to give them a bath. I had to speak with you," he said more seriously, and she was glad she was at his side and not before him then, for she was sure her face would have told him her terror at his words.

Even when they'd reached the privacy of the morning room, she avoided his eye, and looked around the pleasant room instead, and out the windows to the lawns, and only turned her eyes to him at last when he looked away from her. He wore traveling clothes, she noted with a sinking heart as she gazed at him with fear and longing. Aside from his gleaming white shirt, he was all in earth colors today, with a snug-fitting fawn coat that clung like the bark of a sturdy tree to his wide shoulders and long back, and dun pantaloons, and high brown boots, and a scarf knotted about his powerful tanned neck. A deceptive man, looking as solid and rudely healthy as a great oak, rough-hewn and hearty, although the tawny eyes that turned to her before she quickly looked away again were keen and clear, as sensitive as any poet's.

"I must leave after breakfast," he said at once, "and as I suspected, I'm pleased to report that my friend the duke has gladly offered you the use of his home, and extended his hospitality and friendship to you for so long as you may need it. You got on well with Susannah—the duchess," he said, "and as she's soon to be brought to bed with their child, obviously she'd like company and would welcome yours, so you ought never to feel you're imposing. You'd likely be doing her a kindness by staying on with them, in fact."

For all of the beautiful Susannah's friendship and charm, Francesca couldn't see that this last was so. It had seemed to her that all the duchess needed was her duke, and from the way he gazed at his wife, he was hardly likely to let her out of his sight for more than three minutes together until she was brought to bed with their baby. But she didn't doubt her welcome, nor their sincerity—all of their sincerity—she thought as her eyes filled despite her best intentions, and only her anger with her weakness at this crucial moment saved her from the resolve-sapping, easy tears of self-pity.

"But the duke and I spoke long into the night," Arden said, "and he feels, as you've seemed to, that you should have the right to judge me for yourself, rather than judging my estimate of myself . . . if only for your future peace of mind. Although I believe eventually there'll be only one and the same conclusion reached, for you don't lack sense. Still, the sum of it is," he said quickly, "that if you'd like to come with me to Cornwall, you are welcome."

She stopped breathing and then blurted, "But do you want me to?"

He could scarcely say what he didn't know. He wanted her to come with him more than he could recall wanting anything in a life filled with want. But he also didn't want her to, and never wanted her to think he needed her to. He answered the only way he honestly could.

"If you wish to," he said.

"Beware of highwaymen," Warwick Jones, Duke of Peterstow, told them, smiling as he bade them farewell.

Arden nodded, grinning widely, and swung up on his horse as Julian, who'd demanded to drive their coach, taking the ribbons from a scandalized coachman muttering about nobility and their mad starts, saluted him with his right hand, and then, cracking the whip he held in it, they were away.

"Don't fret," Roxanne said comfortably, sitting back in the coach and relaxing, "Julian's an excellent whipster. Why, he told me that he actually drove a public coach once, and not just for the lark, as drunken bucks sometimes do on a spree for the price of a bribe to the coachmen. No, he was down on his luck once, and actually did it to earn his living. Amazing, isn't it," she said wonderingly, "but then, that's our viscount, isn't it? He's never the one for the formalities, is he?"

Understanding that Roxanne was now collecting tales of Julian's eccentricities to buoy her hopes with, the way that other females collected stories of their gentlemen's daring or cleverness to fuel their love, Francesca could only nod agreement. But even if she were told that the Viscount Hazelton had once worked in the fields as a farmer, still she didn't believe he'd ever marry Roxanne Cobb. Not that she doubted he wouldn't fly in the face of convention if he'd a mind to—he and Arden and their friend the Duke of Peterstow all seemed to be men with their own strong minds. They'd all spurn society's highest rulings if it suited their purposes; perhaps that was the very reason the three wildly disparate gentlemen were friends. She believed it a further measure of their individual power and charm that, whether they cared to or not, they'd all still likely get society to accept it, if they wished, as well.

But it was obvious, at least to her, that Julian didn't feel any of the emotions toward Roxanne that were necessary for any form of matrimony—he didn't appear to love, need, or prefer her to all other females; he didn't require her money, opinion, or friendship, either. And though, of course, she didn't know, or care to know, what happened when the bedroom door closed on them, she'd never seen a glance or touch or word from him to the blond widow at any other time to signify that he enjoyed her company in any but the lightest way.

But telling Roxanne that would only net her a sharp retort, or a knowing wink, or some sly sexual innuendo about her own inexperience in such matters. And, Francesca conceded as she sank back in the cushions for the long ride to the Cornish coast, that was true enough. For Roxie could very easily end up the Viscountess Hazelton, with seven beautiful blond children, and she herself could end her days as a companion to the beautiful duchess of Peterstow, and Arden could take to the sea as a pirate, and then her imaginings finally ebbed into a dream of red gowns and green parrots and rolling waves that carried her off into a day of sleep as her uneasy pillow had not in the night, as the coach rocked on down to the southern finger of the kingdom.

They stopped for a light and hasty luncheon on the road, and pressed on again, with little laughter and conversation now, as though they all realized as the time passed that they raced against the night as well as the possible end to a man's life. Arden mightn't speak about his father, nor seem to value him much, but he was hastening to a deathbed, and the fact of it seemed borne in on them as the coach rattled on, Julian bent on driving all the way, Arden pushing his great horse onward alongside the coach.

Though night came later with each soft evening at this time of the year, still it was velvet dark when they stopped at last at an inn on a rocky crag near to the unseen, but faintly heard nearby sea. They ate their dinner with little enthusiasm, for Francesca's head ached trying to think of a thing to say to Arden. He sat in uncharacteristic silence and thought, and toyed with his food, and looked up now and again with what appeared to be a hint of a reassuring smile when he saw her disquiet. That is, whenever he returned from wherever he'd roamed in his mind, and blinking, remembered her, as well as where he was. Julian was physically weary unto death from holding a team of four spirited horses together, after years of not doing so. He'd driven them hard as he'd pushed himself, and once had even helped to change the team in his impatience with the ineptitude of the stable crew at the posting inn near to Bristol.

Only Roxie was in high spirits, but was wise enough to mute her gaiety until she reached the bedroom she was forced to share with Francesca that night. She'd have preferred sharing her quarters with Julian, of course, since there was no one there starched up enough to chide them for it, she told Francesca merrily. But as there were only the two decent bedchambers available, she could hardly ask Arden to sleep in the barn, or suggest that Francesca kip in with him instead, could she? Or could she? she giggled when alone with the dark-haired girl.

But she was content to pass an undemanding night by sharing a feather bed with another female for once, she laughed. Francesca washed and dressed herself for the night, their maid having gone to her quarters in the attics. As she climbed in beneath the coverlets with Roxie, the widow continued to prattle on about her great good luck so far— even though she primely detested the countryside . . . still, once this visit was done, there'd be London, and London would be splendid with Julian, wouldn't it be? . . . and so then it was all worth it, wasn't it?—and Francesca fell asleep nodding agreement to any and every thing she said.

He knew it was real by the scent of it, long before his eyes told him so. The slight salt tang had got stronger as they'd gone on, and now, even as he began to recall that particular ancient tree, that singular-shaped rock, that road with its same cracked milepost, Arden knew he was back to where he'd never wished to return.

The direction they needed to take from this crossroad bore off to the right, but it was the last direction he wished to ride in. And so, never believing he could be a coward, and with no one who knew enough of the land to accuse him of being so, he signaled to Julian to turn the coach to the left—to the left, where his home was—to the left, where he might get word of a respite or even a reprieve. For the old man might have already died.

But he really didn't believe that. Knowing the old man, he knew he'd keep breathing until Arden came to his bedside . . . no, he'd never leave his son's life as easily as he'd given it to him.

Still, Arden lived in hope, he'd had to before, he would again, and he'd a warm welcome coming where he rode now. He wondered, with a stab of guilt, how Francesca would see these simple people he'd soon take her to meet. And then, he laughed to himself, albeit grimly, for, he thought, if these decent people dismayed her, then he might as well have Julian take her right back to Warwick, for they were the best of all the wretched life he was about to unfold to her. And, too, he knew he couldn't continue to worry about her reaction. He'd claimed he'd known what it would be, after all. Warwick had been right in that now he only had to face the enactment of what he'd foreseen in his mind those days ago in France—and those years ago when he'd left here. Even then, he rode away knowing that someday, someone he might come to love, or respect, might have to face what he'd left.

Still, he was well used to pain of every sort, and better equipped than most to handle it. He was, after all, just as he'd been told since he could toddle, a big boy now. Big boys had to develop patience and fortitude as quickly as they grew. They had to grow thick skins in every sense, as well as long tempers, and train themselves in the use of clever words and sly innuendos even as the weakest boy might do, instead of using threats and main force—if they wanted to keep the approval of their elders. And that approval had always mattered to Arden Lyons.

One hurt look from his mother had hurt him far more than all the blows and words from other boys. One harsh word from her husband could cut him to the quick, for John

Dahl was a decent, fair man, and neither praised nor punished without a good cause.

But sometimes he'd forgotten, because when still a boy, he'd sometimes acted as one. He was seven when he gave up that childhood and accepted all the burden of manhood, along with his size and condition, and it was pain that taught him how to best of all. Because as he'd lain in his bed that night aching from the thrashing John Dahl had given him, the look his mother had given him when she'd guessed the reason for his crime and punishment caused him even more suffering. Then he knew that although Tom, Bob, and Jed richly deserved what he'd done to them, and they'd been three to his one, he was three times their size and so shouldn't have taken his revenge so swiftly, openly, and stupidly. Even though they'd earned every bruise he'd dealt them.

For they'd taken pains to ensure that he knew just who everyone knew his father was. And then, though he'd suspected it and hardly cared, under the guise of further friendly revelations they'd taken great care to describe exactly how such wonders were achieved. And though, being a farm lad, he'd already a fairly good idea of that as well, they'd made sure to describe precisely which parts fit where. It was going on to detail specifically what his mother had permitted to be done to her, and where his putative father had placed his hands and person in and upon her in order to produce him, that had been their greatest mistake, and had led to his. Although they were slow and stupid village lads and would only nurse their wounds and grievances, as he lay in bed that aching night, he profited from his mistake.

He'd learned many things that day, and the least of it was that a larger boy couldn't take revenge on a smaller one, however provoked. Having seen the sorrow in John Dahl's eyes even more than he'd felt the strap, he learned the necessity for keeping his temper in check, for good men, he saw, hated to give pain even if it was easy for them to do. Most of all he'd discovered, as he lay abed with his flesh singing from the strapping he'd won for his victory, that certain victories were never worth the winning. Because no physical pain could compare with the pain of hurting the ones you loved.

It had been a day for superior education. He'd concluded that he'd have to discover less obvious means to wage his

wars and win his victories in the future. And he'd understood that if he couldn't defend a thing properly, he'd have
to hide his preference for it, lest it be endangered.

Now, riding down the lane to the neat cottage so familiar
in his memories, he felt all his boyhood lessons borne in on
him again. When the tall woman came to the door of the
thatched house to see the great coach pulling to a stop, and
then flung up her hands and called back into the house, he
held himself in check and waited, and practiced all the con-
trols he'd learned here, and found it was hard, even now,
even so.

When the old man came out, pipe in hand, and looked to
the coach, and then to the huge man on the horse, Arden
finally let slip his reins, and slid from the horse, and went
to the man and embraced him, and neither laughed then,
nor wept, but only sighed, for by so doing he embraced all
that he'd left here so long ago.

He stepped back from the man and looked up to Julian
and signaled him down. The fair-haired nobleman relinquished the reins at last to the coachman and joined them.
Then, after a word from Arden, Julian assisted the two ladies from the coach and they all stood before the cottage,
and Arden introduced them all around. He made the viscount, Francesca, and Roxanne known to a tall rawboned
red-headed woman, introducing her as "my sister Moll";
and the shorter, darker, auburn-haired woman who quickly
joined them "my sister Alice"; and a plump ginger-haired
older woman was "my sister Betty"; and the last woman to
come hurrying from the cottage, wiping her hands on her
apron, a heavyset one who looked senior to all the rest, was
"my sister Jennie." Their eyes widened at the viscount, but
as ever, it was hard to say whether it was at his title or
himself. But after eyeing the two ladies with fascination,
they curtsied as though they'd been introduced to royalty.
Roxanne lifted her chin and nodded regally, and Francesca,
containing her surprise, smiled and held out her hand in
return.

Only then, the old man, slight, stooped, so shrunken with
age his bald head came only to Arden's cravat, his weath-
ered skin so seamed he looked as though he'd been left in
water too long and then dried out in the sun, was presented
to them proudly as "my father, John Dahl."

The viscount didn't so much as blink at any new name
concerning his friend; instead, he proffered his hand and

said on a wide smile, "I'm more pleased than you know to meet you, sir. We traveled as though the devil was on our trail, and I'm glad the rumors were wrong. It's good to see you've recuperated."

"Thankee, my lord, but I've not sickened," the old man answered slowly.

"My friend has you confused with my father," Arden explained to the old fellow.

"Ah, well, there you're in good time, but only just," John Dahl said worriedly. "They say he's sinking, but he calls for you, lad. You ought to hurry now, or you have wasted your trip entirely. It's a wonder he's lasted this long. The drinking, they say, and that with the life he's led, and the rage he flew into at the viscount. He fell over and'll never rise again, they say. But he calls for you."

Arden's face grew still and cold. Francesca had never seen him looking so impassive.

"The lassies can stay here with us," the old man volunteered. "Your friend as well. They're welcome," he said as the women ranged around him nodded, and the senior one Arden had named Jennie agreed, "Aye, more than welcome, the men are in the fields but all will be back tonight. You'd be more than welcome."

"I thought to settle them at the Ark, if it still stands, for it was a tolerable inn, before we came back to visit," Arden replied, "because they've traveled hard these past days. My friend the demon coachman here made it in two days instead of three, all the way from Gloucestershire. They'd appreciate a bath and a lie-down on a bed that don't rattle and sway, before all else, I'd think. And," he added, grinning, "I'm sorry, but the beautiful young gent, my sweet sisters, would no more let me go off by myself than fly. I've hired him on as bodyguard," he confided, "to keep the ladies away—they swarm around me even more now, if that's possible," he sighed, "since I've made my fortune. Aye, and I have. And besides, Jennie, my pretty, can you see Jim's face when he comes home from an honest day's work to find you lounging about the parlor with a prime article like yon blond Adonis? Ho," he said over all their laughter, " 'you'd be more than welcome,' indeed! Poor Jim! You've not changed, have you minx?" he asked as Jennie put her hands on her hips as though to face him down, but then fell silent and colored up like a girl as Julian smiled at her and said earnestly, "Ah

. . . but don't you think you could go on alone—just this once, Arden?''

And so Arden must actually be his name, Julian mused as he resumed the coachman's seat and they prepared to leave again after giving assurances they'd be back with the night. Or at least, he thought with interest as he gave a light flick of the whip to his weary left wheeler's ear so that the great gray horse and his yoke-mate could move up on the leaders and they could begin to move the coach out and down the road again, Arden must be one of the real names one of his fathers had given him.

Arden said nothing as the coach slowed and came to a halt in the wide circular drive. He'd spoken little since they'd left the Ark, and Francesca and Julian, who sat to either side of him, exchanged a look at each other then. In that mutual look they'd seen as well as sensed that they both felt the same—as though they were in fact the bodyguards he'd jested about. For each felt the same sort of alert and edgy protectiveness toward Arden. His distraction and tension communicated itself to them, and seeing no danger, but feeling it all around them, they unconsciously closed ranks around him.

Roxanne had been only too glad to remain at the inn; the thought of meeting another bucolic gent, father to Arden or not, left her unmoved. But she'd have done anything Julian approved, and so his suggestion that she rest and repair her looks had worked so well there'd been no need for him to have issued it as the order he would have if she hadn't complied. Though Arden himself hadn't barred Roxanne, nor even seemed to note her existence since they'd left John Dahl's farm, Julian decided that Arden's life shouldn't be open to her.

Francesca had said only, "Please, may I come?" and when Arden had nodded, had pleaded one moment to remove the dust from her clothes. She'd been as good as her word, and had returned to the common room as quickly as they themselves had after refreshing themselves. But Arden had done it all in silence, washing, changing his shirt, tying a new neckcloth, brushing back his thick and springy hair, all as if by rote, the way, Julian noted uneasily, he always did before he went into danger.

Now, in front of the great rambling gray manor house, Arden smiled at last.

"My real father lives here," he said. "Now, children, you'll see why I've invented so many others for myself. Any of them would be preferable, actually"—he shrugged—"but a man can't choose who pushes him into this life, any more than he can who pushes him out of it. Come along, then, if you wish. 'The play's the thing,' but 'judge not the play before the play is done . . . ' '' he quoted, "and if 'the last act crowns the play,' as they say," he added on one last look to Julian, and one long, sad one to Francesca, "it ought to be, if nothing else, entertaining."

And then because he could say no more, or do no more, and because he'd given his word that the beautiful dark lady could see and judge for herself, and as he trusted Julian to always do the kind, if not the right thing, he left his two guests to the hands of the fates, and girded himself. And left the coach at last.

"Sorry, Hopkins," he said to the butler at the front door, "but I've guests today, so I won't be coming in the servants' entrance with all my brothers and sisters."

"Good afternoon, Master Lyons, his lordship has been asking after you, it's good to see you again, sir, it is," the old man said, leaving off his official air, and, taking the hand Arden offered, and shaking it sincerely, added, "for myself as well as for his lordship, sir, believe me."

"Thank you, Hopkins," Arden said gently, but then, his voice growing cold, he added, "Please tell the earl that I'm arrived, but add that I've brought two friends: the Viscount Hazelton and the Honorable Miss Francesca Carlisle. And inform my father, if he's still in good enough case to hear, that if they aren't welcome, I shall judge that I'm not."

"Oh, never fear, Arden," a slurred voice said bitterly, "you could have come with a detachment of Spanish guer-rillas or some of your London scum, and the old man would welcome you. He hangs on to life only in the expectation of seeing you. 'He'll never come,' I told him. 'Shut your gob,' our lovely father spake, 'he'll come. I asked it of him.' The old fiend's a better judge of character than I thought. But then, he told me I was a worthless cur, and he's the right of that too."

"My lord," Arden said, eyeing the tall thick-set older gentleman who stood in the doorway to the drawing room, watching them, the decanter in his hand verifying the state of the man who held it, "how are you keeping?"

"Oh, well, well, considering," the man laughed. His

thinning hair and blurring jawline gave as much mute testimony to his condition as the burgeoning belly the fashionable tight clothes he wore could scarcely conceal. He was some decade older than his guest, and tall, but not so broad as Arden; he was drunk, but not so foxed that he could not sneer and speak clearly as ever. He looked Arden up and down, ignoring the others, as he added, "Considering that I shall be an earl within hours, and then will be able to toss you out whenever I choose."

"I don't choose to be here now, my lord," Arden said softly. "You, of all people, ought to know that."

"So you say, dear brother-by-blow," the gentleman laughed, "so they all say—all the stableboys and farmhands and kitchen help and ruff and scruff of the countryside my father has amused himself by dragging before his dying eyes in the last weeks. But they come, hat in hand, hoping for something, and it's not his final blessing, I'll swear. All his get, all his bastard sons. To show what a man he was? No, Arden-got-lightly, never think it, rather to show me how little he thinks of *me*."

"And your brothers, Lord John and Lord Robert? And your sister, Lady Millicent?" Arden asked.

"John trembles. Robert prepares for the worst. Rightly so, they leave with the coffin, just as they fear. Millie has her own home, and much she cares. But the rest of you will clear out then too, my legitimate brothers as well as all you bastards, and none of you with anything but his final curse— that's all he's got for any of us. Although I, as firstborn, take the prize away—this house, his name, whatever's left of his fortune," the gentleman said.

"And welcome to it," Arden replied softly.

"Ah, yes, you've funds now, I hear," the gentleman said, and then, frowning, added, "You left in your pride and came back with a fortune. Get on with it then," he said angrily, "and let me know when he gives notice to quit. I wouldn't miss it for all the world," he said, laughing again as he retreated to the library.

The staircase wrapped around the great hall, and as they ascended, Francesca gazed around herself. Without having heard any titles given, she'd have known she was in a noble house. Nothing they passed was new, but nothing, from the furniture to the myriad paintings hung upon the stretched-silk-covered walls, was anything but of the finest. Julian walked silently beside her, gazing around as well, as Arden took the stairs in their lead. But when they'd gone down a long hall studded with immobile footmen, and paused at last at a door, Arden knocked upon it, and absently took up Francesca's hand. Then, as though startled from his interior musing by how cold that delicate hand was, he smiled down at her, and tucking her hand entirely within his, he placed it on his arm, and after they'd been bidden to enter, walked in with her, his warm palm still sheltering and keeping her as close as his own right hand.

It was a huge bedroom, dominated by the great canopied bed. The man who lay in the center of it would have been the focus of the room even if he weren't propped up on several pillows, even if it weren't for the doctor hovering near him, the tall, plain-faced woman seated at his bedside, and the servants grouped nearby, waiting for any order. He didn't look as though he was dying. He was, or would be, tall, if he stood, for he took up a great deal of bed. His hair was white and his complexion, once tanned, was the yellowed shade such skin turns when the touch of air and sun fades from it. But there weren't many wrinkles on the long aesthetic face, and he radiated command and awareness, and the bright eyes were alert and clever. And when they turned to the door, it could be seen, clearly, that they were the same glowing hazel as the pair that gazed steadily at him from the doorway.

"Arden!" the plain-faced woman said with apparent relief as she began to rise, and no sooner had Arden smiled and replied, "Millicent, my dear," then, "Arden! My Lion!" the old gentleman cried, interrupting them, only his breathlessness between words giving the hint of his true state of health. "You've come."

There was such glad welcome in the old face, such a world of joy and pleasure in the hasty words, that both Julian and Francesca looked to each other again. This lean old gentleman was giving Arden the sweetest welcome any son could ask, and yet Arden looked down at him coldly as he entered the room, as if he gazed upon a serpent on a rock, not a sick old gentleman upon his pillows.

"I knew," the old man said on a laugh as Arden didn't reply, "that you'd want to be in at the kill, if only . . . if only"—he paused to get his breath—"to be sure I was done for. Wise lad." He nodded. "You know me well."

And so he did, Arden thought, looking at his father, and wishing he could feel even so much as hate now, instead of this drear numbness. But he could summon up nothing but thoughts of the dead and all that was dead and gone as he looked upon the still-living man.

He'd come to this house and met this man decades ago, on the occasion of achieving his first full decade of life. But he'd known the man the moment he'd set eyes on him. For he'd seen him before, many times. This was the man who had watched him from his horse as he'd played in the street, this was the gentleman they all bowed down to in town, the one who asked the schoolmaster after him, the one who'd watched him with opaque eyes and not so much as a muscle twitching whenever he'd seen him about the town, about the woods, or on the road. This was the man who owned everything for miles about, in property or persons. This was the man they all said was his father, the one that had made his mama an outcast even among her rough fisherfolk kin, the one who'd made her bear the Earl of Oxwith yet another of his bastard children, so that she'd be grateful for the rest of her life to the man who'd wed her honestly, three years later. She'd been nineteen on her wedding day.

It seemed to Arden that he'd hated this man forever. He hated him for all the taunts from other children, despised him for all the other hapless children who'd been pointed out to him as his brothers as they worked in nearby fields or held the gentlemen's horses, or swept out the stables, as well as for his three legitimate brothers whom he'd no right to address, and who'd never addressed him because they hated him perhaps even more in their turn. He'd hated him for every outsize thing about himself, for there were no such giants in his own house. The slight widower John Dahl had brought three children with him to his wedding, none Arden's size, and his mama and John had yet more, none Arden's size. Yet for all he hated him, he'd come here on his tenth birthday, to stand before him, his hat, before him, in his hand.

Arden's mother had him dress in his finest, and she'd gone with him to the great house, and it was the first time for both. For she'd met her noble lover in the fields, and been wooed by him by the shore and by the hedges, and conceived their son in the forest, and had never set foot within doors with him in all the time they passed together. Now, eleven years and four legitimate children later, she would at last stand beneath a roof and speak with him, because she knew she had to do so.

John Dahl knew it too, although he'd cursed his own circumstances for it, and had slammed out of the little cottage
the night before, and paced the night away, passing the night
without his wife for the first time since they'd been married
because of it. And all for his sake, Arden had thought in
shame. And all despite his protests, for his mother was resolved.

"He shall not go wasted," she'd said to John Dahl. She'd
stood tall, and she was a sturdy red-headed lass, and even
if her husband had not adored her he would have had to
admire her. After five children and the years as a farmer's
wife, the only hint of the wild young sprite she'd been was
in her wide dark eyes and flaming hair. But she still had a
way about her, and dressed up a treat, and she knew her
worth as she stood in her plain shoes and her best dress and
planted her feet apart and looked straight at the smiling lord
she'd given herself to all those years ago, not recognizing
anything but the clever glinting hazel eyes now, and that
perhaps only because she saw them each day in his son's
face. She was no longer the girl she'd been; he was, to her
older eyes, now clearly what he'd always been—a cold and
cynical gentleman who loved making love, and who took
the same effort to strew children about the countryside that
her own honest John took to set out his vegetable seed in
the springtime fields. So, too, his harvest was for his pride,
and to flaunt in his lady-wife's eyes. That was why he received her here this day, and his lady locked herself away
abovestairs, again, as she did every day until she died.

For the earl had found a way to make his indiscretions
work for him years after he'd committed them. A parade of
chance-got children came through his ancestral home, it was
always open to them, so long as they came in the servants'
entrance and never looked him directly in the eye. The
Countess of Oxwith would always regret her lack of appreciation of her husband's marital favors.

Arden had watched his mother closely that day, both appalled and proud of her nervous but bold insistence.

"The schoolmaster says he's taught him all he can. He
can cipher and read and write. He's sharp. And the schoolmaster says it would be a waste to let him linger on the
vine. He's got quality," she persisted, her face flushed to
the memory of the breathless, lovely child she'd been that
brief summer, for she was unused to begging favors. She'd
never asked him for anything since the boy had been born,

and had sent back the money he'd sent to congratulate her for having him. The only thing she'd ever taken was the name he'd given her for the boy, for it was a good and clever one, and spoke of his unique history.

"Arden," he'd said when he'd heard of the birth and sent his valet to look down upon the babe and verify his existence. "Arden, his lordship says," the valet had reported tonelessly, " 'for the magical night in the forest.' " It had made no sense, but the sound of it was good. "Arden Lyons" it was, then, with her own decent family name to back it up.

But now she'd a favor to ask, for her pride was as nothing to the boy's chances in life. She could neither read nor write, but the boy was a wonder at his lessons, and everyone knew it. Especially the earl, Arden thought, watching his father narrowly, remembering his long conferences with the schoolmaster of late.

"Well then, boy," the earl had said at last, looking to Arden with great amusement as he said, seemingly amazed, "But ten? Only ten? Are you sure this one is mine, my dear? We met eleven years ago, and look at this great lump of a lad! Perhaps you'd been to the woods once before? Hmm?"

"Please, your lordship," she'd said, red to her ears, and if she'd not needed his favor she'd have taken the boy and marched out, and if he'd not sworn to obey her, he'd have been gone from this room long before. "Please," she said, "you know better than that."

"Oh. Well. Do I?" the earl had said, laughing, showing all his white, strong teeth. "After all, a little shudder, a cry, a grimace—and as for other evidence, it might have been your time of month, mightn't it?"

"Please! The boy," she'd said, her lips tightening, holding Arden by his shoulder till her fingers dug into him, but the earl was still laughing, so she couldn't give up yet.

"Well then, boy," the earl said, never rising from his chair as he addressed him for the first time in his life, "here. Do you know that I am your father?"

"I've not told him—" she said, but he raised his hand as Arden said plainly, "I do now, your lordship."

"Ah," the earl said, hearing what lay beneath the civil words and growing genuinely interested. He looked at the tall, strongly built boy and gazed long at the cold glittering hazel eyes he so admired. "Your mama wants you to be well-educated. But what's the sense of educating a bastard, or a farmer, I'd like to know? What do you want to achieve in your life?''

''I want to acquire a great deal of money, sir,'' Arden answered evenly.

''A gentleman does not discuss money,'' the earl chided.

''But I am not a gentleman, am I, your lordship?'' he'd answered, taking in his flaming rage, tamping it down, smoothing it with keen reason, tempering it to cold, killing steel, as he'd learned to do.

''And what,'' his father asked, smiling widely now, enormously entertained by the answer as well as by the control he saw, ''do you hope to achieve with all that money?''

''Anything I wish, sir,'' he'd replied steadily, staring unblinking at his father, ''except, of course, be a gentleman.''

''Yes,'' the earl said after a moment, ''yes, the schoolmaster was right. He'll go far. My word on it. And further with an education, I think. Leave the room, boy. Go to the kitchens. They're used to entertaining my bastards there. I have to discuss some details with your mama. Some . . . delicious details that she may remember, do you think, my dear?'' he'd asked her, and from the lazy tone of his voice and the look in his eye, Arden had known perhaps even before she had, and had known, in some fashion, that half the pleasure was in his knowing as well.

''No!'' Arden had cried then, wild-eyed, losing his control, and then she'd known, and after a moment when her head had gone up as though she'd smelled fresh-spilled blood, she'd taken a deep breath, and turning to her son, cuffed him on the ear and said distinctly and loud, ''Go now!''

''She'll be back in an hour,'' the earl had said slowly, softly, as he'd backed away from his mother. ''Maybe two, eh, my love?''

He'd gone away to school, for she'd insisted, but it had been a long while until he could look at his mother again. It had taken him years to understand that her degradation had been his punishment as well. She vowed she'd not gone back to the house again, after, and for all he knew, it was so. John Dahl was not a fool, and even the earl would go only so far. It was the nineteenth century now, after all, and all the serfs had gone. Some of them, Arden realized, had even gone to school.

Oh, not the top-flight one, where the earl's legitimate

children had gone and the youngest still went, but a good enough one so that his sons would know that there was a bastard doing as well as, perhaps better than they had. That was their punishment.

He'd thrown it all over when she'd died, of course. He'd been sixteen, and he refused to take anything from his father once she'd gone. But a year in the dregs of London's stews had shown him what education could do, and when he'd lost Meggie, he'd realized that losing everything that the only two females he'd loved had so badly wanted for him in no way hurt the earl, and he'd returned to learn all he could.

The earl offered to buy him colors when he left university, and though he'd been interested in pursuing a study of law, quite naturally then, he'd enlisted himself. And within a few years gotten higher than the commission his father could have bought him. Until he gave it all up, realizing that the bloody business wasn't for him, and so much as he thought he was foiling the old devil, he was actually going his way, only taking the harder way to do it.

Then he'd given up everything and gone to London to live in the cesspit again, until he'd become so successful at it that he knew he'd only been dancing to the earl's tune once more.

And now he stood by his father's bedside and wondered if the old man's death would finally free him, or if it would take his own to do so.

"You, Arden, my Lion," the earl sighed, never taking his eyes from him, for although Francesca stood next to him all the while, it was as though the dying man never registered her presence, he was so busily drinking in the sight of his huge son, "you," he said lovingly, "my chance-got giant son of a common fishwife, my beauty conceived of a sweaty child at the base of a tree, you, Arden, look at me!

"You," the earl said, as both Francesca and Julian understood at last that evil can wear a thousand faces, "you are my best son. How bizarre! With all that I sired. And how you hate to hear that!" the old man crowed. "Even more than my other sons do. Because you're the only one, got in or out of wedlock, with wit and a heart as big as yourself and the courage to despise me fully with both. Of course you hate me. But hear me well, boy: she went with me of her own will, every time. *Every* time, do you hear? We all of us have our dark places, even you, eh? But why tell you? You've made good coin knowing it. Oh, I know of your sins, Arden, as well as your triumphs. I paid good money to keep hearing word of you all these years. Bow Street could have applied to me, my boy, I knew your every move. Clever, clever. My son," he laughed, and then stopped, gasping.

"Here," he said, laboring for breath, taking something from his night table and thrusting it at Arden, "take it, take it! Yes, it's all I can leave you, of course. The legitimate eldest gets the house and title, he'll drink away the one and forget the other, the others get the cold side of his tongue, and it will shrivel them, and so in a generation there'll be nothing left except perhaps the name. Because it's yours too now. You can't fight God. I've made my confession and finally entered my name on that blank bit of the paper. Oh, yes, you're a bastard still, but one with a name. I claim you. It's Arden Lyons Graham now, twist and turn as you may. With all my sowing I've reaped nothing worth the living after me. Except you. The ring's my seal, my coat of arms. It's yours too, like the name, like it or not."

The earl lay back panting, and smiled at him.

"It's not necessary to love me," he said then, in a thready undertone, "but at least now you can never deny me."

"I deny you," Arden whispered, but because he was who he was, however sincerely he meant it, still he said it only when he knew it was too late for his father to ever hear it.

"Arden?" Francesca said, tears in her eyes, calling him away from what was over, at last, "I'm so sorry."

"Ah, yes, so I thought you'd be," he said then, returning to her, patting her hand that he'd never relinquished as he led her from the room. "I understand. And so now you see, of course," he said, loosing her when they'd got to the hallway.

"And now you don't, of course," she sighed, taking his hand firmly in hers again, as Julian, coming up behind them, saw her action and smiled, and in that moment, loved her almost as much as Arden did.

16

"THIS," Francesca said wonderingly, as best she could as soon as she'd swallowed, "is amazingly good chicken."

"Well, I should think so. Imagine trying to choke down the victuals they usually hand you here," the red-headed woman said with a sniff, and then to Francesca's curious look she said in a satisfied whisper, "I brought in three platters of it this afternoon. I got cracking soon as I could once I heard you was to be stopping here after the last rites. "It's true," the woman confided, "that there wasn't enough room for everyone at the cottage, and no one in their right mind would want to go up to the manor, so we put our heads together, we women, and that's why the food at the Ark today is nothing like the rubbish they usually serve."

"It was very kind of you," Francesca replied.

"Stuff!" the woman said. "There's nothing we wouldn't do for him," she added lovingly, gesturing with her glass toward where Arden stood near the cold fireplace, towering above a group of people, all seemingly wanting to tell him things at the same time.

Francesca couldn't remember the proud cook's name. She'd been introduced, but then she'd met so many of Arden's sisters, both legitimate and not, that she could scarcely recall any one of their given names, much less surnames, and this one had also been wed. But since the woman in question had not found any complaint with the liquid refreshment served at the inn, she scarcely seemed to mind that her half-brother's elegant lady-friend never called her by name. She herself called everyone "dear" anyway, Francesca noted as the woman drifted away into the crowd of people massed in the great common room of the old inn, looking for further compliments on her excellent chicken.

"Arden's family have done him proud with the funeral meats," Julian said as he came up to Francesca and noted the direction of her gaze.

"Meats and chickens and jellies and cakes," she answered. "I'm having a marvelous time, but is it quite right

239

to have so much pleasure after a funeral?'' she asked worriedly, wondering at how jolly the assembled persons were rapidly becoming.

''Nothing became the old man in life more than his leaving it, I gather,'' Julian said on a smile, around the glass of ale he was downing, ''and I think they're here more to see Arden than to plant their dear departed earl anyway. Earl and father—lord, the fellow left behind more replicas of himself than Charles II did. Sorry,'' he said quickly, seeing the sudden pain in her eyes. ''Does that bother you?''

''Only because it bothers him,'' she said fiercely, raising her chin and looking toward Arden. ''Myself, I'm grateful to the old lecher. I am, Julian, don't laugh. For if he'd been a decent man, there'd be no Arden, would there?''

''And that would pain you,'' Julian said, smiling at her so warmly that Roxanne, who'd been having some sport dazzling a few local lads, cut herself off in mid-sentence to look narrowly at the light gentleman and the dark-haired lady chatting by the windows.

''And that would pain me very much,'' she agreed solemnly.

''I'm very glad,'' he replied, just as seriously.

''Come, come, my friends,'' Arden said, coming across the room toward them, ''everyone is wondering why my beautiful guests are so somber.''

'We're unaccustomed to funerals,'' Julian reported. ''Tell me, is the dancing to be before or after dinner?''

''In London,'' Arden said imperturbably, though he did look to Francesca keenly as he spoke, ''after a funeral everyone goes off, very sadly and restrainedly, to lift a few thimbles of spirit to take off the graveyard chill, and then they nibble a few cress sandwiches before they get down to the good gossip, catching up on all the peccadilloes of the various family members and friends they haven't seen in years. Here, it's simpler. Moreover, the old earl died full of years and spite and malice. There wasn't a wet eye in the chapel, you know, save for my two legitimate brothers, and they only because they dread eviction. No, knowing the sort of man he was, or rather, not really knowing, thank God, I'd imagine he'd be astonished if anyone grieved for him. Although,'' he said ruminatively, ''perhaps there may be not a few females present with some well-concealed regrets at his passing. He was, for all his sins, eminently pleasing at his chiefest one, I'd guess. For it had to be more than his money that accounts for all my siblings.''

''Oh, yes, now tell us of your legacy, and how it runs in the family.'' Julian grinned.

''Not you!'' Arden answered, much offended. ''What sort of a fellow do you take me for? Now, Francesca, is there someplace dark and secluded where I can tell *you* about it?'' he asked anxiously.

They all laughed, for it was meant for humor, but Francesca wondered what he would have done if she'd agreed. She wondered what she would have done too.

Then, as a pair of brothers accosted Arden on one side, and their wives tried to take his attention on the other, and she saw him bend down to greet a collection of half-nieces and nephews he'd not known of, she watched him closely. These were, as he'd said, simple people. But she'd never seen so much simple affection given to anyone before. He'd sent some of them funds, it seemed, he'd solved some of their problems in the past, it transpired, but it went beyond his money and his opinions. They knew he'd grown beyond them, it was in everything they said of and to him, it was in the way they looked at him and up to him. But they trusted him, and were proud of him, and they every one of them respected him, this half-brother of theirs who so easily carried so many of their confidences and burdens, even as he'd carried his own, uncomplaining, for so many years.

The more she grew to know of him, the more she valued him. And yet, each door he opened, he warned her against. But each time, looking within, she saw none of the dreadful apparitions he'd promised, but only more of the difficult past of an amazing man whose heart was as big as he was, and who had transcended each of the real difficulties life had dealt him. And still, and yet, he believed himself unworthy. The Earl of Oxwith, she thought with futile anger, had more than his lechery to answer for in whatever court he would be hailed into now.

There was a stir at the door to the inn, as yet more guests attempted to wedge themselves into the overcrowded room. But this couple was given room immediately. The tall, simply but elegantly dressed plain-faced woman was another sister, but this one was bowed and curtsied to by all her half-brothers and sisters as well as the other townfolk, even if they'd all just seen her at the cemetery, for she was the late earl's only legitimate daughter, the Lady Millicent.

Her husband, a tall, round-faced, pleasant-looking older gentleman, greeted Arden effusively. As though they'd been asked, the others in the room crowded back, some flowing into the other room of the inn, so as to give the newly arrived pair room in which to confer with their brother.

So many people wanted his ear, Francesca thought, that she'd scarcely seen him by herself since the old man died. Each night he'd met with various relatives, riding out to their farms or cottages, or having them to the inn, and even when she'd gone with him, she'd passed the time with Julian and Roxanne. With Julian, she corrected herself. For Roxanne was bored, and her boredom made her testy, and so she was no good company for anyone, least of all herself. The countryside vexed her, she said, and surely death and all its attendant formalities did too, and it might also have been that what she perceived as Julian's growing and obvious disinterest bothered her as well. Because here in the countryside, ringed around with conventions and the trappings of a funeral, she could do none of the things she excelled at, in public or private. Julian had decreed it.

For there were things a gentleman did not do. And while he might sleep with ten females clad only in beauty while in the midst of London, he'd explained to his fretful mistress, he might not embarrass a friend in the smallest village in England by so much as kissing his unmarried companion beneath the stairs. Julian didn't even share his room with Roxie now, at this inn, he didn't dare, he told her, not when he was under such close scrutiny by all of Arden's relatives and friends, which were, he jested, all of Cornwall.

Because he was sure, he'd teased Roxie, for her ear only, that if the strain got to be too much and he was forced to steal away with her and take her out on a rowboat to have his way with her, a fish would leap up and cry, "My word! So that's why the boat was rocking. Come see what Arden's fancy friend is doing, lads!"

But Roxanne didn't so much as snicker at that; she only flounced away, mumbling about what she'd given up to follow him, and see what such foolishness had earned her. Francesca didn't know what her following Arden had earned her either, except for an even more profound longing for his good opinion, company, and personal attentions. She gazed at him now, and saw him loom even larger than ever in her life. She could not now imagine life without him, but then, she couldn't imagine it with him either, for he seemed not to have changed his opinion of her opinion of him, whatever had happened.

Julian knew, and Julian sympathized, and while that was comforting, it was every bit as embarrassing as it was welcome. Because the blond viscount's friendship earned her only Roxie's distrust, and what ever his intentions, it was lowering to have anyone know where your heart lay, as though you'd not a secret to your name. She was, in fact, thinking longingly of how lovely it would be if Arden mistook her friendship with Julian, or fancied she loved any other, envisioning herself as a languid lady with dark eyes full of humid secrets, when Arden's voice, as though in answer to her innermost fantasies, said in her ear, "What delightfully evil things are you thinking, my dear Francesca? You looked like the most wonderfully corrupt Madonna just then."

"You," she said, and then, horrified, stammered, "you . . . you startled me."

The smile he bent upon her was so amused and understanding that she wanted to both fling herself into his arms and tread on his toes, and conflicted as she was, it was just as well that he brought her to the attention of Lady Millicent again just then.

"My sister would like a word with you," he said easily. "She really wants us to visit with her in Aberdeen, but so much as I love her, and I do, I will not trail up to Scotland now, even with all the haggis and bagpipers and blood pudding and other delights she's tempting me with. See if you can get her to follow on to London, Fancy, there's a good lass, and stay on your toes, for she's desperate and Scotland's lonely, so she may have you trussed up and in her coach in a trice if she decides she likes you. Take care."

As he walked off into the crowd of relatives once more, this time with his brother-in-law and Julian in tow, and was swallowed up by the company again, Lady Millicent laughed.

"Aye," she said, "anywhere is lonely without Arden. For all my contentment—and I've five sons who haven't yet reached their majority, my dear, and so even in the highlands find I absolutely pine for loneliness sometimes—I miss him, I confess I do. I cannot get a straight word out of him," she said suddenly. "Are you two affianced, my dear?"

"Oh, no!" Francesca said. "But I'm not . . ." She hesitated, wondering what the lady would think if she knew they were not, but knowing she knew they traveled together, and so not knowing what to say at all to this tall, prim straitlaced-looking lady, for fear of disgracing herself or Arden. And yet she didn't know how to state the actual truth, which she herself wasn't sure of anymore, now that events were moving so fast. "That is to say . . ." She fought for the right words.

". . . that I oughtn't to pry, as Arden said," Lady Millicent put in nervously, taking off her glove only to smooth it on again, "but he also said you were the daughter of a baron who was a friend of his and that you were a good girl he'd not take advantage of, but when I saw you, I so hoped he would. Oh, dear," she said, putting her half-gloved hand to her mouth in alarm, "I've made it worse," she said uneasily before she hurried on, "I'm not so much plain-spoken as poorly spoken, forgive me. But I've so little time because we leave for home so soon. And you're so very beautiful," Lady Millicent blurted, "the way he looks at you—and I can see you're a lady of some quality, and I adore Arden so—it was not easy being my father's daughter, my dear," she said nervously, "nor my brothers' sister, neither. If it weren't for Arden, and knowing him, and seeking his counsel as all the rest did, for all I'm five years his senior, I don't think I'd have those five sons now, do you see? I don't think I'd have dared trust any gentleman to so much as touch my hand. I'd have gone from Papa's funeral to tending my garden, and never have had to hurry back to my noisy, lovely home in Scotland," she said dreamily.

"But Arden taught me by example what decent men, as well as real gentlemen, were about," she continued, "for all I had to slip out to see him, he was my real brother and friend, and I want only the best for him, you see."

"I do, and so do I," Francesca hurriedly assured her, as Lady Millicent, surely the most unsure and inept lady she'd ever met, went on to beg her forgiveness and entreat her to keep her conversation secret. The late earl, Francesca thought angrily again, had sown a strange harvest with all his license.

"If there is anything you ever need . . ." Lady Millicent said when Arden came back to tell her that her coach was waiting. But knowing that the only thing she needed was something the lady could not give her, and as perhaps the lady knew the same, they merely smiled and without warning, or knowing who began it, they embraced, with much embarrassment as well as pleasure on both ladies' sides, and then Lady Millicent was off and on her long way home again.

"She would have taken you back to live with her as a daughter, or a friend, or whatever you'd wish," Arden said slowly, looking after his sister, and then he looked down into Francesca's worried brown eyes as he said, "But I didn't even ask her," with such wonder in his slow deep voice that her heart picked up. And then, shrugging his great shoulders, he laughed, and then, still laughing, was carried off into the crowd of his relatives again.

The good-byes could well have taken a week to be done with, Arden said, and so he did them all in a night. The last two he did alone, and when they were done he rode back to the inn late in the night, pensive and weary, but well-pleased. Because as he informed Julian and the two ladies at breakfast the next morning, his legitimate brothers had at last been made to see that living together and pulling together was their only hope for keeping their stately old home together, for their fortune was almost gone. And, he added reasonably, with the old earl gone as well, it might just be that they could learn to live with each other again.

And his farewells to John Dahl, he thought as he swung up on his horse as the coach prepared to leave again after that breakfast, had been best done in private, nor were they necessary to discuss afterward. Unlike his true father, John Dahl wouldn't be the sort to send for a son to hot foot across the land when he was given notice to quit. John Dahl was a private man, who would take the end of his life with the same calm control with which he'd taken the rest of it, in the manner he'd taught his stepson the way of. Now, at the old fellow's age, any farewell might well be the last one, so it had to be thorough. Respecting that stoicism and needing it for himself as well, Arden had saved that good-bye for last, and had given it quietly, there in the front yard, and whatever emotion had been involved had been easier for both men to keep close even from each other there in the dark.

Now, he had to express his thoughts, and quickly, as he looked up from his memories to see which road the coach he followed was taking, and startled, reined in his horse even as he bellowed, "Julian, to the left, to the left, we're off to London, not Mecca!"

"To London—via Arundel, my friend," Julian called back, his clear voice ringing in the cool spring morning. "I've a mind to see Elmwood Court—my home. All this visiting, you know," he said in a lower voice as Arden rode up to him, "set me to remembering. But don't worry, it's only a little detour tomorrow, and there are no hordes of relatives to delay us there. I've no family left, nothing but the old Court, and some pensioners I've got living in the old place, keeping it up for me. And it is on the way . . . in a roundabout way," he added more slowly, with a hint of embarrassment that betrayed his casual air.

"I'd like to see it," Arden said at once. "I've been about building a home for myself, by proxy, messenger, and post, for three years now, you know, and can use any ideas I can steal for the place. It's to be a monument to my taste and success, you see," he said, as Julian laughed and his face cleared to its usual blinding serene beauty, and so Arden didn't mention that the house had been finished this past month or more, and instead only stored up this new lie in his memory so that he'd never contradict himself about it.

"Funerals stir up the damnedest memories and emotions," was all he said before he kneed his mount onward again, "so take care! There's a family of ceremonies lurking, don't forget. Weddings," he warned on a giant grin, "are second cousins to funerals, and I won't even mention christenings!"

Roxanne had been on fire to go to London, but during luncheon on the road, when Julian mentioned their new destination, she only widened her eyes and then declared herself enchanted.

"Do you mind the delay?" Arden asked Francesca as he walked her back to the coach.

But as she'd not the slightest idea of what was being delayed just now, and as any day she traveled with him was only another day given to her that she hadn't expected, she smiled and professed herself delighted as well.

"For anyone would want to see his own home," she explained, before she fell silent, thinking that wasn't strictly true, since she'd never had a home to want to see, unless one counted boarding schools or the occasional rented house that she'd come to visit. Even Arden, for all he'd been uneager to share his childhood home with his friends, had at least a home to return to. Yes, she thought as she climbed back into the coach, it would be lovely to ache and long for something real and remembered, rather than something only dreamed upon.

"This is splendid!" Roxanne laughed, swirling around in an impromptu pirouette in the front hall. "We must stay here tonight, Julian, we simply must!"

"We must not," he said distinctly, although he was clearly pleased at her reaction, at all their reactions to his home.

But Elmwood Court was a large and gracious home and would have been difficult to fault. Even with most of the furniture in holland covers, it was plainly a gentleman's comfortable country estate made for living and working, and never pretentious or an architectural-folly. Its drawing rooms and salons were filled with light, the bedrooms were large and equipped with sufficient fireplaces to keep winter at bay. It even had a tolerable ballroom, and a kitchen commodious enough to withstand any siege of visitors. Only its music room, lovely as it was, showed any pretensions, and that, Julian explained as he showed his guests around, was only because the third viscount had had a wife who thought her voice her greatest attribute, and to judge from the fair-haired beauty's portrait which still adorned the room, it must have been lovely indeed.

Francesca gazed up at the ornate ceiling above them. She'd made out the curious sight of a great many ox skulls in among the swirling designs, and asking Julian if that emblem was on his coat of arms.

"No," he said, gazing up with her. "Actually, it's the architect's own coat of arms and symbol. Mr. Adam liked to include his own signature on everything he did, you see. I'll admit they bothered me as a child, and I didn't know why my mother was so proud of them. I was very proud of our name, I think, and couldn't understand why my ancestor wanted our home adorned with someone else's mark."

"Well, why would he?" Francesca asked.

"How else would anyone know how much money he spent?" Julian asked her, smiling at her incomprehension. "Adam was a very expensive chap to haul cross-country just to do a music room, and they were proud of it."

"But that's foolish," Francesca protested. "It would be like wearing a famous dressmaker's signature upon one's

gown. There are some arts that should speak for themselves
. . . why, see the fellow advertises himself forever this
way.''

''Precisely,'' Julian laughed, ''and how much he charged
for the treat, as well. That's the whole point of it. One look,
and all the neighbors, even the ones who didn't know a
cornice from a column, fell into transports of envy, without
a word having to be spoken.''

''What a good idea!' Arden said enthusiastically. ''I think
I'll go one better and have my architects set their names in
the tiles on my floors and chisel their bills on my walls—
for those of my neighbors who are a bit dim, do you think?''

They laughed at the thought, and had some sport with the
idea of famous gardeners trimming their portraits into the
topiary hedges, and had gone onto wonder about chefs pip-
ing their initials into the crusts of their pies, and might have
gone on so for hours, had not Julian checked his watch and
announced that speaking of pies had made him hungry, so
they ought to start out once again.

''But, Julian,'' Roxanne protested again, ''it's late, and
you've so many bedrooms, although,'' she added on a low
laugh, ''we only need three, so let's stay. Oh, come, Julian,
what fun! I'm tired of riding in the coach, and we're already
here . . .'' As she kept on pleading, Arden took Francesca's
arm, and opening a long glass door that led to the gardens,
strolled out-of-doors with her.

''Domestic squabbles,'' he explained as he walked her
over a garden path, ''and the best place for a guest to be
during them is gone.''

They walked in a comfortable silence for a while, down
winding shell paths past herb and flower gardens, and everywhere about them bright daffodils and tulips nodded over
primrose and violets sheltering beneath their more blatant
beauty.

''Julian's pensioners are keen gardeners, I see,'' Arden
said as they strolled on. ''The place is well-kept-up—he's
every right to be proud of it.''

Before Francesca could answer, Arden sighed, and while
still looking at a bank blushing with cerise flowers, said
quite plainly, or else she mightn't have believed her ears,
''It's not too late. You can still go back to Warwick, or I
can put you in a coach and get you to my sister Millicent
before you've had time to think of three excuses for not
bothering her. I was going to take you on to London, it

seemed a good idea at the time, there are things you ought to see there if you are to believe me as to my monumental unsuitability for you, but now, knowing what you do, it would be quite all right to end the charade at once.''

"Knowing . . . what?'' was all she managed to ask. His mood had turned so quickly she'd difficulty fathoming it. And too, although he'd said he'd keep her with him so that she could judge him for herself, she imagined that to be a ruse, because, and she'd worked this out in one long night, as she came to know more of all his talents and abilities, it made far more sense that he was going on with her so that he could make up his mind as to her suitability for him. Evidently now he had, she thought miserably. She looked up into his stern face and never knew that her own confusion and disquiet were so clear upon her own countenance that he had to look everywhere but at her.

"I am a bastard, got of a nobleman or not,'' he explained, watching a cloud with the shape of a torn beast as it drifted by beyond the budding beech tree behind her shoulder.

"Oh, and that matters greatly,'' she said.

"It ought,'' he said, "my dear the Honorable Miss Carlisle.''

"Oh, yes. Of course. Absolutely, the Honorable Miss Carlisle, with her honorable mother who married two men at the same time to save time, no doubt, and so died birthing another bastard babe of her own, and her honorable father who would have been pleased to dice for the pennies they put on his wife's eyes, no doubt—if he'd thought of her at all when she died, that is,'' she said, not knowing that she could speak so well through clenched teeth, so angry that she was trembling.

"I love the way you speak,'' he said, looking at her with mock ardor, his eyes brimming with laughter, "but why are you so angry?'' he asked, his voice gentling. "Is it at my presumption?''

"At you, yes!'' she raged. "At your presumption, yes! At your presumption of your unworthiness, when all about you are far worse, and when you are so very good—''

"No,'' he said, sobering, "that I'm not, you'll see.''

But as he looked down and watched her shuddering with the effort of controlling herself, he quite naturally, without any other intentions, reached out to console her. But at the feel of her delicately boned shoulders shaking beneath his hand, and at the look she gave him then, half-invitation, half-alarm, he lost his own control. He drew her close, and as she didn't protest, he kissed her, marveling at the warmth and taste of her mouth, so moved by it that he took his lips from hers at once and only held her close—that much control, thank God, he thought, he still had.

When he realized that holding her so was achieving the precise opposite effect upon himself that he desired, he stepped a pace back and stared down into her eyes.

She thought he'd apologize, or speak of love, or talk of their foolishness, or jest so they'd forget it. But again she found she couldn't predict him.

"Sometimes," he said wonderingly, brushing a large finger so lightly against her cheek that she felt it no more than she might the wing of some small flying creature skimming past her, "sometimes," he breathed, gazing at her finely textured lightly gilded skin, and at the blushing mouth he'd just touched with his own, "I'm afraid that when I touch you I'll rub some of the gold off on my fingers, and so when I do, and then I dare look at you again, and find you still unblemished, I can't quite believe it."

She was still staring at his firm, wide, unsmiling mouth and wished that however beautifully he spoke, he'd use his lips again as he'd done before he spoke, and so she could say nothing.

But he only took in a long breath and let it out to ask her back to the house with him.

Julian was standing, restlessly looking through a book on a table as they entered the music room again, and Roxanne, at the other end of the room, was looking decidely put-out. But there'd been no valid explanation he could give her, Julian thought as he thumbed through pages that went unseen, or at least none he could offer that, reasonable or not, wouldn't have wounded her. Because reasonable or not when she'd asked, he'd known at once that he didn't want her in his bed in this house. Not this house. It made far less sense to him that it would to her, because she'd doubtless take it as the insult it was not.

It wasn't because of their lovemaking, nor because of her position as his mistress either. They were alone here, after all, to all intents and purposes, at least with no one to judge them. And they'd made love often enough before. But he was always alone in some fashion, and when alone with himself, he judged himself constantly. And this was his childhood home, and his father's childhood home before him, and so on back in time to the good old king who'd made a forefather a viscount for some service, giving him enough reward along with the title to build this old house. And he'd never had a woman beneath this roof, day or night, and would not, he expected, unless she had his name as well as his love.

So he'd told her it was because Arden was anxious to get to London, and he'd explained it was because he'd not ample servants for such a stay, and he'd mentioned that it was because Francesca might be shocked at the situation and feel compromised by their solitude and intimacy. All of which was true, but as all of it was given as reason all at once, Roxanne knew none of it was the real reason, of course.

Julian was glad to take up the reins again, and as he started the coach and headed for a nearby inn for the night, he decided that though he could probably convince her of his continued favor most easily between the sheets, he'd still book separate accommodations for himself and Roxie again, so as to give credence to some of his excuses. This mistress, he told himself ruefully, was fast teaching him why he'd never had one before. She was amusing in bed, and amusing outside of it when she chose to be, but taking on the responsibility for a female wasn't at all as easy or pleasant as meeting one on her own terms for an affair, or taking her on for a merry night. In fact, now that he had a mistress, he didn't know why having one was such a popular diversion.

He was pleased to be sitting on his high coachman's seat, and not the least of it was that he didn't have to exchange so much as a word with the former coachman who sat beside him. In fact, he thought, still musing about his mistress brooding in the coach he drove, having such an arrangement with a female had all the disadvantages of wedlock, and didn't even give a fellow the freedom to be honest in his boredom or occasional distemper, as he might be if he were lucky in his choice of wedded wife.

Most of all, he realized suddenly, thinking of his friends Warwick and Arden, the one wallowing in domestic bliss, the other tossed on the horns of love and desire: if one were even luckier, of course, there was that other element to some marriages that was supposed to make it all worthwhile, that ingredient that was singularly missing from his arrangement with Roxanne—love.

Arden, riding lost in thought beside the coach, was also pondering relationships and rooms. There'd been a time when he'd been loath to return to London, for the good reason of not wishing to be reminded of certain activities he'd been engaged in there, or having others reminded of certain evidence subsequently laid against him for it there. But now he'd heard the wind blew from other quarters, and two years was a literal lifetime in yet other quarters, and too, he'd become a different man. No, what he'd feared most recently had been the judgment of those matters by the lady in the coach he rode beside. At the moment he was even more worried about her proximity, for now he was thinking that separate rooms in London might not be enough.

Separate cities, he thought, might do better—if he wished to keep the lady safe from himself until he could present all the evidence London would offer to her so that she could make a fair, informed decision about him. Which, due to witchcraft, he began to believe, mightn't be enough to hang him, after all. It might only be enough to transport him, to a different and unbelievably better future.

For he now began to imagine—oh, witchcraft certainly, he thought, good Cornishman that he was, remembering her black, black hair and the limitless depths to her golden-brown eyes—that all that evidence might still not be enough to end the new life he dared to imagine he might yet be able to begin with her. He admitted, to himself at least, at last, that he devoutly hoped so, for he began to doubt he could ever have one at all without her.

But then, the closer he came to London, and the more realistically he looked at the matter—and he was a realistic man—the more, of course, he knew that bright dream would fade as all fresh, country-bred things did in the sullen sooty city air. So he decided to ride on toward London as a man ought when facing his execution, as the best brave lads had done on the way to Tyburn hill—proudly and with head held high, full of jest and gallows humor, determined to give the crowd their money's worth and at least leave all the tender-hearted ladies with a smile as well as a tear in their eye for the end of the bold, bad rogue, for all his sins.

17

SHE'D BEEN to London twice before, but this was a different London than she'd ever seen. The Duke of Peterstow had sent word to have his town house opened to receive guests, and Francesca and Roxanne remained there, while Julian and Arden stayed on at Stephen's Hotel for gentlemen nearby. But every day they'd meet to tour the town, and every night now, for a week, they'd been taken out on the town with the two gentlemen. And what a town! Francesca thought.

They'd gone to Drury Lane and Covent Garden to see the latest plays, and then to the Sadlers Wells Theater and the King's Opera for ballets and concerts. And having expressed her disappointment at missing the exhibition of the marbles Lord Elgin had brought back from Greece when she'd been in London as a girl, Francesca had been delighted when Arden found a lecture on the subject that very night, and she'd been able to hear about all she hadn't seen. Then the next day he'd taken them all to a private exhibition of the marbles at Lord Elgin's home, where the statues remained until negotiations to remove them for permanent display could be completed.

But those were only the highlights she could immediately remember, for there'd been other art exhibitions and visits to galleries, and musicales at the most proper homes in the best districts as well. It seemed that between Julian's connections by dint of his birth and title, and Arden's by reason of all the unexpected people he knew, the entire city was open to them, as if they knew the secret password to some magic cave filled with unequaled fabled riches. Francesca was thrilled.

Roxanne was not.

That was why this night was to be different from the others. "She's right, of course. There's more to the city than its culture, far more city than culture, in fact," Julian had jested when Roxanne's plaints had grown too loud to ignore. And at that Arden had looked thoughtful, and curiously sad.

It was time, and past it, he'd thought, watching Francesca's rapt face from the shadows of their box at the theater that night, for he'd found he could follow all the play there in her expressive eyes and receptive expressions as well as or better than watching the strangers on the stage. This had been a week for himself, really, and never just for her, for he'd stored up each memory of their days together, knowing soon he'd have to show her the rest, and so soon he'd need those memories of her.

He was lost, he knew. There was little sense denying it now. And he'd soon lose her as well. Not a grain of sense in refusing to admit that. But he was a clever fellow, and had delayed the moment, passing the week in the pleasure of her pleasure the way he often enjoyed the jests in a play that he knew would end tragically, finding the mirth all the richer for what he knew came after. Best too, he realized, as he agreed with Julian and they decided to show the ladies some of the more thoughtless merriment to be had in the great city, to ease her into the pit. The shock of what he had to show her eventually would be bad enough; yes, best, he thought, to prepare her by degree for it. For it *was* a matter of degree, the same slow descent that even the most highly placed in the city took when in search of ever-new mindless pleasures. Such joys were always in demand, and always available to those who sought them. And the best of it, which was, of course, the worst of it, was all of it in his former domain.

Roxanne was delighted at the change in plans, for although she was sure the entertainment so far had been very uplifting, a girl liked a good laugh, to be sure, and a chance to kick up her heels. In fact, though she didn't say it, she'd been bored to flinders the past week, and she would have said it too—to any other gent than Julian. For he was the sort of gentleman who'd enjoy such pursuits from time to time, and she'd better get used to it, she'd thought, as she'd suffered through the lot of it. But it was a far cry from the gaiety of Brussels or Paris, or the gaming hells she'd frequented abroad, and that she let him know, for she knew very well that even the noblest gent likes a bit of sport now and again—or else, she asked coyly, making him laugh, why would he have taken up with her in the first place?

Today had been much more like it, for she'd adored shopping and then going to Madame Tussaud's amazing waxfigure display. Tonight, still in high good spirits, she'd dressed to the nines in a bright new crimson gown Julian had got her, and she sparkled and posed and fairly danced into the waiting carriage, and then was surprised to find two large boxes, one with her name upon it, the other for Francesca, awaiting them on the seat.

"No, no, hands off, for later," Julian warned mysteriously, giving Roxanne's eager fingers on the string a light tap so that she'd let the bindings be, before he directed their coachman to take them to the Sans Pareil Theater in the Strand.

"Now, this," Roxanne said an hour later on a great satisfied sniff as the lights came up at intermission to find her carefully wiping off the streaks of kohl running down her cheeks from her tear-drenched eyelashes, "is theater done to a turn. Not that the chap in black face last night didn't have his troubles, to be sure, but this was lovely. The part where her father threw her out into the storm with the baby was much more affecting, don't you think?"

"Absolutely, it didn't snow in Venice, or else I'm sure Shakespeare would have loved to use that bit of business," Arden replied enthusiastically. "I know I'd have found Desdemona sniveling out into the storm very gratifying as well. Othello would have quite liked it too, come to think of it."

They all laughed then, Roxanne as well, for she was never sure when Arden was mocking her, but always wanted him to think she knew what he was about, even if she didn't. Still, the next act, a riotous knockabout farce, was even better than the melodrama they'd just watched, and so by the time the lights came up again, she was in charity with the entire world, even the clever, subversively amusing Arden Lyons. And then, after the spectacular closing display of artificial fireworks and a stageful of singers and dancers, Roxanne felt as though her evening was complete. Francesca was sure it was, and so was surprised when the gentleman told them to open their parcels when they got to the coach, for they'd other stops to make.

"The night's just begun," Julian said, smiling at Roxanne's cry of delight when she flung apart the papers to find a great red-feathered flower of a domino mask within.

And Arden looked down at Francesca's confusion as she lifted her enormous gilded sun-faced mask, its rays all streaming golden feathers.

"It's for a masquerade," he said softly, "and it's so a

lady can't be recognized, because the high and the low go in costume there—that's the fun of it, you see.''

"Oh, champion," Roxanne gurgled, putting the giant flower over her face, spinning round and holding her hair back, and commanding Julian to tie her strings at once. "I've heard that they're delicious—why, a duchess might go off with a sweep, and a clerk can catch himself a countess there.''

"Or his own wife, by mistake," Julian laughed as he took out his own mask as well. It was a long black silk one, not unlike a hangman's, covering over all his face, to leave only that portion beneath his bottom lip exposed.

"Jack Ketch come to the party?" Arden grinned.

"Of course, and you?" Julian asked loftily, noting his friend's abbreviated black eye mask.

"His finest catch—the haughtiest highwayman of them all—Gentleman Jones," Arden answered on a smile.

"But don't you have to be completely in costume?" Francesca asked, and Arden sighed, for the sun mask was magnificent, and yet he longed to see the face beneath. Still, it was enchanting to hear that foggy broken voice issuing from the grand mask, and so he told her, adding, "I'm afraid you'd never be able to speak, lest you give away your identity. But no, although some come in amazingly good costume, some, like us, just come to see the sport and so don't need more than these."

"Just to see the sport?" the huge red flower mourned.

"That's tiring enough, but then we're off to see more, don't fret," Julian promised. "We intend to exhaust you completely before we let morning come."

He was as good as his word. The masquerade, a great public subscription spectacle, was crammed with party-goers. Francesca saw a half-dozen prancing Harlequins and a clutch of dairymaids and a dozen devils and even more queens and kings of ancient lands, all crowded together in the huge assembly hall. They'd done with eating, obviously, for the tickets included a meal to be served earlier on. Now they drank, and sang and danced and cavorted together, and from where she stood at Arden's side, Francesca was enchanted. This was, she told him, very like being part of the theater they'd just come from.

And so she would have enjoyed it, taking it just in that spirit, as Roxie and Julian obviously were, as they danced into the throng. But Arden grew still, and then, taking her hand, he walked her round the room, showing her things she'd not have seen, telling her more she'd never have known. It was, she thought, when she could, as though he'd picked up all the glorious theatrical masks to show her all the common, naked, sadly human flesh beneath.

For the three giggling medieval wenches standing in a row, chatting with a royalist soldier, a monk, and a Harlequin, were Covent Garden-ware, he whispered, standing in costumes they'd rented for the night from their bawd, and discussing their price for other delights of the night. And as they watched, one by one the girls went off with their gentlemen, two to leave the festivities altogether, the third, on a shrug, to leave her Harlequin in order to engage a jolly sweep in more flirtatious chatter. And the frolicsome knight in shining armor, who spoke only in rhyme, had drunk so much that if one listened closely one could tell he only prated nonsense, and the beautiful fairy queen grew stiff as a stone when she seemed to recognize the bawdy miller across the room as he romanced a Cleopatra, and so she fled with her own Antony, and all the while in the shadowed corners, couples embraced in ways that showed they'd forgot they were in public, in ways Francesca, averting her eyes, had never even seen in private.

"Time to go on," Arden said at once, seeing her reaction, for though he meant to open her eyes, he never meant to hurt them.

They went to gather up Julian and Roxanne, but Roxanne was having such a merry time, dancing and watching the other celebrants, trying to guess which of them were noble and famous and which were "nothing at all," that Arden, teasing her for her lack of enthusiasm for the new adventures she'd been craving, relented, and told her she ought to stay, and told Julian they'd meet later, at the town house.

"They're likely off to better sport," Julian said almost wistfully as he watched Arden shepherd the spectacular sun mask out the door.

But Roxanne had him to herself now and was delighted, whatever finer spectacles they might miss. She felt more secure when alone with him, and although she knew his friendship with Arden was something she couldn't yet sunder, she could at least make the best of whatever time they had alone together. It was time, and past it, to further secure her position.

"We can make our own sport," she said breathlessly,

fluttering her lashes as she gazed up at him, remembering only when she felt them brush against the buckram that she still wore her enormous mask. "Dancing," she continued, taking his arm, "or just chatting or . . . however you wish. We haven't been alone," she said pointedly when she saw him paying little mind to her as he looked to the door, "for the longest time, Julian. And I begin to wonder," she said, with a bit more annoyance as he sipped his drink, "for see—over there—that Spanishy-looking fellow?"

"The failed bullfighter?" Julian said with amusement, looking at the thin young man who'd been staring after them since they arrived, the same one that he and Arden had noticed at the theater these past nights when he hadn't worn a hastily rented, badly fitting costume. "The spindly one who looks as if he'd have a difficult time in a bullring if faced with a ravening rabbit?"

"He looks rather nice," she snapped, "and he is no less than a *Graf*, which is very like a viscount where he comes from. And he also came all the way from France because of me, because he followed me, he says," she said haughtily, "and will to the ends of the earth, he vows," she added triumphantly. She hadn't wanted to produce her ardent young German to tease Julian into attentiveness until she had to, but it seemed, she thought grumpily, eyeing Julian's amusement, that now she had to. A bit of jealousy worked wonders on most men, but Julian, she thought, watching her golden gentleman, his expression unreadable beneath his mask, was not most men. That, of course, was why she wanted him.

Julian knew of the smitten young man—he and Arden would scarcely have permitted themselves to be followed more than an hour in a park without knowing that much— and it spurred him to more pity than jealousy, for he remembered what it felt like to be a lovesick young boy with more fantasies than facts to base love upon. But it did inspire another emotion in him, far more basic than love, although it often went by that name. He looked down at Roxie with all the attention she could have wished then, and if it wasn't precisely the sort of interest she had angled for, at least he was old enough now to know what its true name was, wise enough not to make excuses, even to himself, for it, and bored enough to be enchanted by it.

"It has been a very long time, has it not?" he breathed,

bending to her ear. "And as I recall, there are satisfactory rooms to let, abovestairs, right here, my dear."

"But there are so many empty chambers at your friend the duke's town house, I vow the place echoes at night," she protested.

"But never to the sounds of our pleasure," he said lightly, "for it's a friend's home, and so I cannot use it to that purpose."

"But your hotel—" she began, as he cut in a bit more harshly, "—is for gentlemen, and if you were one, Roxie, I'd never bother, would I? Do you care to come with me now?" he asked with deceptive casualness, for he was tensed and waiting. "I think it's a fine way to end our evening," he added, looking down to her.

She'd have preferred for him to take her to the Duke of Peterstow's town house for their lovemaking, for she knew as well as he did that pleasuring her there would be a statement of an intent other than mere pleasure. Even a respectable hotel would have signified a different sort of admission. But he was waiting for her answer, and so she shrugged to herself. Some things took time, and a milksop or a bore wouldn't find herself with that time to use to her benefit.

"Of course," she laughed up at him, "but, now?"

"Can you think of a better time?" he asked as he looked for the proprietors of the masquerade to make arrangements for the use of their more private facilities. He deliberately didn't look in his mistress's young swain's direction as he left with her, for although another man's desire had fed his, he knew he wasn't so callous yet that the sight of the deluded lad's grieving wouldn't take the edge from his excitation, robbing him of his fun before he had it.

She began to take off her mask as he closed the door to their room behind them, but he said "Don't" at once, and as he then immediately began to help her out of her other garments, she didn't protest. He hurried, and so she soon stood before him clad in nothing but the mask. And when he stepped back a pace to look at her and saw the white form of a naked, ruddy-nippled, round-bottomed woman, her only other coloring the fair hair curling over the slight slitted mound of her sex and the bright hair framing the great plumed red flower that was all of her face, save for those other inviting lips, he was amazed to discover himself enormously stirred at the sight, for it had begun as a mere fancy. He didn't stop to consider the phenomenon, or wait to allow her to do so, because he began to divest himself of his own clothing even more quickly.

"You want me to leave it on even now?" she asked when they reached their rented bed, amused and more than a little thrilled with the way she obviously thrilled him as she'd not for weeks. Moments later she laughed the louder. "But don't the feathers tickle?" she asked merrily.

"Do they?" he asked, his voice muffled beneath his own mask. "Show me."

But as she did, he never laughed at all, or replied in words, and realizing how moved he was, she fell silent and continued, with his slightest touch as her guide, until he drew in his breath sharply and moved her up at last and then beneath him, and then with him. She was pleased at how tremendously eager and rapt in her he was. Yet then, as she watched his lips, the only facial feature now free of his mask, as they parted to let his breath come quicker as he strained to her, she became curiously displeased. Not at his methods or his manner, for as ever, he was expert even in his extreme arousal, even in his urgency, he was a gentleman. Rather, she was remotely disturbed at how well their disguises suited his mood, at how her fanciful flower face pleased him far more than her own appreciative face ever did in their most ardent lovemaking, which, withal, had never been so ardent as this night had become through their pretense of anonymity.

He didn't even attempt to recreate the moment. After they'd rested, he arose and put on his clothes again, even as he left on his own mask.

"We paid for the night," she said drowsily, watching him through slitted eyes through the mask.

"But I promised to meet Arden, remember? If we don't appear he'll imagine us carried off by villains, quite the little mother he is, you know. Come, stop languishing," he ordered, tapping her on the rump, "Off with you.

"But not off with the mask," he corrected her as she began dressing. "Best if no one knows we stopped off here," he explained.

At least he thought of their reputations, and that was all to the good, she thought as she retied the flower again, noting, with a little chagrin—for she always liked to appear in her best looks, masked or not—how dented and sparse its plumage was now. It might be only his own fame he cared for, but since a gentleman seldom made excuses for

even his worst behavior, she fancied it could even be that
he wanted to keep her face and name from curious stares
and comments. Still, there was something in his odd start
tonight that nagged at her. The masks had been amusing,
for all she preferred to see his face and let him see hers
when they made love and she put on the mask of ecstasy
that he needed. But she was never one to think too deeply,
life was hard enough, she'd always said, without complicat-
ing it more by looking for worms in the roses.

However, it did bother her greatly when they left the masquerade. For it was past midnight then and most of the
guests had unmasked. She finally saw the other revelers for
what they really were as she passed by them. She'd have
preferred they'd removed the damned things then, reputations or not, she thought, if only so that the others could all
get a good eyeful of who she was, and then be forced to pay
her due attention and respect when they beheld the true
glory of the face of the gentleman she was leaving with by
her side.

"It's late, we've promised ourselves to Julian, and if we
don't meet at a good hour, he'll call out the troops, good
as any nanny is our Julian," Arden said as he settled in his
seat after giving directions to the coachman. That had taken
time. There'd been some protest on the fellow's part until a
look from his passenger, along with a coin slipped into his
hand for his pride so that he'd be able to tell himself it was
the bribe and not the terror that made him go against his
better judgment, ended the matter and started them on their
way.

"But we were already here this evening," Francesca observed, peering out the window as the coach slowed and
began to inch down the long cobbled street.

"Just so," Arden agreed, his voice a comfortable low
rolling thunder in the quiet of the darkened coach. "I'd best
be careful to blindfold you when I abduct you—you've a
good eye for detail. Yes, there's the theater where we saw
that superior production that would've made Shakespeare
gnash his teeth in envy, this entire district is for such entertainment—and more. It's rather like the reverse effect of
the mask you wore tonight. Even though it was magnificent
in its own false and theatrical way, it hid your human, and
so more beautiful, features. Here, it's only when the mask
of respectability is dropped that a more glamorous, less hu-

man face is shown. When we arrived earlier it was playtime, but now it's another sort of playtime.

"There are twin Londons, Francesca," he said softly, "and it's this other face beneath that smiling face that I must show you tonight, so that you understand what I've been talking about. It's been like that old story of the blind man and the elephant with us: I speak of the beast; you see only what has touched you. You'll never understand me if I don't," he said, almost to himself, "Although God knows I'd rather not."

Then he spoke up in a cool strong voice very like that of the tour guide her father had once engaged to show her the Tower on that long-past last visit here.

"Do you see those two women, there in the shadows?" he asked, and without waiting for answer, he went on, no judgment or emotion save for bleak humor in his voice: "Not a mama and child, as you may've thought. Come now, how could you think it? At this hour? And loitering so? Any female afoot at this time of night is for sale. No, the elder's a whoremonger, and the child's for rent to any man for less than the price of a handkerchief in his pocket. She's too old to pass off as a convincing virgin, for all she likely cries at her work, for she's already all of ten, I'd judge. No, there are few untouched around here at any age, and so it's left to the professional maidens to simulate that desirable state to any good effect. It's a profitable ruse, for fools believe such sexual congress cures the pox. I imagine what it cures best are their heavy purses. No matter, that child has a thousand competitors, and a thousand thousand more to take her place when she succumbs to the diseases that share her bed and body for no fee at all.

"There," he said dispassionately, "see those other, older females in the alleyway? And the lads? All at the same trade. Walk the alley further if you dare, to find still more, or the nice men who give them room to sleep out of the rain for the favor of luring their customers so far, so that they can be relieved of their purses, boots, and watches instead of their desires. In all," he said in the hardest voice she'd ever heard from him, "they're more fortunate than the gents who achieve their goals, for they only lose their valuables and not their health, or life.

"And can you hear all those pretty ladies singing out, almost as nicely as those other painted ladies did on the stage tonight? Only don't listen, my dear, for what little you'd understand of their offers would upset you. Some only deliver what they promise. Others have friends to deliver their patrons' keys and home addresses to while they sport, so that the fools can return home to find their silver, art works, or furniture missing, for each thief here has his specialty.

"For example," he went on, "that little rat-faced chap who sidles rather than walks—there. He's got no female to provide for him, but he makes do. He don't need keys to get into pockets. The big fellow there in the doorway, the one almost my size? He sells his power to any purpose you have in mind, for he must eat to keep up all that strength. They all must eat to live, God knows why, for they're not wellborn, after all," he said harshly, in an angry undervoice. "And so nothing goes to waste. Not here in this end of town. There's a market for everything here, from wet sheets stolen from a line, to stealing a man's breeches with him still in them—if his family won't come to ransom, and if his flesh don't tempt a gent who fancies that sort of pleasure, why then, living or dead, it might interest some medical chaps, and when they've done with him, his very bones can go to the burners, and all for a profit. That's what it's all about: profit. Not lust, or anger or perverse cruelty. They're far too hungry for those luxuries. Don't look at me like that!" he commanded as she stared up at him with wide, frightened eyes. "I didn't invent all this. I only profited from it. But you couldn't know that if you couldn't see this. And still you don't, so we must go on.

"But don't worry," he breathed in a suddenly gentler voice as the coach slowed at last to a halt on a tumbledown street, "no harm shall ever come to you through me. That," he said on a sad exhalation, "is precisely the point of all this."

She followed him out of the carriage. Although she was alarmed at where she found herself, and the sounds of merriment—raucous singing accompanied by fiddle music—coming from out of the scabrous-looking Golden Rule Coffee House, as the sign proudly proclaimed the place to be, she took his hand and stepped down the small stairway that had been let down so she could alight, without faltering. Arden was with her, after all, and he'd protect her, he'd said it, she never doubted it, although she badly wanted to doubt the reason for their visit here tonight.

It was Arden who paused for a deep breath before he drew

himself up to his full, formidable height and entered the
back-street pub with her.

Within, it teemed with life, so varied and colorful and
loud that for a moment Francesca believed they were back
at the masquerade they'd just left. Indeed, she noted what
seemed to be a few of the same class of gentlemen here in
evening dress in among the truly ragged, filthy common
folk.

Arden noted the direction of her gaze. "Oh, yes, the
quality does love a show," he said knowingly as he led her
to a corner table. He stared down at the two men at it until
they stood up in a crouch and slid away, and then he seated
Francesca and himself. "It's lively enough here," he continued nonchalantly, as if that was the way he always ob-
tained a table. "It may name itself a coffee shop, but they
sell gin by whatever name it goes under and sport of every
sort, and its inmates call it a 'flash house.'

"For all it delights and titillates the venturesome bucks
who dare come down here," he explained, "it's a respectable place of its sort. There are ballad singers and peddlers,
coal heavers, beggars and thieves, pickpockets, whores and
their fancy-men all present, to be sure. But for all their
several interesting occupations, they do work. So for all
their rags, they do eat. There are many worse places. But
those I would never show you by moonlight, and dislike to
even mention to you by day. I know them all, and well.
They were my employment bureaus. Do you see now?" he
asked all at once, staring at her.

But she did not and could not and so she only shook her
head, beginning to be afraid. He sighed.

"So be it," he breathed. "We'll go on, tomorrow. For
now, I believe this is both enough and not enough, so . . ."
He looked about. He arose, beckoned to her, and led her to
a table where a grimy man sat with a huge female and an
ancient blind beggar. Arden stared down at the old man
until his two companions stopped talking and shifted nervously in their seats. At that the old blind man looked up.
He took off his cracked black spectacles and slowly rose to
his shifting feet, so staggered by what he saw that his old
dog beneath the table began to growl.

"Gawd innis mercy!" the old man quavered." 'Tis the
Lion rose hup from t' dead!"

"Never dead," Arden answered softly, as the music and
laughter in the room came to a dead stop. "But yes, risen

again. Who has the running of my old haunts now, old man? Is it Whitey Lewis or Gamy Leg Bob who's got the Spital-fields–Whitechapel ken, from Houndsditch to Petticoat Lane?''

''Whitey's lagged, Gamy Leg crapped,'' the old man whimpered.

''Ah,'' Arden said thoughtfully, as Francesca tried to puzzle out what language the beggar spoke, even as she attempted to breathe shallowly, for the stench of fear had joined with the other odors emanating from the old fellow and it was becoming overpowering. ''Transported and hanged, eh?''

It was much as he'd expected. Lives didn't grow long here. So many would be gone. The women soonest, since their lives were the hardest and what disease didn't take, childbirth would. The men would be gone to sickness, accident, and murder, as well as the hulks and the hangman. But enough would remain. He looked to the stricken old man.

''Don't tremble,'' he said more gently. ''I've no quarrel with you. And don't talk flash, neither, I've a lady in tow. Who runs the district now, then?''

''Portwine John has hisself a big piece, and Ben-be-good's got 'nother, but it's Sam Towers got the biggest share,'' the beggar whispered, as his two companions at the table nodded fiercely, as though their bobbing heads drove in the truth of the old man's utterances.

''I know Towers, and knew Portwine when he was a boy,'' Arden mused aloud. '' 'Ben-be-Good's' new to me, but it don't matter. Tell Sam I want to parley tomorrow, noon. I'll have a lady with me, so I'll come in peace, and go quicker if he comes quiet and fair, though it will go hard for him, my word on it, if he betrays my trust,'' Arden said, and then, taking Francesca's arm, he strode to the door with her.

''You have the night to think it over,'' he finally told her after riding with her for long moments in silence. ''You never have to come with me. You've already had a glimpse of my past, or part of it. And that's why I cannot offer you what in truth I wish I could. It was mad, I see it now, Warwick was right,'' he muttered, ''a man needs new eyes now and again, but in my case they only show the filth and slime to me the clearer. It was insane to even offer for an older experienced, widowed Francesca. But then,'' he said, at last raising his head to look at her, "I didn't know you then, did I?" Nor did I love you to distraction then, he thought.

"I'll be ready," she said softly, "in the morning, because, Arden, I don't understand at all."

And I must, she thought. For I'm far more afraid of your leaving me without my ever knowing precisely why than I could ever be of discovering what it is you're so deeply shamed about. But there was a great deal of fear in all she was thinking, and brave as she was, she was only human, so she remained silent, even as he did, as they rode back to the clean, safe section of town and her temporary home.

She'd dressed in a green sprigged-muslin gown for their outing and he didn't know whether to weep or to shout with laughter when he saw her. Her jet hair was dressed simply and charmingly, pulled back in two raven's wings to the side of her smooth, wide-eyed face. She looked so lovely, so sweet and gold and green and young and clean to him that she belonged, he thought, in a meadow, and never in Warwick's sophisticated London town house, or in the filth he was about to take her to today. But she was as she was, he thought, as he bowed over her hand, delighting at least in this last opportunity to see trust and friendship in her eyes before he ended it, as he was shortly to do, forever.

"Are you sure you ought to do this?" Julian had asked him worriedly the night before.

"No," he'd answered truthfully, "but I know the right thing to do."

And so he did, he thought, as he helped her into the coach wordlessly, and so he would, he sighed, as he sat beside her, sorrowing too much to speak. But a man ought not hold a funeral until the corpse stopped kicking, he remembered, and as the streets outside grew meaner and grayer, and they approached their destination, he tried to explain again.

"This is the lowest part of the city, although there's great competition for the honor, and many such districts," he said in a low calm monotone, for there was no gaiety to be made of this human wretchedness, and no sense trying to pretend to it. "Here the Golden Rule would be considered a pleasure palace. Here dwell those who've lost everything or had nothing from the start. London is rife with the poor, but here, those who look to a future beyond tomorrow are rich, for they have at least hope. I lived here, twice upon a time," he said softly, "once when I was a boy running from my dear father's bitter charity. And then again when I'd grown and seen enough of war, finding the supposed over-world's prime sport too filled with savagery parading as no-bility and honor for my taste. I came here for old time's sake then, seeking temporary oblivion, and found myself thrust into a new career instead, because, I suppose, I was used to command. But no excuses. The first time I learned to survive here. The second, I learned how to make a profit out of survival.

"I owned this place once," he said suddenly, loudly, "I held sway here, and was king of the underworld, king of the dungheap. That is a truth, now I take you to a gent who'll swear to it, so you know without a doubt it's so. Although," he said in normal accents, his sense of humor never deserting him for long, even as his heart seemed to crack as she finally averted her head from his steady gaze, "it's truth he'll swear to anything if paid enough, as any sane fellow down here would do."

The Hole in the Wall was grimier than the pub had been last night, she thought, following Arden as if in some strange dream, although, perhaps, she reasoned as she sat in a crooked chair that didn't stick quite so much to the filthy floor as the others he'd pulled out for her had done, it was just that the sunlight that finally managed to filter through the streaked windows wasn't kind to any sort of squalor. A few drunken creatures lay snoring on the straw-covered floor, a few sat at back tables and ignored them, or seemed to do so. She scarcely minded. Arden was here; she kept her eyes upon him. If he'd taken her here, he'd a rea-son, she supposed, because all he'd said meant nothing to her. If he'd been or done something in his past, she knew it would have been the right thing; he was, after all, of all the men she'd ever met, the most honorable. She could not be wrong in that. She mightn't know life very well, she'd conceded that in the long sleepless night she'd just passed, but she knew him.

He stood and gazed out the window now, as comfortable here as he seemed everywhere, from gambling hell to stately home to squalid tenement. He'd dressed as a neat gentle-man, in a handsome tight-fitting new biscuit jacket she'd never seen, fawn pantaloons, and high brown topboots. His ginger head almost touched the low ceiling and his wide shoulders hunched suddenly as he saw the men troop into the pub, but then he straightened and was his amiable self again, so amiable, in fact, that she knew he was at his most dangerous.

The four tall men who swaggered in were so proud and radiated such authority that if it weren't for their shabbiness, she'd have taken them for some sort of royal guard. But they looked at Arden and then away, and from their expressions, for all their bravado, she knew they'd taken his measure and were wondering if the four of them were enough. The king they protected entered after them. He was a slight, whey-faced, dapper man with straight light hair and a crooked smile. And he smiled as much as Arden did when he saw him, and for the first time Francesca was frightened.

"Lion!" the small man said with great pleasure in his voice and face, extending his hand. "Then the rumors were so, eh? I'm glad of it, I am, so I am."

"Of a certainty," Arden said pleasantly, "just what everyone wants, when the dead resurrect and threaten the living. But have no fear, I've not come to reclaim my throne—it's yours, and welcome to it . . . no, I speak the truth, I swear it. I've a different ken now, Sam, and want no part of the past—except for the truth of it—told to this lady here. Only that, for old times' sake, that favor."

"Favor?" Sam spoke in wonder. "Likely, eh?"

"No, I mean it, indulge me please, tell the lady what I was to you, and who I was when you last knew me. And then I'll leave you in peace and with my blessing, lad, and from what I hear you'll need it," Arden said.

"There's truth," the smaller man murmured. " 'Ere, lads, be off. Lion and I are old news. Let us be."

The four men slouched off, if no further, Francesca noted, than outside the door, leaving them entirely alone, for they'd removed the other patrons of the pub who hadn't disappeared under their own locomotion, hauling them out by the scruffs of their necks as simply as putting out the cat. " 'S truth? You want me to spill to the gentry mort?" Sam asked Lion then.

"Aye, but she is a lady, so I'll not introduce you, if you don't mind, lad, and no flash patter, neither, for she won't understand a word of it. Take your time and say it right, and spare no details. It's important."

"Aye, well then, lady," Sam began, taking no umbrage at his lack of introduction, as though he quite agreed with Arden and wouldn't have considered her a lady if he'd got-

ten one. He spoke carefully, and well enough, when he
didn't hurry and lapse into accents difficult for her to understand. "See here," he said, "the Lion was top of the
heap, see? He ran it all. Aye, well, not all. He'd have no
part of Mother Carey nor none of the fiercer bawds, for he'd
take no share of any house where they was unhappy workers, pressed into service, so to speak. Nor any part of the
kid lay, see? But as to the rest, why, he saw to it and us.
And he did it fair. He was best o' the best. Aye, Lion," he
said, turning to Arden suddenly, "no fooling, you're a sight
for sore eyes. Things ain't been the same since you gone.
It's divvied up betwixt three of us now 'n we fight like dogs
for the scraps. We could use you here, that's truth. Here,"
he said, dropping his voice to a whisper, "I'd work for you
again, I would, for I'd rather have a sure safe slice of the
pie 'n keep my neck than try for all 'n lose it, I'm nobody's
fool. So what do you say, Lion? Is it a go?"

"Sam, I meant it. I'm retired now. But tell the lady about
me, and spare the flattery, eh?" Arden said impatiently,
like a man angry that his noose hadn't been tied securely
enough.

"It ain't no flattery," Sam protested angrily, then in conciliatory tones went on, "I'm telling true. You was good to
us, 'n we need you again."

"Tell her what I did, exactly," Arden roared at him, so
loudly that the four men out-of-doors looked in the windows
and looked glad when their master waved them back again.

Sam shrugged. "You want me to nose on you? Fine. He
done, did, all the crafts, lady. Or that is to say, he watched
over all of it: the resurrection game—that's all in the south,
Lion, we don't see a cent in it no more—the scamps 'n
cracks 'n sneaks,the hoists 'n rushers—"

"I sold dead men for anatomy lessons," Arden broke in
to translate coldly, "and might have created some, for I
took care of the pickpockets and thieves and burglars of
every stripe—from those who entered through windows to
those who only stripped slow-moving wagons, I held the
reins on every pander and whore, every counterfeit and fence,
I saw to every criminal here, save, as Sam said, for the more
perverse and vicious of them, for I had some vestigial morals left then, but don't absolve me of it, for I don't. Because
I could afford those scraps of honor, my dear, since I made
a great deal of money without more," he concluded, lean-

ing over the table and staring into Francesca's eyes, his face
cold and hard as his voice had become.

"Just so!" Sam cried exuberantly, rising to his feet in his
excitement, " 'n you did it good, Lion. That's what I'm
trying to tell you! You kept the boys from the topping cheat,
'n kept them from being teased 'n lagged too. No hanging
nor whipping nor transporting the lads when Lion saw to
us, lady," he explained, turning his attention to Francesca.
"That I can tell you. You kept us safe, Lion," he told Arden
feverently. "Why, half the lads you knew are in Edinburgh
cut into ribbons, or moldering in potter's field since you cut
out on us. Come back, Lion," the pale man pleaded in a
low whisper. "There's need of you now!"

Arden was so taken aback by this round commendation
and offer that for once he stood speechless. Francesca sat
still, as appalled as she was amused, and yet never surprised, for she knew that whenever Arden did something,
he did it well.

"No, thank you, Sam," Arden finally said, taking Francesca's hand and helping her from her chair. "I'm out of
the game. You might try the same if things are getting too
hot," he added.

"Aye, and do what?" Sam said on a thin smile. "Become
a gent like you? Likely, eh? You was always a true gentleman, Lion. I'm born 'n bred to the rope. Still, think on it.
If ever you want in again, you call on Sam Towers, hear?"
he said, his air of insouciance returning, his swagger and
his mocking smile back in place, no hint of his desperate
pleading to be seen as he finally took Lion's offered hand.
" 'N we'll see what we can do, eh?"

"Take care, Sam," Arden said gravely as he led Francesca out into the street again.

The four men and Sam Towers left as well, and as quickly
as a shadow crossing the sun, they were gone, blended into
one of the many twisting alleyways behind them. But Arden
stood and looked down at Francesca, his face unreadable,
his voice soft as he bade her farewell.

"Go on home now, Francesca," he said evenly. "Now
you know. I'll walk awhile, and then return to see you safe
enough, never fear. I'll send you to Warwick, or my sister,
and they're clever enough to invent some tale to cover the
fact that you've traveled with me these weeks, and one day
you'll thank me, as well as your lucky stars, for my forbearance. But this is the last time we'll really speak, I

promise you. I wanted you, Francesca Carlisle," he said on a sigh, "too much to take you, in any way. Remember that. Such memories warm a lady in her declining years, I hear, so remember it well, and don't forget the big bad man who loved you as well." He smiled and touched a finger to her quivering chin.

"Nothing has changed," she said staunchly, refusing to plead with him as Sam Towers had done, but refusing to leave him as well.

"I was a criminal," he said angrily, "and low as any I sheltered, even if I didn't do precisely what they did. At that, did you know how I met our friend Julian? Ah, well, then it's time, is it not? Warwick knew him from school; I encountered him at a different sort of lessons. We met one night as my associates were at the job of half-killing him for a fee, for a nobleman afraid to dirty his hands. I saved Julian's face as well as his life, by terminating the contract, for there was cruelty and dishonor in the work that I wanted no part of. But I was no better than the men who held him so that he could be so soundly beaten."

"But Julian is still your friend," she said, her lip quavering, unable to say more in the face of his rage, unable to take it all in, only clinging stubbornly to her inner perceptions which told her without doubt that this man she wanted so badly needed her every bit as much as she needed him.

"We made our peace when I took up his cause, but it makes no matter," Arden said, his eyes bleak as he tried to wrench them from the sight of her, for she weakened his resolve. "Men pride themselves on their hardiness and can excuse anything in the name of that masculinity," he said on a depreciating smile. "But you . . . Francesca, my one wild little Fancy," he said tenderly, "I'd never harm you. But my past might, don't you see? Even if all else could be forgiven, repented, and washed clean, there's still that. I made enemies, and I'm glad of it. For a man with no enemies can have no true friends, and certainly no morals. But my enemies are legion, and they come no lower. No, I can't put you in such danger. You're young, you'll find another, worthier man. Have done, my Fancy, and let me go now, so that I can go on later.

"Get into the carriage, love," he said softly, lowering his head to hers for a last kiss. But he tasted salt tears on her lips, so he pressed his mouth to her clean, scented hair instead, and then let her go. He stepped back, and then turned, and then, never looking back, strode off to one of the dark, turning alleys that led away from where she stood, her hand to her mouth, in front of the coach that would take her away.

"Arden!" she called as he strode to the mouth of the alley. "Lion!" she cried, such wretchedness in her voice that low as it was, he heard it, as though he'd been attuned to her every breath, for it was a soft voice, not made for such efforts as shouting, nor made to bear such distress. "Don't leave me!" she cried, and he turned at last to look back at her. And he stood at the mouth of the alley, wavering, and gazed at her, indecisive then, as she stumbled forward, her heart clear to read in her eyes, her eyes only upon him.

And that was why neither of them saw the man step from the shadows of the doorway behind Arden, although both heard the blast from the gun he raised, straight-armed, and fired. When the smoke thinned, Arden still stood tall, his eyes no more filled with pain than before, but he shouted, "Go! Go now, Francesca!" as he came forward at a run to warn her off.

He managed to take her arm and pull her to the coach and push her within to safety before he turned to seek his assailant and fell at last to his length in the gutter, blood welling from the back of his ruined new biscuit jacket, to pour in a thin runnel down among the broken cobblestones.

18

HE WAS BREATHING. She could ascertain that much, for though nothing else moved, and indeed it seemed as though the world itself stood still as Arden lay in the street, she could see that the huge frame rose and fell, and it was that motion as much as anything that caused the blood to trickle from the wound she would not look upon. She averted her eyes from the back of the fine new jacket he wore, because she knew that if she saw it close, she'd lose all her control, and she needed it all just then.

She tried to think as he would.

"Coachman . . ." she called. "Coachman!" she shouted, going up to him and tugging at the ends of his long coat as he sat upon his box and stared, stupefied, at the giant man downed by the side of his carriage. "Go now, at once, you hear? Go, and tell Julian Dylan, the Viscount Hazelton, of what has happened. Go to Stephen's Hotel if he is not at the house where you picked us up this morning, and tell him. And tell him to get a physician and wait at the town house for us. Go now," she said desperately, "or it will go badly for you, I vow it will!"

That seemed to reach the coachman, and he raised his whip as though in a daze and then brought it down hard on his team and the coach leapt away. Then Francesca turned to see the crowd that began to appear, inching up out of the shadows of the maze of alleys. She sought out the brightest pair of eyes, the most nimble frame. "You," she commanded in her husky voice, pointing to a sharp-looking bone-thin boy of indeterminate years, a boy with a face like a ferret's all quivering whiskers and pointed ears, "a golden guinea for you, my word on it. If you go at once to Sam Towers—aye, him—and bring him here double-quick, and tell him the Lion is shot and downed in the street," and as the boy prepared to race away, she added harshly, "But he lives, tell him that the Lion still lives, be sure to tell him that."

For, she thought, trying to think like the man at her feet, although she doubted Sam Towers was responsible for this, she could not know it. But guilty or not, he'd come running, he'd not dare do otherwise—if he knew Arden still breathed. A request with a threat bedded deep in it, like the hook beneath the breadcrumb that she'd used as a child when angling for little fish, she thought giddily—that took the place of reason half the time, it seemed.

She bent down over the quiet man, and then she sat down upon the cobbles and drew that great heavy head up, and stroked the dirt from the side of his cheek as she rested it in her lap, and refused to look at the wound as she spoke low to him about how she was there, and all would be well. For she didn't dare think otherwise, she simply would not think it. And so she waited, watching him breathe, counting the breaths so as not to think about it.

Sam Towers came running seconds later, days later, she

could not know, and he'd his four strong men with him, and more, and they carried a door between them.

"He lives," she said defiantly as Sam looked down at her.

"O' course 'e does," Sam said quietly.

She must have told him where she wanted them to take Arden, she thought, as Sam helped her to her feet at last, and she must have warned him to be careful, for he was still swearing he meant no harm and asking her please to step aside, when she realized what he was saying, and stepped away to let them lift Arden and place him on the door. And then, somehow they must have bundled Arden into that great open funeral coach they'd gotten from somewhere, and she was still shaking with anger and wild laughter over it, for Arden was alive, she reminded Sam over and again, as they pulled up to the town house door and Julian, his face white and his eyes wild, helped her down from the ancient vehicle so she could follow Arden into the house.

But when they'd laid their burden down upon the bed, and the fattish little man with his sleeves rolled up that Julian called a surgeon began to strip Arden's coat from him, Julian took her by the shoulders and walked her to the door, to Roxanne, who had appeared from nowhere to cluck her tongue and widen her eyes and say nonsensical things as though they would comfort her.

"I'm not leaving," Francesca said, wheeling about. "He would not leave me," she told Julian.

"Very well," he said, and she came to stand with him over Arden then.

"Not the lung, for see, the blood's not red and bubbling, there's luck," the surgeon muttered as he cut the last of the shirt away to expose the broad muscled back, with the great bloody dimple newly sprung in it, "and yet not out the other side, so we must dig to see where it is. Against the bone if we're lucky, but at least he's out, it would take a team of horses to hold him down else, and I don't want to take the time to strap him to the bed, so we'll act at once— hold her head down, my lord," he went on in the same low drone as he cut deep into the smooth tanned flesh, and Francesca saw the world blacken around the edges and lost the sound of his voice in the throbbing thunder that filled her ears.

"No," she said when Julian sat her on a nearby chair and let his hand up from the back of her neck, and she heard

him ask someone to help take her away, "No," she protested on a sob of a breath, fighting up from darkness, "let
me stay, I won't look at it, but I must stay with him,
please."

She came round to the head of the bed then, as Julian
suggested, and held on to one of Arden's outstretched hands
and looked down only at the still face, sidewise upon the
pillows, as the surgeon continued his work. And that was
when she saw the perspiration on that broad forehead, and
saw the lashes twitch and the clear eyes open to look blankly
at a distant shore.

Then he gazed at her, as though he'd felt her stare, and
he returned to his pain-drenched eyes then and something
like a smile flickered across his broad mouth.

"Canny girl," he whispered, "brave lass," and the surgeon stopped in mid-stroke at the utterance. But then the
surgeon shook his head and grunted, "Sorry, my friend,
but I must," and Arden tried to nod permission. " 'Lay on,
Macduff,' " he recited, " 'and damned be him that first
cries . . .' " He drew in his breath as the surgeon grunted
and bore down upon his knife. And then he closed his eyes
on a shuddering sigh and lay still. It wasn't until Francesca
heard a new indrawn breath replace the air he'd sighed out
that she breathed again herself and stroked his forehead and
whispered, " '. . . Hold enough . . .' " to finish the quo-
tation for him.

Time, the surgeon said, time, the surgeon promised would
answer all the questions modern medicine could not. "We'll
know how serious it is in time," he'd said, for though the
ball was out, and the broad bone it had lodged against still
whole, for the fellow who'd loaded the ball into the gun had
mercifully not notched it beforehand so that it would splin-
ter into a dozen deadly shards on impact, still only "if the
fever leaves and he does well will we know more," he'd
proclaimed, though Francesca couldn't see what more there
was to know beyond discovering if he'd ever come back to
them. For this third day, after one spent in drugged sleep
and another passed in unnatural, restless dreams, he slept
on still and spoke now and again in a language she didn't
know to people who weren't there.

"*Querida, por favor, dame un poco de agua,*" he said
now, and Francesca looked from his flushed face to Julian's
drawn and white one, for the viscount hadn't left his side,

except to wash and eat and catch an odd hour of sleep, she knew, for he relieved her after those times.

"He asks for water again," Julian said wearily.

"Who is 'Querida'?" she dared ask at last, jealous of the lovely lady with the beautiful name he kept calling to.

"It only means 'dear,' and is only a light term of endearment. He was wounded once, in the Peninsula, and I expect he believes he is back there again now. Hello, Julian, how are you, my dear Francesca?" the tall, slender long-nosed gentleman said softly as he came in the bedroom door, stripping off his driving gloves. He stopped then and looked down at Arden. "Oh, how are the mighty fallen," he murmured. "I was hoping I was mistold or it was exaggerated, all the way here," he mused, never taking his brilliant dark blue stare from the man on the bed.

"Warwick!" Julian said with sudden gladness sparking like lightning across the shadows in his handsome face, "But Susannah . . ." he protested as he looked at his newly arrived friend. "I sent word, but never thought you'd come."

"Susannah is well, and well rid of me, for she says she's had enough doting to last her through another confinement, and begged me to see to Arden, to get some surcease and time to herself at last as well as to aid him. She delivered my heirs the night you left, friends, yes—two—lavish lady that she is. A handsome young gent to fill my shoes and a pretty little sister to tell him how to go about it. And as the house is brimming now, since they arrived early and so we must engage a wet nurse as well as nurses—aren't these details enchanting?—I ambled along to see what a pest of myself I could be here, at yet another bedside."

But then the duke stopped jesting, although the joke had never reached so far as his eyes, and he'd never taken those eyes from the bed. "How goes he?" he said then, softly.

"Who knows?" Julian replied.

"You might ask me," a faint rumble of a voice said querulously.

They grouped around the bed and looked down into the exhausted face that wore a faint triumphant grin.

"You must always have the last word, mustn't you, my Lion?" Warwick asked, shaking his head as he took his friend's hand.

"You bring out the worst in me, Duke," Arden answered, his white teeth bright against the rusty stubble that had begun to cover his jaw, looking like a weary pirate as he smiled up at them. "Be sure to invite him to my wake, please, Fancy, so that I can come back to lift a glass with him."

"What? Leaving so soon after you've arrived again?" Warwick asked.

"Have I returned?" Arden replied, and then wincing as he tried to sit up, he nodded. "Aye, I have."

"We'll leave you to get some sleep," Julian said at once.

"Oh, I believe I've had enough," Arden said, attempting to rise again, grimacing as he failed, and then putting up a hand to forestall Julian's objections. "Don't fret, nurse, I learn quickly, I'll be still. But not sleeping, not just yet, for I've a mystery to solve or I'll never be able to sleep easy again. I must know who came for me, you know."

"I imagine whoever it was isn't sleeping too easy neither, my gentle friend." Warwick laughed. "I'd think anyone who aimed for you and missed would be a trifle . . . restless now. But don't worry, we'll aid and comfort you in every way we can."

"In every way you *may*," Arden carefully corrected him. "I don't wish to share my sickbed, you know."

"Selfish beast," Julian muttered, and the gentlemen all laughed.

But Francesca didn't, and it was as if Arden heard the absence of her laughter louder than he'd heard the rest.

"And you will stay on here with me, please, Francesca," Arden said softly, and as her spirits rose and a great smile began to appear on her face, he added, "nor will you set foot without this door, I think, until we have the rogue in hand. Then, and only then, you may leave."

Her smile faltered and she cast her gaze down, looking so troubled that Arden frowned and searched his blurred mind for something consoling, but not misleading, to say.

"Very officious for a man we can easily take advantage of now, don't you think?" Warwick asked Julian lightly, looking a different question at him with one thin dark slightly raised brow.

"Well, I don't know," Julian replied, nodding slightly, as Arden continued to gaze at Francesca. "I think we might ask a few more fellows in to sit on him, even so, but then, if you like, I'd be glad to help take advantage of him with you. So for now, since we're about six strong men short, if you don't mind, Arden, you may plot, or plan, or read a book, or ask Francesca to dance, if you wish. But I," he said on a huge yawn, "having actually for the first time in my life sat up with a sick friend for several nights, am for bed at last, thank you."

"Yes," Warwick agreed, "for it may be dawn to you, Arden, dear beautiful dreamer, but I rode for the better part of a day to get here, and having left at dawn, I feel rather like a centaur now, the bottom part, that is. I'll see you in the morning, my Lion. Francesca," he said on a sketch of a bow, and then put his arm about Julian's shoulder and went to the door with him.

"But wait! Ah . . . yes," Arden said, gathering his wits together, for it seemed he was, as his friends had guessed, still wearier than he knew. "Tell me, the twins, how are they? . . . Lord, who are they? And whom do they resemble?"

"The girl, poor thing," Warwick said sadly, turning round to show his grieved expression, "looks like an angel, fair and blond as my lovely bride, but just like her deprived mama, she's got the same lack—hardly any nose to speak of at all, poor little mite."

"Perhaps it will grow," Julian said sympathetically, as Arden grinned.

"Not much hope of that"—Warwick shook his head with a wonderful show of regret—"for her taller, darker brother, who came into the world a half-hour sooner, entered nose-first, thank heaven, like his papa. A great, lovely appendage he has already." He sighed gratefully.

"Ah, Warwick, bragging about your appendages again," Julian chided him, and laughing, after apologizing to Francesca, who was trying mightily not to smile, they left the room together.

"You did well," Arden said to her after they'd gone. "Getting me here, ordering everyone about—my kind dictator. Come stand here, next to me, as you did these past days, for I saw you, you know, even if I couldn't reach out of myself to tell you so. Yes," he said as she came to his side again, "just so." He took her hand, and closed his eyes. "Embarrassing," he rumbled "to make a fine renunciation speech and then fall in a faint at your lady's feet."

She heard the "your lady" and stored it up before she answered carefully, weighting each word so as not to distress him or herself.

"I worried for you, Arden," she whispered, "although I didn't dare say it aloud, but I did so worry that I might lose

you—before and after your fine speech,'' and then she grew
very still, for she'd said it, at last, however subtly, just as
she'd promised herself she would if he survived through the
long days and nights as she'd watched his struggle for a
purchase on life again.

He was silent, and she thought he might have drifted to
sleep, when he murmured,"Foolish chit. Only the good die
young, you know.''

But he'd not argued about the other part of what she'd
said, so she only smiled, and held his hand the tighter, until
his even breathing told her he was at last in a healthy, healing slumber, and she dared hope his slight smile as he slept
told her more.

She stayed a moment to watch him, feeling oddly self-
conscious now as she hadn't during the past days, because
now she knew those amberine eyes could open and actually
see and know her and recognize all the emotions he might
surprise in her face. Odd, she thought, how powerful he
looked now that she knew he was himself again. She remembered the shock of seeing how diminished and vulnerable he'd seemed when they'd brought him here senseless,
for all his size, and for all his size that was when he'd frightened her the most since the day she'd met him. For she'd
been terrified as she'd hovered at this bedside begging every
deity she could remember for favor as she waited for the
heat to leave his restless, turning brow, for the swelling to
fade from that grotesque violation that marred the clear
tanned skin on his muscular back, for strength to return to
those inert limbs, and awareness to dawn so wit and charm
could animate those closed, craggy features again to make
them more exciting than any man's she'd ever seen.

He was no beauty as Julian Dylan was, nor so elegant as
his friend Warwick, not light and winning as Harry Devlin
had been, nor as facile and insincere as her papa. No, he
was big and complex and unique and different, her Arden
Lyons. When he'd laid in this bed so close and yet so entirely gone from her, she'd realized that all she'd ever wanted
in a man was gone then too. Then she'd been surprised at
the depth of her feelings, but no longer. She accepted the
rush of fierce protectiveness she felt even as she gazed down
at him now. For his size meant nothing; she'd seen how
quickly life could be taken from the most robust of men.
And his size was as nothing to the measure of her emotions
for him. Whatever he'd done, he'd never done a cruelty—

that she was convinced of. Whatever he'd been was as nothing to what he was now and could be. And no matter what he planned, or what chanced next, however they parted, or for however long, while she lived he was hers, and would always be; she knew that now.

And yet when his eyelids flickered, if only at some bothersome moment in a passing dream, she caught her breath, and fled the room, lest he open his eyes to fathom what she now knew before she could conceal it decently, and so pity her, or worse, deny her yet again.

Two days later, against doctor's orders but for the sake of domestic tranquility and everyone else's sanity, the first visitor Arden summoned to his bedside came to call. After long years in the Duke of Peterstow's employ, his long-suffering London butler didn't so much as blink at the apparition which presented itself, hat in hand, at the front door, but to go so far as to announce him as a "gentleman" was more than he could suffer. "Mr. Sam Towers," was all he said on the best-repressed shudder as he eyed the visitor's finery—a snug mustard jacket, accompanied by canary pantaloons, tan topboots, and an extraordinary striped violently green waistcoat with gold buttons.

But Mr. Lyons said he thought his visitor looked fine as fivepence, straight off, and the duke and the viscount also nodded complete approval with perfectly straight faces, and Francesca rose up to greet him with great warmth, leaving only the butler and Roxanne to stand amazed.

As soon as the butler had left, Sam Towers spoke up, ignoring the compliment on his splendor. He faced the huge gentleman clad in a silken robe, propped up on a bank of pillows upon the bed, and looked him straight in the eyes.

"It wasn't me, Lion," he said. "My word, it wasn't me."

"I know," Arden answered.

"Because," his visitor went on, eager to have the thing out and said, "if I was vexed with you, Lion, I'd do you, certain, but back-shooting ain't never my way."

The ladies might not have been comforted by this reasoning, but the gentlemen all took it in the spirit in which it was offered.

"I know it well, Sam," Arden said, "and never thought it was you for a moment. In fact, I have you to thank for your quick action in getting me here to my sawbones."

"Didn't have a choice." Sam grinned, sliding a look to

Francesca. "Your lady would have done for me if I didn't hop to it."

"True," Arden laughed, but then looked at Sam keenly, and for all the big man had lost flesh in his recent illness, so that the strong bones in his face showed hard and clear, his eyes were as bright as ever and perhaps even more piercing by the way they dominated his face now. "But now, of course, I need your help again."

"I reckoned"—Sam nodded back—"and I ain't been dozing. I nosed it about, but didn't need to, it's all anybody's been talking about, Lion. You got friends, man." Sam shook his head. "I knew you was respected, but I didn't know how much. People owe you, Lion, 'n everyone wants to pay up. If we knew who it was, he'd a been served up on a plate to you already, depend on it. The word is he's a stranger."

"But a clever man would hire a stranger to do dogs' work," Arden mused.

"Aye, I been there and back ahead o' you," Sam agreed, "and I'm looking 'n listening, 'n soon's I hear, you will, my word on't."

"Your word is good enough for me," Arden replied, and this praise caused Sam Towers' thin, pale face to light up like a boy's and he flushed in his pleasure as he said in an impassioned whisper, "Anytime, Lion, anytime you want in again, like I said, 't would be an honor."

And then, refusing food or drink, and backing away as he would from his king, Sam Towers promised word as soon as he had it, and bowing, left them.

"Sam told me no more than I expected," Arden commented after his visitor had left and the company sat in silence, thinking of what they'd heard, "but I expect more from others, and as I can't go to them because of my officious jailers, I must have them come to me until I know the score. No man has more than a pair of eyes and ears, but I've access to a city full of sniffing noses, and I'll need to interview them. And some of them are . . . ah, exceptional, for all they'll come here in all their finery and on their highest manners. So I think it best, Duke, if I remove to Stephen's Hotel again now, for it won't do to let the trail grow cold."

"If you really think so, I'd think it best you remove to Bedlam, Lion," Warwick said pleasantly. "Is it my reputation or my silver you worry about? I am a duke now, as you never allow me to forget, as well as embarrassingly rich. So though it grieves me to say it, knowing the standards of the *ton,* I believe the only way I could ruin my reputation now would be to paint myself purple and waltz nude into Almack's. And at that, I might set a style, money and title being wonderful guarantees of acceptability. And as to the safety of my silverplate, I doubt any of your guests would so much as pick up a pin they thought you'd a care for. So, in fact, lodging you here will ensure my home being burglar-proof for the next sixty years, I'd think. If you attempt to leave me now, dear Lion,'' Warwick summed up sweetly, "I'll shoot you in the back again myself."

Arden nodded. "Are you thinking of a career in politics now, your grace? You've got a most persuasive tongue. I'll stay then, since I don't care for more perforations in my pelt. But as for the ladies—I only let Francesca stay because she knew Sam, but from now on, ladies, from intimate knowledge of some of the players who'll be presented here, I think it best we deal you out of this game.''

Roxanne shrugged, and was about to say it was no treat she was being denied, but Francesca's glowing cheek had grown pallid at his words, and now she spoke up, shy but determined, struggling for the right words so as not to seem too forward, troubled because she was aware that too-careful consideration might make her seem backward.

"If it's my sensibilities that you worry for, Arden, I remind you that I am my father's daughter. If it's my personal safety you're concerned with, I'd think they'd have to shoot you dead to harm me with you here . . . but then again, as the duke says, with you here I doubt they'd dare so much as look at me crosswise. Anyway,'' she said in a rush, remembering her recent success with persuasion and that the sweetest reason had succeeded best with a threat within, "I'm curious, and so I can't promise that I won't listen at the door if you ban me.''

"Oh, marvelous,'' Julian crowed.

"You've been keeping bad company, my child,'' Warwick chided her, as enormously tickled by her threat as he was by the way she expressed it in her rough, low little voice.

Arden looked amazingly pleased, so he sighed, and shrugged until he realized such gestures were beyond him until his bandages came off, and so managed a truly pained expression as he said helplessly, "So, see then, how I am coerced. It's a terrible thing to be at other people's mercy."

And Roxanne laughed gaily and applauded and thought glumly that there went her chance to do some more shopping, because if Fancy stayed on and they all thought it wonderful in her, what choice had she but to stay and enjoy whatever it was that was supposed to be so interesting.

They were, even Warwick had to agree, an interesting collection of humanity, those few who were assigned to speak for so many as they made their pilgrimage to Arden's bedside.

Portwine John, so named obviously for the birthmark that adorned the right side of his face, had obviously not deemed it necessary to bathe as carefully as he'd dressed for the occasion of his visit to his old friend, the downed Lion. For though his garments were so beautifully cut and fashioned that even the duke's butler could find no fault in them, from the scent of the beautifully dressed tall dark-skinned fellow it was altogether possible that he was not half so swarthy as he appeared to be.

He paid his respects, and commiserated on Arden's condition, while all the while everyone else in the room save the patient, trapped in his bed, subtly shifted position to get safely upwind of the visitor. But for all he gave his sympathy with as much force as he did his ripe aroma, he shed no new light on the identity of Arden's assailant.

"I dunno who done you, Lion," he swore in his whispery voice. "It ain't no one I know, that's sure. But it won't be easy to find 'im, neither. As much as you want the bastard—s'cuse me, ladies, but I'm a plain-spoken man—there's many another who'd like to tear 'is legs off and beat 'im over the head with 'em. You've that many friends, Lion, and it ain't no secret you're missed in the game. I'm looking," he said at the last, ominously, as he bowed himself out, and Julian and Warwick rushed to the windows to throw them open.

"He may be a captain of crime, Arden," Julian breathed as he drew in great gulps of wet spring air, "but I doubt he got his start as a sneak thief or pickpocket, however stealthily he moves. You could tell his coming for a mile without ears or eyes," he gasped.

"But he's clever and resourceful and as wonderfully devious as he is soiled. He mistrusts water, but I'm honored.

For I do believe,'' Arden said with great hauteur, ''that he dusted himself off entirely before he came here.''

They never laughed when Mrs. Crowell came to call. Julian was enchanted by the sweet old woman and Roxanne and Francesca hung on her every perfectly articulated syllable. She was an ancient diminutive creature, dressed all in grays and lavenders and scented as softly as a whisper of potpourri wafting from a cedar press.

''How glad I am that you survived, my dear,'' she told Arden after she'd greeted him, pressing her handkerchief to her soft gray eyes. ''What a turn I got when I heard the news. I've asked all my children to keep an eye and ear open for suspects, but all to no avail. The only clue I've gotten, and that from a drunken fish seller and a hint more via a dustman, is that he's a stranger, and that only because one has been seen in the rookery with too much sobriety and caution for the role of poor artist he plays. I'd like to be the one that finds him, dear,'' she said softly as she rose to leave, ''for I vow I'll hand him to you without his ballocks if I do,'' and still sweetly smiling, as Francesca and Roxanne gaped at her, she drifted out of the room.

''She is,'' Arden explained to the ladies with an admirably straight face as Warwick and Julian fell about with laughter, ''quite a successful bawd, as you know. Or rather, as you ought not to know.''

Barthelomew Bell brought a bower of flowers, along with word that he was on the trail; Fishhouse Jim brought greetings from all the denizens of his ken, along with a sack of mackerel as a gift to confound Warwick's cook and appall his butler; Jenny Gently wept at seeing Lion again, and bawled the harder when she admitted she'd nothing but rumor to offer him along with all her best wishes and a quantity of gin. They came in great numbers, they came in their best attire and on their best behavior, they came for brief visits, bearing odd gifts and awed reverence, as pilgrims to a shrine, but they all, to a man and a woman and a child, came empty-handed when it came to real word of Arden's would-be assassin.

It was on the third day that someone arrived whom Arden did not know, and so did not so much weep with joy at his recovery as he came to meet him and offer up some news.

Ben-be-Good was such a handsome young man that Roxanne sat up sharply as he bowed his way into Arden's sickroom. Slender and jaunty, well-dressed as any blood on the town, with a cocky smile on his fresh young face, he bowed to the ladies before he addressed the gentlemen and made himself known to Arden.

"You don't know me, sir," he said, sounding every bit the gentleman, until one listened close to hear the too-perfect enunciation that told of the hard work that shaped his speech, "but I remember you well. I ran messages for Whitey Lewis, and did the odd job for whoever tossed the highest coin for me. I run several interesting industries now, and want more, but then, who doesn't? I understand you're done with the business, and can't say I blame you. But you're missed, sir, I can tell you that. You saved my life."

"Much as that pleases me, for I can see it's an estimable life I was about preserving, I can't say I remember you," Arden apologized. "I'm sorry."

"You wouldn't," Ben-be-Good said on a little smile, "and I ought to have said you saved my life several times, and yet even so you wouldn't remember, for you never knew it, or me. And you are the estimable man, sir." He leaned close to Arden then, ignoring the others in the room to look at him with concentrated intent. All his good humor vanished, his face so serious that Warwick and Julian became alert and tense, his face so grave that it could finally be seen that without his ready laughter, it was a slum child's ageless face, with the overlay of pain and wisdom that robbed it of its youth.

"I count it five times I survived because of you," he said earnestly. "The first, when I'd lifted my first silk handkerchief from an old gent as he was about bargaining with a tart, and when I went to sell it to the fence I'd been told about, Mother Daltry, I found she'd been warned out of the business—by you. Because you discovered she'd been selling little chaps like me to bigger gents. Again when I tried to join up with dashing Lawrence French, whom we boys so admired, only to find he was out of town permanently after you found he was bundling his lads out to the navy for a fee. Again when you closed down Martha Love for paying off her boys with opium instead of extra cash, and I was of an age and a mind that I wouldn't have minded until too late, and then again when you shipped George Gibbons for taking money for information on us lads, along with our jokes and brag at the flash house he ran."

He paused, his eyes downcast.

"That's four," Arden said quietly.

''And again when you thrashed my father for daring to try to sell you a corpse that was far too lately living,'' he said quietly, ''so that he feared you more than going without drink, and left us, my mother and me, to go off with his cronies and never returned, and so let us, my mother and me, live. You looked after us all, Lion, in like fashion, all of the unknown little rats of the East End. And when you left, it all fell apart. I'm building it up again. I'm trying to be like you.''

''Good God, lad, do not!'' Arden said angrily.

''Who else will look after the little villains, sir?'' the young man asked with a twisted smile. ''The judges and the hangmen? It's death to steal a watch, as you well know, and transport for swiping a cheese, the rope for forging a pound note, and to the Antipodes for eternity with those who borrow a meal without asking. No, I didn't come for permission, but only to say thanks, and to try to repay you with word of the man who shot you, for he offended us all when he did.

''He's gone from his lodgings, so I can't give you that, nor his name, for it was doubtless a false one he used, nor have I ever set eyes on him myself. But he wasn't one of us, nor hired by any of us, neither. For even your enemies would not dare, not if they have to live among us. It's a gent from your new world, sir, and an Englishman too, for all he says he's French, and—''

''Ben, my boy,'' Arden said quickly, ''I'm sorry to cut you off, but could you hold that thought?''

Ben-be-Good stopped abruptly, and as Arden went on to say in an urgent whisper, ''I heard a noise outside in the hall, please look, Julian.'' and as Julian did, no more than a look passed between the young man and Arden, but it was enough, for the young man was quick.

''No one . . . I think,'' Julian reported in a worried tone when he returned, although he flashed quite a different look to Arden, for he was quick as well.

''But that doesn't mean it's not possible. I'll have the staff kept from this area unless on business,'' Warwick said, frowning, for he too was never slow to hear that which wasn't said. ''We may have been too casual, your life was threatened once, my friend, and I'll not have it again, and certainly not in my house, until we know more of this mysterious gentleman.''

"But there is no more to say, at least that I know. I'm sorry," young Ben-be-Good said.

The company all grew still then, before Ben began to reminisce with Arden, and flirt a bit with Roxanne, and entertain them all wonderfully. All except for Francesca. For she, too, wasn't slow to comprehend. And knew, of course, that there was more Arden didn't wish for her to know. There'd been no noise outside the room; she sat closer to the door than Arden, and she'd swear to it. It was the conversation in the room Arden wanted immediately stopped. The possible reasons why troubled her almost as much as the fact that she was being deceived, even if he thought it for her own good. Most of all, sensing Arden's thoughtful gaze upon her, she knew that he wouldn't have sundered their intimacy and friendship by excluding her for anything but what he'd think was good reason. Any of those reasons she could imagine were hard for her to bear, harder still because now she knew she'd have to bear them alone.

He walked with his head down, and didn't venture out until dusk, but still the dark was too light for him. He walked quickly; it was a brave thing he was doing, and it frightened him enormously, but it had to be done. When he reached the end of the street, he paused and looked up at the town house in one quick nod of his head, almost as if he'd a tic, before he lowered his chin and marched on again. So that was the house, he thought, so that meant it was impossible for him to do more until the giant left the house again, since simply coming to see it had taken up all his courage for the day.

Still, he was proud of how far he'd come, because every step had frightened him. But each time he survived the fear he felt, he grew stronger and so knew he was doing right. When he'd fired the gun he'd thought his own heart had split from the sheer terror of it, and there was no shame in it for him that he'd waited until the man's back was turned. Because even that had been beyond his ability once before, when that same back had been turned, as both a challenge and an insult, upon him. But this time he'd grown brave enough to finally answer that dare, if belatedly, and as courage grew from courage, next time, he thought, he'd be able to do even more.

He'd be able to free Francesca, he thought, rescue her and take her back to France with him, and live in peace and love with her, as he'd always thought to do before fear had chased all joy from his heart that terrible morning. Because fear, he was discovering, could be overcome. Thinking of that, he began to walk tall again for the first time in a long time.

"Excuse me, sir . . ." the gentleman passing by said, pausing in the street to gaze hard and questioningly at him.

"I speak no English," Harry Devlin said in a rush, and ducked his head, and scuttled down the street and away into the shadows again, leaving the man to wonder what he'd done to frighten the foreign gentleman so badly, and whom he could ask the time of next, for he'd mislaid his watch and if he was late to dinner again, his wife would never forgive him.

19

"HE MENDETH the fastest who walketh the soonest," Arden insisted, holding the banister tightly.

"He flattens the soonest whose foolish friend falleth upon him," Julian countered, standing on the step below. "Walk if you must, idiot, but not on the stairs. Warwick hardly needs a dungeon in his front hall, and if you crash, you'll go straight through to the basement, you know."

"But I wish to receive my visitors from a chair, below-stairs, like a living man, not lying in state on a bier," Arden explained, clinging to the rail, for his back throbbed as though someone was drumming on it now, and the stairs had become treacherous since his feet refused to acknowledge his head, "and I refuse to be carried down like a log, thank you," he added, as Julian offered his arm, and with the surprising strength he concealed so well, helped hold him up as he negotiated the rest of the stairs.

When on solid ground again, he sighed and straightened his cuffs, for he'd just passed an entertaining hour putting on his clothes without falling on his face, and didn't want his work to go for nothing now. And then he looked up to see Francesca arrested in mid-step in the hallway, staring at him, her hand to her heart, her eyes wide and troubled.

"No, truly," he said at once, "it's a certifiable fact. I noted it in the Peninsula, those lads who got to their feet the fastest kept their health the best. Bed's fine for many things, but not recuperation," he added, hoping his unexpected reaction to a pang of pain would be taken for a leer.

"Oh, lovely," Warwick said, coming into the hall behind him. "War stories to justify suicide now—what an entertaining houseguest you are, to be sure, Lion. Do you have a thrilling deathbed speech prepared, as well?"

"I'm rehearsing a more mundane farewell, which I hope to deliver soon as may be," Arden growled as he made his way as steadily as he could toward the drawing room and a chair he focused on, hoping he'd arrive there before his entire field of vision became as dark as the edges of it were growing.

He found Julian on his left, and Warwick on his right, and without another word they walked him to his destination. The pain of settling in the chair was as nothing to the effort of concealing it, and it was a moment before he spoke again. And then he laughed.

"A damned fool thing to do," he conceded, now that he'd achieved his goal. "You're right. But it had to be done. And not just for the look of it, because it's true that lying about after injury brings worse evils, or so I saw it then. And true too," he added, with a look to Francesca, who still appeared stricken with concern for him, "that because of it I was afraid to remain in bed."

"Very fearful is our Lion," Warwick agreed.

"It doesn't take courage to try to save your own skin," Arden said testily, before he laughed again and commented, "Lord, now I understand how old gents get so crusty—it's damned annoying to have to creep about and listen to yourself creak as you do. Maybe that's why the good die young—it serves them the embarrassment of old age. At any rate, Warwick, I *was* thinking of you, believe it or don't. Because the sooner I'm quit of you, the sooner you can get back to the bliss of dandling your infants on your knee and frightening Susannah with the prospects of more, or whatever it is that you do in your countrified fastness. Since you refuse to leave until my problems are solved, the gents I'm seeing today should help me in removing myself from your tender mercies the faster."

"Major Kern, Lieutenant Adjutant Miller, and Captain Shipp," Warwick said, "all late of his majesty's Light Dragoons, and each given an hour's audience. Wouldn't it have been simpler, considering how well you're feeling, to have them all to tea together?"

"Easier, but far less effective," Arden sighed. "When old army men get together, lock up the port, get out your nightcap, and put out the cat, for they blather on for an eternity with reminiscence that grows progressively fantastic, and enlivening only to each other. No, the three of them in the room together would be amusing, but I wouldn't get a sensible word from any of them. It'll be hard enough as it is, so I'd like to make it as unsociable an occasion as possible."

"I'll withhold tea, refuse them water, and have the footmen remove the chairs," Warwick promised promptly as Julian eagerly offered to insult them roundly too.

"Not quite that unsocial, I believe," Arden sighed, "but nearly so." He gazed at Francesca with a show of regret. "So pray don't take it amiss, Fancy, that you're not invited to join us. A pretty lady is all an army man needs to get him to ignoring everyone else in the room, twirling his mustaches and coming all over coy, and then hanging about until she gets too weary to say no."

"But," Francesca said, speaking up as innocently as she could, though her eyes had narrowed during Arden's excuses for her coming dismissal, "I'd like to hear about your army career."

"A gem of a girl," Warwick confided loudly to Julian.

"My dear," Arden said blithely, "it wouldn't do. Once they'd seen you, I might as well leave the room for the day. Remind me to tell you my army experiences tonight, at dinner," and as Julian and Warwick groaned loudly, he added, pointedly ignoring them, "Until that fascinating moment, suffice it to say I was clever and bold, brave as I could hold together, and a brilliant tactician. I kept my boots shined beautifully too," he added smugly.

"Our Lion was no less than a bona fide hero," Warwick commented, ignoring Arden's scowl as he went on, "for all he's pleased to jest. He's enough medals to start his own pawn brokerage, and commendations enough to paper over Napoleon's drawing room, for he rose to a colonel in his majesty's service, before he was pleased to sell out."

"I was more than pleased, I was ecstatic," Arden snarled,

eager to change the subject, and began to ask his host what keyholes he'd snooped at when Julian added merrily, amazed and amused yet again at how Arden squirmed at praise as he'd never do at pain or injury, "Yes . . . Fuentes de Onoro, Badajoz, Ciudad Rodrigo . . . his itinerary in Spain wasn't one for idle tourists, it reads like a dispatch from the battlefront, and his name was mentioned in many of those dispatches too," he added, his face growing more serious as he gazed down at his friend with pride.

Francesca sat quietly as she listened, unwilling to make a sound lest she call attention to herself and interrupt this odd, touching, and honest moment among the three friends. Because although they'd supposedly begun these revelations about Arden for her benefit, she doubted they thought of her at all now. This was for each other. There was a bond among them, she perceived, that supported and greatly pleased them all, for all they jested about it. It was a sort of love, and it was as good to behold as it was rare. She wouldn't say a word lest she miss one that was spoken, for when they weren't jesting, these three spoke truth, and spoke it so as to aid each other.

"*Et tu*, Julian?" Arden murmured unhappily. "But how did you discover it? And not a word of it to me until now?" He shook his head in dismal wonder.

"Oh," Julian said simply, grinning, "I'd a friend who taught me that the best gamesters keep their best cards concealed until they need them. And as to how—why, Warwick told me so."

"Am I any less than you, my dear Lion?" Warwick asked before Arden could speak. "Would you sit down to play with any man until you know the cards he held? And as to how—why, Wellington told me long ago."

"With you, my devious duke," Arden said, nodding, "it's entirely possible. Although I'd think it more probable that you had it from Harriet Wilson's pillow."

"Such a monster of vanity," Warwick scolded, "to think that the great Wellington had nothing better to do than whisper praise of him into his mistress's ear! At any rate, I never enjoyed anything but dear Harriet's displeasure, even in those salad days when I so much as looked at other females. She was both too expensive and too cheap for my tastes. But enough salaciousness, for look—our clever Francesca, all a-lurk and a-listen, is still quiet as a mouse but now red as a rose!"

"True—I'm afraid you'd make an inferior spy, Fancy," Arden said ruefully, though he smiled at her. "You've got the silence down very well, but whenever the talk got warm, you'd glow in the dark."

Knowing the best way to deflect attention from herself was to call it back to him, Francesca, hoping her blushes, if for nothing else but that attention, were fading, only said, "I'm glad to hear of your glorious career, Arden, however it was divulged."

"Oh, yes, glorious," he said, all laughter fled. "So glorious I tried to leave all memory of it in Spain when I left there. Battle's nothing but savagery, and the aftermath of it in Badajoz showed me how killing fever's infectious and in some cases incurable once it's set in. No, medals for competency in killing are not my idea of fashion."

"But for all I don't know a great deal about the army, despite my brother's having been in it," she said just as seriously, for she sensed his denial of his honors had more to do with his distaste of how he'd earned them than of the honors themselves, "I know they give medals for bravery, not slaughter."

Warwick and Julian looked at her with approval and fell silent. And Arden smiled at her again. Then he shrugged, and scoffed, and the moment was gone, but it had restored something to him, for he seemed easier in his mind.

"Oh, bravery," he said lightly. "It's much misunderstood. It's only doing something you'd rather not, but think you ought. Extreme bravery is doing something you'd *really* rather not, but know you must. Fools confuse it with daring or recklessness, but it's nothing but duty. Good army men don't think about it at all. And the gents I've coming here today may talk about war itself in passing, but mostly they'll want to forget the battles to remember all the gossip and little incidents to do with weather and supplies and other men. Talk of battles and bravery is for those who were chefs and onlookers—fighting men speak of trivialities and leave history to judge what they did while at work."

But Francesca doubted that Major Kern, Arden's first visitor, had only gossip on his mind when he came to call. She'd a look at him when she was introduced as he was announced, and a lingering glance at him as he sat down to confer with Arden—and Warwick and Julian. For neither of the other men left the room, and Major Kern was unsmiling and efficient-looking and still in uniform. He looked as determined as any officer about to ride into battle, and never like an old army chum come to chat about the weather that amusing day in Spain.

She'd a father who was a master of lies, so Francesca quite naturally doubted anything told to her, and for all that Arden, who might well have been able to sell her father London Bridge if he'd a mind to, had been so blithe with his excuse of army friends come to call for tea and tall tales, he hadn't seemed entirely comfortable with it. Or rather, she thought, as she pretended to look at letters left on a table in the hall, so a passing footman would think her occupied, he'd seemed far too comfortable with it. It might have been because of her experience with her father, or even because she dared believe she might be becoming someone Arden couldn't be easy about deceiving, but mostly it was that she was too alive with speculation to take any excuse for her banishment easily. She wanted to know what was going forth in the drawing room more than she'd wanted anything in her life but Arden's life before.

But the moment she drifted past the drawing room, coming close enough to hear the low vibrations of active conversation through the closed heavy oak doors, the duke's butler appeared like a genie from a bottle, out of nowhere, to ask if there was something she needed, just as she was seriously thinking about resting her ear against the door and calling it a fainting spell if that door should swing open. But a fainting spell with that astute butler watching closely would avail her nothing but salts waved under her nose and the housekeeper called to see her to her bed. And it was the front hall and the drawing room she wanted to see. So remembering that the library lay diagonally across the front hall, she murmured something about seeking a book to read, and trying to look earnestly studious, she made her way there, found a chair facing the open door, and waited.

Major Kern left after his appointed hour, looking as grim and determined as he'd been when he arrived. She'd hardly time to actually look at the book she'd opened when the front door was opened again to admit Lieutenant Adjutant Miller, a comely young man with an easy smile and the evident gift for making others merry as well, for long after he was shown into the drawing room and the door closed behind him, Francesca could hear the rumbling vibrations of masculine laughter coming from the room. He'd stayed for his entire hour when Francesca, who'd kept careful count of the passing minutes, laid down her book and arose. Her timing was almost as perfect as the lieutenant's, and her tread was much more deliberate, so by stopping to look at her slippers and dawdling as she retied them, she imagined to be passing by the drawing room just as his hour was up, and was pleased to appear all surprise and delight when she came face-to-face with him as the door opened, and was introduced, at last.

She received a flatteringly appreciative smile from the young man as all of his handsome face lit up, including, she would swear, his signature army mustaches, but nothing else for her pains except for such a rueful, knowing look from Arden that she dared not linger so as to meet his third guest. She returned to the library only after Captain Shipp arrived and had been shown into the drawing room. And there he stayed. And remained past his allotted hour, and half again the time. Not daring to prowl the halls again, Francesca found herself poised on the edge of her chair, the leather cover of the book she held grown damp and warm in her hands, but still he didn't reappear. No sounds of laughter came from the room, nor did the butler stray far from it. At last Francesca, ablaze with curiosity and jangling with tension, rose, and ventured into the front hall again, prepared to face Arden's amusement and to swear to any probable thing to save face, if only to get a hint of what was going forth. And then the door swung open and she got far more than that.

"Very well. When you're ready, Colonel," the tall, thin office said, looking back into the room he was about to leave. "My word on it. I'll have his direction by nightfall, I promise you, and shall return as soon as I do, As you ask it of me, I promise I'll not confront him, but by God, sir, only because it is you who ask it of me. Bad enough what he did that day, but to compound such ignoble cowardice by attempting your life! He ought to be twice hanged, for that as well as for his—"

"Ah! Captain, may I present the Honorable Miss Carlisle," Warwick, who'd been standing closest to the door, quickly said, cutting across the captain's angry utterances, "a dear friend of ours and our friend Arden, and a lady with the most convenient restlessness. Arden, I know how you wanted these two to meet—how lucky that she anticipated your wishes."

"Singularly fortunate," Arden agreed as he rose to his

feet, suddenly paler due to the sudden effort, or to Francesca's unexpected appearance.

"No," Captain Shipp, bending over Francesca's hand, refuted promptly, "it is I who am most fortunate, ma'am."

He uttered the requisite flatteries, gave Francesca an even measuring stare from his cold blue eyes, and then, reassuming his rigid height, nodded, his smile gone, his face all neat planes again, even to his luxurious but symmetrical mustaches, and casting Arden a last significant look, he bowed and took his leave of them.

Francesca felt the force of three pairs of assessing eyes upon her, and knowing her guilt, yet nurturing her self-justification, and worse, beginning to accept something else she'd far rather not, she turned her head and looked down to her toes.

"I believe it's time for a light luncheon," Julian said after a silent moment, "that is, Warwick, if your kitchen staff's recuperated from the effort of filling our invalid up this morning."

"Recuperated?" Warwick asked, incredulous. "Say, rather, inspired. He's exalted my chef to new heights, and here I thought it was only motherly country cooks who admired a hearty appetite. But Antoine is in raptures over the first really appreciative audience he's had since leaving France, and I'd best look sharp or he'll elope with Arden in the night."

"The trick is not in gluttony," Arden said, sounding much offended, while all the while he watched Francesca carefully, "for I've sent back the odd dish or two, when I had to. Rather, it's all in paying due homage to what is done right."

"Sent back a dish?" Julian hooted. "Why, was it still moving?"

"Hush, lout," Warwick advised his blond friend. "Antoine will be after you with a cleaver if he hears you depreciating his favorite guest. I think it's time for us to pay our own homage to him. Coming along, Arden?"

"Shortly," Arden answered, "soon," but he didn't move or leave with them, nor did he speak until they'd gone.

"Half-heard is all misheard every time, you know," he said, trying to read Francesca's expression as best he could as she stood with her head bent, her face half-hidden beneath the sheltering wings of her dark hair. "A great many very bad plays have been written on just that premise," he went on gently, ''and a number of amusing ones. Still, farce is fine in a theater, but less so in life. Captain Shipp is helping me look for my assailant, that's true. But he doesn't really know anything as yet. He likes to sound positive—it made him a good soldier, and makes him an excellent hand at cards, for I've seen him bluff a man out of a hand flushed with royals with that air of certitude. It makes him a good gambler, and that's lucky for him, since he does little else when he's not playing at war,'' he said on a grin, before he added more seriously, ''but it don't mean anything, not yet, Fancy.''

''And when it does, Arden, will I know of it?'' she asked quietly, raising her head and learning more than the half she knew by his expression then, and the way he left off looking at her and gazed elsewhere, anywhere, around the room.

''In time,'' he said at last. And she thought she knew almost all then.

Arden set himself to entertaining her at luncheon, to chase away her drawn expression. Warwick and Julian aided him, and when Roxanne arose at a fashionable hour to join them, their task was made easier. Roxanne declared herself vexed to discover she'd missed the morning callers Francesca had seen, since, she said, casting a flirtatious eye to Julian, they'd all been stalwart army men, after all. Then Arden was pleased to commiserate by describing them to her in terms of such manly desirability that even Francesca was distracted from her interior fears and had to look up to smile at him.

It was when Arden was relating how the Spanish ladies had thumped their French lovers on the head and become partisans after one look at Lieutenant Adjutant Miller that Julian broke in at last, with outsize annoyance.

''Yes, Roxie, it may be so, but pull in your net. For there are a few details he neglects to mention. The charming lieutenant may well be a pretty fellow—though never half so lovely as I, of course—but he's far more fickle than Yours Devoted too, since he complains that he's only got seven nights in his week and eight ladies to share it among just now. That other bit of glorious manhood, Major Kern, who wouldn't know what a smile was if he tripped over one, has a wife and more drooling babes underfoot than Warwick can claim. And our noble Captain Shipp fancies himself a Captain Sharp, because the gaming tables are his favorite battlefields and his best tactical efforts are waged at his club, Watier's, and every lesser gambling hell in London.''

"Sheer jealousy," Arden declared, shaking his head sorrowfully, "although I'll admit the lieutenant has a busy bed, and the major a crowded one, and the captain does prefer a table to a bed—for some sport, that is to say.''

They laughed, and Roxanne, delighted to hear the conversation get warm, proceeded to take it too far, or at least far enough so that Julian had to give her a warning look, which she ignored, and then Warwick had to deftly turn the topic again. And Francesca went back to her brooding and turned her problem round and round in her head until it whirled.

After luncheon, Roxanne retired to her rooms to rest, the gentlemen went back to the drawing room, and though they invited her to join them, as if by tacit, unspoken agreement Francesca refused them graciously. Instead, she retreated to the library again, this time solely for the solace of the thoughtful solid silence in the book-lined room. For she didn't dare eavesdrop again. But she never had to. The afternoon was not too advanced when Captain Shipp was readmitted, and although Francesca could only see him stride toward the drawing room, she didn't have to strain to hear the note of exuberant triumph in his deep voice as he announced, poised on the threshold, "Success! I have him, Colonel! As I thought, he's been seen and recognized, and we have him, or at least, his direction, now!''

And then the door closed sharply on his next words.

But Francesca didn't need them.

Roxanne's voice was querulous when she called an answer to the tapping on her door. When she entered, Francesca was surprised to see her own maid brushing out Roxie's hair as the widow peered into her glass. She'd given the girl the afternoon off but hadn't realized Roxie had given her some coins to tend to her immediate needs.

"Lemon juice and crushed soap and a bit of ash from the fireplace, rub it in, and wash it out, and the hair gleams gold as new. But not for you, Fancy, for you'd only need to pat on a bit of boot polish if you spotted a gray hair," Roxie sighed.

"Roxie, I have to talk to you," Francesca said bluntly.

"I'm here," Roxanne answered absently, staring deep into her mirror with a critical frown, investigating her face as though it were that of a stranger. Then, realizing from the dark-haired girl's silence that it was a matter of a personal nature, she brightened somewhat, and inventing a wrinkle in a frock that needed a touch of the iron, watched the maid gather up the offending gown and sat quietly until she'd left them alone.

"At your service," she said brightly then.

"I need you to come someplace with me this afternoon," Francesca said carefully, "and I need you to stay mum about it, with never a word to anyone, ever—your word on it."

"Sounds lovely," Roxanne laughed. "Tell me more."

"First, your word," Francesca demanded.

"Not until you tell me more, for I may not approve."

"Then there's no point in saying more." Francesca shrugged, turning to the door.

"Have done," Roxanne said disgustedly. "You've learned from your old man, haven't you? At least, how to play people, because you know I can't resist a secret. All right, stay on, my word on silence about it—at least on hearing you out."

"I need to meet with a gentleman. One of the army men Arden's seen today. He's downstairs again right now. And I don't want Arden to know," Francesca said quickly.

"Whoo!" Roxanne cried. "Some sport! Don't color up, peahen, it's not pleasure you're after, I know."

"It's not, it's information," Francesca said softly.

"And I suppose you think you'll ask pretty and know all? Stuff, Fancy, save your breath and my time. If Arden won't spill it, no friend of his will," Roxanne answered, turning her attention back to the mirror with a disgusted sigh.

"I know," Francesca said sadly, for she did. She'd thought of little else all afternoon. But she had to know more, and soon.

She knew who Arden's would-be assassin was; to her despair and her shame, twist and turn as she might, she couldn't escape knowing who he was well enough, by now. Too much pointed to it. No one from Arden's past hated him enough, or was brave or cowardly enough to shoot him in the back. Low as those men were, they had a code. And why else would he summon army officers to aid him in his search? Who else could this "Englishman who says he's French" be? And if by some miracle it wasn't as she thought, why then would Arden take such pains to keep the name from her?

Perhaps he thought she loved Harry Devlin still. Perhaps

he knew the shame she'd feel if it was her former love who'd done such a thing. Or it might even be that he believed her to be in danger, because of her love or lack of it, from Harry.

But she knew Harry too well for that now, for all that it seemed she'd never known him before. She knew a great many things, to her sorrow, now. In fact, the only thing she had yet to learn was where he was, so as to save his life. And to preserve Arden's. For a man who had no honor was perhaps the only man who could bring her noble Lion down. She could end that threat, if she could find him. But Arden would never tell her. Men, she was discovering, even poor benighted Harry, had a certain belief in their own power and in the helplessness of females.

Unable to be trusted, unwilling to bring her ideas out into the open for fear of laughter or pity, or even worse, condescension and protection, she'd have to make her way with the only weapons left to a female—guile and craft. She'd never done such, but imagined she knew how, if only because her father had always tried to use these supposedly feminine arts to his benefit. And after hearing about Captain Shipp's one weakness, she believed she knew how.

But she trembled at the thought, for it went against everything she was raised to. It would require brashness and presumption, both of which she'd been trained to abhor. It needed pretense on her part, and though she doubted she'd enough falsity, she had to try. It also took enormous courage. That, she wasn't sure she possessed. But for Arden if she wanted to be worthy of him, she had to attempt it. She'd after all brought Harry upon him, and if she wanted to prove the difference between herself and Harry, to herself as well as to Arden, she'd no choice. She'd her own code of honor.

And still, for all it took courage to interfere, perhaps, she acknowledged sadly, it would take even more not to. She doubted she could be that strong.

She stared at Roxanne, her voice determined.

"He's a gamester, Roxie. There it is. They all say it. He's mad keen for any wager. And my father taught me a thing or two. I may not be able to wheedle the information from him, that's true. But I think I can win it away."

"Devil a bit!" cried Roxanne, astonished. She began laughing. And then she stopped, and looked at Francesca keenly. The girl was as smart as she was beautiful; she'd always known that. But only just now she wondered if she were as clever. If she was, then nothing would stop her. It was amazingly amusing. And dangerous. Because if Julian found out she'd helped the girl despite Arden's forbidding her involvement, she'd lose him entirely. It was bad enough that he seemed to be drifting away just as she was trying to land him safely; she couldn't risk having him slip her gaff entirely. But then, if Fancy succeeded, and won all, even Arden eventually, she could be a great help in convincing Julian as to her worthiness. It was a problem.

Roxanne smiled at last. Of course, as she'd learned long ago, all problems had two answers if one were sly enough.

Captain Shipp made his farewells and left the room feeling enormously pleased with himself. It was not an unusual emotion. But today it was even stronger. He'd gotten wind of the vile bounder who'd tried to kill the colonel, and he'd been promised he could be in at the kill of the wretched creature as well. It was well. Colonel Lyons was an admirable man, and for all he'd chosen to give up his commission, he remained one, and he was as pleased as his friends were appreciative. For all that Nappy was safely bound up again, so that glorious war was done, Captain Shipp felt he'd won yet another encounter with evil and so felt a warm glow of self-esteem as he left the town house. As he did so, a footman came out upon the stair and handed him a note.

After he read it, his spirits plummeted. And he chewed at the end of his mustache as he hadn't in years as he slowly walked back to his club.

Jermine's was a new gambling hell. Not so reputable as any one of London's best clubs, nor so fine as Watier's grand establishment where a man might get an excellent meal while he lost his life's savings, nor reputable as Boodle's or White's, or so deliciously wild as some others where he might chat with debauched poets as he gamed, nor so exciting as any of several dozen gambling rooms and brothel combinations where it was jested a man could lose his breeches and only save himself the trouble of removing them later by doing so early in the evening, nor so dangerous as any of dozens of more fly-by-night high-stakes gaming establishments where a man might lose everything he'd entered with early or late. For London loved to wager, and

there was a game and a place for every gamester to patron-
ize.

Jermine's was in a decent neighborhood, and it was singular in that it was patronized by ladies as well as gentlemen
of the *ton*. The ladies weren't permitted in most of London's
better clubs, and the sane ones wouldn't venture to most of
the others. But there were some that catered to them as well
as to the gentlemen, and the sage retired butler that had
opened this establishment knew he filled a purpose with his
house rules, which insisted on luxury and anonymity and
provided several private rooms to ensure it.

Francesca held her head high and stepped out of the coach
with her maid following in her wake, and entered Jermine's.

"Captain Shipp is expecting me," she said hoarsely as
she came into the main hall. It was late afternoon, and so
while she could hear the sounds of several voices within,
since ardent gamesters know no external hours, still it was
not so busy as it would doubtless be later, just as Roxanne
had said when she'd advised her to come here, and taken
care of all the arrangements.

"Certainly, madame," the proprietor said, and checked
his ledger, scarcely looking at the young woman who had
come to repay or incur a debt. As he'd got an earlier message, he made a tick against the name with his pen and
promptly bowed the young woman and her maid into one
of his smaller private rooms.

It was, Francesca thought with relief, as yet unoccupied.
And it was furnished richly, and in the most prosaic fashion,
with everything luxurious and nothing speaking of sexual
license. There was a gilt gaming table, several slight chairs,
as well as two more comfortable but unexceptional-looking
ones. For all that Roxie had assured her of the place's virtue, she'd expected it to be embarrassingly sensual, a haven
of silken poufs and beds and chaises. She didn't known that
rooms for secret sexual purposes were so easily got in London that the proprietor, a wily gamester himself, had opted
not to compete with what he couldn't win against, and had
instead furnished his rooms solely for their one function.

Francesca had scarcely got her maid settled in a chair,
put her things down upon the table, and taken a deep steady-
ing breath to fortify herself when Captain Shipp was escorted to the room. He stood tall, implacable and rigid as
one of the rifles he'd once carried, and looked at her, she
thought, as he might an approaching foe's cavalry unit.

"My lady," he said, bowing over her hand so stiffly she wondered he didn't creak upon arising, "you asked me to meet you here on a matter of utmost secrecy and urgency, and so I am come. You also implied that the colonel didn't know of your intent, and so I must ask immediately if this is still the case. I should dislike," he said, his lips beneath his mustache scarcely moving, "to have him discover me here with you in secret, as much," he said on a sneer that contorted that mustache far more than his lips, "as I dislike to come here myself."

Forget yourself entirely to become who you would become, her father had said once when describing how he'd convinced another gentleman he'd a bundle in his pocket when he'd already lost all but his last copper penny, for if you want to be believed you must first not doubt yourself, he'd declared. And so, Father, I shall not, she thought. And so, behold, here I am, she decided, before she closed her eyes and opened them as a new Francesca, and moved, and spoke so.

"Oh, Captain," she breathed in her soft throaty voice, now colored with a deeper lisp, "pray, oh pray do not misunderstand. But where else could I speak privately with you? I shouldn't vex dear Arden for all the world, no, how could I? But I had to have your ear and I was told by a friend that this was as good a place as any."

"This?" asked the captain, only his brow raised in his stiff face, gesturing with a hand as though pointing out all the features of a seraglio.

"But where else?" she cried in consternation, thinking: prig. "The park, where there are all eyes? The dear duke's house, where all seek to protect me? A public restaurant?" she asked shuddering. "A theater, where my approach would seem . . . unseemly? Your rooms?" she asked in horror.

That pleased him, as she'd hoped. And so she hurried on, "I must know what you've discovered about Arden's assailant. I knew you'd find out. Everyone knew you'd be the one to discover him," she said, watching the captain's face grow nicely pink, "but alas, everyone seeks to protect me from the world and myself. But I am not a child. You don't think I am, do you?" she asked worriedly, destroying the haughty image she'd just created, and causing his mustache tips to slip upward over a poorly concealed grin.

"Of course not," he said kindly now. Poor chit, he

thought, beside herself with worry for the colonel, and see what she attempts on his behalf. She was a handsome creature, he thought, and wellborn. Trust the colonel to find himself such a stunning female. Dark of eye and hair and graceful as a swan, from what he remembered, that was, for he couldn't see anything of her figure now, as it was all swathed in a proper concealing gray pelisse.

"But they're right in that, my dear. Never worry, it will all be taken care of, and nothing dreadful will happen again," he said, feeling far more comfortable now that her great dark eyes watched every movement on his face, as though he were spouting the gospel to her.

"But I wish to know about it," she said petulantly, "only that. I want to know the villain's name and direction."

"So that you can thrash him?" he chuckled. "Come, my dear, leave the matter to us. I couldn't possible tell you; aside from having given my word on it, there's the possibility of your doing the evil fellow an injury before we can get to him." This last made him laugh indulgently, and he was only sorry that she wouldn't take his no for an answer, for she began to plead, then pout, and then beg him again.

"Come, come, Miss Carlisle," he said at length, when it began to grow tiresome rather than amusing—really, he thought, that was the besetting fault with all her sex, eventually the most charming of them became boring in their petty importuning. "I can't tell you, for love nor money, it simply wouldn't do. Now you must run off and go along to the duke's again, I cannot like your remaining here with me. Nor will it do you the slightest good," he said, raising one finger, "for I won't tell you."

"Would you care to bet on that?" she asked. "I do mean it," she said, sniffling childishly. "I understand that's how the gentlemen do it. Here," she said wildly, looking about, and finding two packs of cards upon the table, waved them beneath his nose. "Here. Any game for your information. Or, at least," she said sadly, embarrassed, "any game I know. Two games out of three?" she begged. "Ah . . . hearts? No? I know," she said excitedly, "ecarte. I played that with my papa and he always said I was 'devilish' good at it. Is it a wager?" she asked.

She had asked the most thrilling question he knew. He smiled down at her. It was also the easiest, kindest way he knew to rid himself of her company so he could get down to a good night's gaming on his own.

"Done!" he said.

The first game was a debacle. He could almost feel sorry for her—no, he thought, watching her downcast dark head, he did feel sorry for her.

"Oh, fie!" she said, tossing down her cards as he scored his five points. "It's the cards," she cried pettishly. "Here, cut for the deal from this other deck, and we shall see!"

He was so amused by her using the oldest loser's excuse in the gaming world that he scarcely minded that she drew an eight to his seven. He only hoped, from the way she'd played, he thought as he swallowed another chuckle, for there was nothing worse than a gloating winner, that she knew how to deal. He was not so amused when he got his hand.

It wasn't so much that it was a bad one, for when he'd opened it he was pleased to find a jack and a queen holding court there. But as she made him wait, and wait again as she frowned over her cards while she decided whether to exchange them for better ones or not, he chanced to look closely at his jack of spades. And then his eyes widened. He blinked and looked again, and his face grew red. With all the unconcern of a man finding a beetle flailing all its legs in his soupspoon, he folded his hand and fanned it open again to stare at his queen of hearts. Then he put his hand down, facedown. And picked it up once more.

"Ah . . . I play. Do you take more cards?" he asked quickly.

"I cannot decide. May I have a moment more, please?" she asked sweetly, looking up at him with entreaty. "For I can't count very well, you know."

He didn't so much as bend a patronizing smile upon this ingenuous excuse; he only picked up his cards and studied them again. There was no doubt. Their backs had a blameless trefoil pattern; it was the fronts which were ornate, pleasing, almost amusing until one looked closely at the curling forms that made up their suits, and especially when one stared at the royals. For, once observed keenly and with the truth of them in mind, it could be seen that the human figures depicted there were plainly, clearly, and nakedly doing things, however in miniature, that members of royal houses had not done in public since the fall of Rome. It was the most shocking, exciting, and cleverly painted pack of pornography he'd ever held in his hand. In fact, he thought, staring at his queen until he looked cross-eyed to Francesca,

eyeing him over the top of her hand, he'd never really seen
how that was done before, it was actually quite interesting,
he thought with a secret surge of a long-forgotten desire,
until he looked up to see a pair of huge, innocent, wondering eyes fixed upon his.

"Is there something amiss with the cards, Captain?"
Francesca asked worriedly, "I wondered myself, for I've a
jack of clubs with the most curious design, and I wondered—"

"I play," he said at once, red to his eyebrows, forgetting
he'd nothing to play with. "And you?"

Once she'd won that hand, he thought, as he endured her
finally getting a winning hand by chance, he'd change decks
and be done with it. The colonel would never forgive him
for so much as exposing his lady to this vile and fascinating
deck, but how he could wrench them from her now, short
of main force, he did not know.

"Ah," he said at last, "well done. Now," he said, taking
up the discarded deck they'd gamed with first, "let's cut for
the next and deciding deal, eh?"

"Oh, poor stuff, Captain," she said with the most winsome smile on her tender lips, "to make me give up my
lucky pack. Well," she said, shuffling and poking her pretty
nose up in the air as she cut the deck, "I shan't! Pick, sir."

Frozen between a question of poor sportsmanship and
morality, he'd no choice but to agree at that moment. He
would have to forget the designs and play to win fast, he
thought desperately, and so end the matter like a gentleman
without her ever guessing the nature of the cards she held.
But she won the cut again, and dealt him a queen, a queen
and a jack, and then a king and a king, one more lascivious
than the other. He goggled.

Once he almost regained control enough to trade in a
card, when she stopped him instantly by frowning and saying confusedly, "Captain, this king of mine, I don't know
cards very well, but is he supposed to be doing something
to—?"

"He's supposed to be winning for you," he said wildly,
casting out his cards unthinking, and so doing what he'd
just said the vulgar king was supposed to do.

"I won," she said on a great sigh of happiness. "Two
out of three, I won."

It was more than incredible, it was unthinkable. He'd not
felt so crushed since his unit had fallen the first time at

Ciudad Rodrigo. For he didn't wish to pay his penalty; with every grain of his being, he didn't wish to pay his penalty. But he knew as a gentleman he'd no choice.

And all business now, she persisted. Prettily, but she insisted.

"His name," he said at last, beads of sweat upon his brow, "is Lieutenant Harry Devlin, for all he calls himself Georges Donat now. My friend's batman saw him and almost fainted, for he was supposed to have fallen at Waterloo. But he's no ghost, he lives, and stays on in a garret on the northeast side of Gravel Lane, number three," he said as her rosy lips moved soundlessly, repeating and memorizing the information. "God knows why he's angry at Colonel Lyons, they were in different units and never served together—but there it is. And now, my dear, let me take you back to the duke's house."

"Not right now, thank you," she said briskly, scooping up her belongings and signaling to her maid, "for I've errands, Captain, but thank you."

And before he could argue it, she'd gone in a whisper of roses and spice.

"Jermine!" he shouted, raging out from the room a few moments later, hot on the trail of the proprietor, "how dare you stock such cards for your customers, sir? I thought you were a respectable fellow."

Fuzzed cards were a terrible accusation, and the proprietor looked long and hard at the front and back of the decks before he handed them back with a superior smile. Really, the way some chaps carried on when they lost. "There's nothing amiss, sir, that I can see," he said.

"Nothing amiss?" the captain roared. "What do you call this pornography, nothing?" he shouted, and then quietened as he looked at the two blameless, ordinary decks he'd given the proprietor.

"Number three, on the northeast corner of Gravel Lane," Francesca commanded the coachman she'd hailed, "and please don't argue, for I do want to go there," she said as she hurried her maid within the carriage and then seated herself. And thank you, Father, she said soundlessly, for your legacy. It might be all you ever leave me, but it will do, she thought as she gazed at the dowager's pack she'd secured in her drawstringed reticule again. It *has* done, thank you. And now I must do half so well.

20

DINNER WAS ANNOUNCED and she wasn't there. But then, she hadn't been belowstairs for the past few hours. Arden had known that, of course. He'd felt her absence like a rebuke, and so avoided asking after her. For he dreaded the hurt questioning look she'd give him, the mute suspicion he'd earned as she wondered why he'd suddenly locked her out of his confidences. But he could no more tell her why than he could tell her who it was who had brought him so low.

He was a coward; he acknowledged it as he made light chat with Julian and Warwick and as he jested with Roxanne and looked beyond her shoulder, watching the doorway, hoping she'd be there, hoping she'd not. And of course he'd earned a coward's reward for it, suffering all the remorse and pain he would've if he'd faced her rather than hiding from her, by thinking about little else all the while.

Still, he reasoned that it wouldn't have been any easier enduring her silent hurt, nor could he see how it would have helped her, either. When it was over, well, by then he might have found a way to tell her about her old love's act of cowardice. Or if not then, then perhaps someday long after, when she was content and happy enough in whatever new life she found to afford to be forgiving and understanding of an old memory, and of both her old, mistaken loves. Until then, he was prepared to endure, as ever, because he had no alternative.

But there was a limit to even his endurance. Because Roxanne was here, their sherry had been taken, their dinner growing cold, and still Francesca was absent. Warwick looked oblivious, Julian chattered on, Roxanne was oblivious, and it became clear that as he was her sponsor, and as they suspected he was far more, they all thought the next move up to him. Now he began to grow more worried than guilty. This no longer looked like petulance, or even spite. It was altogether unlike her.

He sent word to her room, asking for her presence or her

excuses. And the word that came back was that she wasn't there. Or within the house. She was gone, without word, and without leaving a word behind her.

"At least her maid is gone as well," Julian said, as Arden called for writing paper, and Warwick called for all his servants, so that they each in their different ways could begin the search.

"Oh, yes, great help a maidservant will be to a lady in the night in the heart of London," Arden agreed, writing out his fifth hurried note, his face so grim it was as though a rock chose to speak.

"Does she know anyone else in town?" Julian asked as he paced, and hearing his own question, he grew still, as did both Arden and Warwick, and they all looked to each other.

"There's no way she could know . . ." Warwick said, thinking aloud while rapidly reviewing all the leakages and boltholes in his great house. "I had this door closely watched all the while Shipp was here."

"But it is possible that somehow Devlin got word to her," Arden exclaimed bitterly, crushing the note he'd just begun, as though he closed his hand over the thought. "Yes. And who knows what he told her. She's so trusting . . . Good God," he vowed, "I'll kill him twice over if he harms her."

"Don't be a fool, Lion," Warwick said coldly, as Arden rose to his towering height, his eyes glittering with fury. "You're in no condition to go coursing out into the night to do vengeance yet."

"Oh, yes," Arden replied as he strode to the door, "I suppose I should call in Bow Street? And after they take the information down in their occurrence books and after they take my coin, and after they nose out the street and wharf rats who'd tell me the time straightaway, and get lied to by them—why, then they'll find her right enough . . . in a year or two, dead or alive, safe or defamed. Oh, yes, Warwick. Well, Duke, I leave that course to you, for I'm on my way now."

"But not alone," Julian spoke up. "For all your wit, dear Arden, you can't drive a coach even when you don't have a hole in your back. And two heads are better than one hot one, or have you forgotten our partnership along with your pistol? Or were you thinking of facing the night barehanded?"

"And were you both thinking of facing it empty-headed

as well?'' Warwick asked acidly. When they turned to look at him, he went on, ''I applaud your zeal, and am moved to have my man fetch my hunting clothes immediately too, but first, I'd like to know just where you're going. Even if she's met with him, where would that be? He'd hardly ask her to his rooms. He's in the lowest slums now, and as he's supposed to love her, he'd scarcely let her see him there, if not for her good opinion, then if I estimate him correctly, because he'd fear the task of protecting her from his neighbors.''

''I've half a hundred villains to interview this night,'' Arden said tersely, ''but believe me, one will know her direction. Nothing happens in this great city without some of my old lads sniffing it out. London may be vast and wide, but it's small enough for those who make their livings from such knowledge. She may be as a pebble dropped into a lake, Duke, but trust me, there are those who watch for every ripple on it. Though it takes until dawn, I will know.''

''Yes,'' Warwick agreed, actually smiling, ''it never does to underestimate you, Lion,'' and as he tugged at a bellpull, he added, ''but tonight it does to ensure you don't overestimate yourself. You're immensely threatening, my friend, especially when in full roar, indeed you even terrify me now. But precisely because you do, you're exactly what's needed to make the fellow pull the trigger without waiting for you to turn your back this time. I thought you'd learned that size and virtue aren't proof against bullets. I'm coming to, of course, just as soon as my man fetches my pistols, and yours.''

Roxanne stood silent and watched the three men arm themselves and send word for their carriage, and all the while she chewed her bottom lip and thought furiously. She might have spoken when they turned to go at last, but then the front door was opened to admit a visitor.

Captain Shipp had lost weight and gained years in the few hours since the other gentlemen had seen him. Or at least it seemed he stood less tall and bent at every straight angle, although it might have been only the amount of alcohol he'd taken on that made it look so. He was wilted, and seemed even more so as he'd tried to pull himself together to face Arden.

''Col'nellyons, surr,'' he slurred, and then, red-faced with the effort or the embarrassment of it, he pulled himself up a fraction higher and went on, ''A ghastly thing happened after I left you. I lost a wager . . . with a lady," he said quickly, in the smallest voice Arden had ever heard an officer use, unless he were dying.

Arden was a man of endless patience, he'd made many friends by the hard-earned forbearance he'd been trained to, and with the agonizing patience he'd cultivated in order to exist in a world of men of slower minds and smaller size. But he was at his endurance's end now.

"*What in God's name are you blathering on about, man?*" he shouted, making the tiny Dresden shepherd and shepherdess on the edge of the Duke's mantelpiece take tiny shaking steps forward toward their doom.

Captain Shipp grew a white face to contrast with his red cheeks, and standing stiffly at attention now, made a staccatoed report from whatever front he'd been lost upon. "The lady, your lady, Miss Carlisle. She sent word to me and met me at Jermine's this afternoon. She . . . gamed with me for the information I delivered here today."

"Well, then," Arden sighed, turning to his friends, "there's hope she's not in danger yet. For it seems she's only after knowledge, and poor lass, if she's got her maid with her, all she's got to lose is her money, her time, and her temper."

"I lost," Captain Shipp said, wincing.

When they all stared at him, and Arden did not so much as utter a word, he found the courage, for he was a much-decorated officer himself, to go on. "I lost to her, Colonel. At ecarte. I never lose at ecarte," he babbled, as he'd done to himself as he'd armed himself with enough spirits to come here to confess, "but there was this extraordinary pack of cards, I couldn't let her see them clear, so I couldn't keep my mind on the game, so as to divert her—"

"Like father, like daughter?" Julian asked, frowning.

"Hardly," Arden said thoughtfully. "It seems she's a good gamester."

"No, Colonel," Captain Shipp protested, "never. She's dreadful. Threw out a jack she needed, tossed away all her royals whenever she'd got them . . . that's what overset me. You ought to have seen them." He fixed his boiled-egg eyes on Arden, desperate to make him understand through all his shame and the mists of good clear gin, as with juniper-scented breath he explained, "The cards. They were . . . so creative. So . . . unique. The royals, y'see, were at the rites of Venus," he whispered, looking to Roxanne. "They were rogering madly . . . they were having at each other in incredible ways,'' he moaned loudly at last, ''but not so plainly as to note all at once, mind, it was all hid in the design, and I never wanted her to see. When she left, they were gone with her. But I didn't imagine it, for I'd never seen the like of those cards, they'd have made my fortune in the Peninsula, and I'd only taken on some claret before, I never broach my second bottle until sunset . . .'' he explained, as he'd done to himself over and again since it had happened.

And then Arden's great grim face gave way to comprehension, and incredibly, he threw back his head and roared— with laughter.

''Good God!'' he shouted to the startled captain. ''She's got hold of a dowager's deck! The wench, the cheat, the adorable cheat,'' he said to a vastly amused Julian, ''and she pulled it off, too!''

''Packs of naughtiness, portable pornography,'' Warwick mused. ''I've heard of them, but never met a lady with enough dignity and desperation to use them—a rare, heady, and winning combination.'' He smiled, as though congratulating Arden for Francesca's guile, as Arden continued to chuckle.

''And so in all honor,'' the captain said, unsmiling, ''I had to tell her all.''

The laughter fled from Arden. ''Who he is?'' he asked incredulously, as the captain nodded miserably. ''Where he lives now too?''

''Forgive me,'' the captain said humbly.

''No need,'' Arden answered absently. ''You were gulled. Go home, sleep it off, and remember never to trust a female any more than you'd trust a man, and count yourself fortunate that it was only your information she was after. But she,'' he told Julian and Warwick as the captain bowed and slunk off, ''may yet regret that hard-won information profoundly, if we don't make haste.''

''You don't believe he'd harm her?'' Julian asked.

''Will he, won't he?'' Arden's face was drawn. ''I won't play that game. But he lives on Gravel Lane, a bone's throw from Leadenhall Street and Angel's Alley, between Whitechapel and Spitalfields, and whatever he will or will not do, I shouldn't want her there at dawn with my cavalry unit behind her, much less alone at night. We must hurry.''

''I didn't know!'' Roxanne spoke up at last, in a high,

frightened voice, causing the men to pause in the doorway and turn back to look at her. She might as well have it out now, she reasoned as she trained her great blue eyes on Julian, for sooner or later they'd wonder how Fancy got to Jermine's even if Fancy kept her word and kept her mouth shut. And anyway, she decided, see how they admired Fancy for her derring-do, obviously a cheat in a good cause was acceptable to them. She'd think about that useful bit of knowledge later, for now she'd a clean breast to make of it before Julian found out for himself.

"I thought it all a lark," she said in a shaking little voice. "She said it was a jest, so I told her of Jermine's and promised to keep mum. Oh, dear, is she in any danger?"

"You knew all along," Julian asked, amazed, "and yet listened to us wait and worry and never said a word?"

"But I gave my word," she said, as though amazed at his question, ". . . of honor," she emphasized, in case he'd forgotten the way his friend had just forgiven the errant captain for the sake of honor.

"Oh, Roxie," Julian sighed, knowing it was too late to go into the matter of wisdom and honor with her now, as he shook his golden head for her foolishness, if not for her treachery, and left her.

Neither Arden nor Warwick chastised her either before they went, and though she counted herself lucky and saved, as she sank into a chair after they'd gone, Julian knew from his friends' very silence that they considered her not worth their scorn—which was far worse than earning it. But then, he'd expected no less from them, or more from her.

Julian drove, Warwick sat opposite Arden, who sat lost in thought, as though his concentration would speed the coach along. But it wasn't long before he left the reins to Julian, and the concentration to Warwick, and began to let his fears fly away, as a man must do before battle. Instead, he thought of Francesca, and the whole mad coil that had brought them to this night. He'd done everything, even to renouncing her, so as to spare her danger from his unclean past. And the gods, forever mocking him, had, of course, brought her danger from her own blameless history.

It was enough, he thought, remembering her voice, her laughter, her face and form and then her friendship that he'd have given half his life to turn to more. Enough and past it now. No man could be expected to endure more than that. He wanted her. And for all he'd wondered how he could

ever let her go so as to let another man protect her, he knew
now he could not. For so little as he trusted himself, he
trusted no man more. She was his, for so long as he lived,
she was his, he'd known that even as he'd been prepared to
sacrifice his dreams for her, for her safety.

He had learned to do without a great many things in his
life. But there were some things that mattered more than
his life, and she, it seemed, was chiefest among them. Now,
he thought, changing his position in an attempt to ignore
the pain that threatened to bore through his back into his
heart to join the other ache there, he'd had enough of fear,
as well as futile desire for her. That was too potent a combination. If it was possible she could want him—oversize,
illegitimate oaf that he was, with so ruinous a past as he
claimed—then he'd resist no longer, he'd make her his. And
devil take the hindmost. For, he thought, whimsical again,
since the devil was determined to take the foremost, he
might as well make the most of it for himself. Then so long
as he lived, she would be his in name and in actuality, and
not just in his secret heart. *If,* he thought, sitting up the
straighter, despite the pang it caused, if she lived, he must
convince her of this. Because now that he was decided, he
realized it was never enough to surrender; he would fight
for what he wanted now, as ever.

Now she knew why the coachman had argued with her.
But now it was too late. The carriage halted on a street that
the approaching night was kindly blurring. The buildings
that leaned over the street above the coach were more like
ruins that dwellings, but their filth and decay made them
nothing like the marble relics of lost civilizations she'd seen
pictures of, and there was little hint of any evidence of a
higher civilization anywhere in the district they'd driven
through.

Her maid shivered back against the cushions. The poor
creature, Francesca thought sadly, seeing her terror, was
foreign, after all, and didn't understand London. But the
girl had come from just such a place in Paris, and understood all too well.

"You needn't come with me," Francesca told her, and
taking a breath the way a swimmer might take in air before
a plunge, she stepped out of the coach. But she couldn't
hold her breath forever, so her next intake of air told her as
much about her surroundings as her eyes had done. For the

stake, leather-scented, horse-tainted scent in the closed coach was as perfume to what she breathed in now.

"Please wait for me," she told the coachman evenly.

And as she sought and found the cracked bit of marble that surely had read "Three" before urchins had defaced it, she heard the coachman's whip crack, and saw him gone done the street, eyes front, face set, carriage and horses and maid and all but her courage gone with him, even as his had fled.

She wasn't brave in the least, she knew. But she couldn't sit on the filthy street and weep, nor could she pick up her skirt and rush after him, nor would it be sensible to wander away now. There was nothing to do but do what she'd come to do, and, she thought, noting the legless old black beggar inching toward her on his rolling platform, and the two rough-looking young men uncoiling from the darkened doorway where they'd hidden, she'd better get on with it.

It made no sense to rush into the darkened entry of number three. So she walked there, quickly but deliberately, for it made less sense to stand in the street to be accosted. She'd little faith in the protectiveness of strangers in this neighborhood, and knew no one who could help her there, but someone she knew who lived within number three might. If he was there, if he was at home, she thought, her breath and her thoughts keeping rhythmic pace with her slippers as she climbed up the stairs and tried to ignore the sounds of other feet following. There were two of them, and for all her increasingly labored breathing as she followed the spiraling steps higher and higher, and for all her busy, frantic thoughts, she could clearly hear them coming, laughing, laughing ever louder as she picked up speed, although her heart would burst from the effort of it. At the summit, she did not so much as knock as fall upon the single door in the narrow hall, and she beat her fists upon it as the two men, breathless too, both from the climb and the look of their prey close up, came on a level with her.

"Oh, here," breathed one, a young and pale-haired one, so gently her spirits rose, so tender was the look of admiration upon his gaunt, unshaven face. "Oh, look at what we got here, ain't she something? Ain't she?"

"Oh, yes," his companion said, this one less gently, this one darker of eye and hair, and though no older, far bolder of eye and surer of himself, as well. Although just as plainly and poorly dressed, he wore, she saw, a great deal of hair pomade, and the scent of it was as strong as that of her fear as he stepped up to her.

"Me first," he said to his companion, "then you. You take all day," he said disdainfully, ignoring Francesca even as he reached out to clasp her shoulder hard. "I'm ready now, see?" He gestured where Francesca was appalled and sorry she'd looked. "And then you," he promised, still looking at his companion, "*if* you don't take a year at it this time, 'ear? 'Cause then it's to Mother Carey's with 'er, and wiv that in our pockets and 'er under our belts, that'll make a fine day's work."

"But," the young pale-haired one said hesitantly, and she took heart, "ortn't we to hold her to ransom, then? Better profit in it than selling her to Mother Carey."

"Gawd," the dark-eyed one sighed, never looking to Francesca yet, though he still held her shoulder tightly, as he fumbled in his clothing with his other hand, "what 'ave you got for a brain—wot I got in my 'and now? 'Old 'er to ransom where, fool? Inna street, in our lodging'ouse? They'd 'ave word of 'er inna day and take 'er away from us wiv nuffin' but a beating for our reward. Nah, Mother Carey 'll give us sumpt'n for 'er, at least."

Still glowering at his companion, he began to push Francesca backward with the hand that he'd hard upon her shoulder. There was no desire in his voice or face, indeed, he seemed far more interested in squabbling with his companion than in molesting her. But there was no doubt of his intent. She was, after all, fair game. Females who traveled unescorted in the better parts of London were open to insult and invitation. Those who ventured here alone were clearly welcoming abuse. If they weren't for sale, they were mad or misled. It made no matter. Neither malice nor lust really inspired the young men; in their world, where nothing was easily come by or discarded, simply, such opportunity couldn't be wasted.

Even knowing this, it seemed incredible to her that she'd be taken in any fashion, casually or not. She refused to think of being portioned out, or of exactly what it would all mean, for if she did, she couldn't bear it. She couldn't fight them, though she would, she knew, when she had to, whether or not it would avail her. She would beg them too, if she had to, when she had to. But for now, she couldn't give up her one real, rational hope of escape. So she spun around, her shoulder still held in that heavy hand while she beat upon the door and cried, "Harry . . . oh, Harry . . . Harry, I'm here!"

"Oh, yeah, 'Arry, she's 'ere, all right," the bold one said, brusque and impatient as he turned her around and began to pull up her skirt. "'Urry 'Arry," he said mockingly, "or you'll lose yer turn."

"Let her go!" the voice commanded, thinner and higher than she remembered, but determined. "Let her go or die," it said.

She turned in her captor's arms even as he dropped his hand from her, and saw the man standing in his shirtsleeves, in the now-open doorway, his serviceable army pistol lowered, held in two hands, and pointed straight at the dark man.

"'Ere guv, just 'aving some fun," the young man said, smiling in a terrible sham or mirth as he backed away, although not so far away as his companion had already sprung to the head of the stairs. "Just fun, mister, just fun," he said on a rising note as he grunted with the effort and then vaulted the banister and was away, before his terrified companion could try to shoulder him aside, away and down the stairs.

"Harry," she said weakly, "Harry," she said with prayerful relief, "Oh, Harry," she said, coming into his arms and feeling his body trembling as much as hers was.

When she'd got her breath in one long unshaken draft again, she walked with him into the room, his arm still tightly around her. It was a huge, almost empty garret, with a skylight to illuminate the makeshift bed and the few sticks of ancient furniture and an old paint-encrusted easel in the corner.

"I like high places," he said on a shaky laugh, gesturing to his realm with the gun he still held, "and it seems artists do too. Francesca," he said, "oh, my dear, I wish I *were* an artist so I could have had a picture of you to sustain me all these weeks. But I came even without one, I came just with the memory of you in my heart. And now I've you," he said, gazing down at her with wonder. "But how did you find me? Never mind," he said quickly, "we haven't time for that now. We must be gone from here. You never know when they're coming back—I made enemies there," he said nervously, listening, for a moment, to some distant tumult on the lower stairs.

"Later," he said, smiling tenderly. "We've all the rest of our lives for it later."

He looked thinner and worn, not so much agile as slight, not so much fine-boned as fine-drawn now, but that, she thought, as she stared at him critically as he bent to drag his portmanteau out from a corner, might be because her eye had got used to a different sort of masculine ideal and was used to admiring a more substantial gentleman. Then she remembered everything that horror had chased from her mind.

"I cheated and lied to find you, Harry, for I had to find out why you'd harmed Arden," she said as he stopped in mid-motion and looked at her. "They've recognized you—some army friends of his—and I had to connive to discover what they knew," she added as his look of surprise changed to something like the mindless fear she was sure she'd shown only moments before.

"Then we must leave at once," he said tightly.

"Why did you do it?" she asked firmly, standing in front of him. She'd bar him from the door bodily if he didn't answer her, she thought, bizarrely, even to herself. "Why, Harry?"

"For you," he said simply, "all for you. You had to be free of him. I knew. What was it you said back in France? . . . Ah, yes. You told me he was a great beast. And so he is, or was—is that why you're here, is he gone now? I hope so. I had to destroy him for you, to set you free. For you're a lady, Francesca, and life is no fairy story. All your kindness wouldn't convert him from being a beast. And that, you were right, truly was the case."

Well, he knew that, Arden thought as he stood there at the open door, his lips half-open on the glad utterance of her name he'd begun when he saw her standing there safe and whole and alive. Warwick looked away, and Julian, shocked and saddened, looked straight at him, but he didn't move. His back hurt, after all, from his exertions with the two villains he'd met upon the stairs, the two old legless Black Bob had told him followed her here. So they'd all understand his silence.

But it was true, of course. Even if he could admit the pain of it only in little bursts, because the whole of it taken in all at once would kill him, surely. He was never angry at her for voicing it, only at himself for deluding himself for even a moment, thinking he could ever be a lover to that lovely lady. For so he was, he thought, just as she'd said, a beast—a great cumbersome beast. Hadn't the world always told him so? Or would have, if they'd dared, and if he hadn't always saved them the bother by telling them first. And a stupid beast, at that, for forgetting that, he thought, staring at the pair lost in contemplation of each other in this dim, bare skylit room open almost to the sky it lay so close beneath. He gazed at her in that fading twilight as he would at something beautiful come to him in some odd, idyllic dream that was already fading into dawn, thinking how idiotic he'd been to so much as imagine she'd ever have him as anything but a friend or take him close to herself unless she'd been in dire need of a sanctuary. A big, safe one—only that, he thought dumbly. Yes.

She paused and closed her eyes and swallowed hard. But couldn't rid herself of the distaste she felt remembering that lost girl who'd said that, who'd been herself so long ago, those short weeks ago, in France. Then she opened her eyes and yet looked within herself. And so smiled in a sweet remembrance that came to her so clearly it took her breath away, along with the sight of the dismal room and all its contents, and the sour taste of her green judgment made in her green years, those weeks ago.

"And so he is," she said slowly, each word clear, tolling clear in Arden's ears, "And so he is," she agreed, actually grinning now, "And so, thank the Lord, he is—a very great beast is my Lion. Bold and strong and brave and fine is my Lion," she said proudly. "Only no—not mine," she corrected herself hastily, as Harry stared at her, "for he won't have me, Harry, not in any way. You came to free me, you said, and so I've come to tell you that though you may have thought your intent noble, you did a terrible thing. If you want to free me, do it correctly, by leaving me, and let Arden alone. For I won't go with you, Harry, not anywhere. I don't love you. I'm sorry, but there it is. But because I thought I once did, I warn you now—don't you ever attempt Arden again, do you hear? Because if you take his life, you'll take mine—as well as yours. For he is my life, and I vow I'll never rest until I take yours in turn. I, too, can hold a gun. Yes, that's so," she said fiercely, standing stiffly and looking directly at him.

His hands trembled as he gripped his portmanteau and lowered it to the bed. He'd grown pallid as he stared horrified at her, and so she went on more gently, "What's done's done, Harry. Do no more. At least not on my behalf. Because you don't know my heart. It's here, with him, and will always be, whether or not he ever accepts it."

"But I came to England, risked my safety," he stammered, "it took all my courage and put my own life at risk, it cost me anxious days and sleepless nights, and all for you . . ." His voice grew shrill though his face still showed shocked sorrow. "I endangered myself for you, and all for nothing?" he asked, unbelieving.

"For something, Lieutenant Devlin," Arden said as he entered the room, "if only for the sake of knowing that you could run such risks if you felt you had to, that's worth a great deal, I should think. Hello, Francesca," he said affably as she gaped at him. "How nice to see you. Do you come here often?"

It might have been the unexpected sight of the big man walking and talking as though he'd never been shot, as though he were a risen ghost, or it could have been the two other gentlemen standing and waiting in the doorway like patient minions of authority, or it could have been the dreaded sound of "Lieutenant" that threatened him the most. But Harry Devlin raised his pistol, and though he took a step backward, he was still close enough to make a far more decisive hole in Arden Lyons this time if he so chose, if he so much as squeezed the trigger his finger was locked on now.

Arden went on talking, not so much as raising a brow, although there was a sharp intake of breath from the vicinity of the door, and Francesca froze in place.

"Oh, put it down, lad," he said in his deep, smooth accents, scarcely glancing at the death inches away from his eyes. "You heard the lady, she'll be after you like a vengeful fury if you singe my eyelashes. None of us are here to harm you anyway," he continued in accents so calm and reassuring that Francesca began to understand his tranquillity as well as the purpose of his gentle humor. The very commonplace of it made violence seem out of place, and the comfort of sane discourse itself began to lessen the tension that had been almost palpable in the room. She understood that he was a master of many sorts of unexpectedly effective weapons as he went on off-handedly, "Those are my friends the Duke of Peterstow and the Viscount Hazelton who are so rudely gapping at us. They've nothing to do with armies or wars, except for their own private ones. We come to praise Francesca, not to bury you," he said, smiling, "and it's all the same to me whether you go or stay in England, so long as she is safe."

"I shot you," Harry said, but he licked his lips as he was perspiring like a man whose fever had just broken.

"So you did. Don't congratulate yourself on it, neither," Arden said ruefully. "Only a blind man could miss such a fine target, you know."

"In the back," Harry said in a strangled voice, his pistol still tight in his hand.

"So you did," Arden said quietly. "I can't approve that, but so you did."

"Do you despise me for it?" Harry insisted.

"No," Arden answered, "but I believe you do, lad."

"You think I'm afraid to shoot you now, as you face me, man to man?" Harry asked breathlessly.

"No," Arden said, looking at him then, keenly and with unblinking gaze, "not at all. But I think it would take a different kind of courage not to. I think it would be extremely brave of a man to allow another he despised and could easily rid himself of, to live. And I'd thank you for it," he said simply.

Harry lowered the pistol then.

"Thank you," Arden said.

"Is it to be Bow Street or the army court-martial for me, then?" Harry asked, sinking to the bed and not raising his head as Julian removed the pistol from his limp hands.

"Not Bow Street!" Arden said, recoiling. "And not necessarily a court-martial either, Devlin. I've heard Wellington will often make exceptions. There was one chap he recommended for naval duty after he'd fled a battle in Spain. Of course, that's entirely up to you."

"No," Harry said softly, shuddering, "no more war, by sea or land. I want to go back to France and live out my days in peace. I wanted Fancy with me for her brother's sake as well as mine, I wanted to save her more pain."

"As do we all," Arden agreed. "It was brave of you to come so far and put so much at risk for her, Devlin, that is true."

"So you'll let me go?" Harry said then, raising his head and staring at them.

"Of course. Why not?" Arden answered on a shrug.

At a glance from Julian, Francesca recovered herself, and bending to Harry, she whispered a good-bye, and then stepped with the gentlemen to the door. At that Harry spoke again, in a rush. It had been a long while since he'd spoken with his equals, he knew he was in no more danger, and he had more to say than good-bye, for he knew it was the last he'd ever see of them.

"I never meant to turn and run that day," he said hurriedly. "I'd done it before I know. It was ghastly—the noise, the blood, the sounds of dying. You cannot know," he said, speaking to Arden now, and not to Francesca.

"I know," Arden answered softly, "too well. I was in the Peninsula, I was at Waterloo too—only in the night, after it was done. I'd sold out by then, but when we heard of the battle, we came, my friend Julian and I—too late to do anything but help in the field, sorting the maimed from the dead, beating off the scavengers, human and less so. I do know," he said sadly, "and it was too bad, my friend, for most men can go through life and never be tested and so never know if they would have turned or gone forward or not. I'm sorry."

It was the gentleness that did it. For there was one last thing Harry Devlin had to say, because they were leaving, and leaving it with them would relieve him. "Fancy," he said, "that day, I saw your brother fall. That's true. But . . . he fell as he was riding after me, to call me back. That's true. That's all. I'm sorry," he said.

Arden took Francesca from the room then. But as they reached the stairs, Julian cursed beneath his breath. "He could have spared her that," he said furiously.

"It took another sort of bravery," Warwick answered. "It may be there's hope for him yet."

"I'm surprised he let him go," Julian muttered to Warwick, still fulminating as Arden walked a silent Francesca down the stairs.

"I imagine," Warwick said thoughtfully, "that he couldn't think of a worse punishment. Very clever, our Lion, as always. That's why he asked for his life, instead of taking Devlin's, though he had his hand on a pistol in his pocket as he did. He gave the poor creature something to take away with him, rather than taking his life as he could easily have done, in front of his lady. Well done of our Lion, as usual."

There were two recumbent forms in the hallway, and Francesca paused as they approached them.

"Step over them, or on them if you wish," Arden advised, "they won't wake for a while, but no, they've not got anything broken." As she gasped, recognizing the two youths that had threatened her, he added, "I know they did no more than shock and frighten you, and that they're no more, poor idiots, than gutter-bred, desperate children, but I thought I ought to remind them of the manners I expect them to use with those weaker than themselves."

She tiptoed around them, and as they got to the sidewalk and the welcome sight of the duke's coach, an old black beggar on his wheeled platform rolled up beside them.

"Pity the sorrow of a poor old man whose trembling limbs have brought him to your side . . . Oh, 'lo, Lion," he said, dropping his plaintive whine and speaking up in chipper accents. "Did you get the bad lads in time?"

"That I did indeed, Bob," Arden said, bending to drop several coins in his cup. "Thank you, and drink hearty."

"To your health, as always, Lion." The old man grinned. "And to the lucky lady," he added, bowing his head, before he scooped up the coins and knuckled his cart into motion and down the street once more.

"I'll ride with Julian. I believe I can use the fresh air," Warwick said thoughtfully after Francesca had entered the coach and Arden waited for him by its door.

"Oh, yes," Arden agreed, "very salutary tonight, especially here. Your subtlety never ceases to thrill me, your grace. It would be even more impressive if you'd remove that leer."

"But it becomes me," the duke complained before he added lightly as he sprang to the high hard driver's bench with Julian, "I promise not to peek, too."

Arden smiled, then frowned, then shook his head, but his color was still high as he entered the coach.

He said nothing as the coach started up. Francesca felt the silence crowd around her. She'd deceived him, true, but it had been for the right reasons, and she knew he couldn't be angry with her still, at least not for that. Harry had said a dreadful thing about her brother's death, and she automatically shied from it; that would be another thought, for another time, and she doubted Arden hesitated to speak because of that. But he wasn't speaking at all, and as she sought a reason why, she remembered what he'd heard her tell Harry, and held her breath. When moments passed and he still hadn't spoken, she let it out in a sigh. Declaring oneself publicly was bad enough; having that declaration ignored was perhaps the politest way to deal with an unwelcome affection, but also the most embarrassing. She began to speak at once then, on any trivialities, just to fill the silence and show she didn't care, inventing a bright voice as she rambled.

"I didn't really believe you were in the army, Arden, no mustaches, you know, and other army gents are so proud of theirs. Why, Captain Shipp . . ." Her voice dwindled as she spoke of something she belatedly realized she ought not to have.

"Mine always grows in red," he said easily. "Believe it or don't. Too vivid by half, you see, or rather that's why you *don't* see it. Clashed with the uniform," he mused. "Harry didn't have one either," he reminded her.

"He took his off because I didn't like it, or so he claimed," she answered, low.

"That's a relief," he said, looking at her cameo profile, her ivory skin glowing in the dim coach. Then he sighed and looked out the window. "I was king here once. You've seen it now," he commented, "just as I said."

"You took care of them," she answered quickly.

"And myself."

"You protected the innocent," she insisted.

"And the guilty. . . . Fancy, my dear love," he said seriously then, leaning forward and speaking intently, "give it time. Give yourself a chance to see reason. You were looking for a safe harbor, you can't mean to stay with me—"

"If I'd wanted a safe harbor," she cried, angry and amazed at his stubborn refusal to understand, for if he didn't want her, she'd understand, but if he didn't know she wanted him, she couldn't, "there are missions and convents and friendly dukes and doting sisters in Scotland for that, aren't there?"

He grew very still. She didn't dare look at him, but studied the darkening streets with interest instead, as though she could see them.

"I've led a strange and varied life, but I want nothing more than to settle down to my gardening now," he said.

And when she wheeled about to look at him, astonished, he went on sadly, "I've a lovely home in the Lake District, with acres of hilly land and a complex systems of water gardens, and my yellow flags and Chinese peonies flourish there. I've an orangery where I experiment with pollination, and a dozen bedrooms to do more of that sort of thing in, or," he said hurriedly, "to decorate for fellow horticulturists when they come to call, and a drawing room as fine as Warwick's, I'll warrant, and a music room to make Julian's ancestress tear her phantom hair with envy, and a grand ballroom and, of course, a grand kitchen the like of which hasn't often been seen on this blessed isle. That, I can offer without apologies.''

She didn't dare ask whom he was offering it to, but only said, in a high, artificial squeal that threatened to humiliate her, ''Arden, with all your tales, so many that turn out to be true, and so many that must be false, I vow I don't know what to believe of you. What is real, what is true?''

''A problem,'' he agreed seriously. ''I think it's best solved by your coming along with me for the next five decades or so, to keep a close watch on me. And then I think you'll see for yourself. Will you?'' he asked, all soberness now. ''For I've some difficulty in believing my ears too. Was all that you said in there, my poor foolish, deluded Fancy—was all that you said you felt for me true? I'm too famous for my lies to dare tell you how much I love and need and want you. But God knows, if you don't, my love, that I do. Will you marry me, and soon, before you change your mind?''

''Oh, yes, please,'' she said, ''yes.''

He gathered her up in his arms and kissed her lightly, and then, beginning to believe he actually held her and she was really opening her wonderfully soft lips against his and pressing close to him, as though she were afraid he'd get away, he kissed her so thoroughly she still lay back on his arm, eyes closed, breath rapid, when he drew back from her.

''To little, but too much for such a short carriage ride,'' he murmured, stroking her smooth hair to keep from stroking her smooth skin again, ''and besides, I know Warwick's peeking. I'd like to be able to leave here with some little dignity,'' he explained as she opened her eyes to look at the tender, bemused look upon his face, ''but I don't really want to stop. Talk to me,'' he pleaded, ''we're almost there, and I refuse to give the duke so much satisfaction.''

''I love you so much,'' she said.

''Wrong topic,'' he sighed when he drew back from her again. ''Oh, love,'' he said then, smiling so joyously her eyes filled, ''what a marriage it will be. We two—the big bad villain and the wicked little gamester's beautiful brave daughter—why, we'll breed wonderfully sinister infants who have style and guile and grace. And if we can't, we'll be just as happy with our peonies, and what fun we'll have, such a union, the like of which never has been seen, I promise you. Oh, my foolish Fancy,'' he said tenderly, forgetting where they were and all his resolve to deny Warwick the pleasure of opening the coach door to see him entirely lost in her arms, ''thank you. I'll aspire to see you never regret me. And, Fancy,'' he asked several moments later when the coach was still and he finally admitted it had stopped moving, and so reluctantly released her, ''when we're wed, will you . . . could you possibly bring yourself to reveal something . . . ah, intimate for me?''

''What, Arden?'' she asked nervously, sitting up, patting her hair back into place, suddenly aware of an amused oval of a long face at the window, studiously not looking within.

''Well, actually, only after you've gotten to know me and trust me, of course,'' he said softly, ''because it's not an easy thing for any well-bred woman to do, I'd imagine. Still, I'd hoped . . .''

''For what?'' she asked, a little alarmed now, forgetting the fair-haired gentleman also pointedly not looking in at them, for she began to wonder just what personal thing it might be that he'd want of her. For all she loved him, she'd heard of certain proclivities—and was nervously wondering if her love could surmount such unimaginably esoteric desires, when he said eagerly, ''Your cards, Fancy, I really would like a look at the king of diamonds! If Shipp was right, it's something I've always wondered about and—''

Few newly engaged couples were revealed, when their coach door was finally opened, to have the gentleman roaring with laughter as he raised his hands to defend himself against a furious lady batting him with her reticule, but then, Warwick commented wisely to Julian, when he'd a better look at their faces, this would doubtless be a marriage such as few people had seen before anyway.

21

It was a wedding the like of which had seldom been seen, even in London town. It was two weddings, actually. The one in the grand cathedral, and the one outside of it. The groom must be a popular public benefactor, a passerby thought, to judge from the number of celebrant poor who overflowed the sidewalks and capered on the cobbles, dancing to the music of the savoyards with their hurdy-gurdies and the fiddlers and ballad singers, all in full voice and great heart. There were even more varied professionals in the throng. The cutpurses and pickpockets had declared it a holiday, so reticules, watches, and fobs were safe, but reputations weren't. Some of the finest gentlemen mounting the steps to the cathedral with their wives in tow had to avert their eyes from some of the gaudier females who cavorted in the streets. Not for reasons of propriety, as the Duke of Peterstow confided to his own lovely bride as they entered the great church, but for prudence, since half the demimondes in London that the gentlemen regularly patronized were there. Although, he whispered into her delightful ear, he doubted they'd recognize each other in the sunlight.

There was a great deal of sunlight that bright early summer's morning, but it was cool and quiet within the cathedral, as befitted a ceremony attended by so many notables. The groom must be a very fashionable fellow, the passerby commented to his friend as they watched the string of titled persons entering to witness the wedding. There were three famous dukes: witty Peterstow, sly Torquay, and enigmatic Austell were there; a smattering of earls, among them, it was whispered, the groom's own half-brother, the new Earl of Oxwith; a plenitude of marquesses, including the mysterious Marquess Bessacarr and his lovely wife; barons galore, numerous lords, and as for viscounts, there was among them the groom's new neighbor, the Viscount North, whose masculine blond beauty rivaled that of his best man, the Viscount Hazelton.

Of course, the honorable Miss Merriman's spiteful mother

commented, to console her as-yet-unwed daughter, they were most of them notorious in their youth and not a few bore shocking reputations still, no matter how reformed they chose to represent themselves to be. There was even a certain something whispered about the bride's father, in for the happy day from his estate in Cologne, he claimed. Or rather, there might have been something whispered if there weren't far more interesting persons to gossip about than a mere rackety baron.

That the proud bridegroom had been an army officer was evident not only from the way he held his head and marched down the aisle. For what seemed to be an entire unit of army officers and men were there as well, so many that a guest was overheard to say he'd never felt so safe in all his days.

Not all the guests made each other feel as comfortable, for some were decidedly oddly dressed and behaved. There were some gentlemen, such as the one who declared himself a "Mr. Portwine," and others such as Mr. Sam Towers, for example, whose garb was so unusual, as was that of their ladies, that if it hadn't been for that charming young Mr. Begood explaining softly to all and sundry that they were nabobs from the colonies, they might even have frightened some of the more timorous guests.

After the ceremony it was remarked that the groom certainly must be a public-spirited gentleman, for all he was unknown to so many ladies in society, for no less a notable than Sir Conant, chief magistrate of Bow Street himself, came up along the receiving line to congratulate him.

"So that's where you'd got to," Sir Conant said, taking the bridegroom's huge hand firmly in his. "I'm glad to see this happy resolution to your career, Lion. Though in a way," he whispered, leaning close, "I'm sorry to see your retirement from the lists, for I do love a challenge. Still, you've made my declining years so much the easier, and so I thank you, as well as congratulate you, lucky fellow," he sighed when he saw the glowing bride.

He wasn't the only one. Few present had seen such a radiant bride, they declared, and this time, they may even have been right. Certainly her new husband thought so. He seldom took his eyes from her, it was almost as if he didn't quite believe in her presence, so that he had to keep looking back to assure himself she was real. But then, few bridges had such creamy ivory skin to complement a creamy silk

gown, and fewer still had such luxurient midnight-black
hair, the most admired color of the season, to set off fine
features, and fewer still such grace, the ladies admitted, or
such an admirable form, as the gentlemen noted and didn't
dare mention within hearing of the groom.

For although Arden Lyons was beyond impressive in his
immaculate, well-fitted, beautifully made clothes, and his
tawny hair had been brushed and his every ornament was
as fashionable and elegant as may be, he was still the largest
gentleman anyone had seen in a great while, and not the
sort, it was generally feared, to be told of his new wife's
desirability by other fellows, whom he might take it into his
head to resent.

But resentment was the last emotion his face expressed
all through the ceremony and afterward, and by the time the
happy couple had slipped way from the merrymakers at the
wedding breakfast, a long way past noon, it could be said
that it was also the last emotion from his mind. Relief was
largest on his face as their carriage pulled away, unnoticed,
save but the Duke and Duchess of Peterstow and the Viscount Hazelton and his invited guest, Mrs. Cobb. For they'd
arranged his great escape.

"Army men," Warwick explained to his still-smiling wife
as she waved her damp handkerchief at the disappearing
coach as it headed northward, "have unique methods of
celebrating their friends' wedding nights. Arden is a brave
man, but he wasn't prepared to face all that, or have Francesca forced to do so, at any rate."

"Tell me about it!" Roxanne Cobb laughed gaily,
"Banging pans and thumping on the ceiling if they find the
inn you're at, and bawdy songs and suggestions! Lord," she
sighed, not with disapproval, but with fond remembrance,
"how they carry on! Someone always volunteers to take the
groom's place if he finds it hard going"—she laughed merrily, as, faintly, imperceptibly, the lovely fair-haired young
duchess stiffened in dismay—"and another, creeping up to
their chamber door, gets everyone to stamping their feet in
rhythm when he hears—"

"Good heaven," Julian said at once, "Roxie, look at the
time! You did say you wanted to have a word with the baron
before he left again, didn't you?"

As she agreed, eager now to be back in the great dining
hall that had been engaged for the party that no one wanted
to miss, the party that had for his bride's sake firmly estab-

lished Arden in the society he'd likely never wish to set toe in again, Julian looked one significant, helpless look to his friends Warwick and Susannah, and then more properly took his leave of them both, with a promise to see them soon again.

"Without her, I hope," the blond duchess breathed to her husband. "Oh, Warwick, I don't mean to be cruel, and I've no title save for what you gave me at our wedding, but I cannot like her, she's so . . ."

"Common?" the duke supplied lightly. "But don't hesitate to say it, for it's not a quality of birth, it's one of breeding and will. I've meet common countesses and noble beggars, and by the by, the only title I gave you at our wedding that I want you to never forget is 'love.' " And as she gazed at him with an expression of just such wondering love, he touched her cheek and whispered, "Yes, there is something about weddings. Julian had best beware. He's too much the gentleman to be rid of her easily, but too much the man to want her now that he knows her well. And as to celebrating weddings"—he smiled, his thin face illuminated with the sort of joy he'd seen now and again, when he couldn't quite conceal it, on his friend Arden's face today— "are you sure the doctor said it was safe now . . . ?"

"He did," she said, understanding at once, for it was what she'd been thinking all day as well, and smiling said, "and you mentioned you'd those new devices to make it even safer . . . in a way?"

"Oh very well put," he grinned, "I can hardly say if it's your tact or your newly restored body which entices me more now, and I agree we ought to try them because two children is blessing enough for this year, but," he whispered as he led her back to the wedding breakfast, his head bent low so as to tease her without anyone further than her ear knowing why she blushed so nicely, "as to them being 'new' devices, I assure you they've been around for a few centuries. Why, Cassanova himself, they say, carried some in his wallet . . ." he lectured, as the wedding guests who noted them reenter the room remarked on the lovely young duchess' high color.

'We'd never have made it so far as my . . . our home by nightfall," Arden corrected himself with a smile, "and there's no sense exhausting the horses and ourselves," he added as the coach was waved past the gatehouse and slowed as it came in sight of the lovely house set deep in the park. "I'm glad Warwick lent us this place. An inn would be both too impersonal and too easy for some of my old friends to locate. It's an unhappy tradition in the army to make wedding nights uncomfortable for the groom. This way, by the time they admit we've given them the slip, they'll have drunk themselves under the table even if some are fools enough to try to scour the countryside's inns for us tonight—especially if they stop at each inn," he said lightly as he helped her out of the carriage, "but then even I find it hard to believe our friend Warwick inherited so many houses with his title that he could put up the entire lot of them in separate rooms tonight, if they'd asked nicely enough. It is lovely, though, isn't it?" he asked, nodding in satisfaction at what he saw.

They were no more than a few hours' ride from London, but the park was alive with birds and its smooth green lawns led to a charming house, half-timbered and surfaced with many small windows that glinted in the late-afternoon sun.

"He sent servants ahead too," Arden sighed, "so there'll be a bath waiting. I don't know about you, Fancy, but I yearn to be out of these constricting clothes . . ." He stopped then, and as she laughed at him she noted that he grew unusually self-conscious, and for all his sense of humor, never so much as smiled at his unintentional double entendre. Instead, he led her to the house, and took her arm as the housekeeper led them to their rooms.

"Ah, only the one tub here," he said at once, "but I see there's an adjoining room, so if you'll excuse me . . ."

He sounded suddenly stilted, which he'd not been all through the day—no, she thought in puzzlement, which he'd never been through all their relationship—as he bowed like a stranger before he let himself into the room next door. Weariness. It was simple exhaustion, she thought as she sank back in her steaming tub. She felt it now too, along with the greatest joy she'd ever known.

The greatest joy she'd ever known *yet,* she amended, grinning at her soapy toes. For she awaited her wedding night with a delicious mixture of excitement, curiosity, eager anticipation, and a dollop of fear to give her patience. She knew, of course, the basics, of the matter, as there'd been a year or two at school when the girls had whispered of little else. And there were those cards, she giggled now, even though surely, hopefully, she thought, sitting bolt upright at the idea, being caricature, some of them were exaggerated. It made no matter, she decided at last, settling down again; nothing that was part of Arden's person could distress her, as nothing he would do, she was convinced, would ever harm her. She only feared being inadequate to his purposes and expectations. He was an experienced man of the world, and she had only her willingness to learn. But he knew that, she comforted herself as she rose from her bath, and love should count for something, and so she had only to wait for him, she thought, glad that she was between maids as she was between houses right now, for she wanted to be alone to prepare for him.

But it seemed she would spend most of her wedding night alone, even though he was with her. For after she'd perfumed herself entirely and dressed in an elegant but casual flowing gown of midnight blue, he knocked upon her door, and then, himself dressed as nicely as though they were going to pay a social call, he invited her for a walk with him in the gardens. He did know about flowers, she learned, for he lectured to her about them at some length as they strolled in the knot garden, the rose garden, and the kitchen garden until it grew too dim to make out a nasturtium from a delphinium.

Then he took her in to dinner, and made interesting conversation about the wedding they'd just been to, but with little of the high humor that was his hallmark, and with none of the long, lingering glances and sweet smiles that he'd been pleased to visit upon her these last days of their engagement. After several of her jests had gone unmatched, she fell silent, and they sat and watched the fire in the salon grow from blaze to glow before he yawned and arose, and stretched and said it was time, he thought, for bed, since they'd likely to get an early start in the morning.

He left her to change his clothes for bed, and he left her to sit upon her bed and worry, wondering where her Arden had gone tonight. Because it might possibly be that he hadn't wanted to wed her after all, but had done so because of her situation, and all the longing he'd seen in her eyes.

He closed the door to their connecting rooms and closed his eyes. It had been the most difficult evening of his life, this wedding night of his, and he dreaded the rest of it far more than he'd dreaded the battles he'd faced, at home or abroad. Because he burned for her. Every glance, every touch, every glimpse he got of her added to the heat of desire that threatened to immolate him. And yet each time

he gazed at her perfect, fragile beauty, he grew more terrified. He, who'd feared nothing that had ever threatened
him before, feared her disillusion with him to the point of
sheerest terror. Now, at last, he understood that poor devil,
Devlin, for hadn't he turned just now, mindlessly, to run—
from her?

Yes, he told himself as he unbuttoned his shirt, of course
she enjoyed his humor and his conversation. And it was
altogether possible she liked his temperament and tall tales
too. But now their love called for him to involve his body,
and although he'd always been proud of certain of its func-
tions before, he blanched at the thought of doing what he
most wished to do.

For all his past experience, all the things he knew would
please a woman of experience, having to do with matters
he excelled in—such as proportions and stamina—were
things he believed would not matter to a virgin, or even
especially delight her, in fact. He'd never known an untried
female, but it would be rather the reverse with one, he'd
think. It was a daunting prospect. And this was not just any
woman, but his own beloved Francesca. No sooner had he
uncovered his powerful, suddenly regrettable body than he
flung on a robe and sat down to think.

He never realized, as he did so, that the two other attrib-
utes that always went with the ones he noticed—his gentleness and consideration—were the ones his former bedmates
had valued just as much. But "monsterous," "elephantine," and "enormous," and all the vulgar epithets he'd
ever heard used against a big man ran though his head like
the bars of a tune overheard in the street that then refused
to leave all day, and he hesitated to begin his marriage now
that he was faced with the actuality of it, fearing he'd end
her love by doing so.

Oh, yes, he burned, he thought worriedly. But he was a
strong man, an iron man, they said, and so, he smiled
grimly, his humor stealing back to him in his time of need,
perhaps this time he'd have to test his mettle—by dousing
his flame just as he'd temper fine steel, plunging it into a
basin of cold water, rather than as a human lover ought
quench it, by sheathing it in equal heat. For he wasn't sure
she burned as he did, and doubted it, and he wouldn't sear
her tender flesh for all the world, for all his aching yearning.
He waited, he brooded; it was, he thought, smiling even in

his distress at the incorrigible wit that surfaced to cheer him at such times, certainly not a thing to hurry into.

She went from anxiety to self-doubt to dismay and then to fear for him and finally to a combination of them all, with slow anger and a sense of ill-use capping them, as she sat and waited for him. Because for all she was unsure of herself, she was, inescapably, a lady, and so had some small sense of her own worth. She'd put on a delightful filmy night-rail, but she thought, rising at last and pacing to the connecting door, it would be morning by the time he finally decided to so much as say good night to her. He might have fallen asleep, he might have fallen ill, his wound was only lately healed, after all, and he might, she thought at last as she came to the door, have decided to ride back to London. She must know. She knocked.

"Ah, yes?" he answered immediately.

"Arden," she asked softly, "are you all right?"

"Fine," he said, from what seemed to be directly behind the door, "just dressing for bed."

"It's fairly late . . ." she said.

"Is it?" he asked.

"Are you sure you're feeling well?" she inquired.

"Perfectly," he announced immediately.

"I'm not," she muttered. "Is there anything amiss at all? Are you coming in to . . . say good night?" she asked finally, when she heard no reply.

"Oh, yes, soon," he said with a patently false enthusiasm. "I just lost track of the time."

"Arden," she said, beginning to smile, "I thought I was supposed to be doing that. I mean, making excuses from behind the door." She emitted a hastily stifled but distinct giggle.

The door swung open.

"Wretch," he said in the first natural accents she'd heard from him all night.

But then he looked down at her and saw the gauzy night-rail, and the way it didn't quite conceal her high breasts and the way it helped to outline them, as well as the darker halo of shadow that crowned each of them and the patch of deeper mystery beneath, and he looked away, and let out his breath, and said all in a rush, "Good God, I can hardly bear to look at you."

"Why?" she asked, her eyes widening, suddenly frightened.

"Because I want you so much," he answered, lost, gazing down at her helplessly.

"But what's wrong with that?" she asked, disbelieving.

"I don't want to hurt you, or frighten you, or disillusion you," he explained painfully. "Ladies have romantic ideas of love, but it's a matter of bodies as well as souls, and I am rather . . . a large man, and you are a gentle lady and . . ."

"And you are a great fool if you think I don't know that, or if you think I'll break. I doubt I will," she said a little tentatively, for he had planted a fear where there wasn't one before, but then, as she looked up at his yearning face she decided talking would never show her, and so she cast herself upon his great chest and spoke into it as she whispered, "For heaven's sake, Arden, don't you want to risk it? I do. I'm a gambler's daughter, after all. And I do so love you."

This was more than he could withstand, or would endure. He picked her up as though she were light as a snuffbox, which delighted her, for she was not a small girl, and as he held her, his lips to her hair, he whispered, "Which room?" and she, suddenly shy, giggled. "Yours. I don't entertain men in my bed."

He took a long while proving he could see very well in the light of only a few candles, before he gently removed her night-rail to prove he could do more, although by then she was scarcely aware of it, since his touch was so intoxicating. And then he told her in words as well as with his hands and lips of how beautiful she was, and when she was not responding to his great art, when she could think, she was glad of it if it made him do this to her. She'd known of his unexpected grace and gentleness, but never guessed how expert he'd be at the games of love, so much so that he never made her feel foolish or inept as he led her from delight to fear to yearning once more.

His speech was soft, but his body was huge and rockhard, and when he moved she could feel his muscles bunch and slip beneath his skin, beneath her fingers, but for all his power, he was as delicate and skilled as a master craftsman as he molded her to match his desire. He took far more time than even he had ever done before with this beginning of the culmination of their love, to ensure she wanted him, to be very sure of his ultimate welcome in her smooth, sweet body.

It was when he wasn't sure he could bear it any longer,

long after he'd already brought her to temporary peace with his skill, and long after he'd set her to burning again, that he forgot to hold her so that she couldn't see him in his need, his robe being dispensed with, long before. And then it was her indrawn breath that called his mistake to his attention.

She gazed at him and then looked up to his face. She had seen his naked back before, of course, and at that time, glimpses of his great chest with its light fuzz of ginger hair, as well. But now she was, although she'd not tell him this, very glad of her father's gift, for as Arden had said once about the blind man and the elephant, the feel of a thing didn't prepare one for the look of it. Now she saw that the cards hadn't lied, or if they exaggerated, then so did he. And so she wasn't so much shocked as amazed at how she reacted. For she thought, after a moment, that not only was it not so unknown then, after all, and obviously survivable, but it was also all in perfect keeping with the rest of his massive form, and so he was all of a piece to her, glorious in his strength and power in every part. But after she'd wonderingly noted that aloud, and he smiled down at her in love and gratitude, she noted something else, even in the dim room. She giggled, and that stopped his breathing.

"Arden," she whispered, glancing down quickly to that nether thatch again, "at least one thing's true, though I'd not have guessed from your head or your chest, but now I do believe your mustache must grow in red, after all."

And his laughter released the tightly coiled springs of his fear and it fled, and he brought his lips to hers, and his body to hers at last, in joy and unafraid.

He'd prepared her so well for the pain, she waited for it, acknowledged it, and then even as it expanded, discounted it. He waited until she tugged him closer and whispered, "Fine," and knowing she meant it, allowed himself some small abandon, and so it wasn't long before he knew, at last, the greatest moment of this love, and found it to be greater than any he'd known before. She held him as he rocked with the intensity of it, knowing from what he'd told her that she'd know the same someday, knowing from what she felt that simply providing him this and being so much of a part of him was enough and more than she could have asked for, for now.

When they were done, and when he held her near, long after he'd tended to her and assured her that she'd never know such pain again, just at he'd never known such pleasure before, she spoke in dazed wonder.

"Arden," she asked in honest amazement, "how can you do this with strangers?"

"I don't know," he answered, his lips buried in her hair, breathing in her scent as if it were his only source of life, speaking with absolute truth. "Dear God, love, I do no know how I did. For the life of me, that's true. Now, I do not know."

He didn't know why Warwick had warned him about weddings. As he lay back on the bed and watched her readying herself to share it with him, Julian did not know. All he knew was that he must have drunk more than he'd had in the whole of his life, and all it had netted him was a dull headache and a bad taste in his mouth, and unfairly, all before he'd even had the momentary felicity of feeling foolish or giddy or good. As he watched Roxie wriggling out of her gown, he wished for the third time that he'd got himself a separate room when she'd left Warwick's town house when Susannah came to town. For now, all he wanted was sleep, and all she wanted, he saw, was to entice him.

It wasn't that her body wasn't delightful. He watched her through half-lidded eyes and saw the tight skin, the uplift of the little breasts, the nicely rounded line of her bottom, the light flexible swell of her belly. But not even his eyelids rose at the sight. He'd seen it all a dozen times before, and felt it against himself a dozen times more than that, and so he found nothing new in it, and nothing, he admitted, at last, in her. He was bored with her, and felt guilty for it, and dreaded her finishing with stroking her brush through her blond hair, for he wanted nothing but his sheets beneath him tonight, and, he accepted, trying to face the matter bravely, he was done with her, and didn't know how to tell her of it.

This was always the worst part of an affair, worse now, he discovered, because she was his employee, and he'd no idea of how to let her go. Should he offer to write out a recommendation? How much payment did she have coming to her? Mixing pleasure with money was a thing he vowed never to do again, for it complicated an already complicated situation. He realized he'd kept her on the way one might keep on an old retainer long after her services were inadequate to the need, simply because of sentiment, and the nagging knowledge that though hiring her on might have been for his convenience, it was her living. He groaned.

"I'm coming," she said. "Hold your horses . . . or whatever."

"Headache," he mumbled. Coward! he called himself as he rolled over and buried his face in his pillow.

"I've something to make it feel better," she sang, coming to the bed to lean on him, her lips to his nape, her knotted nipples prodding like accusing fingers into his back.

"No," he sighed in a muffled voice, "not tonight, too much wedding, not enough sense." He lay still and hoped she'd leave him to his supposed rest.

"Poor lad," she said, trailing her fingers down his spine. Unfair, she thought as her eyes followed her fingers; even this way, he was beautiful, from the thatch of golden hair that overlong, curled to the nape of that strong neck, to the graceful but lightly muscled lines of his back, to his tight buttocks—he snatched the covers up and covered himself. But she didn't have to see him again to know, back or front, how visually splendid he was. And kind, and gentle, and, tonight, oddly passive. It would do. Weddings did strange things to people, she knew. Although the one today had only hardened her resolve.

"All right," she said. No sense beating a dead horse, and if he didn't rise to the occasion, she thought, he must be half-dead. "Poor lad."

She sat quietly for a moment and then she leaned down again, putting her lips close to the smooth, shining hair that curled next to his ear. The days were getting longer, and she was getting no younger, the time was right. Now or never, she told herself.

"Julian," she breathed, and she saw his eyelids flicker so she knew he wasn't sleeping. "Julian," she said gently, "let's get married, eh?"

He lay so still she thought he might have been sleeping after all, but then she noticed he wasn't breathing.

"What?" he asked, turning around and resting on his elbows, staring at her with astonishment in those startlingly light, startled eyes of his.

"Yes," she said comfortably, "it's a fine idea. After all, what's to do now? You've not got the big man to tool around the world with anymore. Where are you going to go now? Back to your house in the country? Pah." She made a moue of distaste. "To be sure, for a week, and then you'll find

time heavy on your hands. London? But you know it inside
and out. And what will you do? Pick out some simple miss
at Almack's and wed her and give her a babe to remember
you by while you frolic in London again, like the other care-
for-nothings? No, I know you, you're restless, like me. It's
the Continent for us, Julian—this time, Brussels and Rome
and the Germanies and all the fun they're having there. Par-
ties, fetes, gaming and gossip and pleasure. You and I, my
love. What do you say?

"Oh, we'll have your heirs in time, if that's what's stopping you," she assured him as he continued to stare at her,
counting in his mind until he breathed easy again, remembering she'd just done with her courses. She'd realized that
too, bitterly. Because, she thought, regretting again that
she'd moved in with him when the duchess had come to join
her duke, a hint as to that possibility might have turned the
trick. But not only had he been careful of late, but living
so close these last days, even though he'd not requested
sport, he'd have noticed she'd been unable to oblige him
prettily.

"We suit, we do," she said merrily, "and what better
time than the present? And speaking of presents . . ." she
continued far more gaily than she felt, for his silence wasn't
promising. She hopped up and went to her dresser top to
sort through her jewel box. "Here," she said, coming back
to the bed and sitting beside him, holding out her palm with
two small painted ivory circlets on thin golden chains for
him to see. "Look what your clever Roxie had made up for
us whilst you were tending to your big friend all those days.
See? A miniature of me, for you, and one of you, for me.
I had the artist come and stare at you at the opera that night.
But look, he's made you ever so much handsomer than me,
poor lad, he took a fancy to you, I think.

"Here," she said, taking the ivory circlet with the portrait of an idealized Roman god, he thought, and fastened
it about her neck. "Now you can pass all your time lying
on the parts you like best." She giggled but then said
quickly, noting his wide-eyed silence, "All the quality are
doing it—exchanging portraits—some just with pictures of
each other's eyes, can you believe it? I was going to have
him paint ours, but you were far too handsome to waste the
rest, he said, and so he did all, and for the same price. So
here, for you," she said smugly, leaning forward to fasten
a similar circlet with a twin blond lady about his neck,

''there—so when you take off your shirt to another lady, I can keep my eyes on her,'' she laughed.

But then she suddenly sobered, and sitting there, naked, she poked her finger into his chest. ''And if that's bothering you, Julian, my word on it—I'll never interfere. I know gentlemen, after all. No, you go your way, I'll go mine, in time. For nothing stales like a clinging female, I know that. You'll see, once the glow's gone, I'll not hang about your neck—that's what the portrait's for, just to remind you who to come home to, when you're done. So!'' she said, sitting back and smiling at him. ''When shall we do it? It don't have to be a grand affair, just soon, so we can be off for some real fun.''

He breathed in so deeply that her portrait rose before her eyes before it fell as he spoke, slowly, sincerely, and quietly, as he took hold of one of her hands.

''Roxie,'' he said, his light eyes tender, ''it cannot be. We've had our fun. And for all it's been exciting, it's enough now. I never promised more, remember?'' he asked evenly. ''And, Roxie, sweet,'' he said, smiling lightly now, in a teasing, knowing voice, ''you don't expire from love of me, don't pretend to it. I offered some amusement, I took a great deal more, I know. But there's an end to it.''

''Love isn't for people like us,'' she said, relentlessly smiling, trying to make him see the truth of it, ''but we do suit. We have fun and we please each other, and we're neither of us getting younger. See here, my lord, dukes have been known to wed fishmongers' daughters, and I'm no common tart. My father's a squire, no less, and I've friends in high places. But I chose you, and for all you said it was for a night, it became a week, and the week became a month. Let's let it become a year and more and more. You'll not do better, my lord.''

Once, he thought, she might well have been right. Once, before he'd seen how Warwick had grieved and grown through his love, how Arden had agonized and then been exalted in his. He didn't speak of rank or station then, nor of the difference between mistresses and pure young misses, for none of that mattered. He spoke at last from his heart, as much to her as to himself.

''Roxie,'' he said, ''no. It would never do. And it's nothing to do with you. It's just a whim of my own. I want to love madly, foolishly, and completely absurdly when I take a wife. I don't know if I can, but I'd like to try. I've always sought pleasure, and I begin to think it would be the greatest one I've known. You and I know another kind of ecstasy, but what I seek is so much more profound I believe it must be very like suffering in its intensity. Or so I've seen it to be, at times, in my friends. I miss that. I don't know if I can ever feel it. But I believe I need to, Roxie, I really believe I do.

"I wouldn't want to share that love neither, and I think I'd strangle my wife before I'd calmly allow her to sport elsewhere. And"—he shook his fair head ruefully—"I'd hope she'd want to slay me for so much as undoing my topmost shirt button before another woman. It ought to be that sort of mutual passion, I think," he mused, "at least, only that sort would move me to wedlock. In truth, I don't know if I'll ever find it, it may be I just enjoy the suffering in looking for it. But I think I must seek it out, and so I can't marry you, for all you may ultimately prove to be right, for we may well be alike," he said sorrowfully, raising his arms to unclasp her portrait from around his neck and lift it off his golden chest, as he sighed, "but I really think I must."

She didn't entirely understand him, not the most of it, he was often too deep for her, but although not profound, she was quick enough, and knew good-bye however it was said. She snatched the portrait from his fingers and rose from the bed in one swift movement.

"Then I know who'll want this—and me," she said furiously, marching back to the dresser and pulling her clothes on. "I'm not going to wear this willow," she promised as she threw her other belongings into her portmanteau, emptying her dresser table as rapidly as she spoke, "and when you realize your mistake, my lord, I'll be long gone and nowhere you can find me, bet on it. I'm not without friends or opportunities," she vowed, panting from emotion as well as effort as she flung items out from the wardrobe.

"Roxie," he said gently, rising and standing beside her and placing a hand on her shoulder, "no need to tear off like this. We'll have time to say good-bye properly. Where are you going at this hour of the night?" he asked sadly. "It's blowing up for rain, it's late, come to bed, and we'll settle things in the morning."

"No time like the present," she said, shrugging him off, buckling up her bag, and stuffing the last of her things into a smaller case. "I'm off to Southampton, and then to the

Continent, and,'' she said, wheeling around and sneering, ''not alone. Oh, no. You remember my handsome young *Graf?* Well, he's plagued me by courting me for weeks, all unbeknownst to you, and he's a title and a fortune and a yacht, so one word from me, which I'll give him for he's not more than a few streets from here, and we'll be off. And I'll have wedlock this time, depend on it. Well, my lord?'' she asked, ruffled and distraught, pink with anger and disheveled, her hands on her hips, looking, he thought, more charming than he'd ever known her in the honesty of her rage in that moment. ''What's your last word, last chance . . . ?'' she asked, staring challenging at him.

''Don't go,'' he said reasonably. ''Think it over, calmly. But I offer no more.''

''Damn you!'' she raged, and tore the chain from her neck to throw his portrait in his face.

She went to the door as he stooped to pick up the locket, and then paused to look back at the living bit of statuary that had so entranced her. Her eyes narrowed. Now she played her last card.

''I'll wait awhile before we leave,'' she said, as though she grudged it, running her gaze over him. ''His yacht's the *Roxanne*. The paint might still be wet, for he just renamed it after me.'' And laughing at last, she hefted her cases and left him, smiling secretively to herself at the look upon his handsome face, as she hurried down the stairs and into the night.

He drew on a robe and held his aching head and sat by the window for a long while, staring at times at the portrait of the insipid, inhumanly beautiful face of the painted blond man, and at other times he gazed thoughtfully into the cool, sweet-scented early-summer night.

22

IT WAS a fine, clear sunny morning, and yet there were so many present that some more luckless members of the congregation had to crane their necks to get a better look at the incredibly handsome gentleman who stood before them all. There was a great deal to see, from the presence of such thrilling strangers as the elegant duke and duchess and the giant gentleman and his wife that had come from the mainland for the occasion, to the magnificently good-looking young viscount who stood before the minister. Then the minister cleared his throat to commence the service and the company quietened, even there in that quiet place, so as not to miss a word.

But he only said the usual things before he began with the too-familiar service, not adding a drop more to the little they knew already as he gave his sympathies to her family and offered condolences to the blond gentleman who might, if the gossip were true, well have been her bridegroom, instead of her chief mourner this sunny July morning. As they were all islanders, these former friends and neighbors and acquaintances of poor drowned Roxanne Cobb they all grew still, nodding their heads, knowing the vagaries of that untrustworthy sea around them, knowing the same regret for Roxanne and the young German gentleman who had been out on his yacht with her when the weather turned, as they'd felt for hapless family, friends, and neighbors for generations before. Their thoughts then turned, as always, from shocked sorrow to wonder as to whether or not they could have done better with the steering than the unfortunate foreign gent's crew had, so as not to have ended them all cast up upon the shore, with their broken ship, too late.

The blond gentleman did not cry, but then, gentlemen didn't, but he looked, with his alabaster face so still throughout, like one of the carved angels on a neighboring stone. And he could think, all the while, only that it was a pretty place, this green copse behind the white church, even though it was defaced by the thin, tall stones, their names and sorrows picked out with lichens and moss, as out-of-place in this summer morning as rows of blackened teeth in the green maw of the churchyard. As out-of-place as she was here, in this peaceful place, far from the lights and laughter of the Continent, where she'd yearned to be. As he was as he stood as dry-eyed and stony-hearted as a statue of remorse.

Because it had all come too soon. She'd left a note for him, it seemed, in Southampton, and then after they'd broken up in the storm, someone thought to contact him in

London, where he was just beginning to forget her. She'd waited a day for him, they'd said, and finally, laughing too loudly, had gone off with the foolish overeager young man to her death. All, he knew, as he stood and listened, cold and tall and unmoving as any of the stones about him, because of him, of course.

When the ceremony was over and the crowd dispersed to the squire's house for the funeral drinks and sweets and reminiscences, he remained in the churchyard, his hand numb from the many people who'd shaken it, his heart number.

Warwick and Arden were speaking around him, he knew, and he knew he'd best listen, for he wouldn't be hearing their voices again for a long while.

"He'll stay with us, of course," Warwick was saying, "the christening's soon, and he'll be right on hand for it that way."

"But the lakeland is tranquil this time of the year, the peace of it will do him good, he'll travel down with us, Duke, when we come to the christening," Arden insisted.

"He'll be sorry to disappoint both you gentlemen," Julian said then quietly, but they stopped at once to look at him, as astonished as they'd be if they heard someone they were treading on rise up to chat, "but he'll be going off today and so will miss both the tranquil lakes and the merry christening. I really must move on, my friends," he said, smiling at last. For he'd resolved to show them he was whole, and wholly on his way to recovery, or they'd hold him here in England by main force. So he fashioned his mouth into the memory of a smile, and knowing the way that death invited laughter for the living, jested to show them he was undaunted by the woman who lay so still so near, because of him.

"And though I won't be here for it, I insist on my rights as godfather," he said, "except this time, let me get the girl. Arden can have the boy. What's my goddaughter's name, by the by?" he asked, as lightly as if he were standing with them in his club, and not a cemetery. But what better place, he thought, to speak of ongoing life?

It seemed Warwick agreed. "Philippa, followed by Anne, and then a great many more," he said uneasily, but so theatrically that Arden, who was also watching Julian closely, responded with the same outside slyness—the sort, Julian realized, used in pantomiming for the very young or the very grieved, as he asked, "And the boy, Duke, be sure to tell the boy's name."

"Yes, what is your heir's name to be?" Julian said, glad they'd given him something easy to talk about.

It was worth it, when Warwick, on a sigh, muttered, "Buckingham."

Julian laughed naturally and easily for the first time in long days.

"And this from a man who rued 'Warwick' and swore he'd adore being 'Fred' or 'John' in his schooldays?" Julian taunted him, as Susannah, turning from her quiet chat with Francesca, burst in, "But 'Jones,' you'll admit, Julian, is hopeless. The boy needed something to stand up to his father with."

"Never fear," Arden put in, "I'll train young Buck to stand up to the brute," and they all laughed, and stopped only when they realized how empty-sounding the churchyard grew after that.

"No," Julian said then, softly and decisively bringing them all back to what they never forgot but didn't speak of, "I must go now, and put myself back together, you see. This time, alone. Last time, I'd Arden to help me grow up, just as he'll help our new young Buck. But now I must get to know the gentleman I travel with, and so I have to go alone."

"It was never your fault," Warwick said seriously, more seriously than Julian could ever remember him. "You behaved honorably."

"Honorably, yes. Correctly, no. I thought I'd learned from my past, but it seems I need some more past before I can announce myself fully grown. I'm off to find those little yellow birds at last, I think," he said then, determinedly lighthearted, so determinedly that the ladies looked away with misty eyes and Arden and Warwick seemed stricken, "and conquer new worlds as well as this stranger I live with. But I'll write, incessantly. And take it very much amiss if you don't answer back," he warned as he kissed each lady, and then had a private whisper for each. When they left him to the gentlemen, he hugged them hard, as well, first Warwick, and then, after he'd recovered his breath from Arden's good-bye, he said, as they all struggled to be the grown-up gentlemen they were supposed to be, "Don't worry. We'll meet again, and in joy.

"But I'd like to walk alone awhile," he said at last, "so

I'll return to the mainland on the next boat. Good-bye my friends, for now," and turning, he walked away, never watching to see if it was a road or a path he took, for it made no matter, he could scarcely have seen it anyway, the way his eyes were blurring.

The churchyard was in a hollow of a hill that sloped away to trees and bracken before it turned, as every prospect did along the coast here on the Isle of Wight, to the open sea. So he stumbled through the thorny bushes that ringed the churchyard, careless of his fine shining Hessian boots, as he walked through a haze of tears to look out over the solitude of the sea that had taken her, so he could wonder where it would take him next. Then, standing on a tilted rise over the blue-and-bottle-green-patched waters, at last, he wept. For Roxanne, and for himself, and for the fact that he knew she had no more died for love of him than he could have for her.

When he'd done, if, he thought, trying to contain himself, he'd ever be done, he heard the other weeping. Not strange for a churchyard, except, he remembered, curiosity turning his thoughts from himself, that he was no longer in the churchyard, after all. And yet he heard someone weeping. He looked about until a flash of movement in a shallow shadow beneath a tall tree showed him the glow of a fox-brush-colored head, bent over the earth.

She was only a child, he thought as he approached her, a plump little girl in a huddle of her crushed blue dress, so deep in her misery that she didn't hear his boots crunching over last autumn's ragged leaves, but when he actually halted above her, she must have heard something, for she looked up.

She looked up from the brown boots to the strong legs to the jacket and then far, far above, to the face, all in shadow, save for the glowing halo of hair backlighted by the sun she faced, and so thought for a mad moment that one of the angels had come to punish her for weeping, and so she gasped and scrambled to her feet.

"Don't grieve so," the gentle voice said, from so far above her still, for she was not very tall, "at least not for her, she's beyond that now, and you must go on."

"I know," she sniffled, "oh, I do know, and further, I know it's a sin, but I can't help myself, and I can't help feeling it was my fault," she explained, for though no angel, the gentleman was kindly-spoken, and she was well-brought-up.

"Did you know her that well?" he asked softly, seeing how the child was squinting in the full light and moving so that she could see him more easily in the dappled shade.

"Oh, dear!" she moaned then. "You're the beautiful gentleman they were all talking about. Oh, dear, I'm so sorry," she said, and went off into a new freshet of tears.

"Please, don't," he said, much discomfited, putting out a hand to touch her, realizing that as he was a stranger she might take alarm, and so withdrawing it. "I know you must have loved her very well, but don't, you'll be ill . . ."

"But I didn't even know her," she sobbed, "not at all. I saw her now and again, when I was young," she said a little more calmly, fighting to pull herself together, "but no more than that. She was very pretty," she added, trying to open her drenched handkerchief and failing, since it was so sodden and filthy with earth and tears it might never be prized open again. She accepted the one he handed her, and though it was already damp, the very scent of it, lemon and sandalwood, breathed comfort to her.

She straightened herself, and he saw she was, withal her crumpled state, not very prepossessing. For she was small and, he'd guess, far too fond of sweets. But at last, for all they were swollen and red, she'd a fine pair of eyes, large and light-filled light brown, which, he thought, she'd need, for she was also burdened with a mass of tangled curling hair of a glorious shocking shade of red.

"I'm quite all right now," she said with curious dignity. "You might as well go on."

"If you spoke about it, it might help you. And," he added, smiling gently, "me, as well."

"No," she said, shaking her head and looking wretched, "it would only make matters worse. Because we were talking about different funerals. I think you'll hate me," she said miserably, "because that's what I was weeping about." She gestured to a newly dug mound of earth that he saw was partially covered with leaves, and that, he realized, was what she'd been crouched near.

"My dog," she explained, flinching, as though she thought he'd strike her, "just died. She was twelve years old, and I buried her myself, and it was dreadful, for all I'd a box for her. But I know, as Nurse says and Cook says, that it's a wickedness to weep over an animal, and how especially you must think so, having just buried . . . Mrs. Cobb. Please,'' she said, her fine eyes entreating him even as they streamed with new and, because silent, somehow, more adult tears, "forgive me.''

"For what?'' he asked. "For feeling sorrow? Don't ask my forgiveness,'' he said, "for I don't condemn you. And what I said before is just as true. It can't help her . . . ah, it was a 'her'?'' he asked, and when she nodded, he went on, "and can only harm you know.''

It was as she noted his own pale cheeks were streaked that he added, "But why do you feel responsible?''

"I was leaving soon, you see,'' she answered shamefacedly, "for the mainland, and I couldn't bring her and I worried for it, for she'd known me all her life, and I wondered what would become of her without me, for all they'd care for her, she loved me entirely, and when she died so suddenly, it was as if she did it for me. I couldn't help but feel she was solving my problem herself, by ending herself, as though she knew . . .''

Then her grief overcame her, and her obvious suffering overcame his wariness, and soon he held her close and told her to hush. In a moment, she'd recovered herself and pulled away, much abashed, her face now red as her hair, and mumbled something about how she'd chosen a fine burial site, not far from where there was a peaceful churchyard, yet not so near as to be sacrilegious, and yet with a wonderful view of the sea. As she smiled tremulously over that foolishness, she led him up the slope to a clearing where they could look out over the wide waters this soft summer morning.

They stood there in silence for a moment and then she sank to sit on the grass, as he perched on an outcropping of rock nearby and she said in a small voice, "How you must detest me for weeping over a dog, when you've lost your fiancée.''

"Mrs. Cobb was not my fiancée,'' he said softly.

She digested this in silence before she clarified, "But it's wrong to cry over a beast, I know.''

"It's never wrong to weep for love,'' he answered.

"It's not so much the love as the guilt, you see, that's the worst,'' she sighed.

"Oh, I know,'' he breathed, staring out to the sea. "I know it's nonsensical,'' she went on, "because dogs can't read minds, no one can, and I never wanted her dead, only

. . . disposed of conveniently, and so no more bother to me, or weight on my mind. Not dead! Oh, dear,'' she said, scowling fiercely to banish tears.

''You can't be punished for thinking something, child,'' he said, listening to himself carefully, ''not even by yourself. There's enough guilt that we earn by what we do, to bother with what we think. Nor can we always know when we look our last on each other. Someday you'll have another pet,'' he assured her.

''Someday, perhaps,'' she said sadly, ''but it will never be the same. You can't love twice the same way.''

''Better yet,'' he answered. ''You wouldn't want to. You'll have learned to love much better. We learn, those of us who live on, you know. Or,'' he said very softly, ''I pray we do. And leaving will make it simpler. Ghosts, even beloved ones, haunt best in familiar places, and though we bring our past into our future, they're not too comfortable there. I don't know if that's bad or good, but it's so. Where will you be going?'' he asked, to take her mind and his from unhappiness.

''School,'' she said with such loathing in the one word he felt laughter well up in him again, but only cleared his throat as if on an interested query, and she went on glumly, ''They remembered me, you see. I've lived here all my life''—he swallowed a smile again—''happily, with Nurse and Cook and everyone. But Mama came home on a repairing lease, and looked at me and suddenly remembered my birthday, and decided I must go to boarding school in the autumn, as if Vicar's lessons weren't enough. So I'm to leave for the mainland to learn to be a lady, instead of learning Latin and history.''

''Well,'' he said, ''think of how much more you'll learn at school.''

''Oh, yes,'' she sighed, ''watercolors, deportment, and how to walk gracefully. I've four older sisters, sir, I know the way of it. Mama is very fashionable, and so are they. I am by far the youngest. I was lucky they'd forgot me for so long. It'll be ghastly. I'll never be fashionable, I'm bound to disappoint them. How much better if they let me stay on here.''

''Come,'' he said as he rose, feeling ancient as he spoke the elder gentleman's role, ''you're very young yet. In years to come you'll be glad of their decision.''

''Perhaps in ten,'' she said quietly, ''for by then they'll

have given up entirely. I'm sixteen on my next birthday. Not
quite so young. Oh, yes," she said as he stared at her,
assessing her again, but she was still plump and short and
breastless as she was shapeless, for all that her words held
wisdom and her demeanor was quaintly adult. She nodded,
as though she saw precisely what he did. "There's a history
in my father's family for late-blooming ladies, they say, but
they don't bloom regularly or too spectacularly when they
do, either," she said on a sigh. "On Mama's side, they're
tall and willowy, and at thirteen, young gentlemen send
them sonnets. You can see whom I take after. And how well
I'll fit in at school, especially so well-looking as I am, and
coming so late, when everyone else is accustomed to it and
has already made friends, they'll be eager to befriend me,
I should think, don't you?" She sighed. "I wept, I think,
for myself as well as for my poor dog," she said, looking
at him straightly. "just as they say we all of us do when we
grieve overmuch."

He seated himself again.

"My name is Julian Dylan, Viscount Hazelton," he said
formally.

"I am Eliza Mary Merriman," she answered just as correctly. "How do you do."

"Not well, but I've hopes," he answered, grinning, his
handsome face looking years younger as a bit of color stole
back into his pale cheeks. "I'm off from England tomorrow
or the next day," he said thoughtfully, "to the New World,
I think, or wherever the wind blows sweetest. Theres a commonality between us in more than our grief then, isn't there?
We both must travel on soon. My friends, my two best ones,
that is, are both lately wed, and so for all they love me they
quite naturally love their new wives and families more. I've
no other family at all. Do you think I might write to you?
And you to me?"

"That's very kind of you," she said stiffly, growing red
again, "but I hardly think you'd be interested in a schoolgirl's banal gossip. Thank you just the same."

"But I would be," he said, smiling, "every banal word.
Every scrap of gossip, every bit you could think of. Though
I'd hope it would help you, it would profit me too by reminding me of the commonplace of home. I'm rather selfish, you know. And I think I'll be very lonely, and not a
little frightened, if you want to know the truth. It would
help to keep a part of my mind in England, because I do

plan to return someday. I tell you what,'' he said. ''I'll come back to dance at your wedding.''

''You'll have too much arthritis by then,'' she laughed.

''No, no,'' he said, ''you'll grow to be a beauty.''

''Oh, yes,'' she laughed again, ''Overnight. Just like in all those Minerva Press novels Nurse reads in secret.''

''Yes,'' he agreed, ''you'll grow tall and slender . . .''

''As a reed,'' she encouraged him, ''please. And my hair will turn lustrous and dark . . .''

''Just so,'' he said, ''and your freckles shall have faded . . .''

''I don't have any,'' she corrected him.

''Well, you'll get some and then they'll fade,'' he said testily. ''And then . . .''

They chatted and laughed for a long while about her coming transformation and his journeys and other fantasies they invented to stave off thoughts of death and other partings, before she noted the turning of the sun and then they talked all the way back to the road that led to her great white house.

''Please come to the door with me,'' she begged, ''or they'll think I've been dreaming up stories again.''

''I will,'' he promised as he began to stride toward it with her, and then he felt in his waistcoat pocket, remembering what he'd put on Roxie's coffin when Arden had stopped him, scooping it up in one huge hand, and warning,''The living may not bury themselves with the dead, lad,'' before handing it back to him.

''Here's a cure for that in future,'' he said, offering the ivory circlet to her, flinching slightly when he recalled its twin lying somewhere deep beneath the waves, ''and to remember me with, yourself as well . . . no, no,'' he said, as she misinterpreted his shudder, ''no one else wants it, even she did not. And I'll look lovely if my ship goes down and I wash up with a picture of me on my breast, won't I? They'll bury me with a mirror,'' he said, thinking again how remarkable it was that he could laugh again so soon, that death now seemed the easiest thing to laugh at. ''Please keep it, so that at least a part of me remains in England until I come back entirely again.''

She gazed at the small portrait and then back at him.

''You're handsomer,'' she said without thinking, and then, blushing wildly, added with a twinkle, ''and just think of the friends this will win me! Thank you, my lord.''

He stayed to dazzle Nurse, and Cook, and all the house-maids, and not a few of the local tenants' wives. And then after some light refreshment, he said he had to leave. She walked him to the end of the road near her house.

"You've been very kind," she said, "and I understand, you don't have to write, you know."

"I do," he said, looking down at her, small and plump and embarrassed, so oddly young and old, and so very lost. That was another commonality, he thought, one he'd never mention, "and so do you, for I'll send you my direction when I know it. Because no matter how wide the world, or what corner I find for myself in it, if you've ever need of me, I'll find a way to aid you, that's what friendship is all about, so never doubt me. At any rate, I count on you to bring me back to England one day, you know."

"Oh, but I'm sure you'll find happiness elsewhere," she protested.

"How can I?" he asked. "This is my home."

Smiling sadly then, he bowed and walked away. And then a long way down the road, he turned and waved and called out once, "I'll see you again—when we've both grown up," and laughing, he strolled down the long road to the sea, which would take him as far as he had to go, before he could come home again.